IMAGE COMICS PRESENTS

VOLUME 2

CREATED BY
TODD McFARLANE and ROBERT KIRKMAN

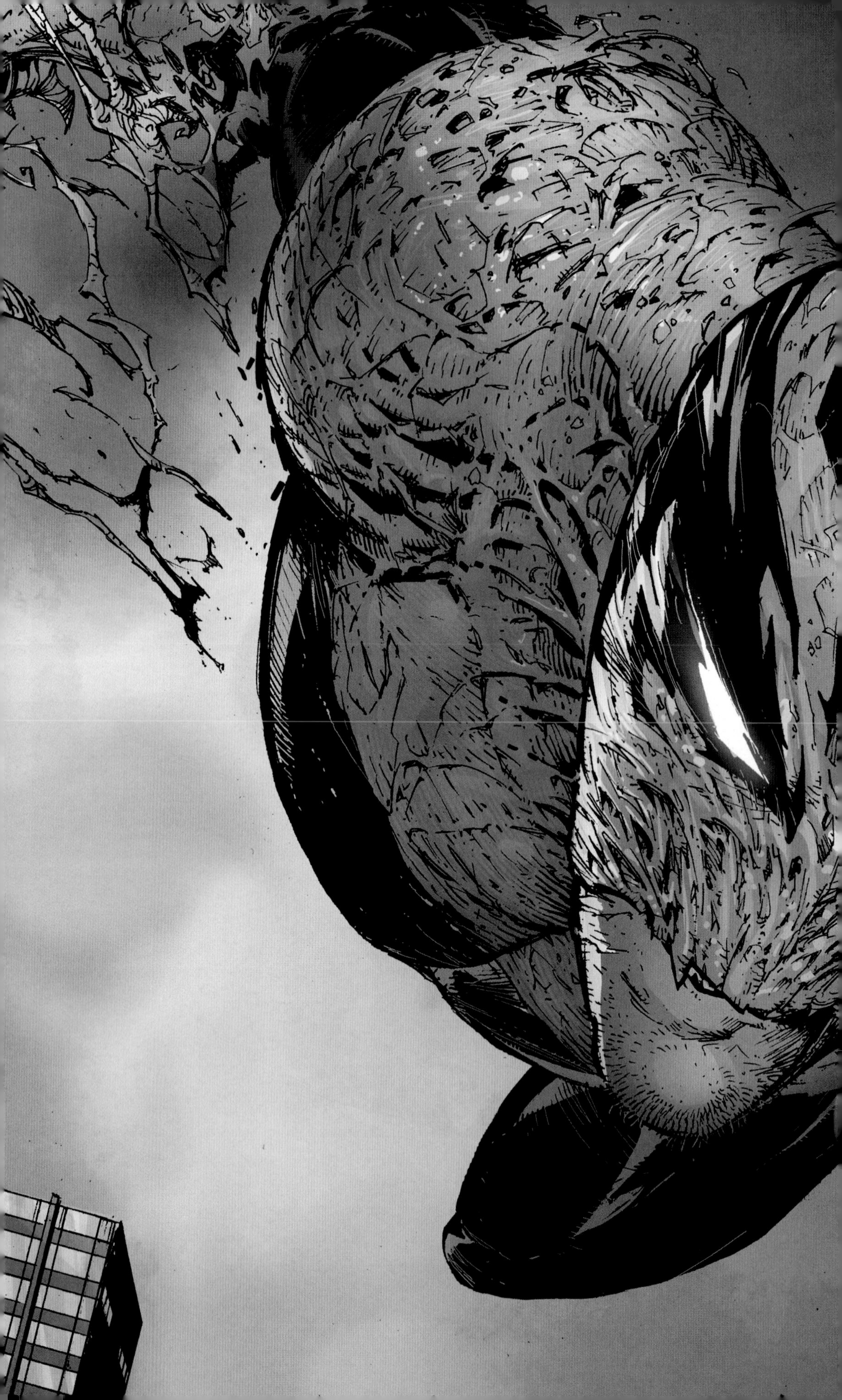

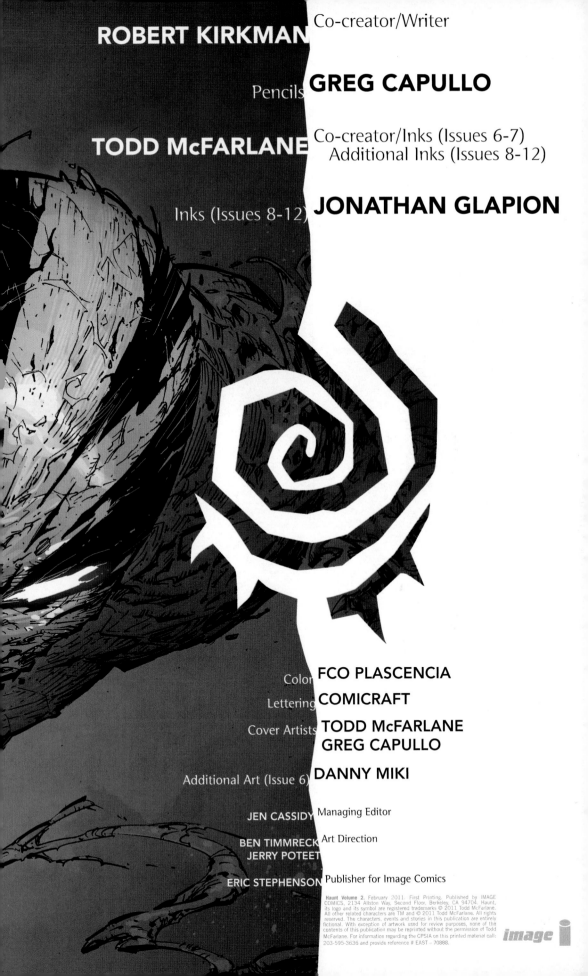

ROBERT KIRKMAN
Co-creator/Writer

Pencils GREG CAPULLO

TODD McFARLANE
Co-creator/Inks (Issues 6-7)
Additional Inks (Issues 8-12)

Inks (Issues 8-12) JONATHAN GLAPION

Colors FCO PLASCENCIA
Lettering COMICRAFT
Cover Artists TODD McFARLANE
GREG CAPULLO
Additional Art (Issue 6) DANNY MIKI

JEN CASSIDY Managing Editor

BEN TIMMRECK Art Direction
JERRY POTEET

ERIC STEPHENSON Publisher for Image Comics

Haunt Volume 2. February 2011. First Printing. Published by IMAGE COMICS, 2134 Allston Way, Second Floor, Berkeley, CA 94704. Haunt, its logo and its symbol are registered trademarks © 2011 Todd McFarlane. All other related characters are TM and © 2011 Todd McFarlane. All rights reserved. The characters, events and stories in this publication are entirely fictional. With exception of artwork used for review purposes, none of the contents of this publication may be reprinted without the permission of Todd McFarlane. For information regarding the CPSIA on this printed material call: 203-595-3636 and provide reference # EAST – 70888.

image i

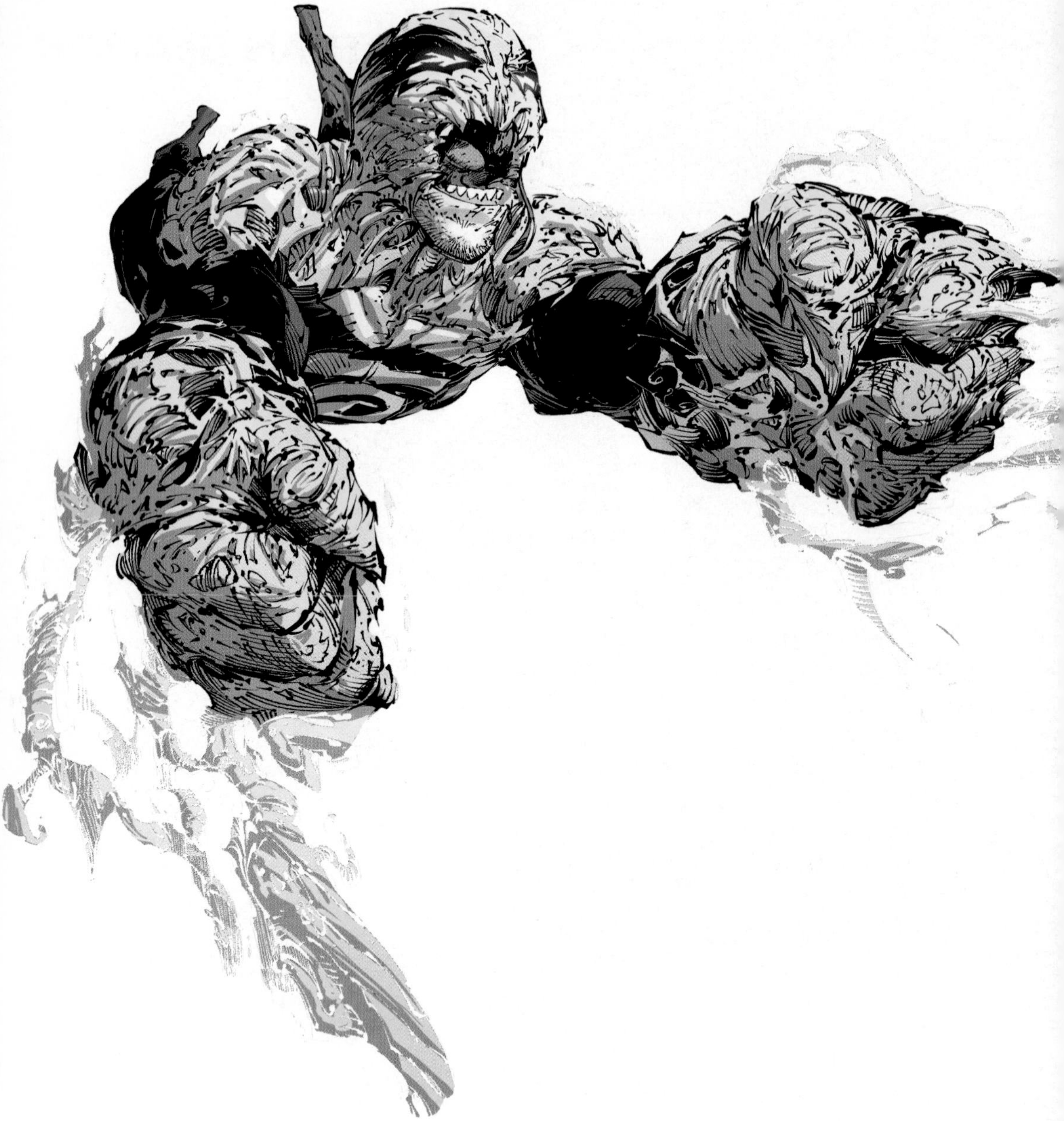

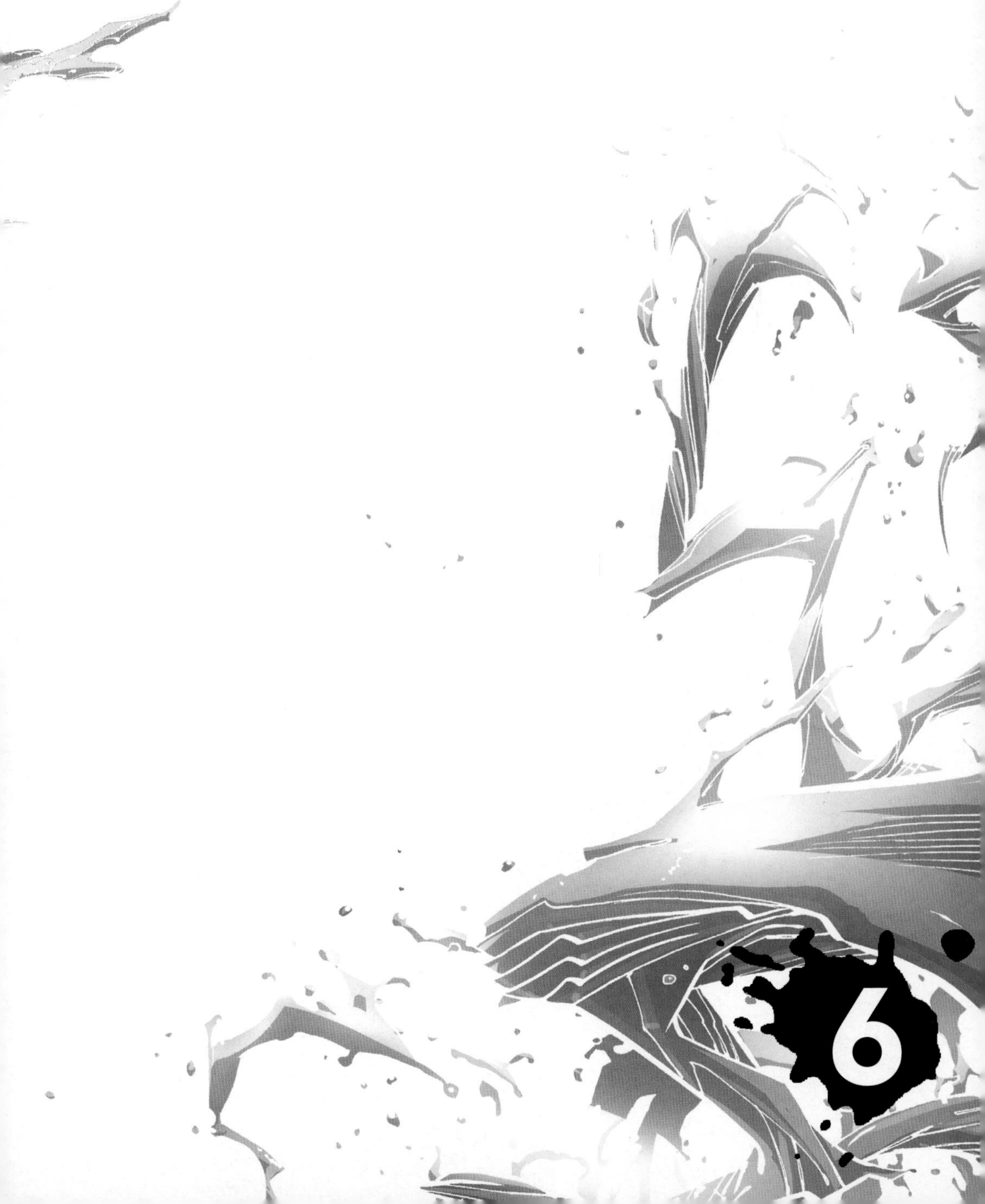
6

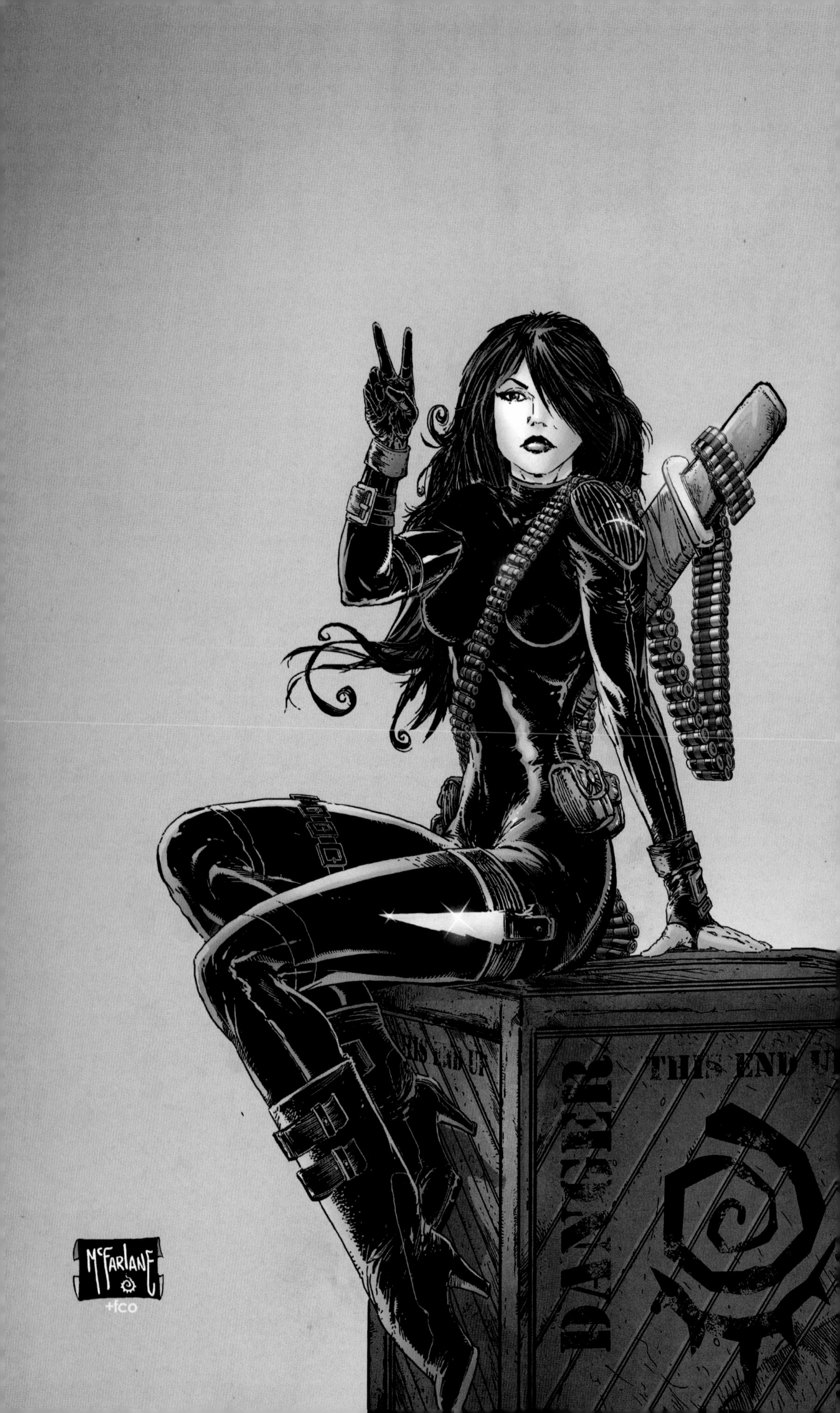
DANGER
McFARLANE
+fco

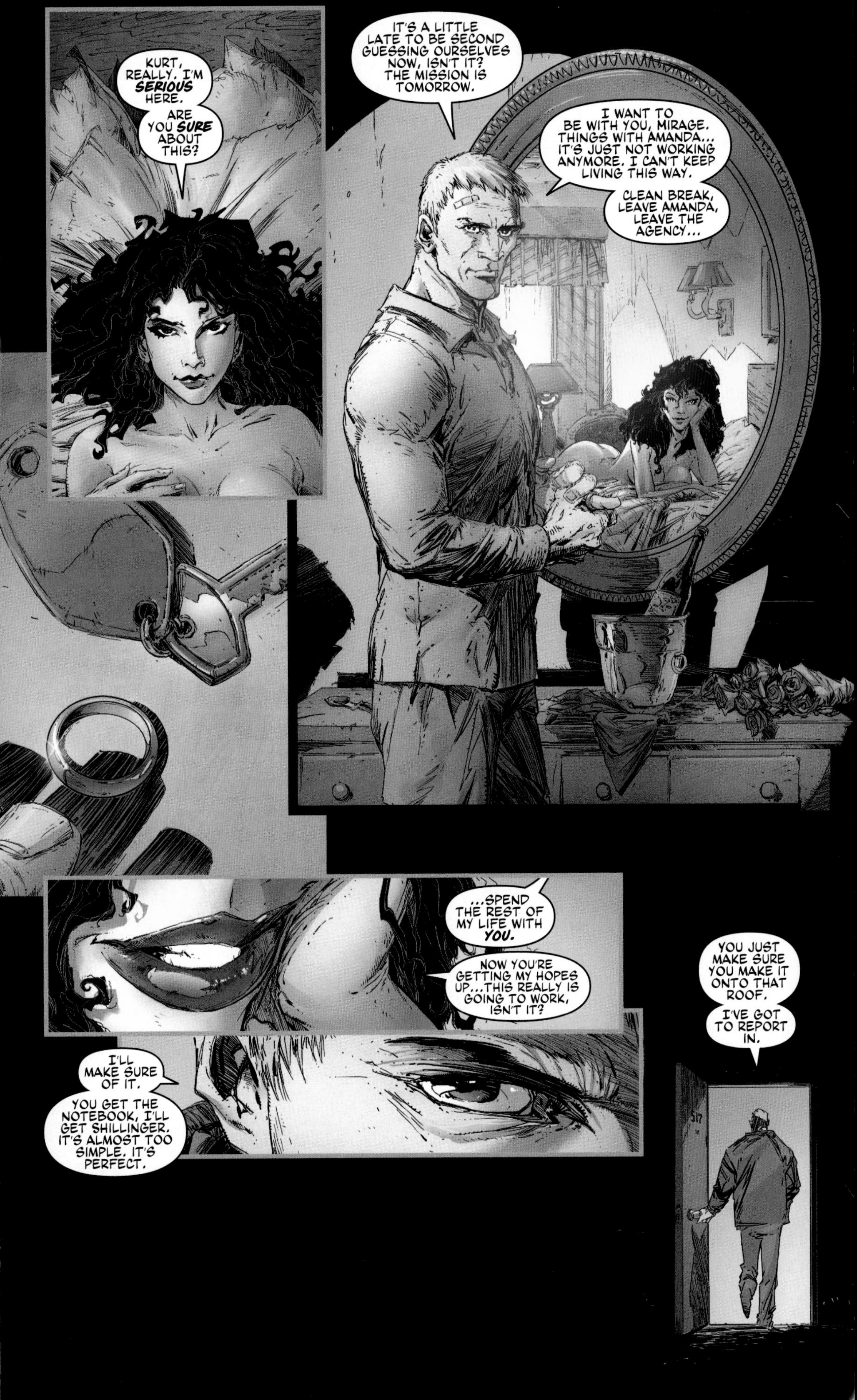

KURT, REALLY. I'M SERIOUS HERE.
ARE YOU SURE ABOUT THIS?
IT'S A LITTLE LATE TO BE SECOND GUESSING OURSELVES NOW, ISN'T IT? THE MISSION IS TOMORROW.
I WANT TO BE WITH YOU, MIRAGE. THINGS WITH AMANDA... IT'S JUST NOT WORKING ANYMORE. I CAN'T KEEP LIVING THIS WAY.
CLEAN BREAK, LEAVE AMANDA, LEAVE THE AGENCY...
...SPEND THE REST OF MY LIFE WITH YOU.
NOW YOU'RE GETTING MY HOPES UP...THIS REALLY IS GOING TO WORK, ISN'T IT?
I'LL MAKE SURE OF IT.
YOU GET THE NOTEBOOK, I'LL GET SHILLINGER. IT'S ALMOST TOO SIMPLE. IT'S PERFECT.
YOU JUST MAKE SURE YOU MAKE IT ONTO THAT ROOF.
I'VE GOT TO REPORT IN.

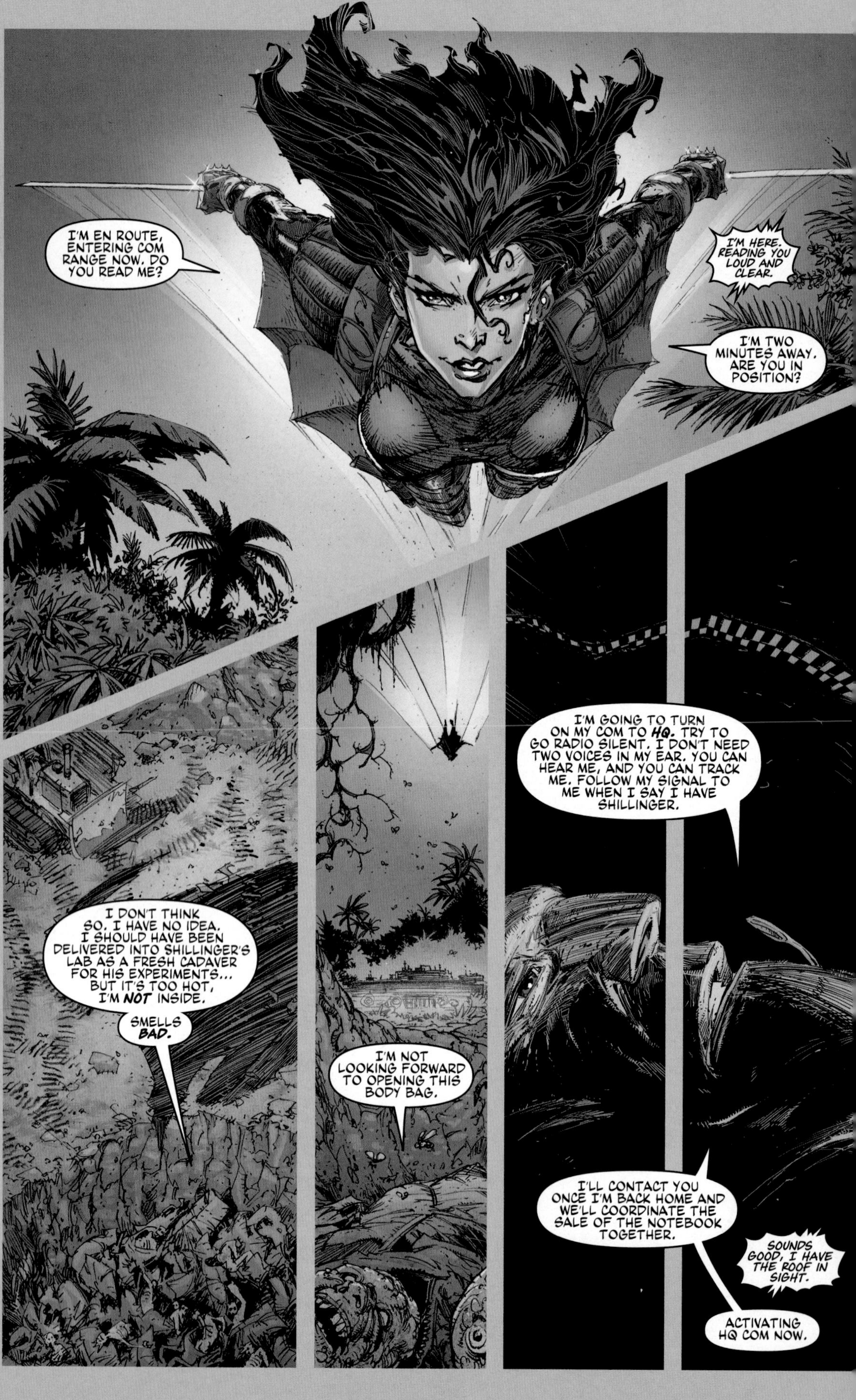
I'M EN ROUTE, ENTERING COM RANGE NOW. DO YOU READ ME?
I'M HERE. READING YOU LOUD AND CLEAR.
I'M TWO MINUTES AWAY. ARE YOU IN POSITION?
I DON'T THINK SO. I HAVE NO IDEA. I SHOULD HAVE BEEN DELIVERED INTO SHILLINGER'S LAB AS A FRESH CADAVER FOR HIS EXPERIMENTS... BUT IT'S TOO HOT, I'M NOT INSIDE.
SMELLS BAD.
I'M NOT LOOKING FORWARD TO OPENING THIS BODY BAG.
I'M GOING TO TURN ON MY COM TO HQ. TRY TO GO RADIO SILENT. I DON'T NEED TWO VOICES IN MY EAR. YOU CAN HEAR ME, AND YOU CAN TRACK ME. FOLLOW MY SIGNAL TO ME WHEN I SAY I HAVE SHILLINGER.
I'LL CONTACT YOU ONCE I'M BACK HOME AND WE'LL COORDINATE THE SALE OF THE NOTEBOOK TOGETHER.
SOUNDS GOOD, I HAVE THE ROOF IN SIGHT.
ACTIVATING HQ COM NOW.

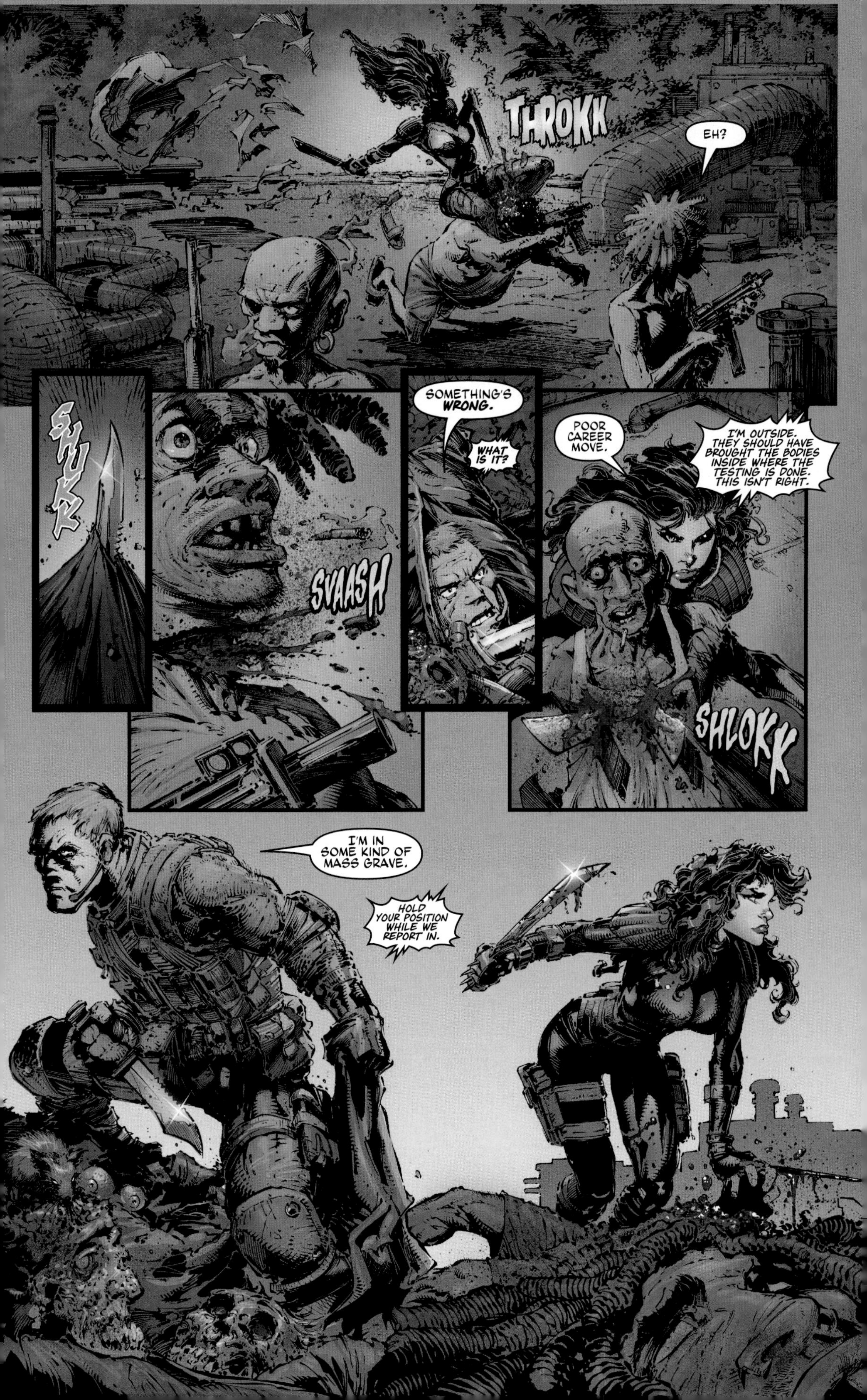

THROKK
EH?
SHUKK
SVAASH
SOMETHING'S WRONG.
WHAT IS IT?
POOR CAREER MOVE.
I'M OUTSIDE. THEY SHOULD HAVE BROUGHT THE BODIES INSIDE WHERE THE TESTING IS DONE. THIS ISN'T RIGHT.
SHLOKK
I'M IN SOME KIND OF MASS GRAVE.
HOLD YOUR POSITION WHILE WE REPORT IN.

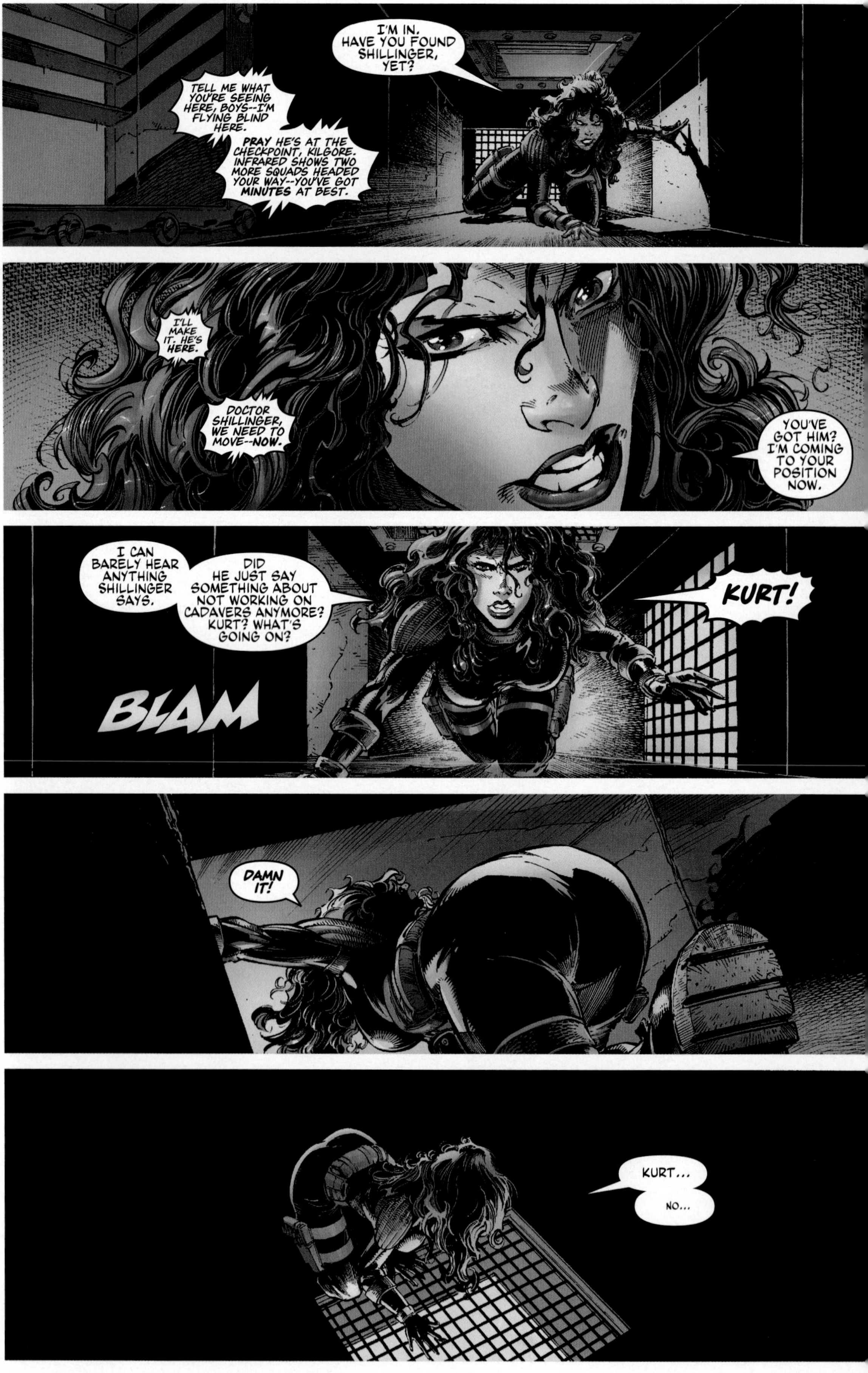
I'M IN. HAVE YOU FOUND SHILLINGER, YET?
TELL ME WHAT YOU'RE SEEING HERE, BOYS--I'M FLYING BLIND HERE.
PRAY HE'S AT THE CHECKPOINT, KILGORE. INFRARED SHOWS TWO MORE SQUADS HEADED YOUR WAY--YOU'VE GOT MINUTES AT BEST.
I'LL MAKE IT. HE'S HERE.
DOCTOR SHILLINGER, WE NEED TO MOVE--NOW.
YOU'VE GOT HIM? I'M COMING TO YOUR POSITION NOW.
I CAN BARELY HEAR ANYTHING SHILLINGER SAYS.
DID HE JUST SAY SOMETHING ABOUT NOT WORKING ON CADAVERS ANYMORE? KURT? WHAT'S GOING ON?
KURT!
BLAM
DAMN IT!
KURT...
NO...

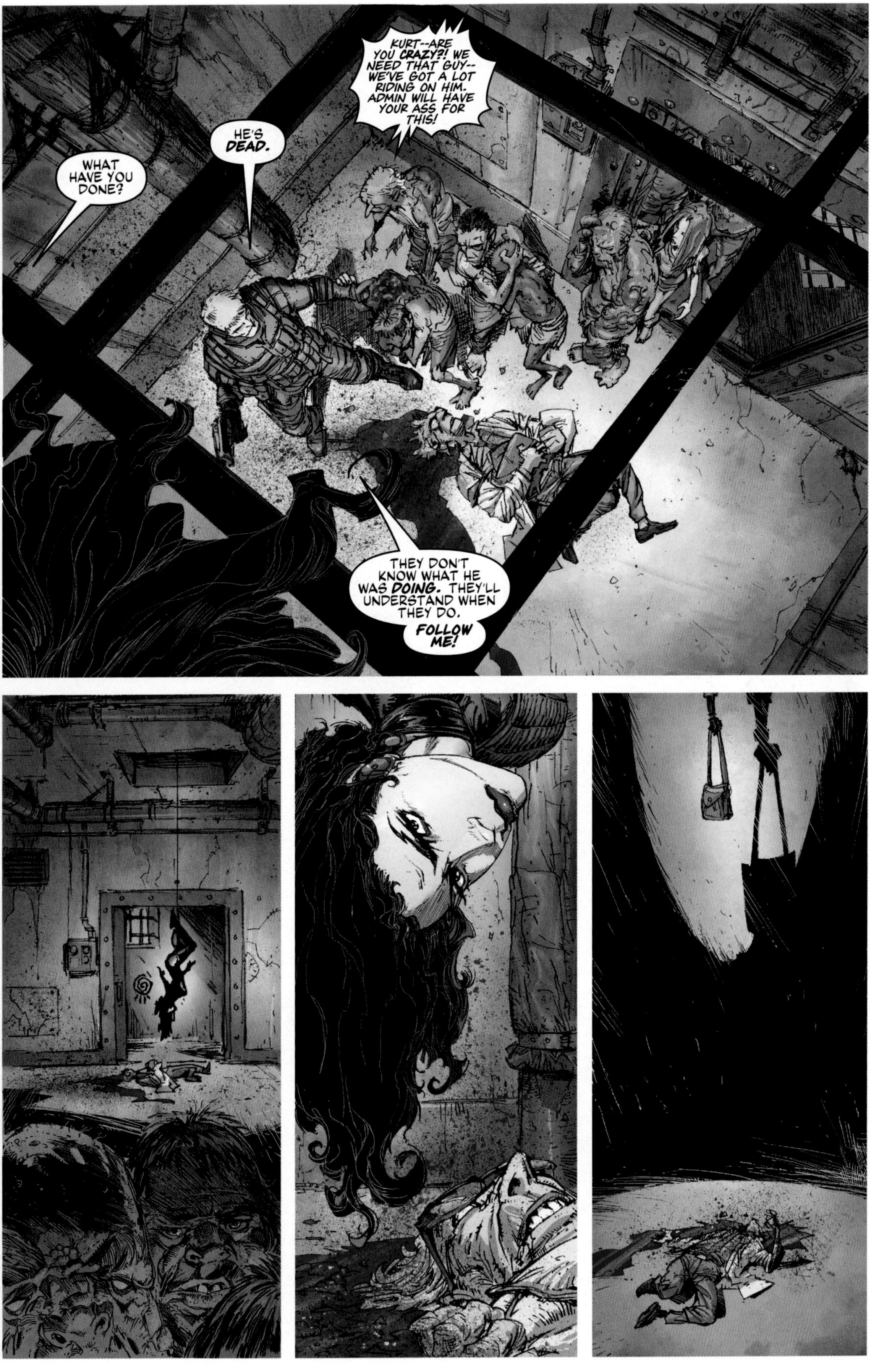
WHAT HAVE YOU DONE?
HE'S DEAD.
KURT--ARE YOU CRAZY?! WE NEED THAT GUY-- WE'VE GOT A LOT RIDING ON HIM. ADMIN WILL HAVE YOUR ASS FOR THIS!
THEY DON'T KNOW WHAT HE WAS DOING. THEY'LL UNDERSTAND WHEN THEY DO.
FOLLOW ME!

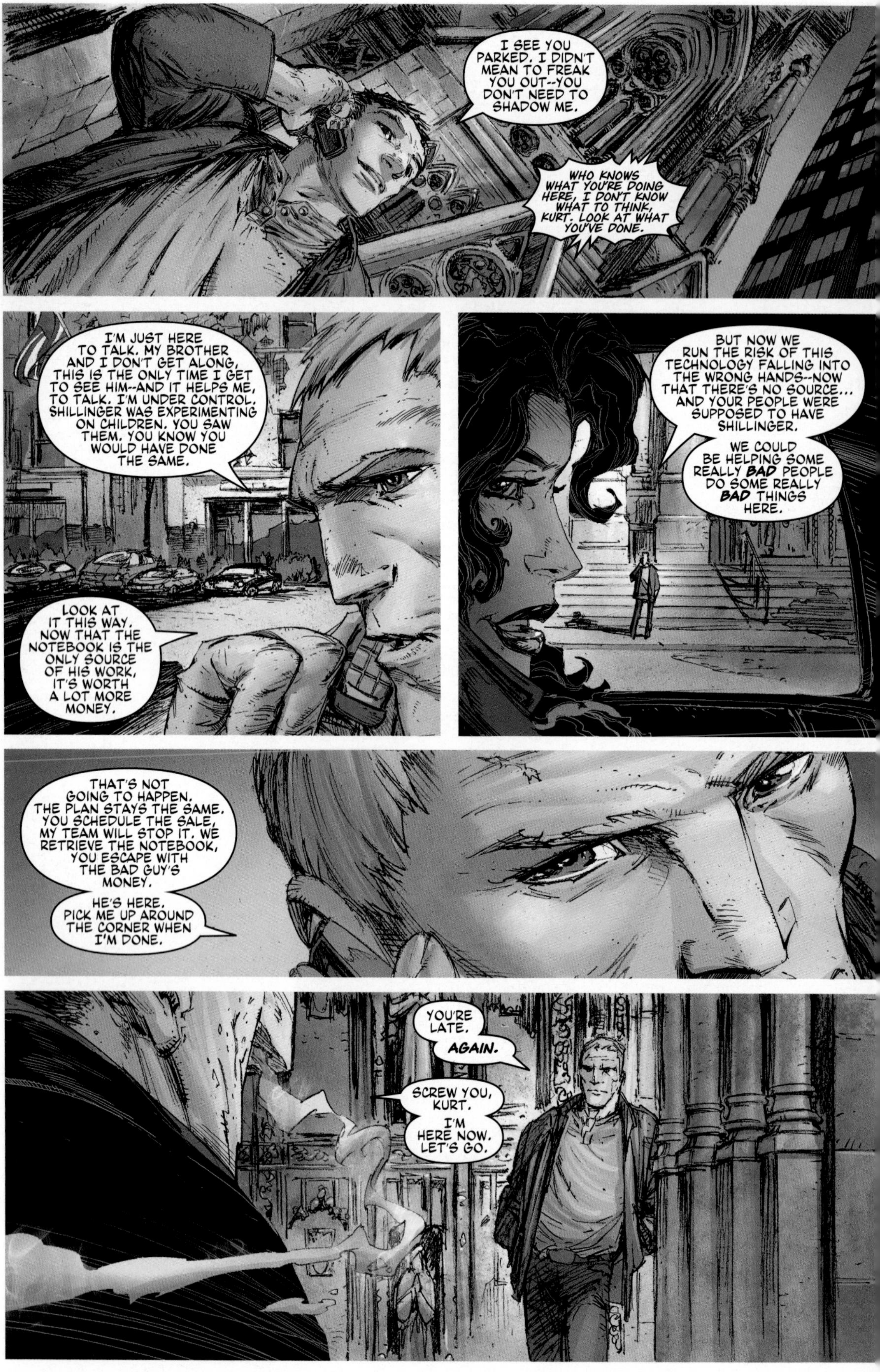
I SEE YOU PARKED. I DIDN'T MEAN TO FREAK YOU OUT--YOU DON'T NEED TO SHADOW ME.
WHO KNOWS WHAT YOU'RE DOING HERE, I DON'T KNOW WHAT TO THINK, KURT. LOOK AT WHAT YOU'VE DONE.
I'M JUST HERE TO TALK. MY BROTHER AND I DON'T GET ALONG, THIS IS THE ONLY TIME I GET TO SEE HIM--AND IT HELPS ME, TO TALK. I'M UNDER CONTROL. SHILLINGER WAS EXPERIMENTING ON CHILDREN. YOU SAW THEM. YOU KNOW YOU WOULD HAVE DONE THE SAME.
LOOK AT IT THIS WAY. NOW THAT THE NOTEBOOK IS THE ONLY SOURCE OF HIS WORK, IT'S WORTH A LOT MORE MONEY.
BUT NOW WE RUN THE RISK OF THIS TECHNOLOGY FALLING INTO THE WRONG HANDS--NOW THAT THERE'S NO SOURCE... AND YOUR PEOPLE WERE SUPPOSED TO HAVE SHILLINGER.
WE COULD BE HELPING SOME REALLY **BAD** PEOPLE DO SOME REALLY **BAD** THINGS HERE.
THAT'S NOT GOING TO HAPPEN. THE PLAN STAYS THE SAME. YOU SCHEDULE THE SALE, MY TEAM WILL STOP IT. WE RETRIEVE THE NOTEBOOK, YOU ESCAPE WITH THE BAD GUY'S MONEY.
HE'S HERE. PICK ME UP AROUND THE CORNER WHEN I'M DONE.
YOU'RE LATE.
AGAIN.
SCREW YOU, KURT.
I'M HERE NOW. LET'S GO.

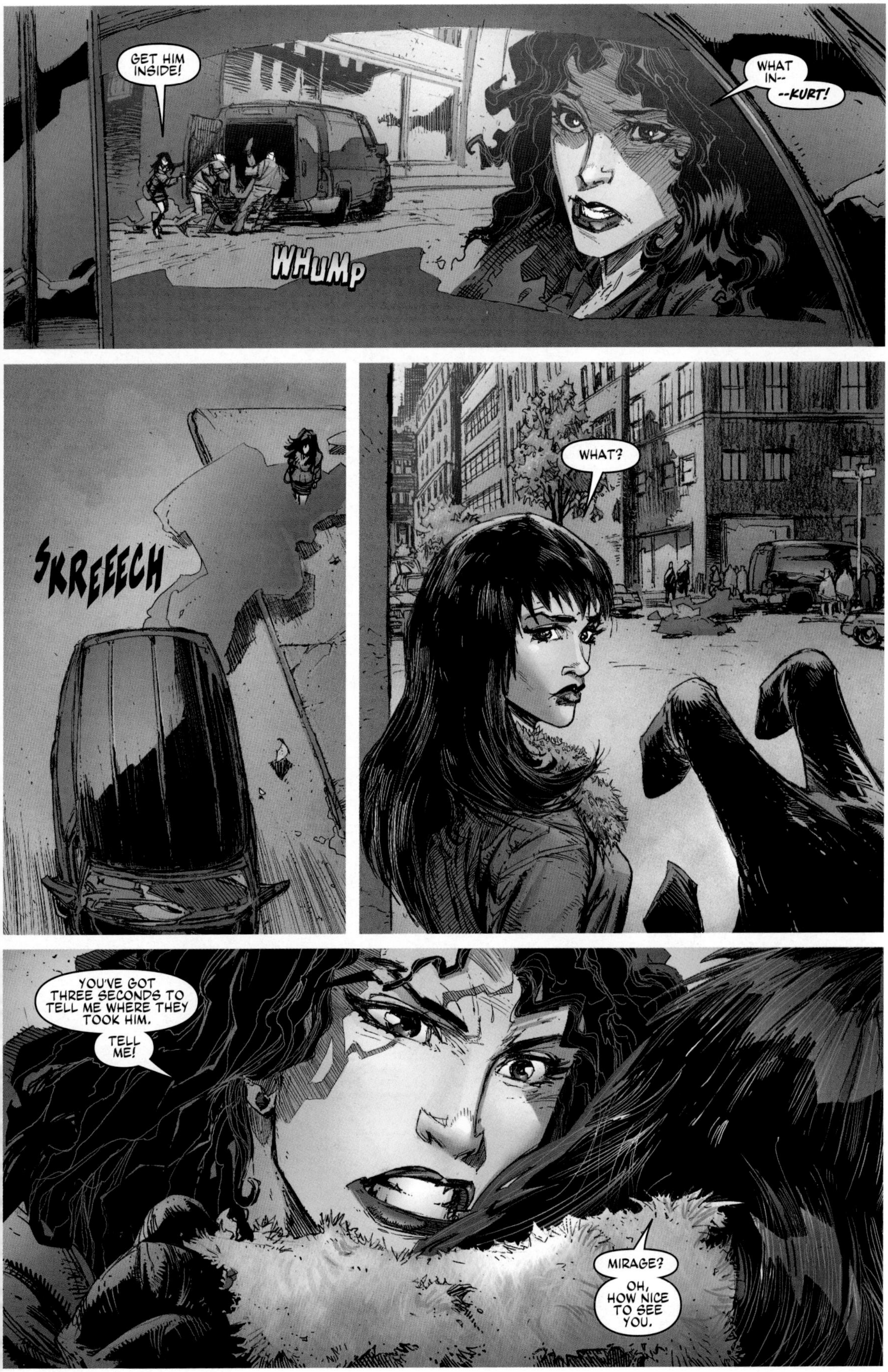
GET HIM INSIDE!
WHAT IN-- --KURT!
WHUMP
SKREEECH
WHAT?
YOU'VE GOT THREE SECONDS TO TELL ME WHERE THEY TOOK HIM.
TELL ME!
MIRAGE?
OH, HOW NICE TO SEE YOU.

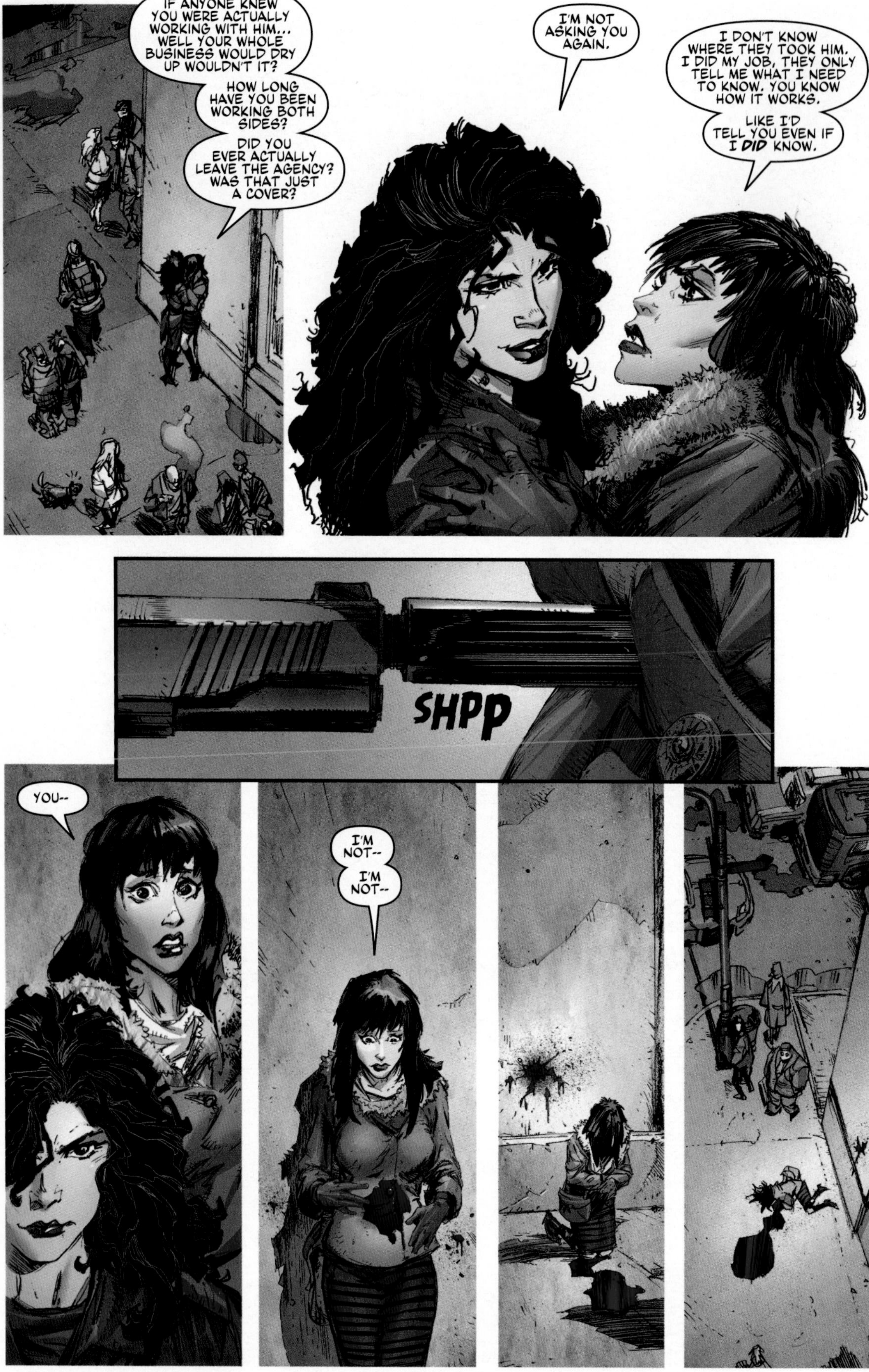

IF ANYONE KNEW YOU WERE ACTUALLY WORKING WITH HIM... WELL YOUR WHOLE BUSINESS WOULD DRY UP WOULDN'T IT?
HOW LONG HAVE YOU BEEN WORKING BOTH SIDES?
DID YOU EVER ACTUALLY LEAVE THE AGENCY? WAS THAT JUST A COVER?
I'M NOT ASKING YOU AGAIN.
I DON'T KNOW WHERE THEY TOOK HIM. I DID MY JOB, THEY ONLY TELL ME WHAT I NEED TO KNOW. YOU KNOW HOW IT WORKS.
LIKE I'D TELL YOU EVEN IF I DID KNOW.
SHPP
YOU--
I'M NOT--
I'M NOT--

I'M PAYING ATTENTION. I'M SORRY. IT'S JUST THAT I'VE GOT A FRIEND OF MINE FROM WORK WHO'S IN TROUBLE AND I HAVEN'T HEARD FROM THEM. I'M JUST A LITTLE WORRIED. BUT I CAN TALK.

IT'S GOOD TO HAVE A DISTRACTION FOR A BIT. BUT I'VE GOT TO STEP OUT IN A MINUTE SO I CAN'T TALK FOR LONG.

A FRIEND FROM WORK? SO YOU'RE STILL GOING TO CONVENIENTLY LEAVE OUT ANY SORT OF DETAILS ABOUT WHAT YOU ACTUALLY *DO* AT YOUR JOB. I SWEAR DEAR, IF I FIND OUT YOU'RE A STRIPPER.

I'M NOT A STRIPPER, MOM. I TOLD YOU, I WORK IN A LAW OFFICE, I CAN'T TELL YOU ANY DETAILS ABOUT OUR CASES. IT'S ALL CONFIDENTIAL.

I MEAN, REALLY--A STRIP--

--ACCIDENT IN MADISON COUNTY CLAIMED A MAN'S LIFE LATE THURSDAY NIGHT.

CNR

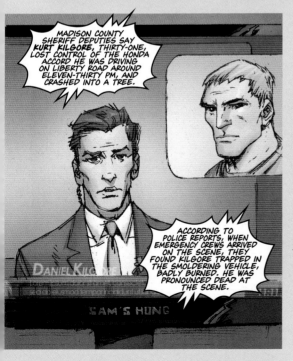

MADISON COUNTY SHERIFF DEPUTIES SAY *KURT KILGORE*, THIRTY-ONE, LOST CONTROL OF THE HONDA ACCORD HE WAS DRIVING ON LIBERTY ROAD AROUND ELEVEN-THIRTY PM, AND CRASHED INTO A TREE.

ACCORDING TO POLICE REPORTS, WHEN EMERGENCY CREWS ARRIVED ON THE SCENE, THEY FOUND KILGORE TRAPPED IN THE SMOLDERING VEHICLE, BADLY BURNED. HE WAS PRONOUNCED DEAD AT THE SCENE.

DANIEL KILGORE

SAM'S HUNG

MOM... I HAVE TO GO.

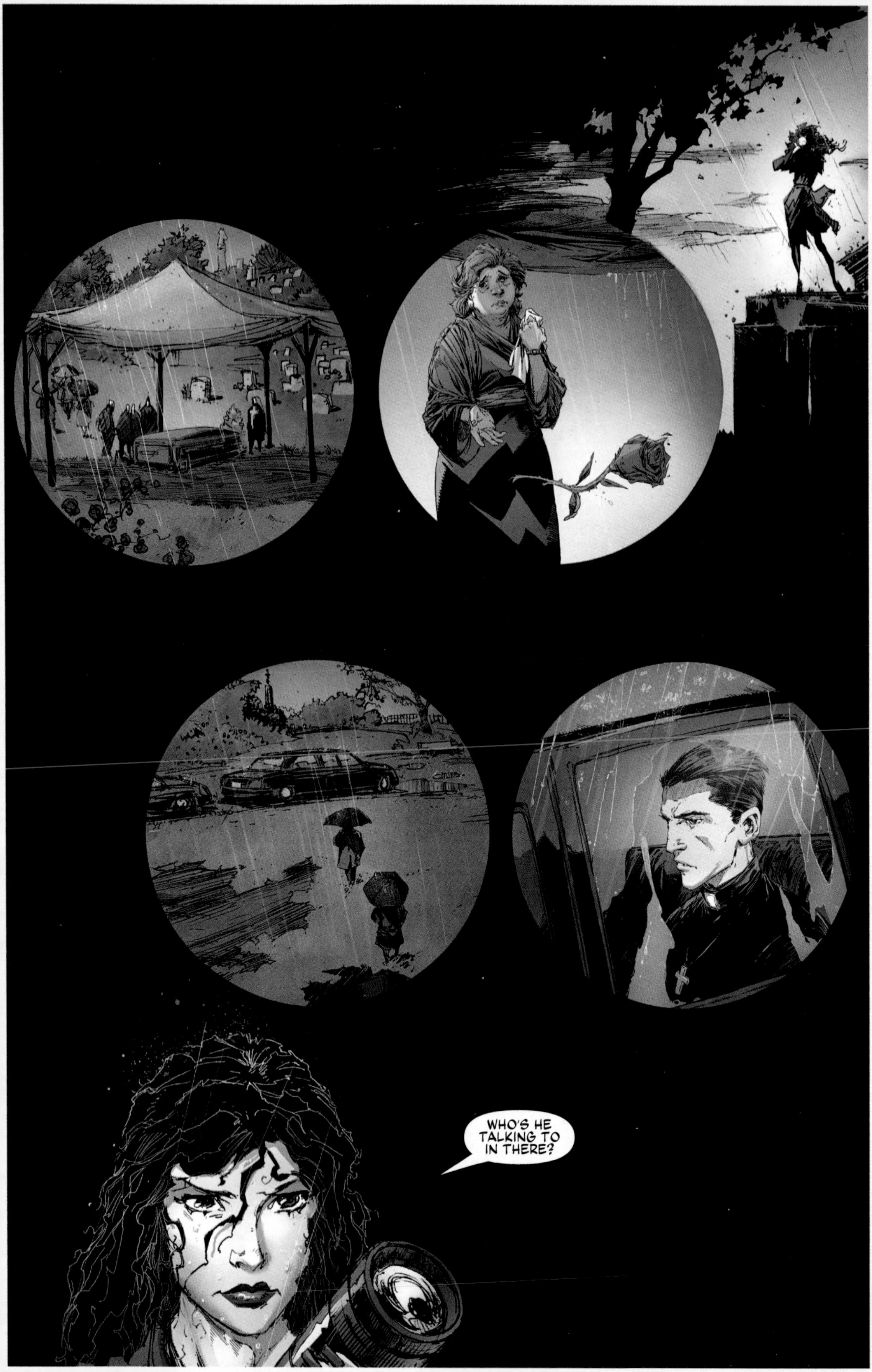
WHO'S HE TALKING TO IN THERE?

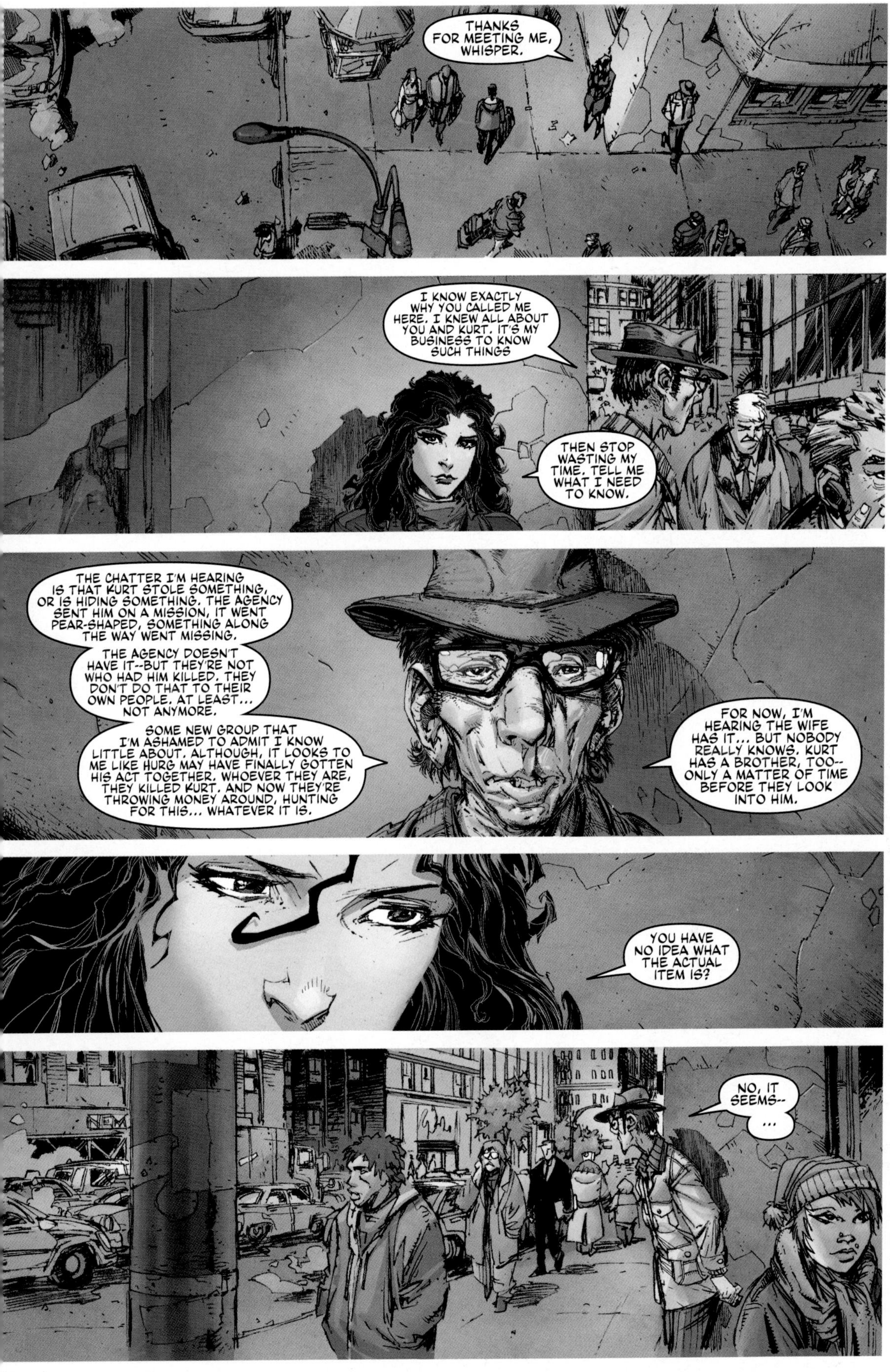

THANKS FOR MEETING ME, WHISPER.
I KNOW EXACTLY WHY YOU CALLED ME HERE. I KNEW ALL ABOUT YOU AND KURT. IT'S MY BUSINESS TO KNOW SUCH THINGS
THEN STOP WASTING MY TIME. TELL ME WHAT I NEED TO KNOW.
THE CHATTER I'M HEARING IS THAT KURT STOLE SOMETHING, OR IS HIDING SOMETHING. THE AGENCY SENT HIM ON A MISSION, IT WENT PEAR-SHAPED, SOMETHING ALONG THE WAY WENT MISSING.
THE AGENCY DOESN'T HAVE IT--BUT THEY'RE NOT WHO HAD HIM KILLED. THEY DON'T DO THAT TO THEIR OWN PEOPLE. AT LEAST... NOT ANYMORE.
SOME NEW GROUP THAT I'M ASHAMED TO ADMIT I KNOW LITTLE ABOUT. ALTHOUGH, IT LOOKS TO ME LIKE HURG MAY HAVE FINALLY GOTTEN HIS ACT TOGETHER. WHOEVER THEY ARE, THEY KILLED KURT. AND NOW THEY'RE THROWING MONEY AROUND, HUNTING FOR THIS... WHATEVER IT IS.
FOR NOW, I'M HEARING THE WIFE HAS IT... BUT NOBODY REALLY KNOWS. KURT HAS A BROTHER, TOO-- ONLY A MATTER OF TIME BEFORE THEY LOOK INTO HIM.
YOU HAVE NO IDEA WHAT THE ACTUAL ITEM IS?
NO, IT SEEMS-- ...

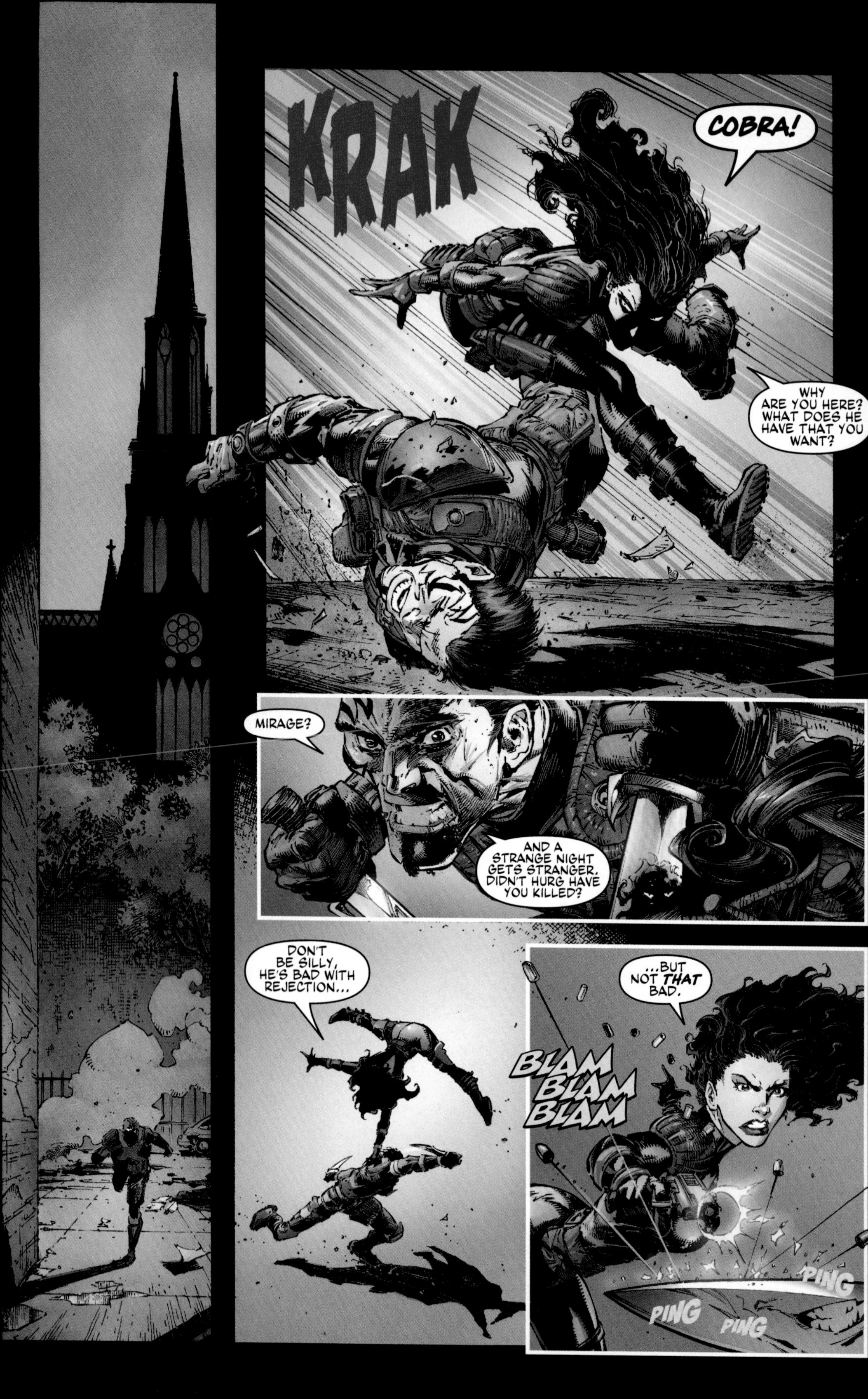
KRAK
COBRA!
WHY ARE YOU HERE? WHAT DOES HE HAVE THAT YOU WANT?
MIRAGE?
AND A STRANGE NIGHT GETS STRANGER. DIDN'T HURG HAVE YOU KILLED?
DON'T BE SILLY, HE'S BAD WITH REJECTION...
...BUT NOT THAT BAD.
BLAM BLAM BLAM
PING
PING
PING

GUESS I HEARD **WRONG.**

SVASSH

YOU--!

YOU THINK I DON'T HAVE THE ANTITOXIN FOR THIS? I KNOW YOU'RE TRICKS.

I DON'T WANT TO KILL YOU ANYWAY. YOU'RE FAR TOO FUN TO LOOK AT--EVEN WHEN WE'RE ON OPPOSING--

OKAY, YOU GOT ME--JUST BACK OFF KILGORE, OKAY? THIS IS MY MISSION, I REALLY NEED THE BREAD THIS IS GOING TO EARN.

I'M ASKING FOR A LITTLE PROFESSIONAL COURTESY, HERE.

WHY KILGORE? WHAT DOES HE HAVE THAT YOU'RE AFTER?

ALL I KNOW IS THAT IT'S A NOTEBOOK, I DON'T KNOW WHAT'S IN IT--SOMETHING TO DO WITH SOME DEAD SCIENTIST NAMED...

...SHILLINGER.

HUH...

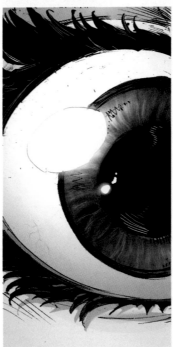

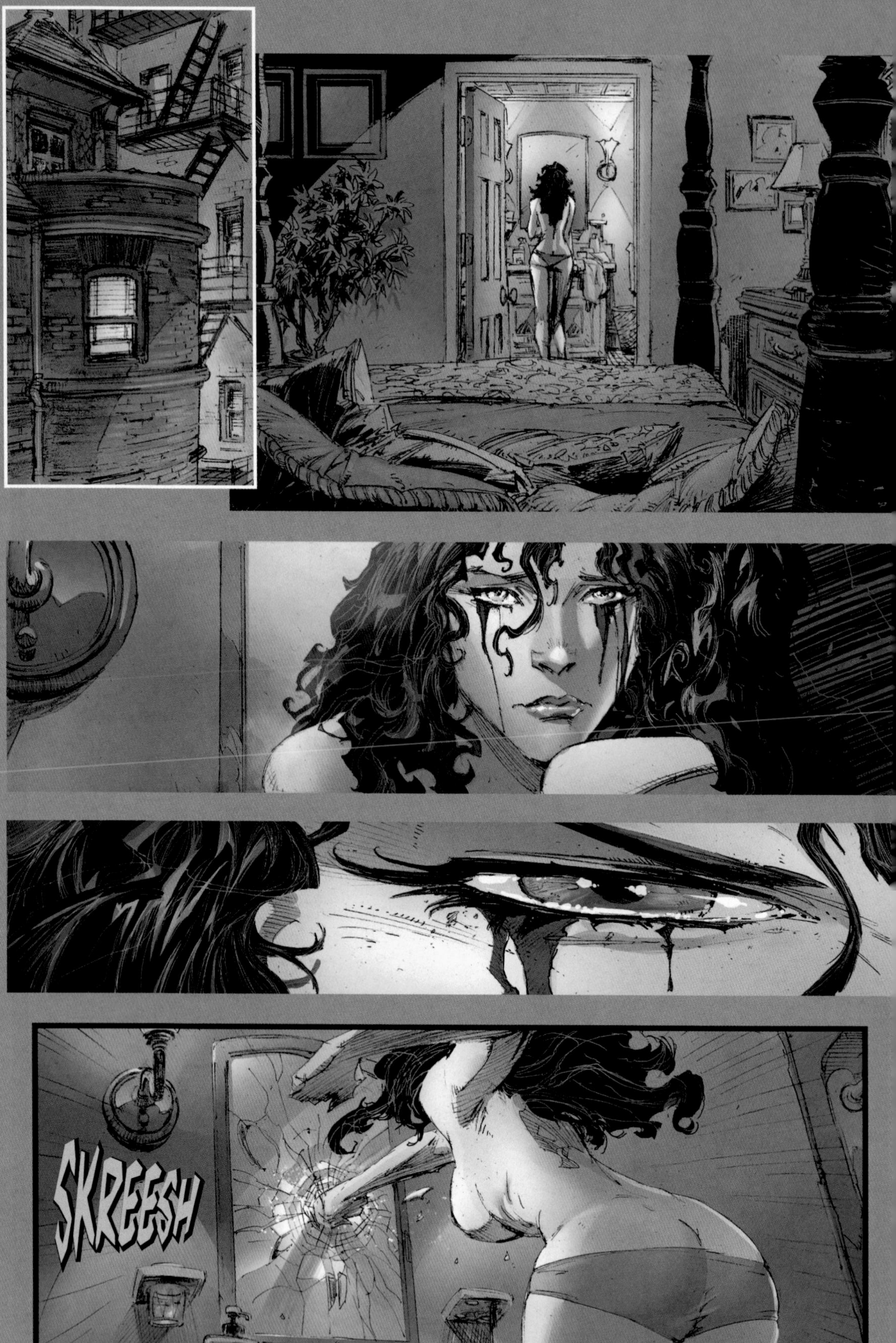
SKREESH

I ASSURE YOU MA'AM THIS IS ALL BEING DONE FOR YOUR SAFETY.

CAN YOU TELL ME WHAT'S GOING ON? HOW LONG WILL I BE GONE?

ALL WE CAN SAY IS THAT YOU'RE IN DANGER, WE'RE SORRY.

LET'S MAKE SURE THE BITCHY MS. KILGORE MAKES IT TO HER SAFE HOUSE...

I OWE YOU THAT MUCH, KURT.

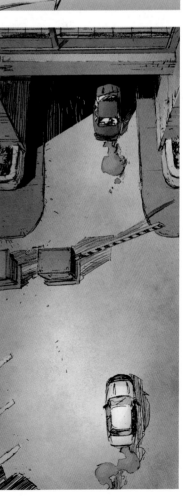

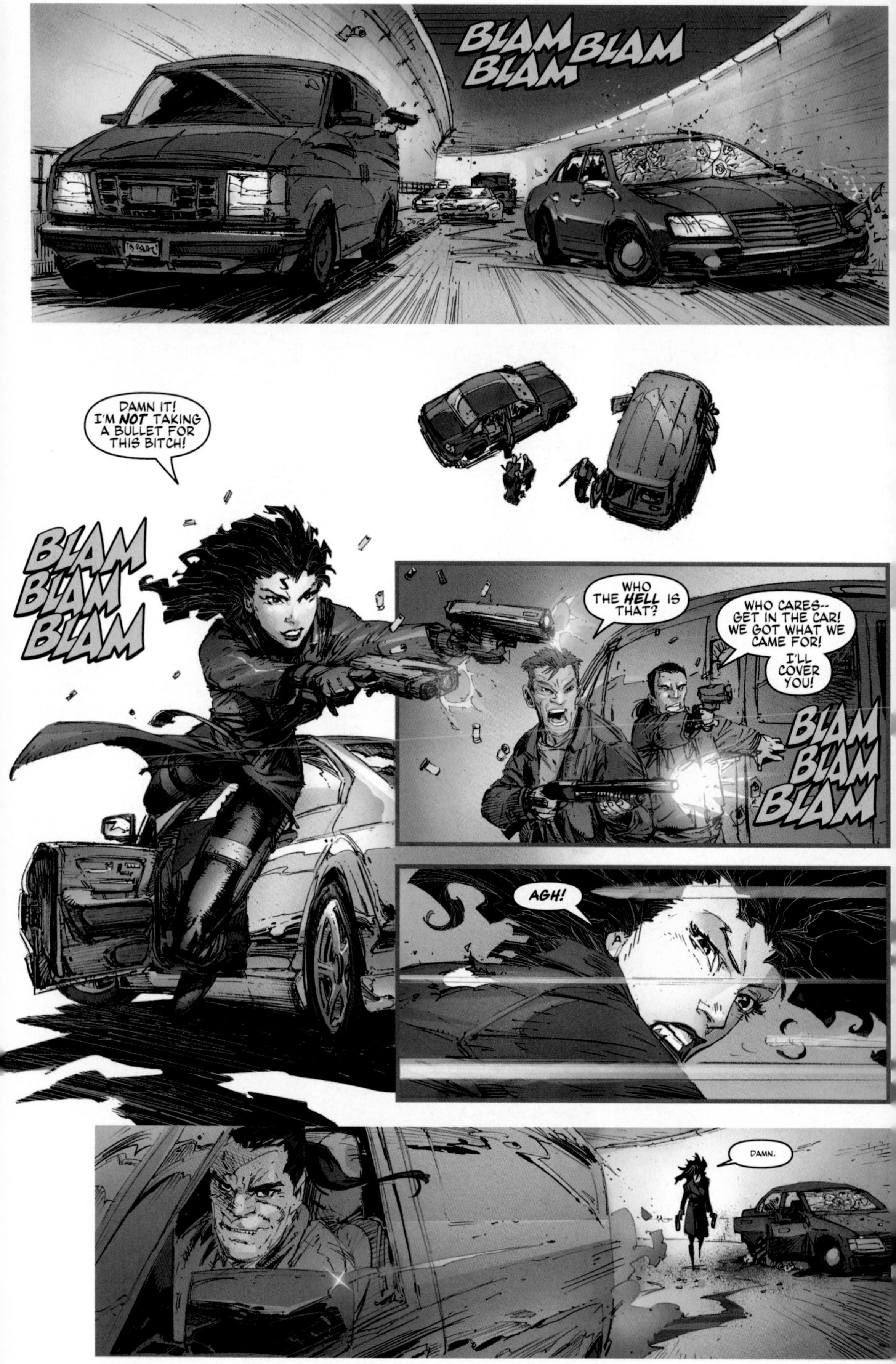
BLAM BLAM BLAM
DAMN IT! I'M NOT TAKING A BULLET FOR THIS BITCH!
BLAM BLAM BLAM
WHO THE HELL IS THAT?
WHO CARES-- GET IN THE CAR! WE GOT WHAT WE CAME FOR!
I'LL COVER YOU!
BLAM BLAM BLAM
AGH!
DAMN.

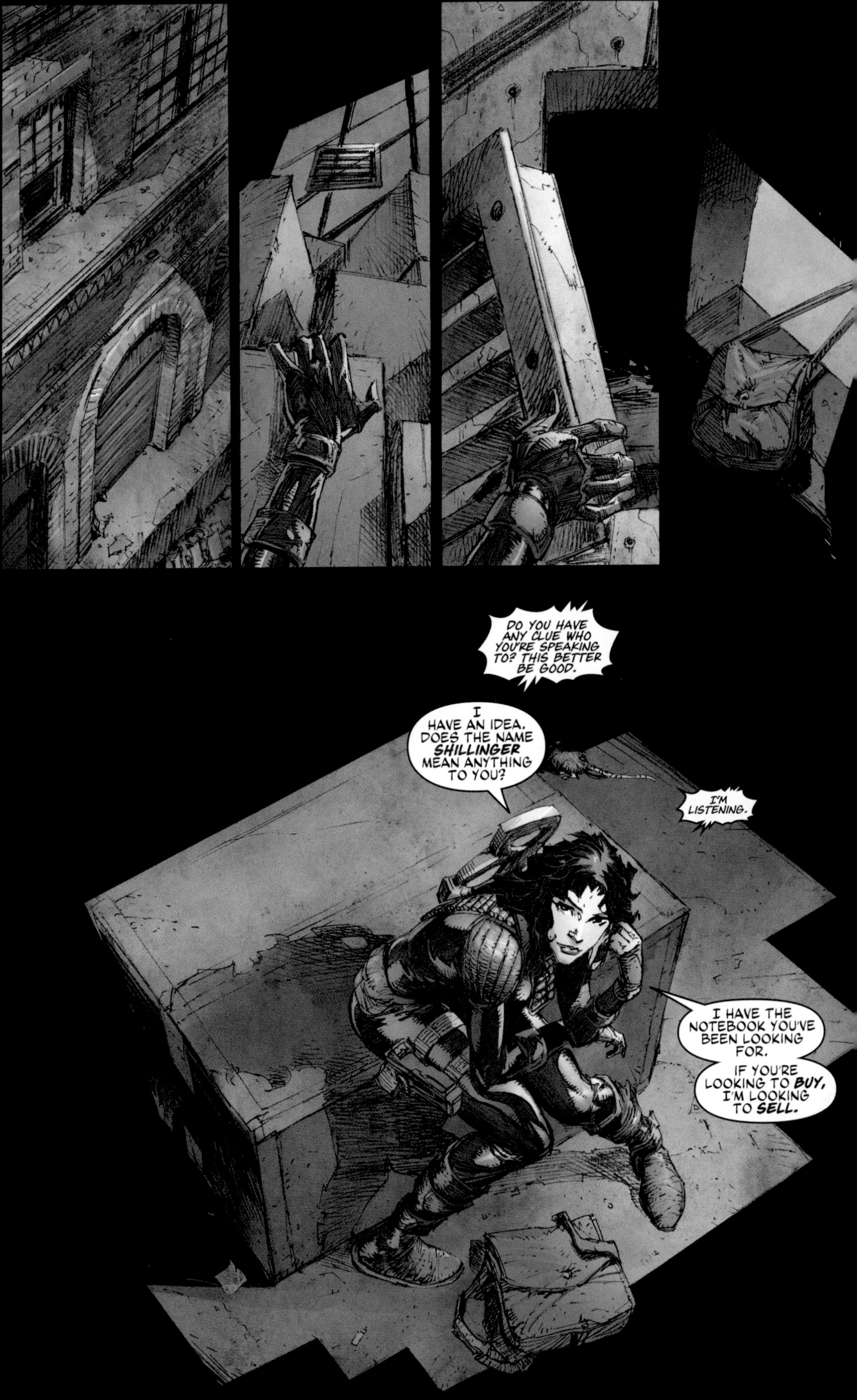

DO YOU HAVE ANY CLUE WHO YOU'RE SPEAKING TO? THIS BETTER BE GOOD.
I HAVE AN IDEA. DOES THE NAME SHILLINGER MEAN ANYTHING TO YOU?
I'M LISTENING.
I HAVE THE NOTEBOOK YOU'VE BEEN LOOKING FOR.
IF YOU'RE LOOKING TO BUY, I'M LOOKING TO SELL.

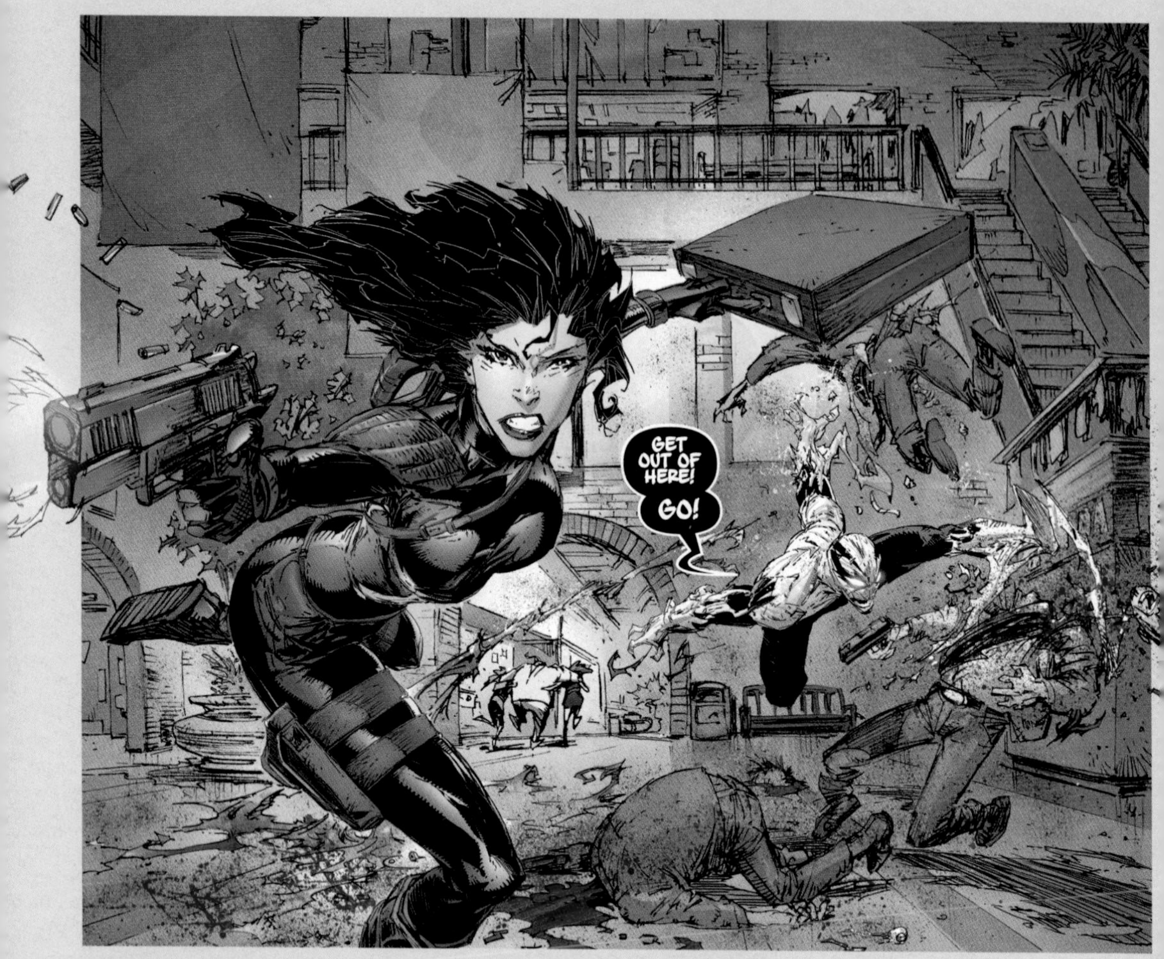
GET OUT OF HERE!
GO!

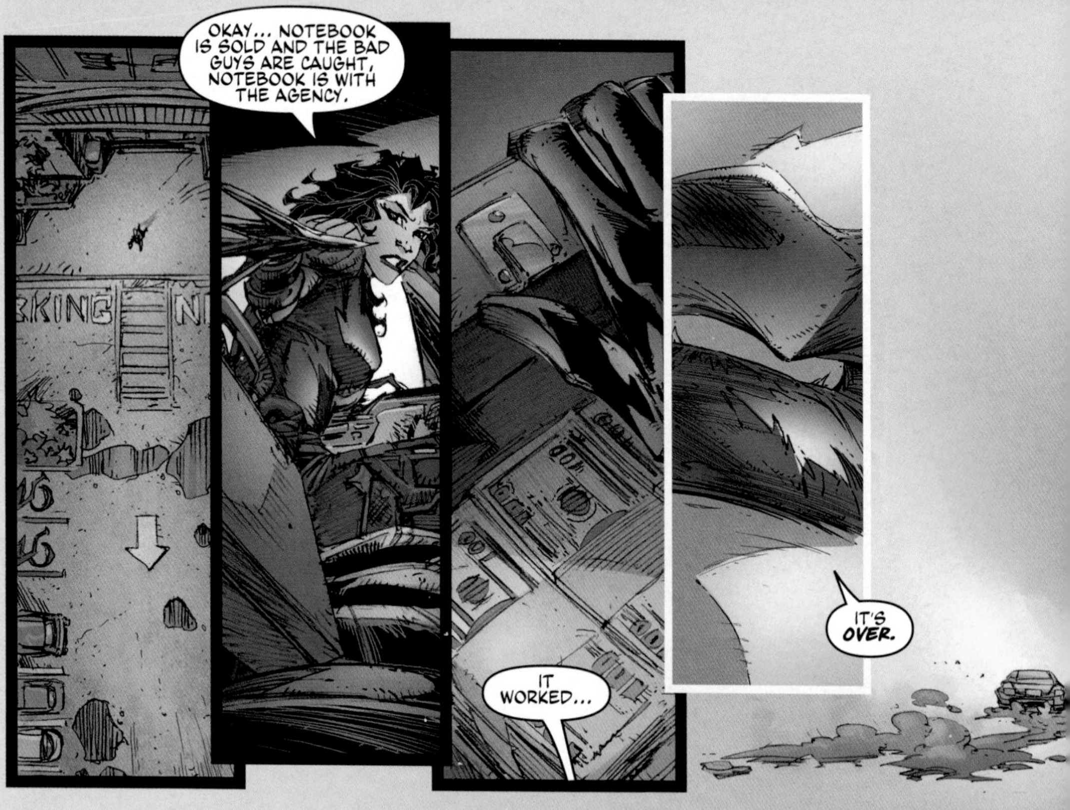
OKAY... NOTEBOOK IS SOLD AND THE BAD GUYS ARE CAUGHT, NOTEBOOK IS WITH THE AGENCY.
IT WORKED...
IT'S OVER.

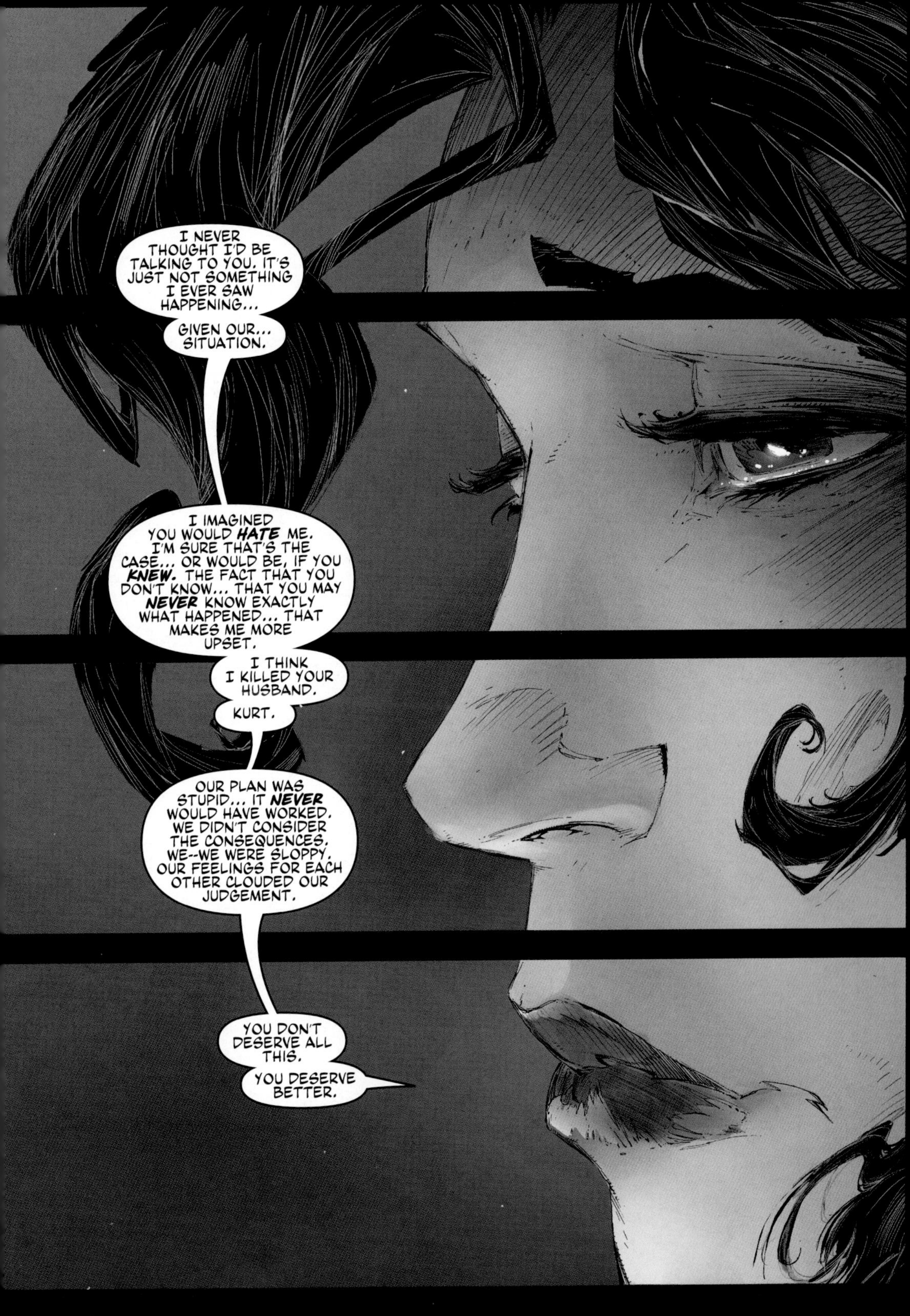
I NEVER THOUGHT I'D BE TALKING TO YOU. IT'S JUST NOT SOMETHING I EVER SAW HAPPENING...
GIVEN OUR... SITUATION.
I IMAGINED YOU WOULD HATE ME. I'M SURE THAT'S THE CASE... OR WOULD BE, IF YOU KNEW. THE FACT THAT YOU DON'T KNOW... THAT YOU MAY NEVER KNOW EXACTLY WHAT HAPPENED... THAT MAKES ME MORE UPSET.
I THINK I KILLED YOUR HUSBAND.
KURT.
OUR PLAN WAS STUPID... IT NEVER WOULD HAVE WORKED. WE DIDN'T CONSIDER THE CONSEQUENCES. WE--WE WERE SLOPPY. OUR FEELINGS FOR EACH OTHER CLOUDED OUR JUDGEMENT.
YOU DON'T DESERVE ALL THIS.
YOU DESERVE BETTER.

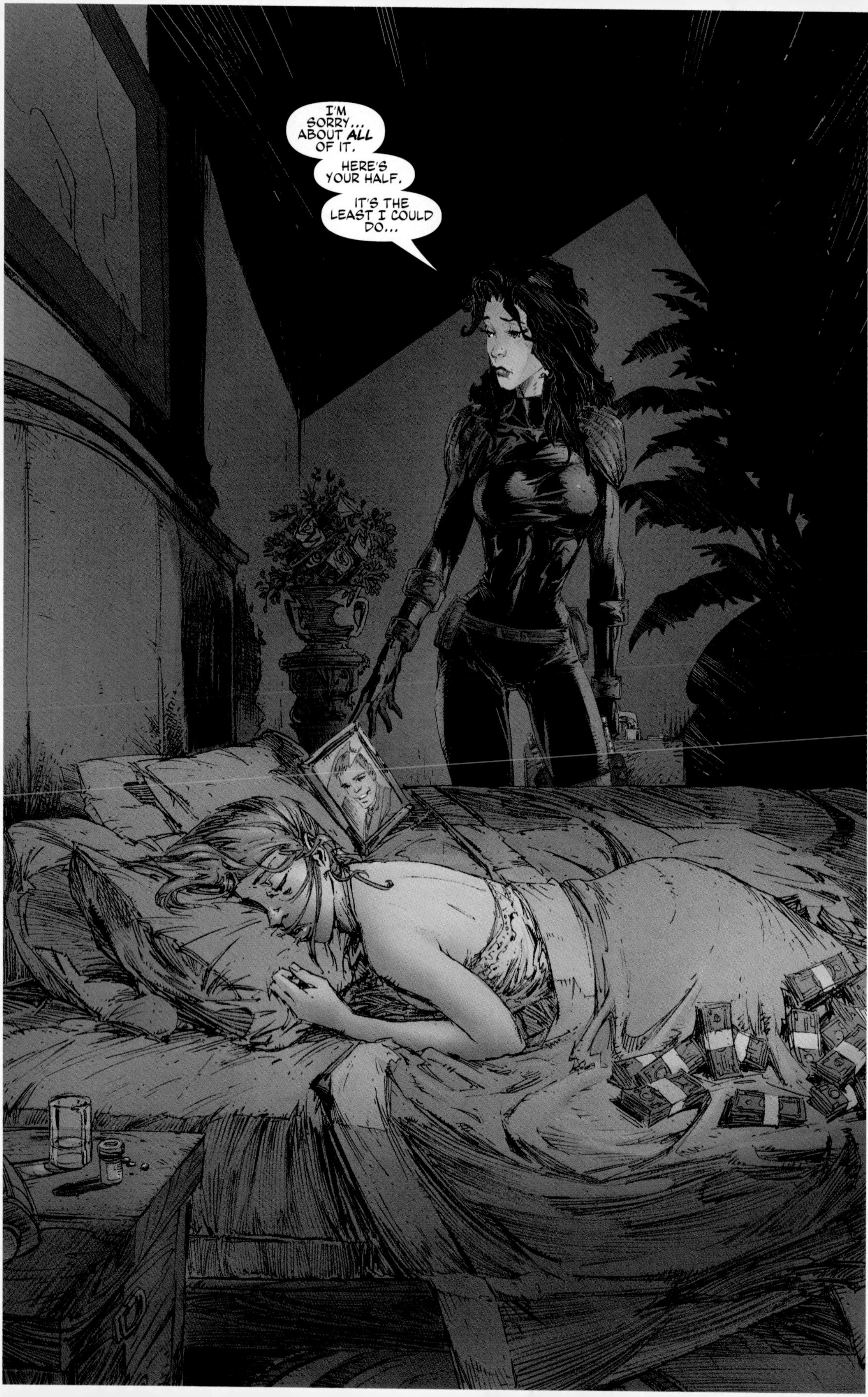
I'M SORRY... ABOUT **ALL** OF IT.
HERE'S YOUR HALF.
IT'S THE LEAST I COULD DO...

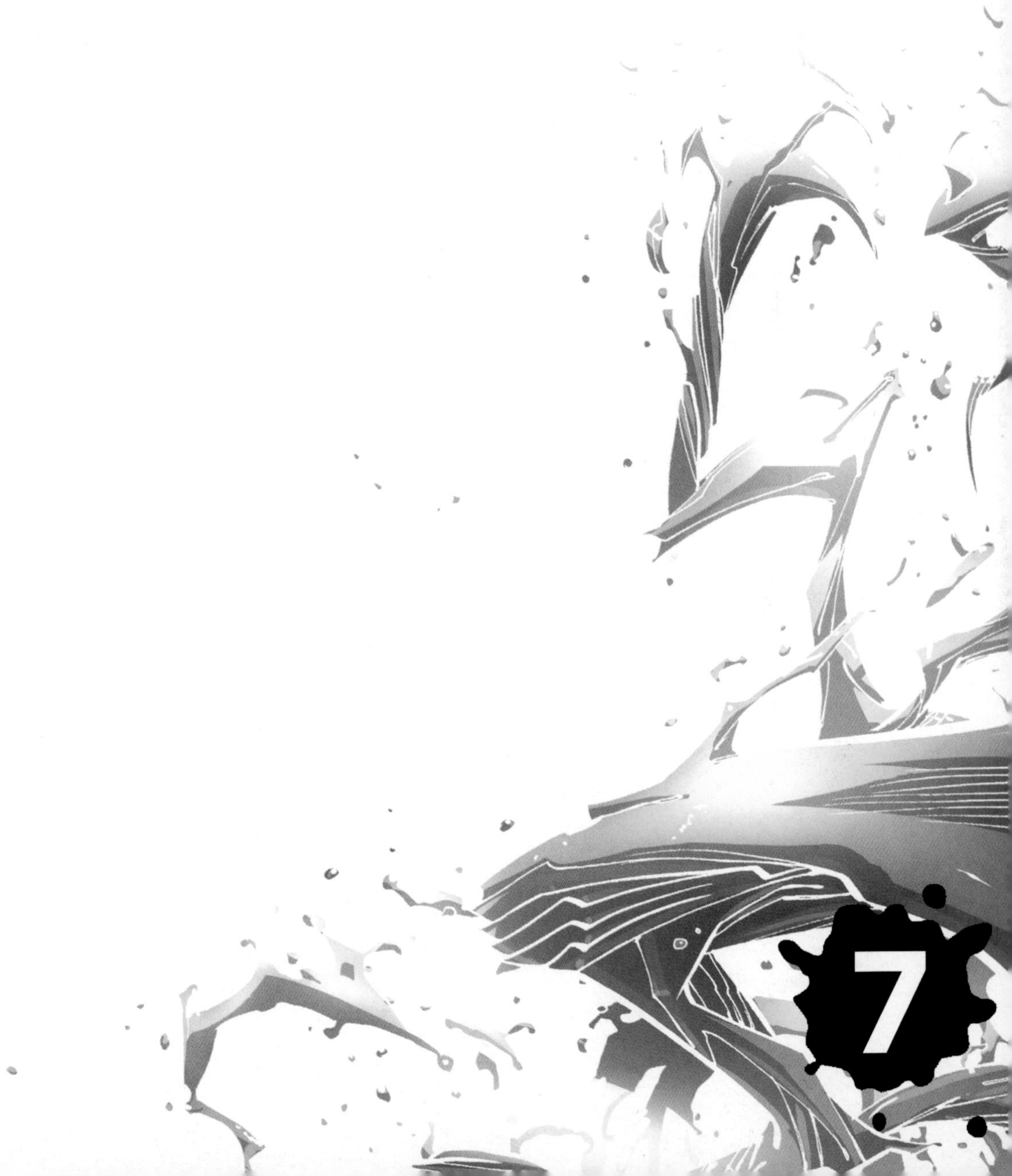
7

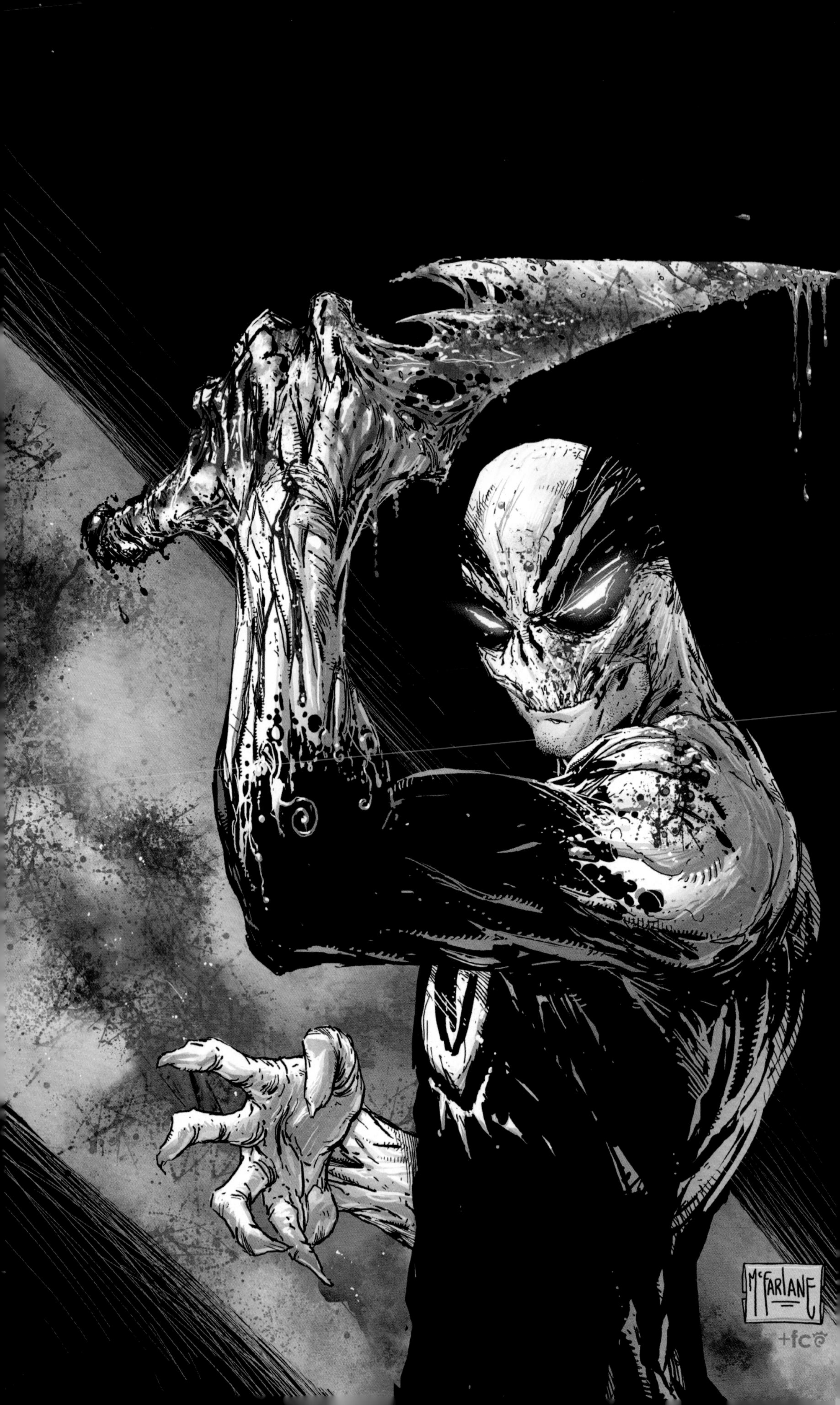
McFARLANE
+fco

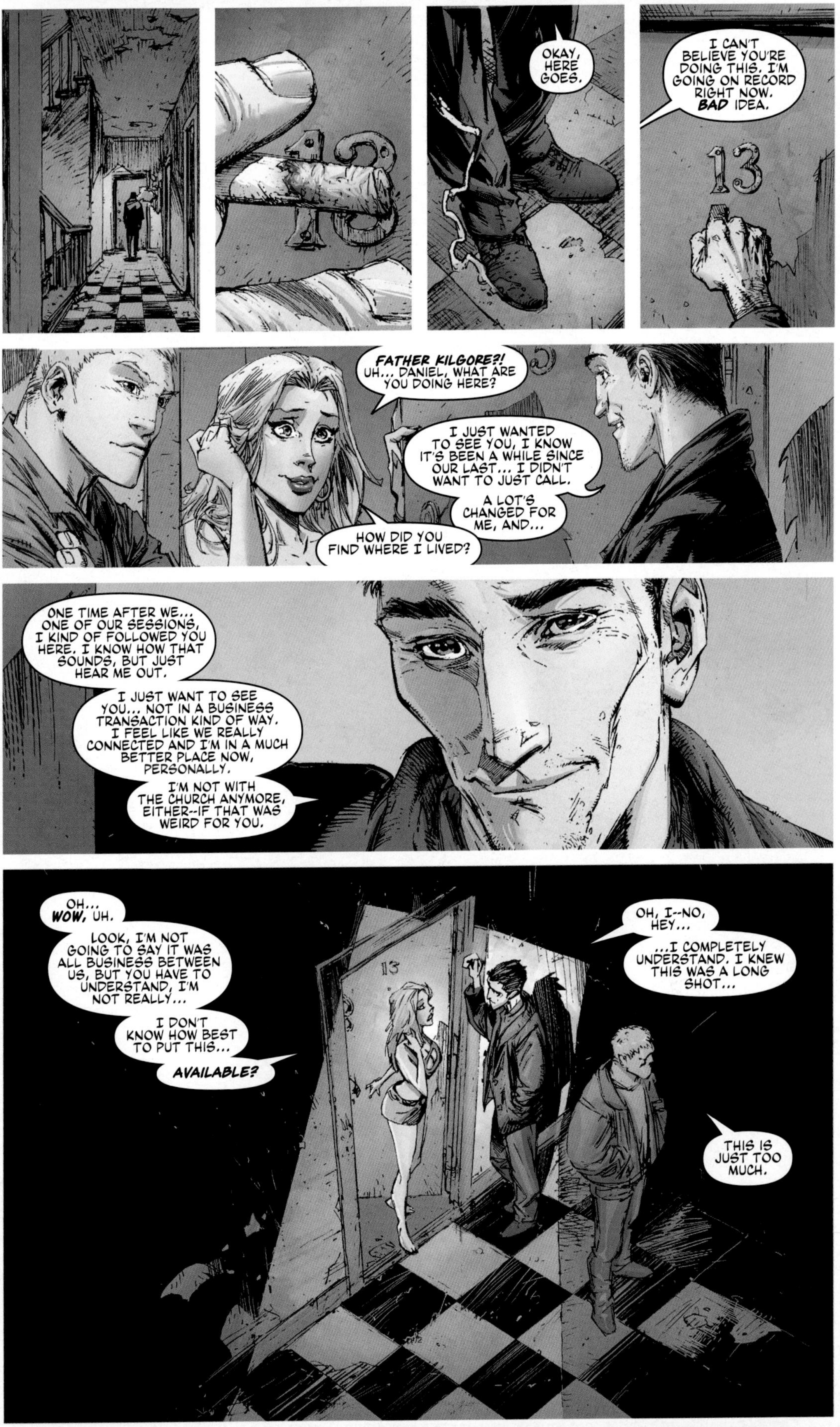
OKAY, HERE GOES.
I CAN'T BELIEVE YOU'RE DOING THIS. I'M GOING ON RECORD RIGHT NOW. BAD IDEA.
FATHER KILGORE?! UH... DANIEL, WHAT ARE YOU DOING HERE?
I JUST WANTED TO SEE YOU, I KNOW IT'S BEEN A WHILE SINCE OUR LAST... I DIDN'T WANT TO JUST CALL.
A LOT'S CHANGED FOR ME, AND...
HOW DID YOU FIND WHERE I LIVED?
ONE TIME AFTER WE... ONE OF OUR SESSIONS, I KIND OF FOLLOWED YOU HERE. I KNOW HOW THAT SOUNDS, BUT JUST HEAR ME OUT.
I JUST WANT TO SEE YOU... NOT IN A BUSINESS TRANSACTION KIND OF WAY. I FEEL LIKE WE REALLY CONNECTED AND I'M IN A MUCH BETTER PLACE NOW, PERSONALLY.
I'M NOT WITH THE CHURCH ANYMORE, EITHER--IF THAT WAS WEIRD FOR YOU.
OH... WOW, UH.
LOOK, I'M NOT GOING TO SAY IT WAS ALL BUSINESS BETWEEN US, BUT YOU HAVE TO UNDERSTAND, I'M NOT REALLY...
I DON'T KNOW HOW BEST TO PUT THIS...
AVAILABLE?
OH, I--NO, HEY...
...I COMPLETELY UNDERSTAND. I KNEW THIS WAS A LONG SHOT...
THIS IS JUST TOO MUCH.

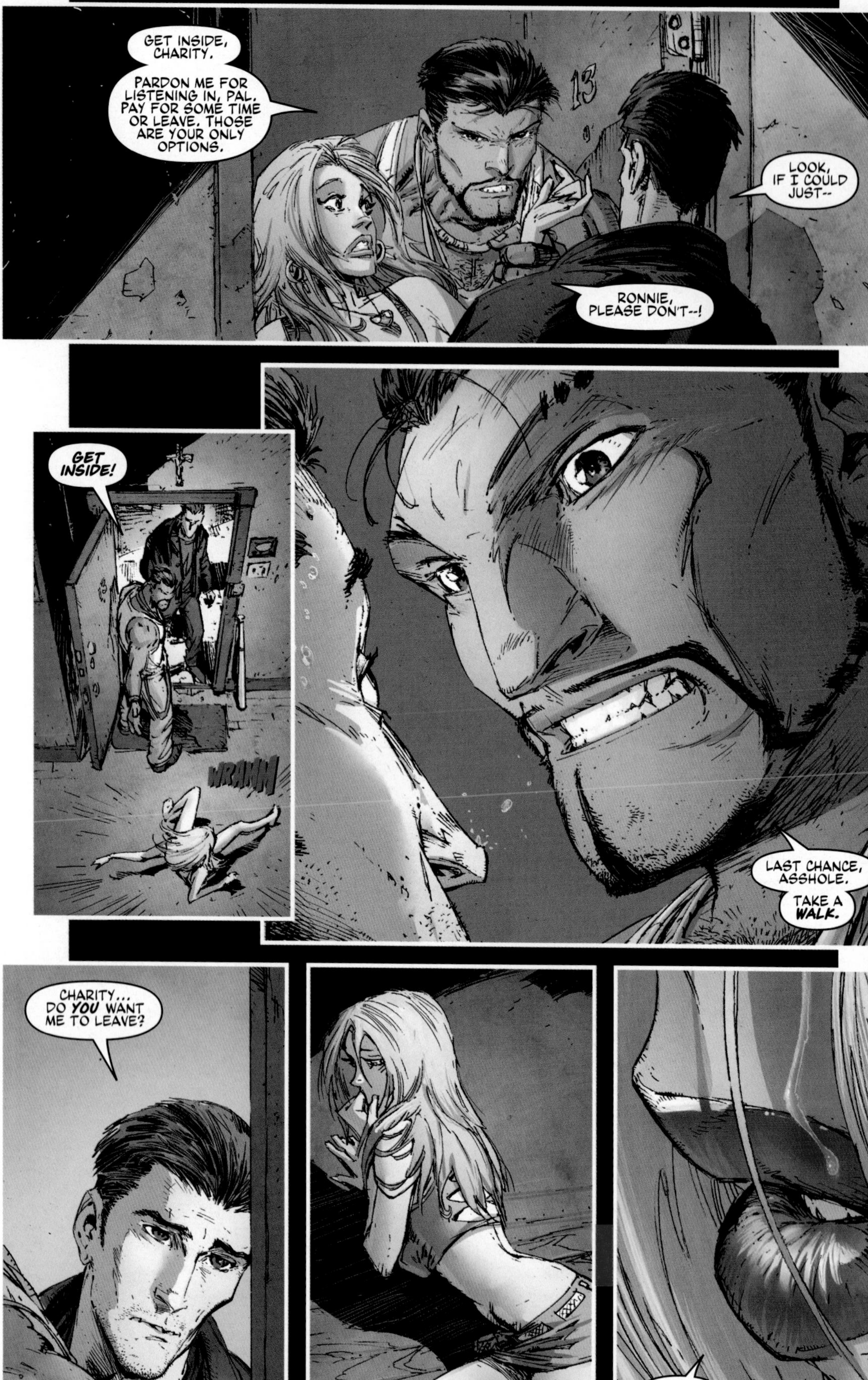

GET INSIDE, CHARITY.
PARDON ME FOR LISTENING IN, PAL. PAY FOR SOME TIME OR LEAVE. THOSE ARE YOUR ONLY OPTIONS.
LOOK, IF I COULD JUST--
RONNIE, PLEASE DON'T--!
GET INSIDE!
WRAHM
LAST CHANCE, ASSHOLE.
TAKE A WALK.
CHARITY... DO YOU WANT ME TO LEAVE?
NO.

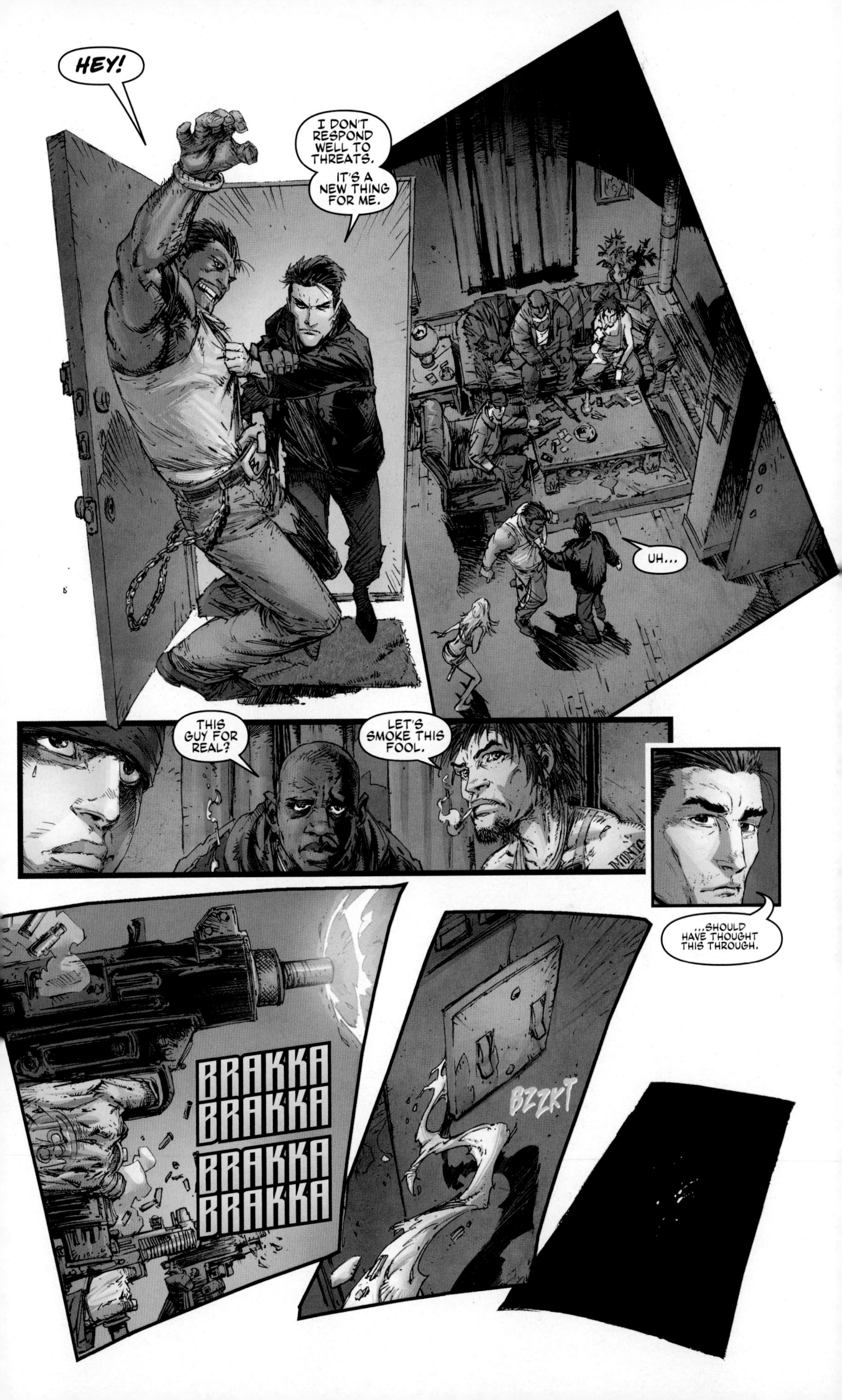
HEY!
I DON'T RESPOND WELL TO THREATS.
IT'S A NEW THING FOR ME.
UH...
THIS GUY FOR REAL?
LET'S SMOKE THIS FOOL.
...SHOULD HAVE THOUGHT THIS THROUGH.
BRAKKA BRAKKA BRAKKA BRAKKA
BZZKT

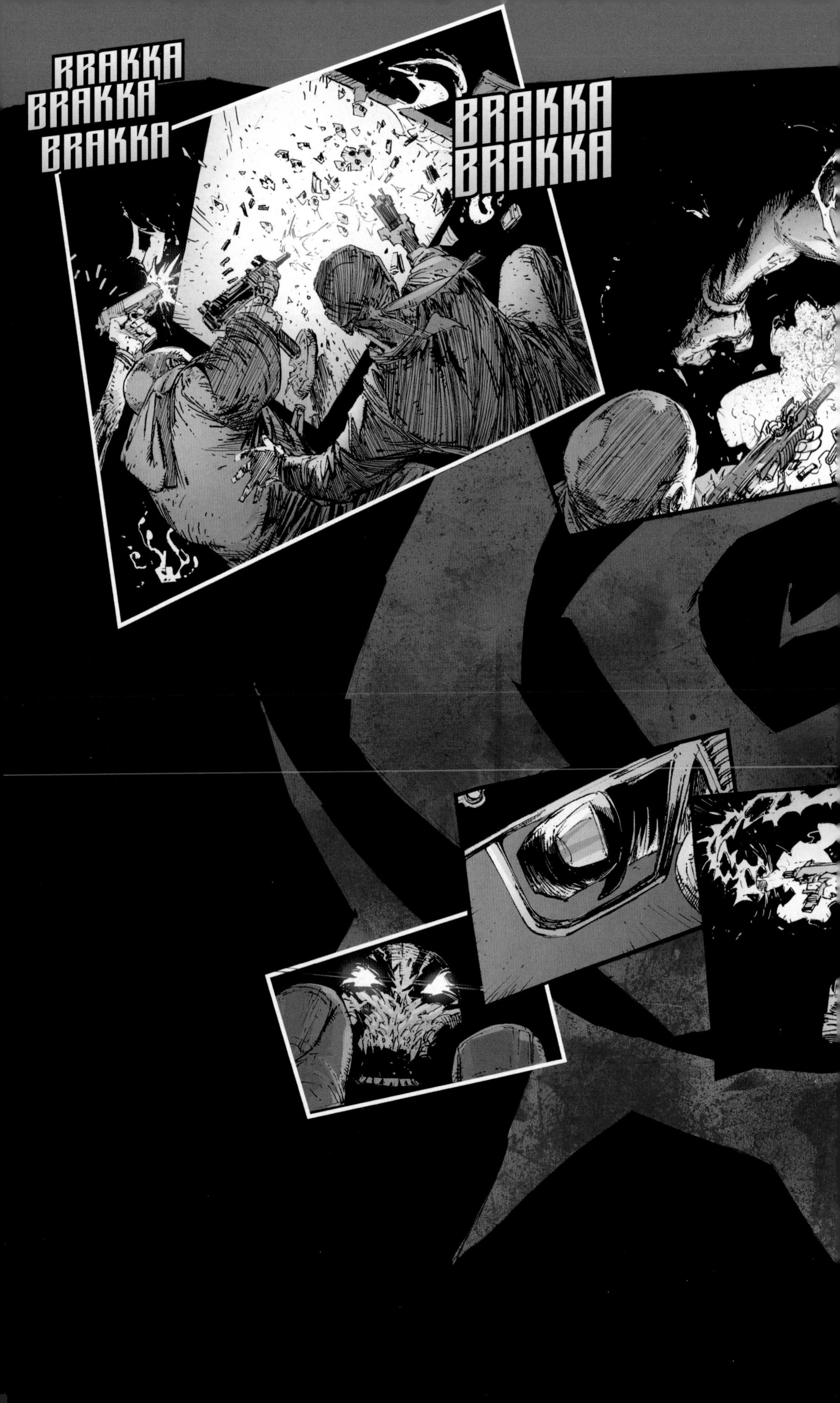
BRAKKA
BRAKKA
BRAKKA
BRAKKA
BRAKKA

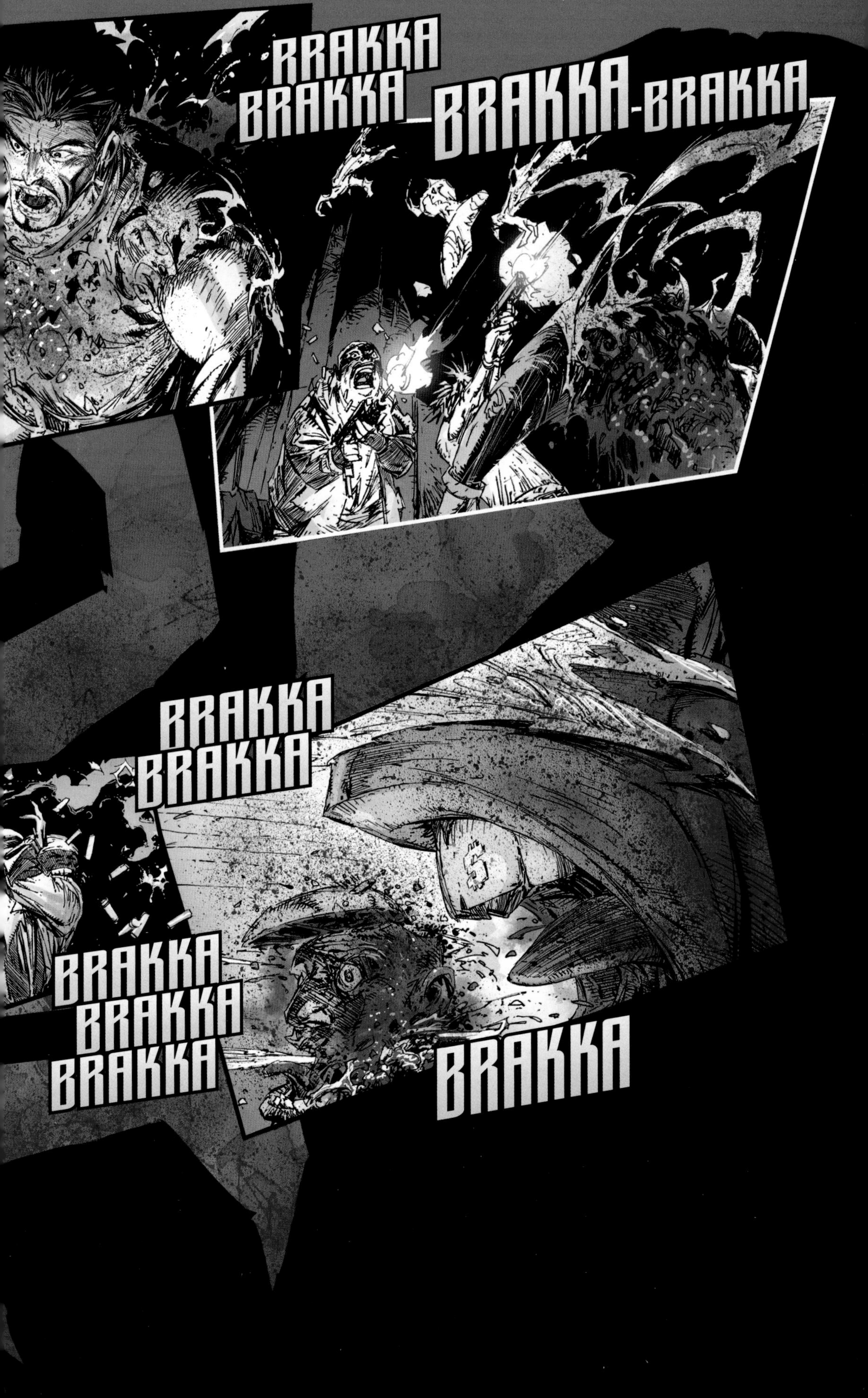
RRAKKA
BRAKKA
BRAKKA-BRAKKA
BRAKKA
BRAKKA
BRAKKA
BRAKKA
BRAKKA
BRAKKA

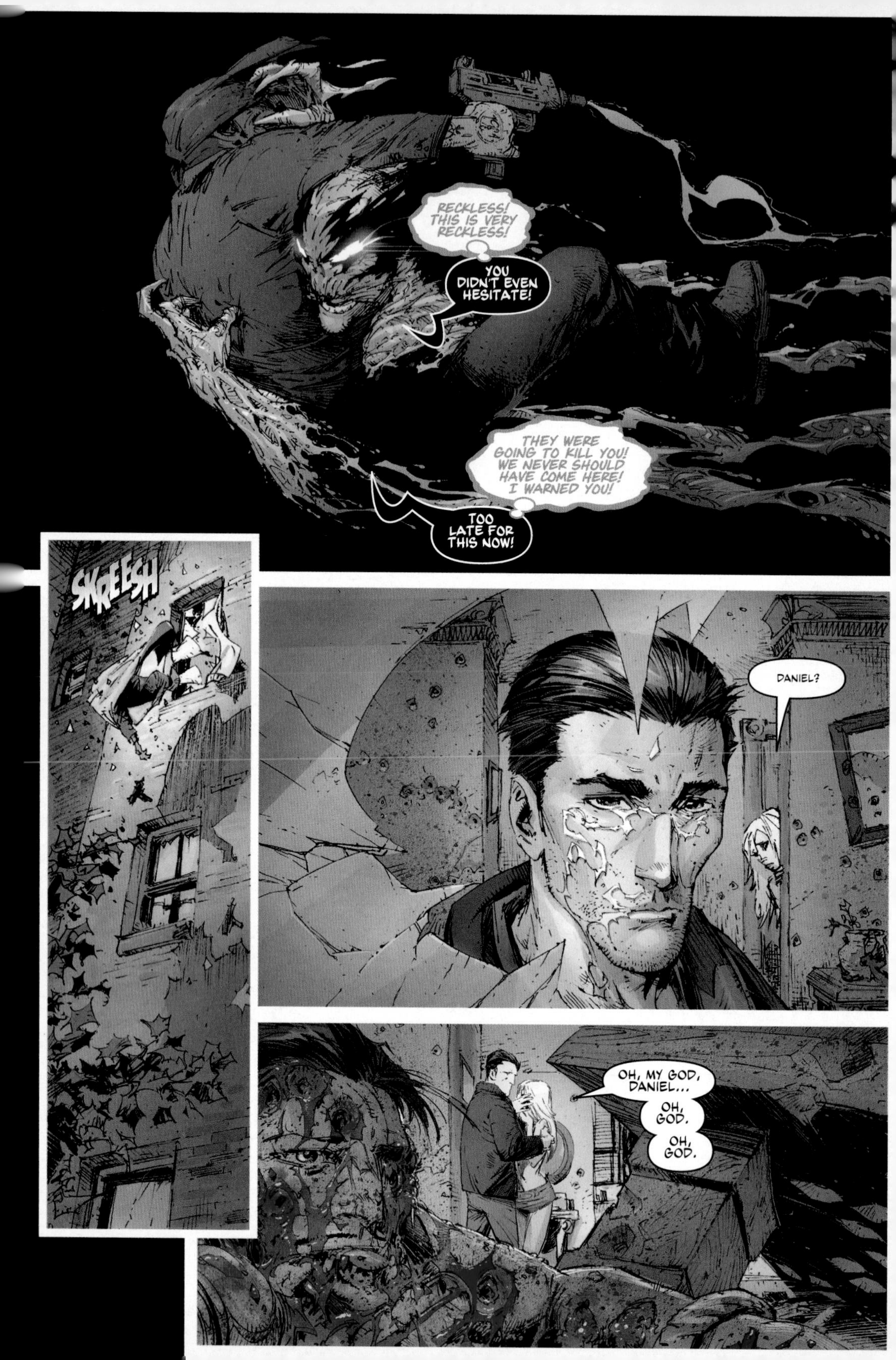
RECKLESS! THIS IS VERY RECKLESS!
YOU DIDN'T EVEN HESITATE!
THEY WERE GOING TO KILL YOU! WE NEVER SHOULD HAVE COME HERE! I WARNED YOU!
TOO LATE FOR THIS NOW!
SKREESH
DANIEL?
OH, MY GOD, DANIEL...
OH, GOD.
OH, GOD.

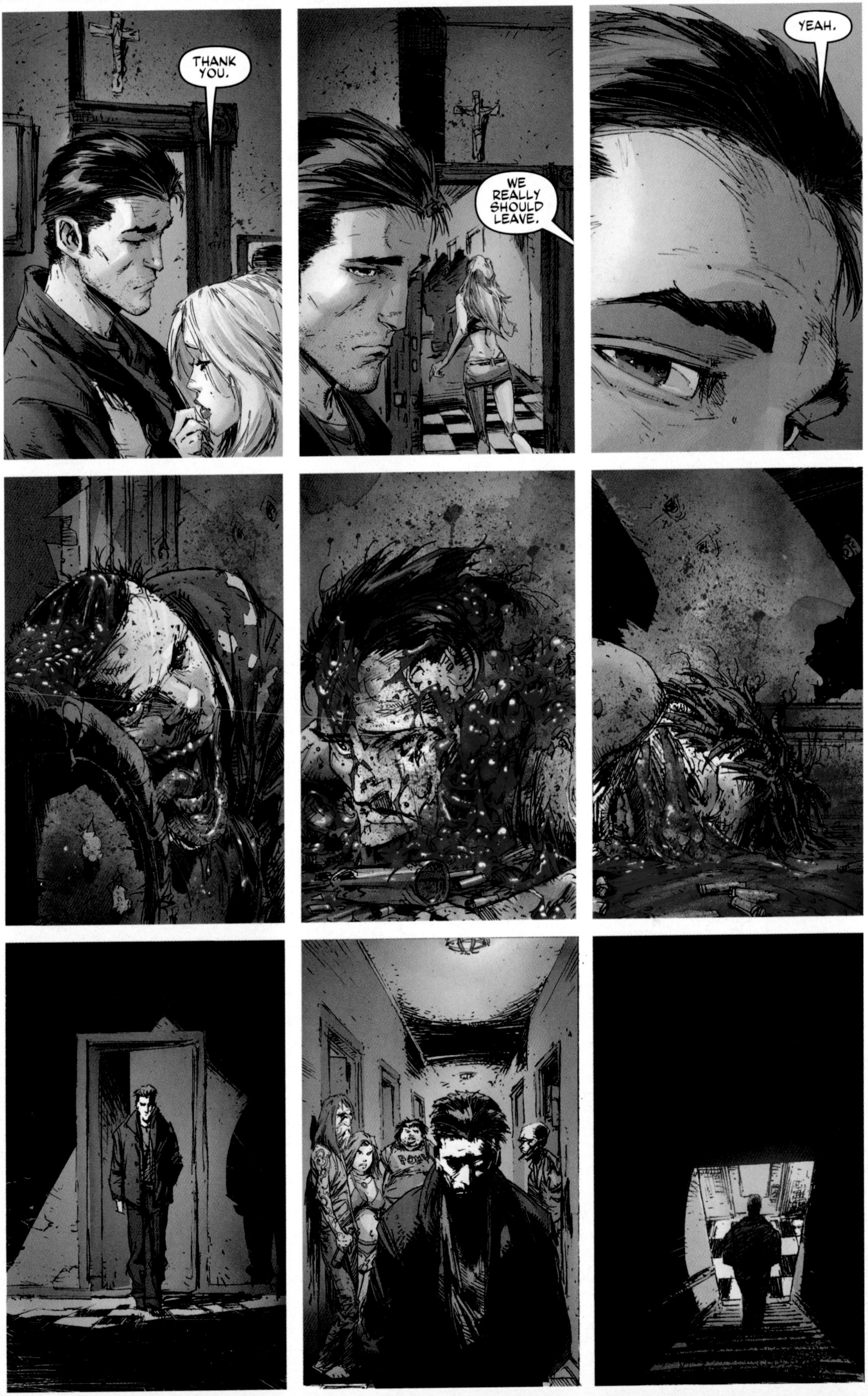
THANK YOU.
WE REALLY SHOULD LEAVE.
YEAH.

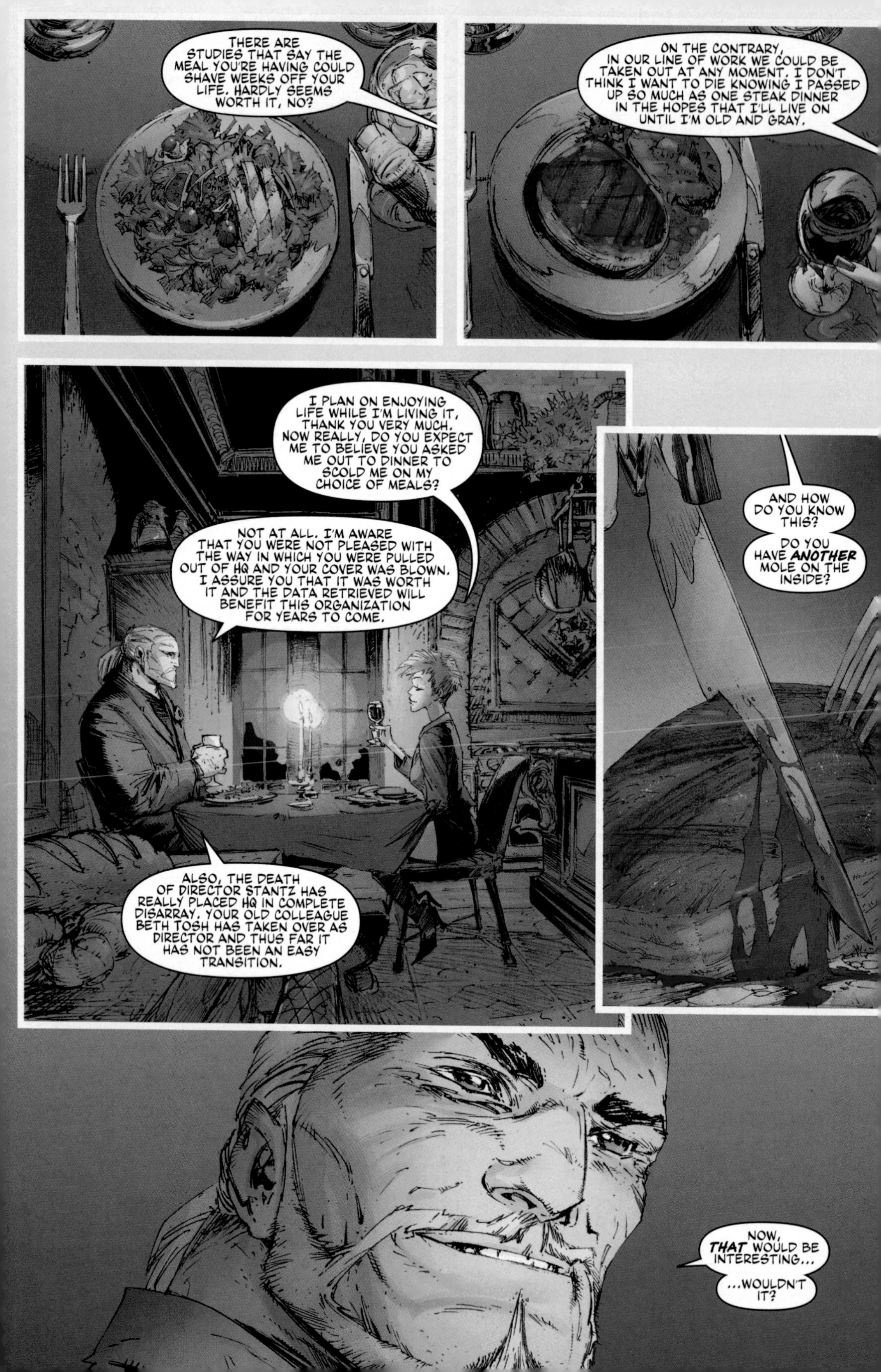

THERE ARE STUDIES THAT SAY THE MEAL YOU'RE HAVING COULD SHAVE WEEKS OFF YOUR LIFE. HARDLY SEEMS WORTH IT, NO?
ON THE CONTRARY, IN OUR LINE OF WORK WE COULD BE TAKEN OUT AT ANY MOMENT. I DON'T THINK I WANT TO DIE KNOWING I PASSED UP SO MUCH AS ONE STEAK DINNER IN THE HOPES THAT I'LL LIVE ON UNTIL I'M OLD AND GRAY.
I PLAN ON ENJOYING LIFE WHILE I'M LIVING IT, THANK YOU VERY MUCH. NOW REALLY, DO YOU EXPECT ME TO BELIEVE YOU ASKED ME OUT TO DINNER TO SCOLD ME ON MY CHOICE OF MEALS?
NOT AT ALL. I'M AWARE THAT YOU WERE NOT PLEASED WITH THE WAY IN WHICH YOU WERE PULLED OUT OF HQ AND YOUR COVER WAS BLOWN. I ASSURE YOU THAT IT WAS WORTH IT AND THE DATA RETRIEVED WILL BENEFIT THIS ORGANIZATION FOR YEARS TO COME.
ALSO, THE DEATH OF DIRECTOR STANTZ HAS REALLY PLACED HQ IN COMPLETE DISARRAY. YOUR OLD COLLEAGUE BETH TOSH HAS TAKEN OVER AS DIRECTOR AND THUS FAR IT HAS NOT BEEN AN EASY TRANSITION.
AND HOW DO YOU KNOW THIS?
DO YOU HAVE *ANOTHER* MOLE ON THE INSIDE?
NOW, *THAT* WOULD BE INTERESTING...
...WOULDN'T IT?

I MUST SAY, MISTER HURG...

...YOU NEVER FAIL TO IMPRESS.

PHONE CALL FOR YOU, SIR.

THIS BETTER BE GOOD, I'M HAVING A MEAL.

IT IS, SIR. IT IS.

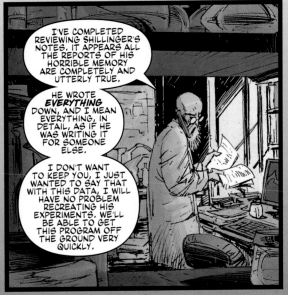

I'VE COMPLETED REVIEWING SHILLINGER'S NOTES. IT APPEARS ALL THE REPORTS OF HIS HORRIBLE MEMORY ARE COMPLETELY AND UTTERLY TRUE.

HE WROTE EVERYTHING DOWN, AND I MEAN EVERYTHING, IN DETAIL, AS IF HE WAS WRITING IT FOR SOMEONE ELSE.

I DON'T WANT TO KEEP YOU, I JUST WANTED TO SAY THAT WITH THIS DATA, I WILL HAVE NO PROBLEM RECREATING HIS EXPERIMENTS. WE'LL BE ABLE TO GET THIS PROGRAM OFF THE GROUND VERY QUICKLY.

EXCELLENT. THANK YOU FOR THE UPDATE, DOCTOR.

WAITER, I'M IN A GOOD MOOD, SO I'M GOING TO SPLURGE. BRING ME A BOWL OF STRAWBERRIES.

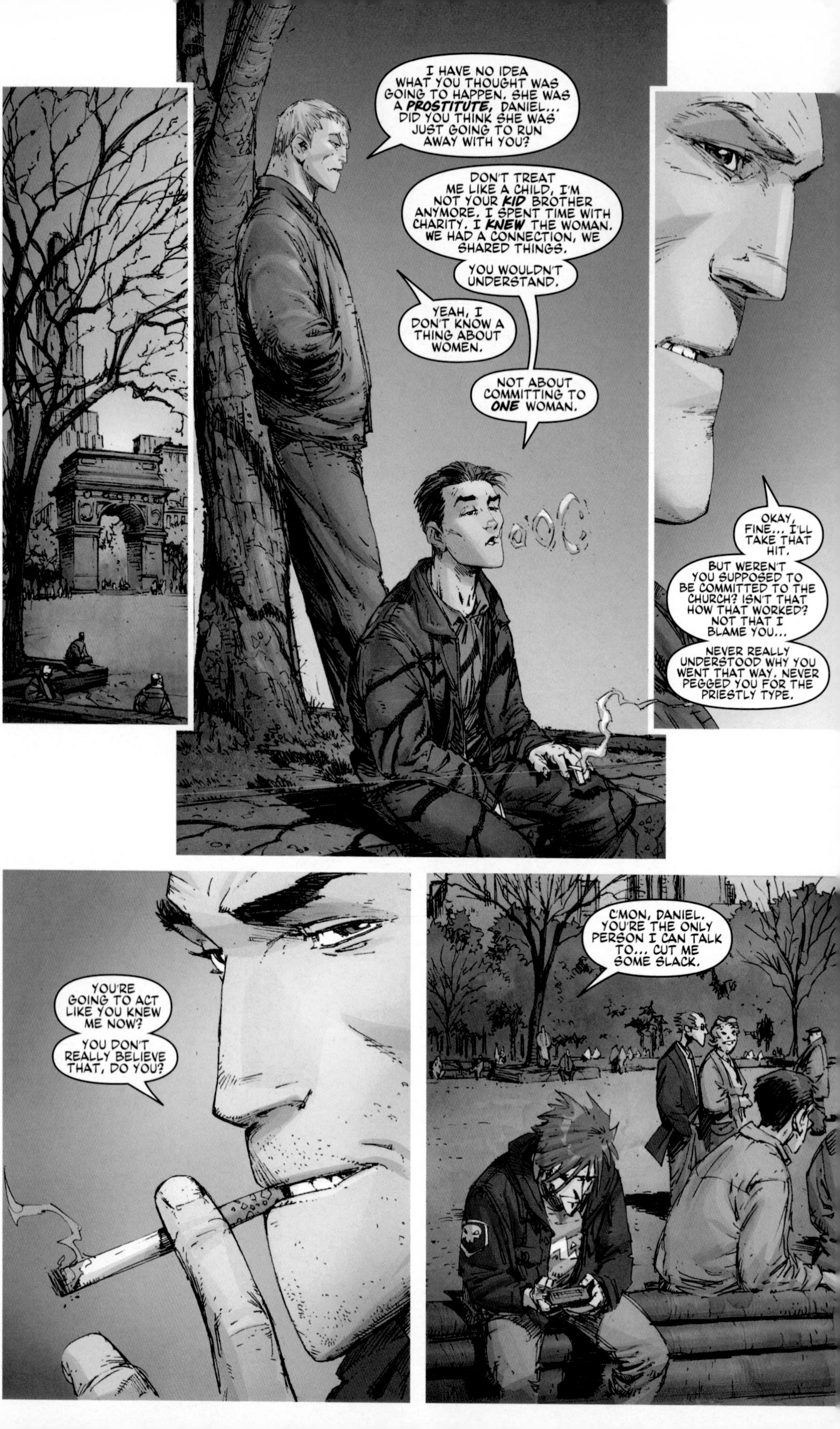
I HAVE NO IDEA WHAT YOU THOUGHT WAS GOING TO HAPPEN. SHE WAS A PROSTITUTE, DANIEL... DID YOU THINK SHE WAS JUST GOING TO RUN AWAY WITH YOU?
DON'T TREAT ME LIKE A CHILD, I'M NOT YOUR KID BROTHER ANYMORE. I SPENT TIME WITH CHARITY. I KNEW THE WOMAN. WE HAD A CONNECTION, WE SHARED THINGS.
YOU WOULDN'T UNDERSTAND.
YEAH, I DON'T KNOW A THING ABOUT WOMEN.
NOT ABOUT COMMITTING TO ONE WOMAN.
OKAY, FINE... I'LL TAKE THAT HIT.
BUT WEREN'T YOU SUPPOSED TO BE COMMITTED TO THE CHURCH? ISN'T THAT HOW THAT WORKED? NOT THAT I BLAME YOU...
NEVER REALLY UNDERSTOOD WHY YOU WENT THAT WAY. NEVER PEGGED YOU FOR THE PRIESTLY TYPE.
YOU'RE GOING TO ACT LIKE YOU KNEW ME NOW?
YOU DON'T REALLY BELIEVE THAT, DO YOU?
C'MON, DANIEL. YOU'RE THE ONLY PERSON I CAN TALK TO... CUT ME SOME SLACK.

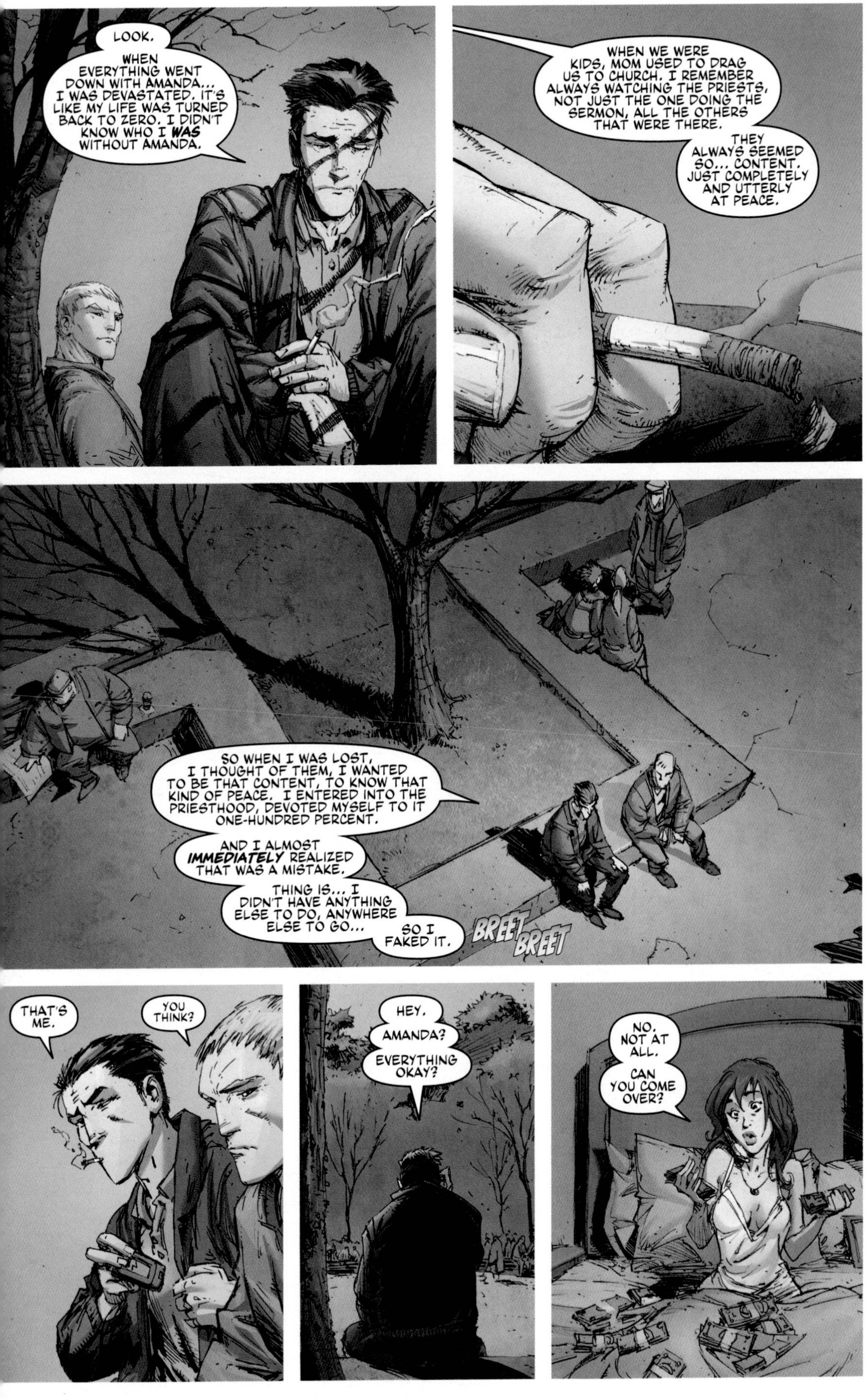
LOOK.
WHEN EVERYTHING WENT DOWN WITH AMANDA... I WAS DEVASTATED. IT'S LIKE MY LIFE WAS TURNED BACK TO ZERO. I DIDN'T KNOW WHO I WAS WITHOUT AMANDA.
WHEN WE WERE KIDS, MOM USED TO DRAG US TO CHURCH. I REMEMBER ALWAYS WATCHING THE PRIESTS, NOT JUST THE ONE DOING THE SERMON, ALL THE OTHERS THAT WERE THERE.
THEY ALWAYS SEEMED SO... CONTENT. JUST COMPLETELY AND UTTERLY AT PEACE.
SO WHEN I WAS LOST, I THOUGHT OF THEM, I WANTED TO BE THAT CONTENT, TO KNOW THAT KIND OF PEACE. I ENTERED INTO THE PRIESTHOOD, DEVOTED MYSELF TO IT ONE-HUNDRED PERCENT.
AND I ALMOST IMMEDIATELY REALIZED THAT WAS A MISTAKE.
THING IS... I DIDN'T HAVE ANYTHING ELSE TO DO, ANYWHERE ELSE TO GO...
SO I FAKED IT.
BREET BREET
THAT'S ME.
YOU THINK?
HEY.
AMANDA?
EVERYTHING OKAY?
NO. NOT AT ALL.
CAN YOU COME OVER?

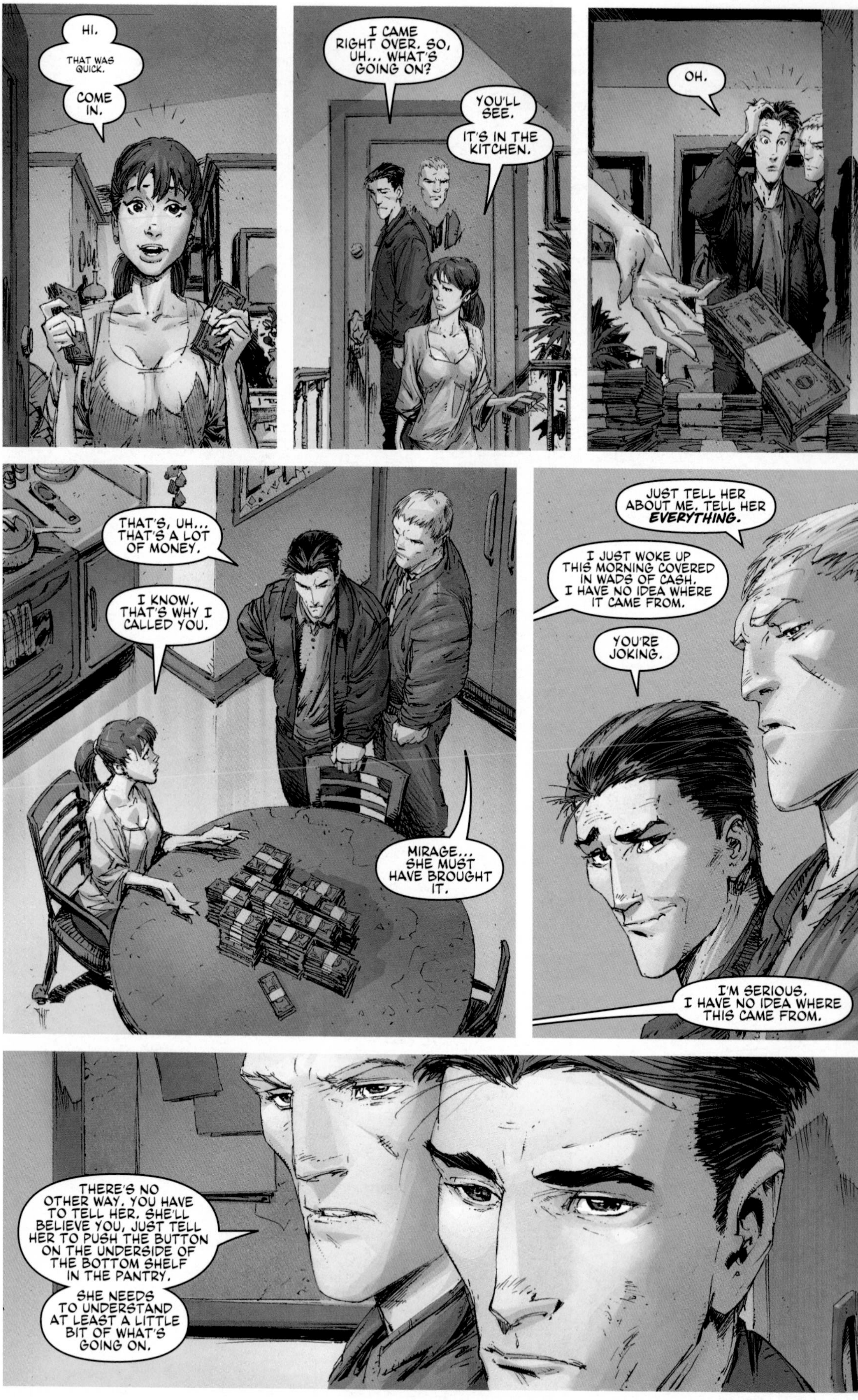
HI.
THAT WAS QUICK.
COME IN.
I CAME RIGHT OVER. SO, UH... WHAT'S GOING ON?
YOU'LL SEE.
IT'S IN THE KITCHEN.
OH.
THAT'S, UH... THAT'S A LOT OF MONEY.
I KNOW. THAT'S WHY I CALLED YOU.
MIRAGE... SHE MUST HAVE BROUGHT IT.
JUST TELL HER ABOUT ME. TELL HER EVERYTHING.
I JUST WOKE UP THIS MORNING COVERED IN WADS OF CASH. I HAVE NO IDEA WHERE IT CAME FROM.
YOU'RE JOKING.
I'M SERIOUS. I HAVE NO IDEA WHERE THIS CAME FROM.
THERE'S NO OTHER WAY. YOU HAVE TO TELL HER. SHE'LL BELIEVE YOU. JUST TELL HER TO PUSH THE BUTTON ON THE UNDERSIDE OF THE BOTTOM SHELF IN THE PANTRY.
SHE NEEDS TO UNDERSTAND AT LEAST A LITTLE BIT OF WHAT'S GOING ON.

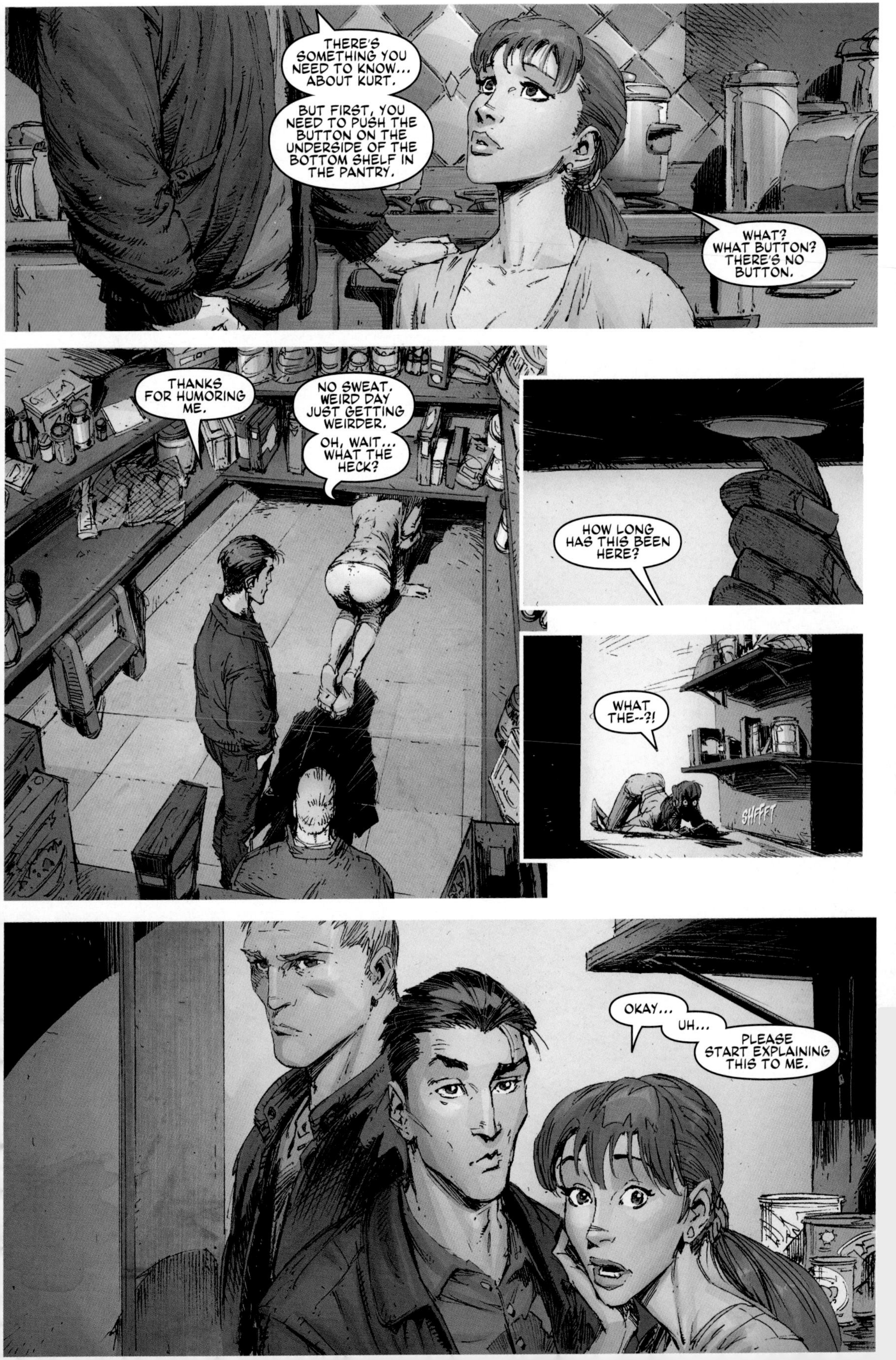
THERE'S SOMETHING YOU NEED TO KNOW... ABOUT KURT.
BUT FIRST, YOU NEED TO PUSH THE BUTTON ON THE UNDERSIDE OF THE BOTTOM SHELF IN THE PANTRY.
WHAT? WHAT BUTTON? THERE'S NO BUTTON.
THANKS FOR HUMORING ME.
NO SWEAT. WEIRD DAY JUST GETTING WEIRDER.
OH, WAIT... WHAT THE HECK?
HOW LONG HAS THIS BEEN HERE?
WHAT THE--?!
SHFFFT
OKAY...
UH...
PLEASE START EXPLAINING THIS TO ME.

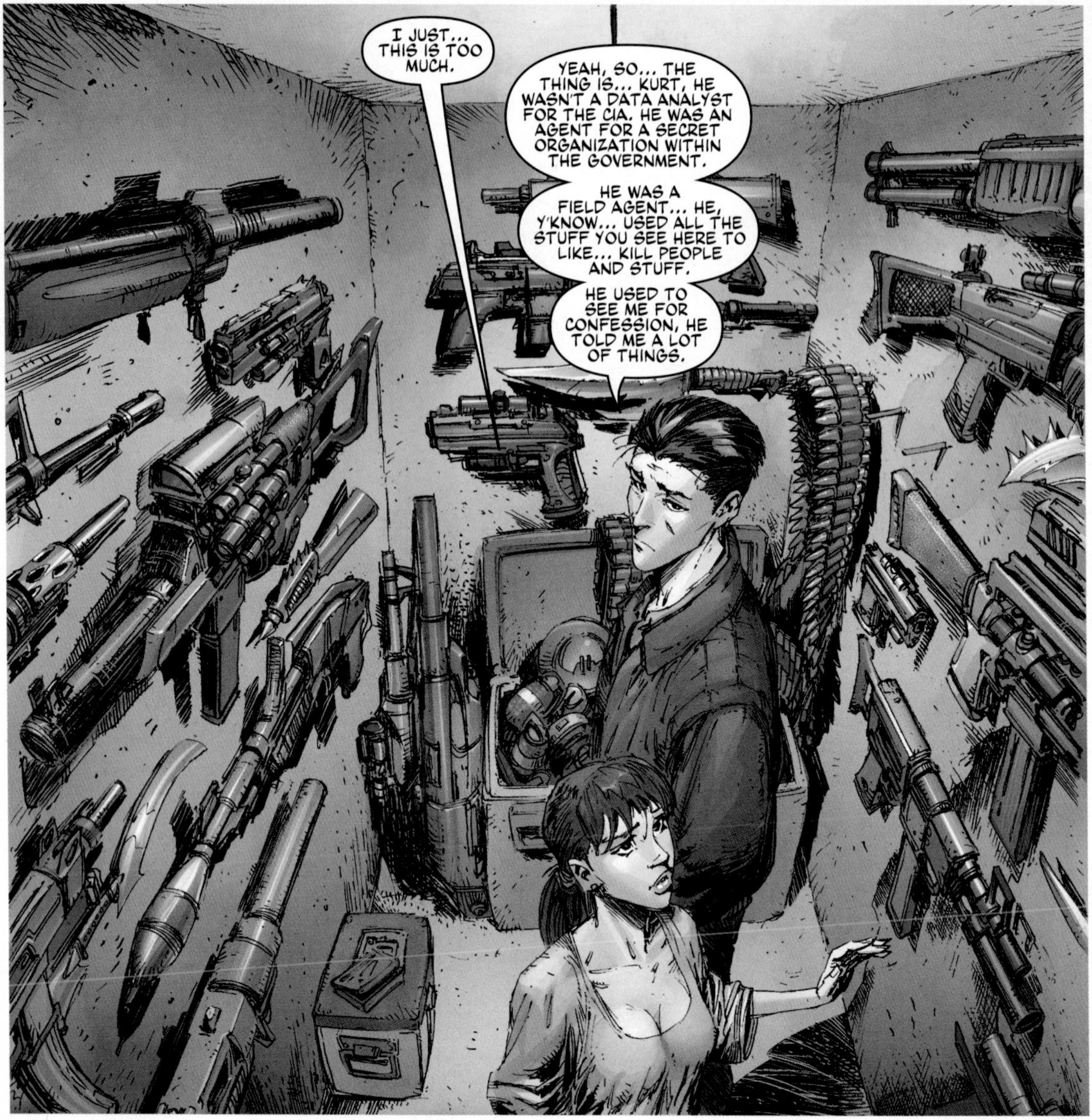
I JUST... THIS IS TOO MUCH.
YEAH, SO... THE THING IS... KURT, HE WASN'T A DATA ANALYST FOR THE CIA. HE WAS AN AGENT FOR A SECRET ORGANIZATION WITHIN THE GOVERNMENT.
HE WAS A FIELD AGENT... HE, Y'KNOW... USED ALL THE STUFF YOU SEE HERE TO LIKE... KILL PEOPLE AND STUFF.
HE USED TO SEE ME FOR CONFESSION, HE TOLD ME A LOT OF THINGS.

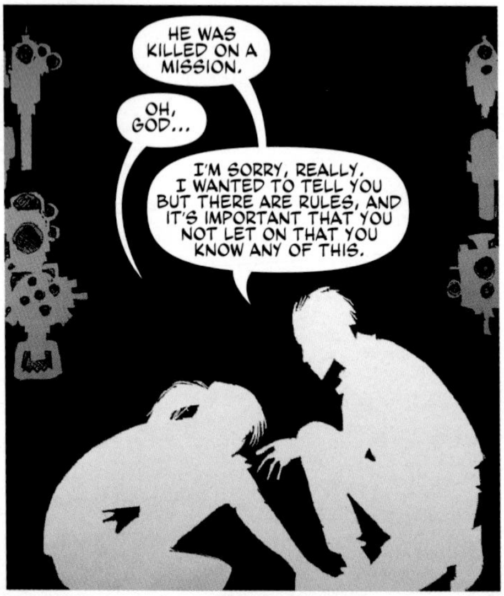
HE WAS KILLED ON A MISSION.
OH, GOD...
I'M SORRY, REALLY. I WANTED TO TELL YOU BUT THERE ARE RULES, AND IT'S IMPORTANT THAT YOU NOT LET ON THAT YOU KNOW ANY OF THIS.

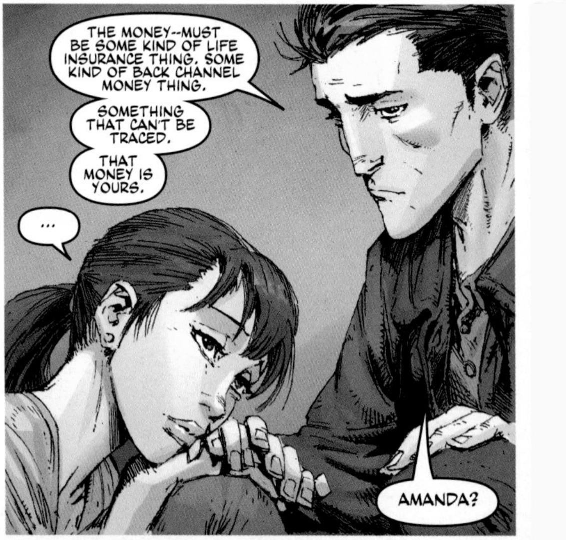
THE MONEY--MUST BE SOME KIND OF LIFE INSURANCE THING. SOME KIND OF BACK CHANNEL MONEY THING.
SOMETHING THAT CAN'T BE TRACED.
THAT MONEY IS YOURS.
...
AMANDA?

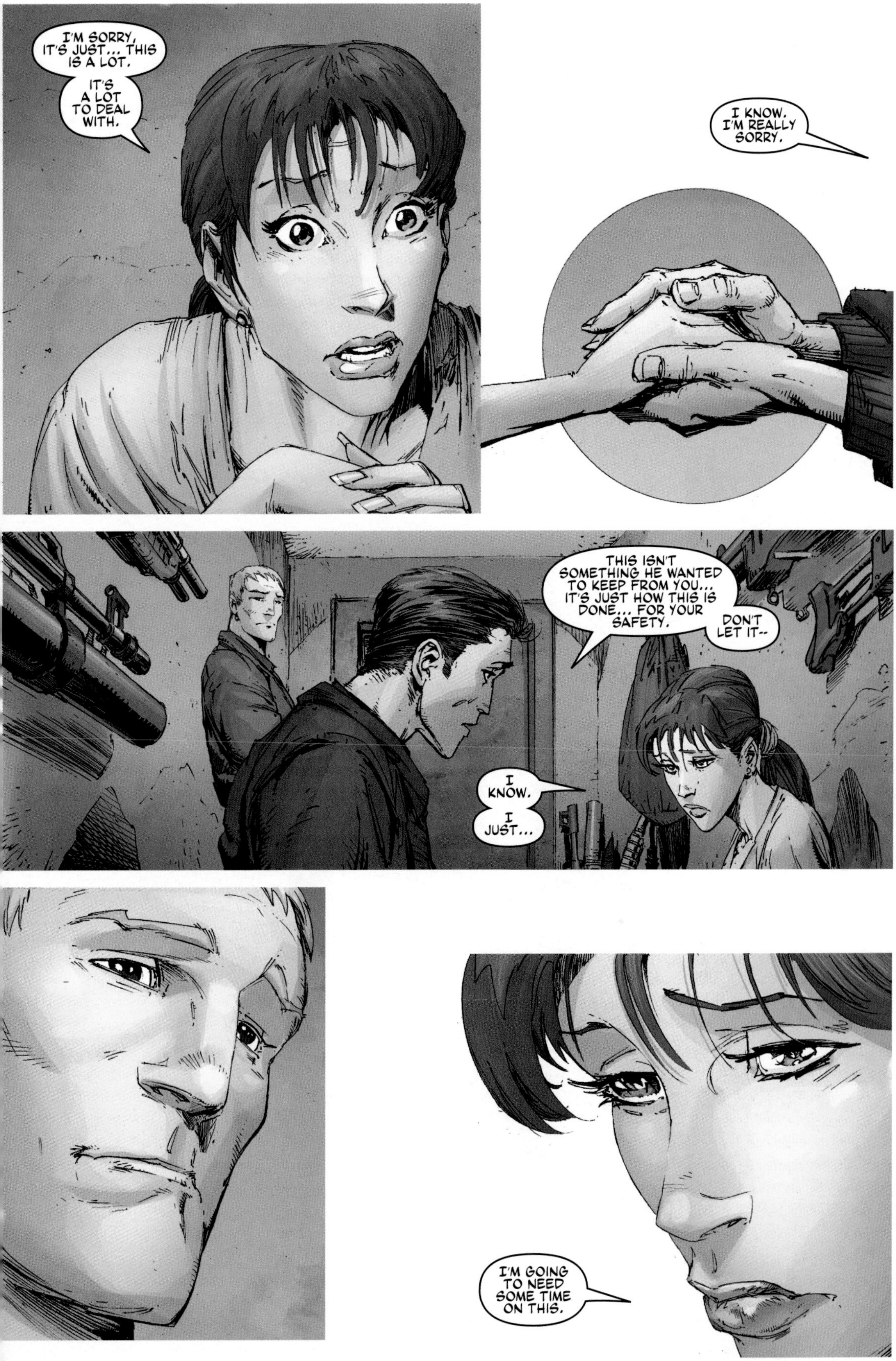
I'M SORRY, IT'S JUST... THIS IS A LOT.
IT'S A LOT TO DEAL WITH.
I KNOW. I'M REALLY SORRY.
THIS ISN'T SOMETHING HE WANTED TO KEEP FROM YOU... IT'S JUST HOW THIS IS DONE... FOR YOUR SAFETY.
DON'T LET IT--
I KNOW.
I JUST...
I'M GOING TO NEED SOME TIME ON THIS.

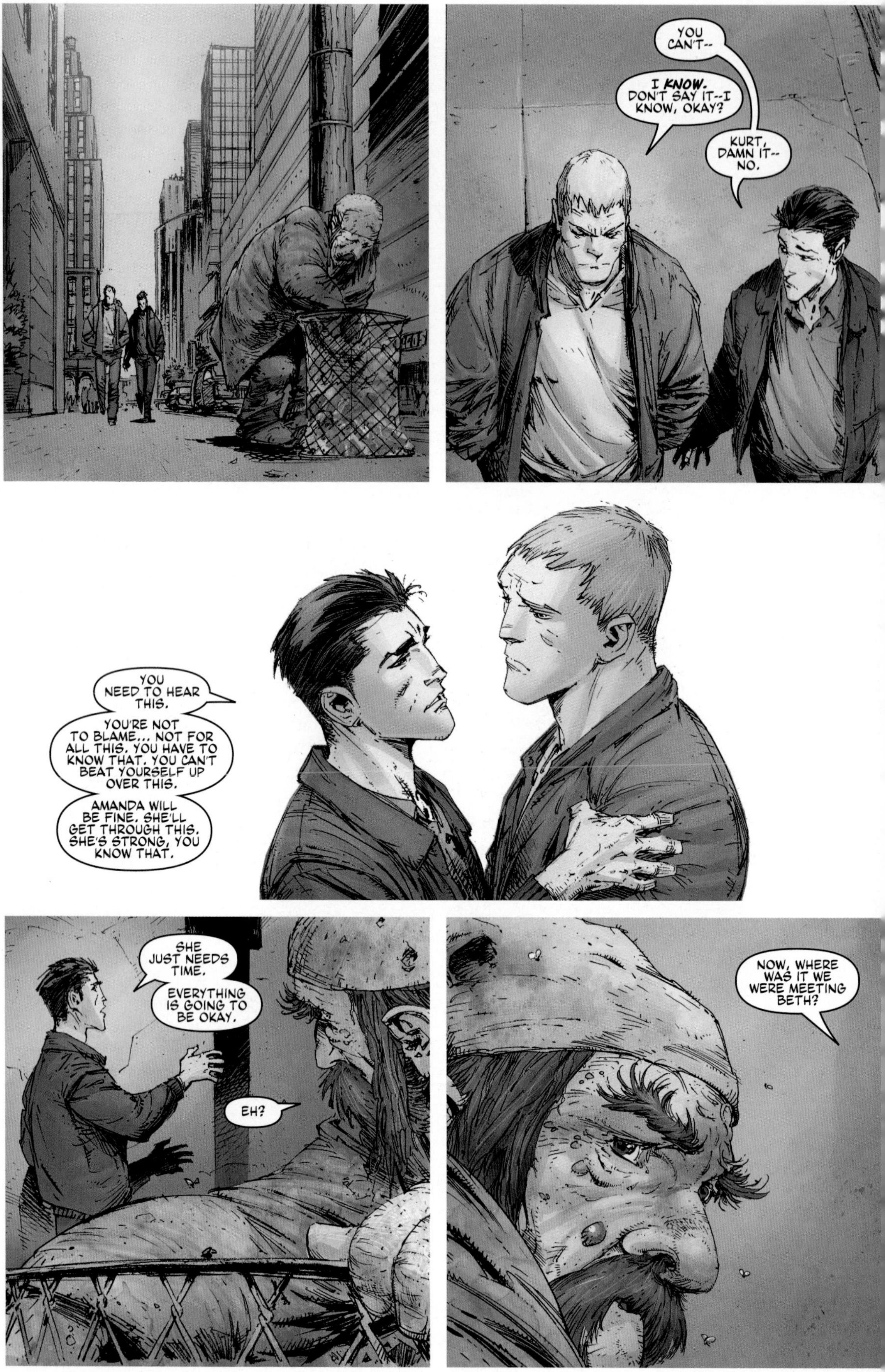

YOU CAN'T--
I KNOW. DON'T SAY IT--I KNOW, OKAY?
KURT, DAMN IT-- NO.
YOU NEED TO HEAR THIS.
YOU'RE NOT TO BLAME... NOT FOR ALL THIS. YOU HAVE TO KNOW THAT. YOU CAN'T BEAT YOURSELF UP OVER THIS.
AMANDA WILL BE FINE. SHE'LL GET THROUGH THIS. SHE'S STRONG, YOU KNOW THAT.
SHE JUST NEEDS TIME.
EVERYTHING IS GOING TO BE OKAY.
EH?
NOW, WHERE WAS IT WE WERE MEETING BETH?

DANIEL, WELCOME. ON TIME, GOOD START.

ON TIME? REALLY? WASN'T KEEPING TRACK.

THIS IS EDWARD WILLIAMS. HE'S OUR TRAINER. WE'LL BE OPERATING OUT OF THIS BUILDING FOR THE TIME BEING.

NICE TO MEET YOU, EDWARD.

PLEASE, CALL ME EDDY.

SO WHERE DO WE START? GUNS? KNIVES? KUNG-FU?

WHAT'S IN STORE FOR TODAY?

TODAY'S GOING TO BE VERY EXCITING. OUR WEAPON TODAY WILL BE THIS.

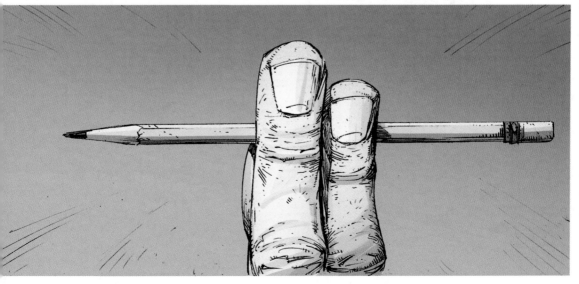

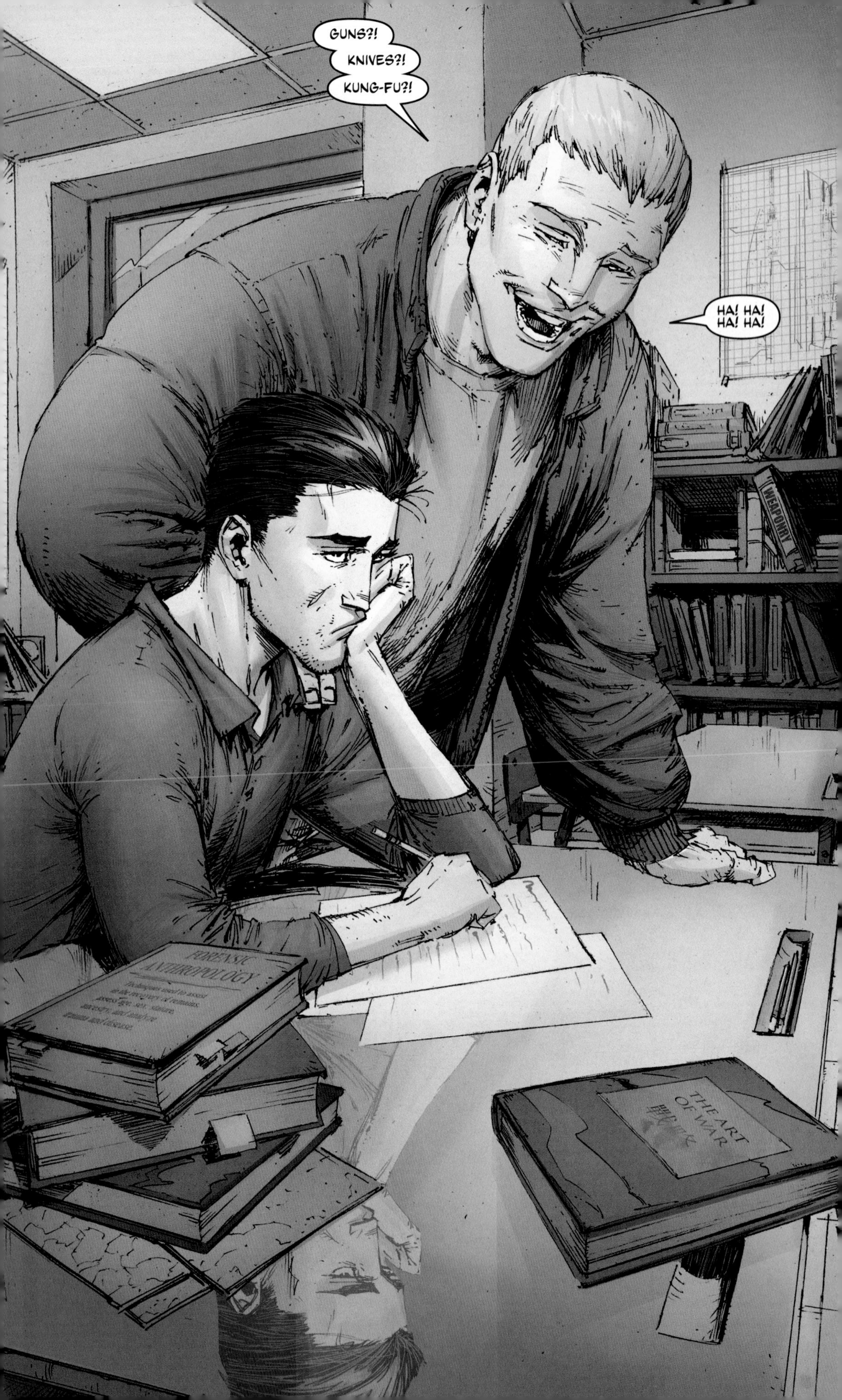
GUNS?!
KNIVES?!
KUNG-FU?!
HA! HA! HA! HA!
WEAPONRY
FORENSIC ANTHROPOLOGY
THE ART OF WAR

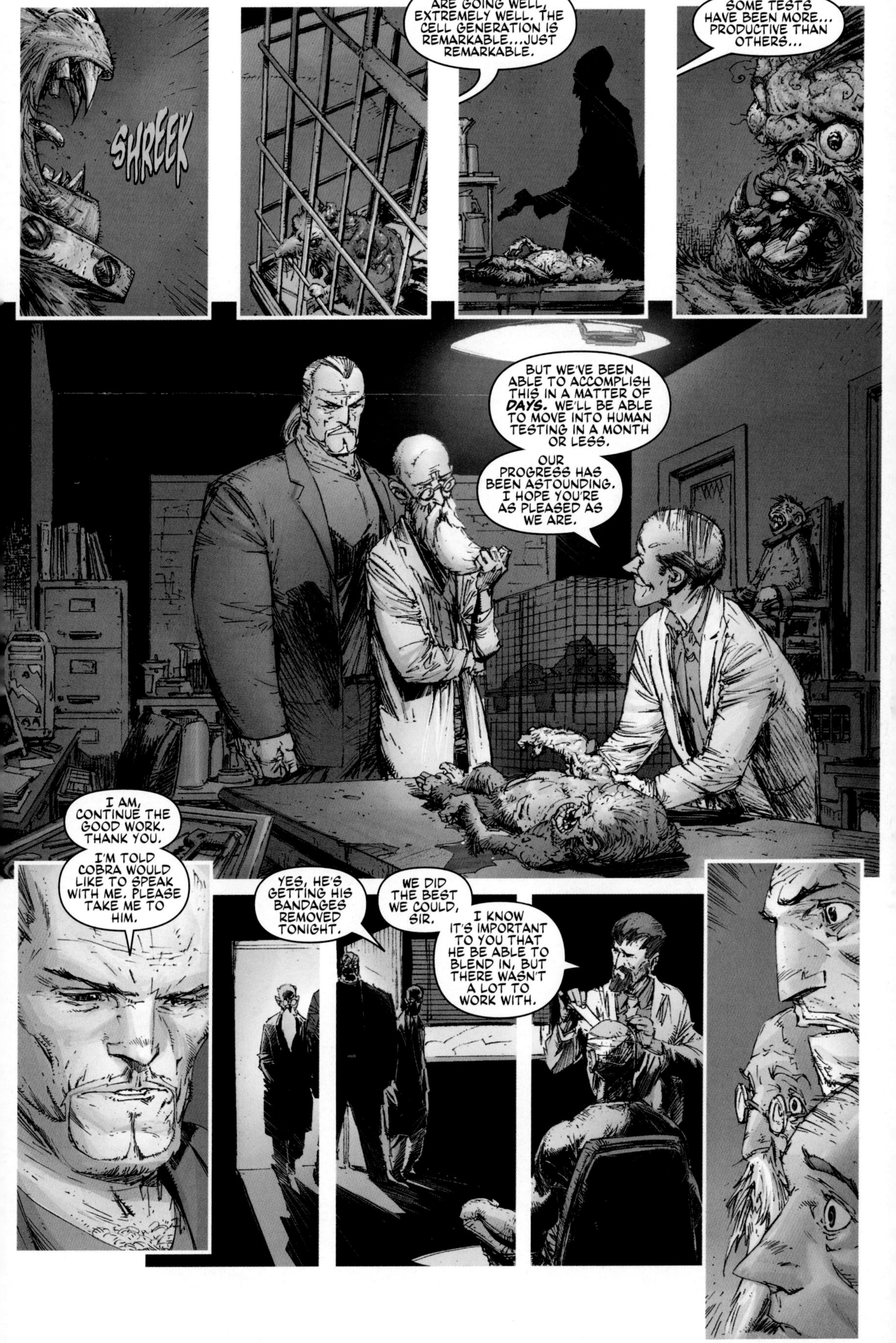
SHREEK
THINGS ARE GOING WELL, EXTREMELY WELL. THE CELL GENERATION IS REMARKABLE...JUST REMARKABLE.
SOME TESTS HAVE BEEN MORE... PRODUCTIVE THAN OTHERS...
BUT WE'VE BEEN ABLE TO ACCOMPLISH THIS IN A MATTER OF DAYS. WE'LL BE ABLE TO MOVE INTO HUMAN TESTING IN A MONTH OR LESS.
OUR PROGRESS HAS BEEN ASTOUNDING. I HOPE YOU'RE AS PLEASED AS WE ARE.
I AM, CONTINUE THE GOOD WORK. THANK YOU.
I'M TOLD COBRA WOULD LIKE TO SPEAK WITH ME. PLEASE TAKE ME TO HIM.
YES, HE'S GETTING HIS BANDAGES REMOVED TONIGHT.
WE DID THE BEST WE COULD, SIR.
I KNOW IT'S IMPORTANT TO YOU THAT HE BE ABLE TO BLEND IN, BUT THERE WASN'T A LOT TO WORK WITH.

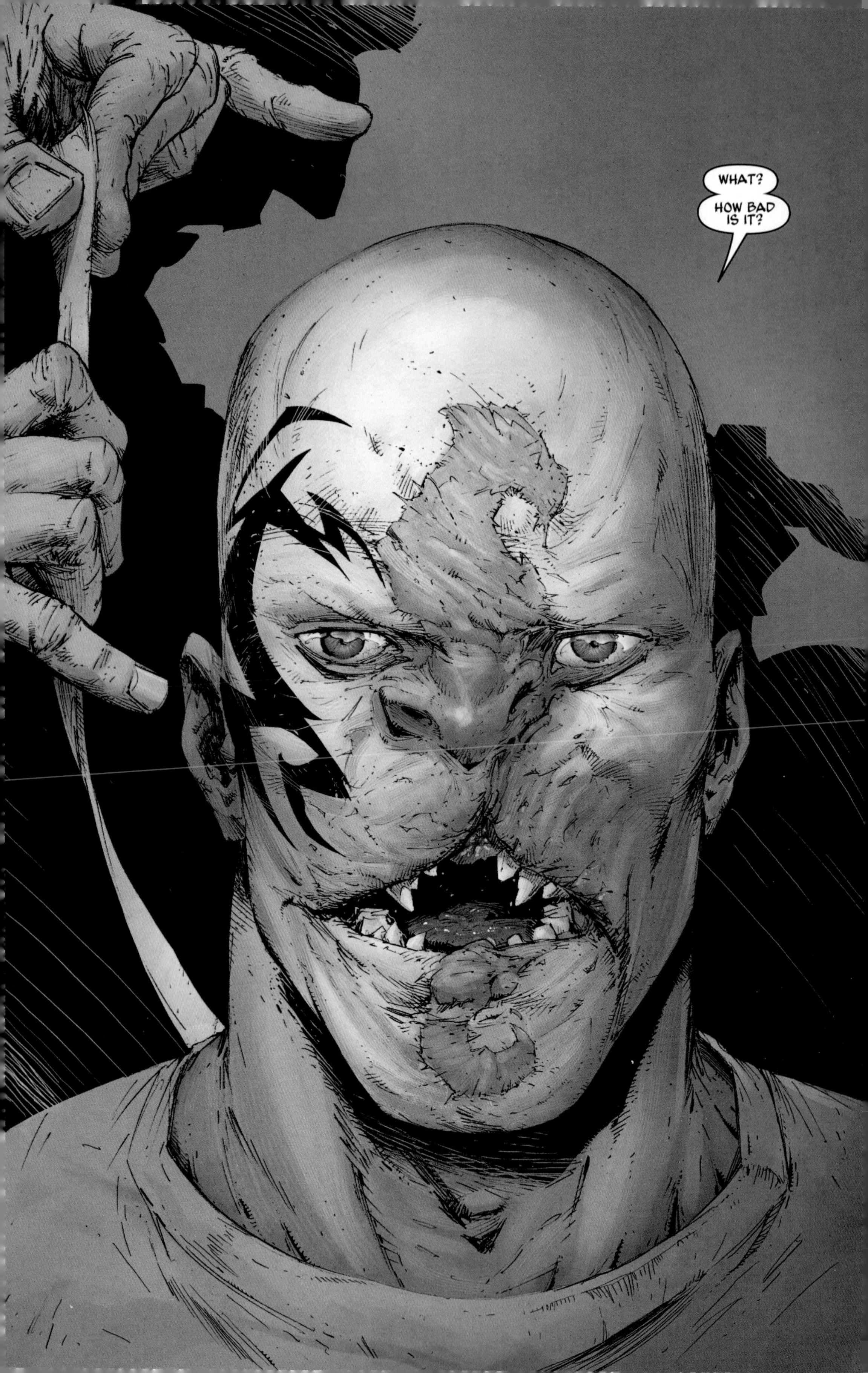
WHAT?
HOW BAD IS IT?

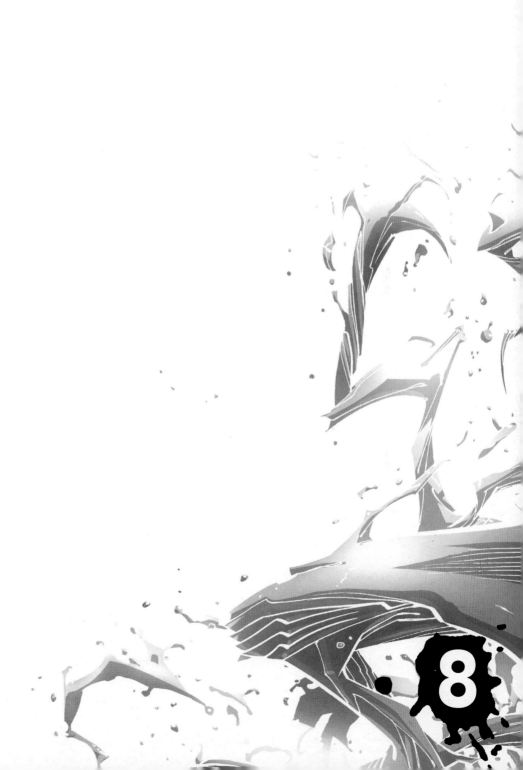

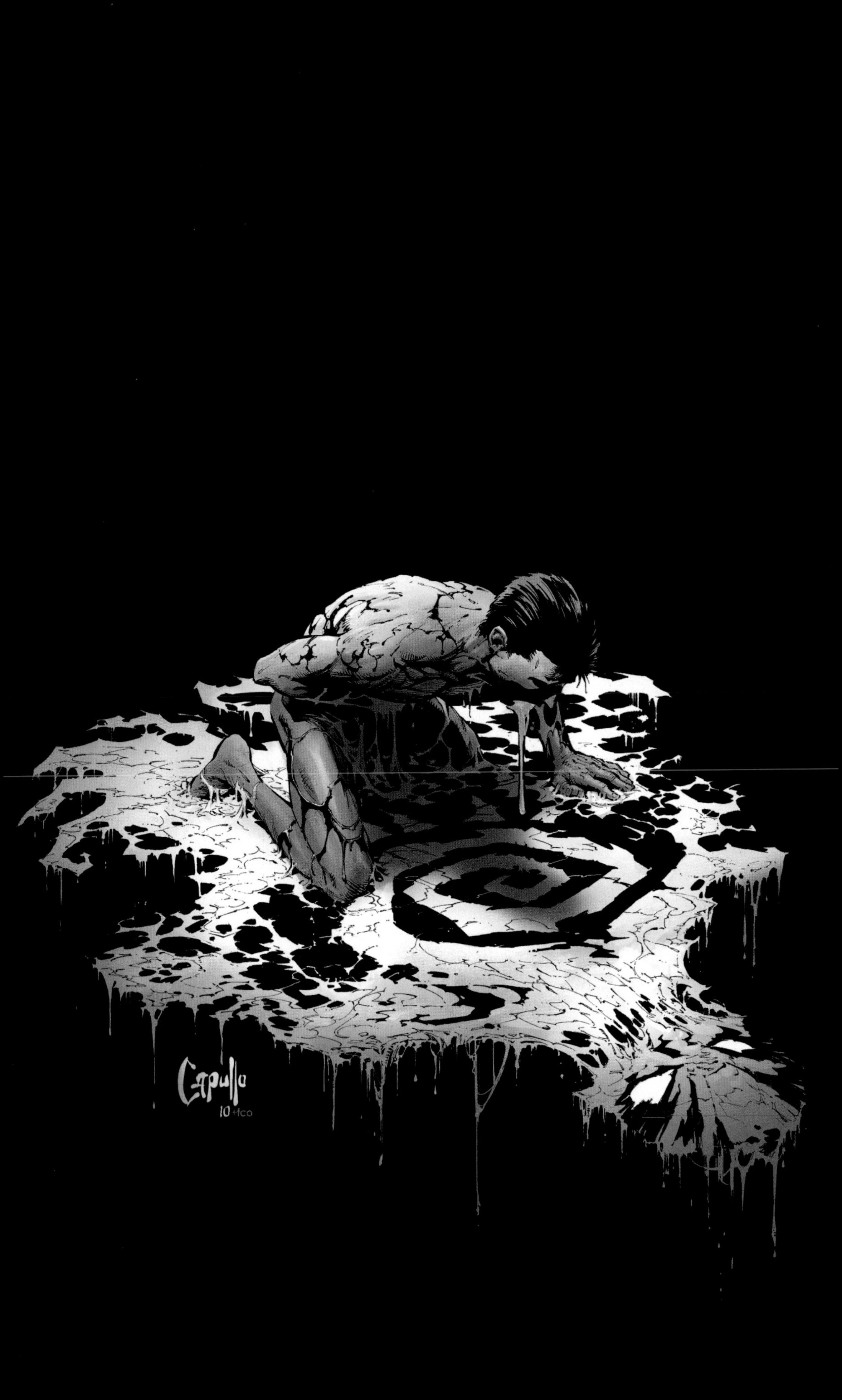
Capullo
10 +fco

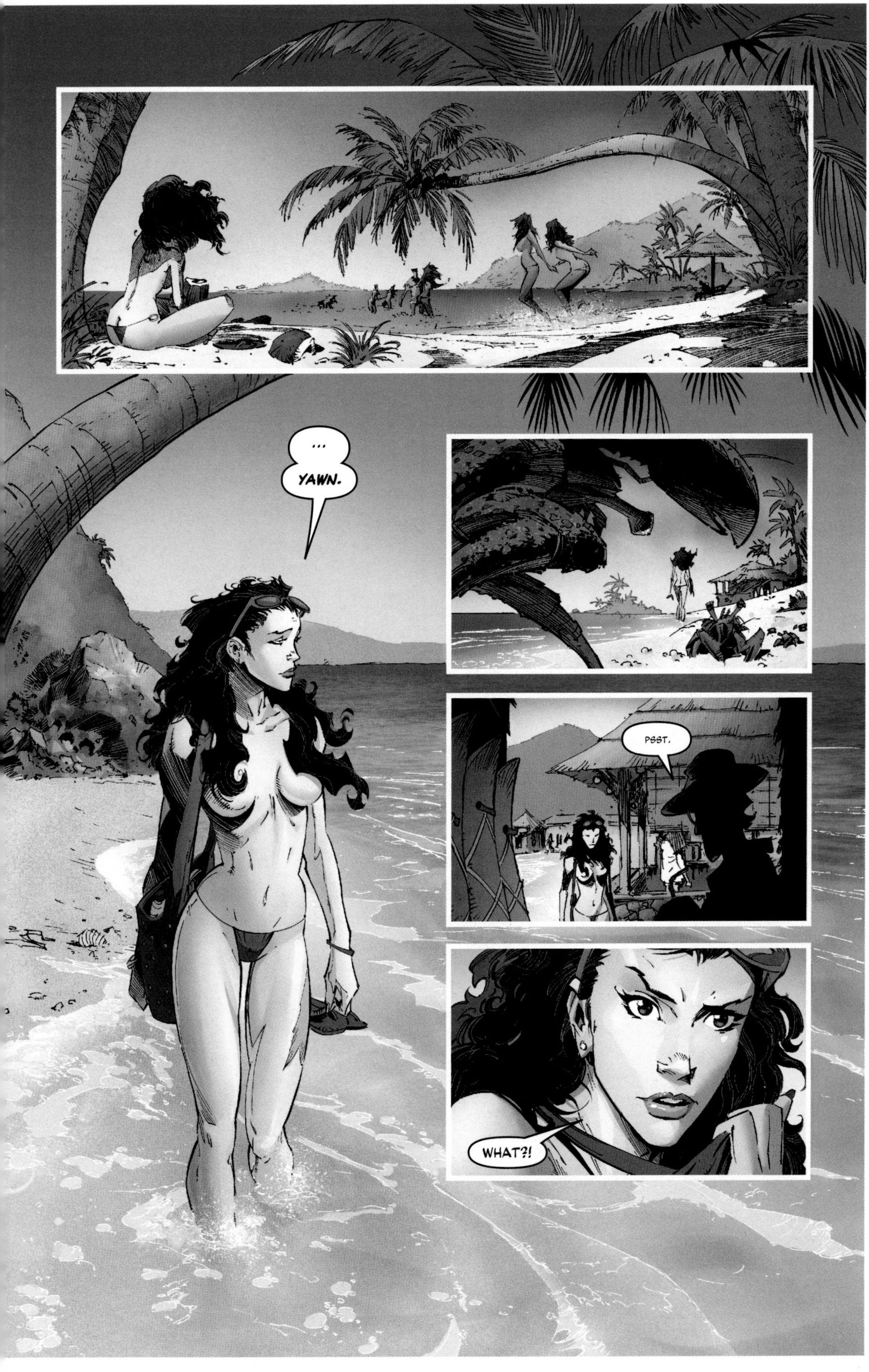
...
YAWN.
PSST.
WHAT?!

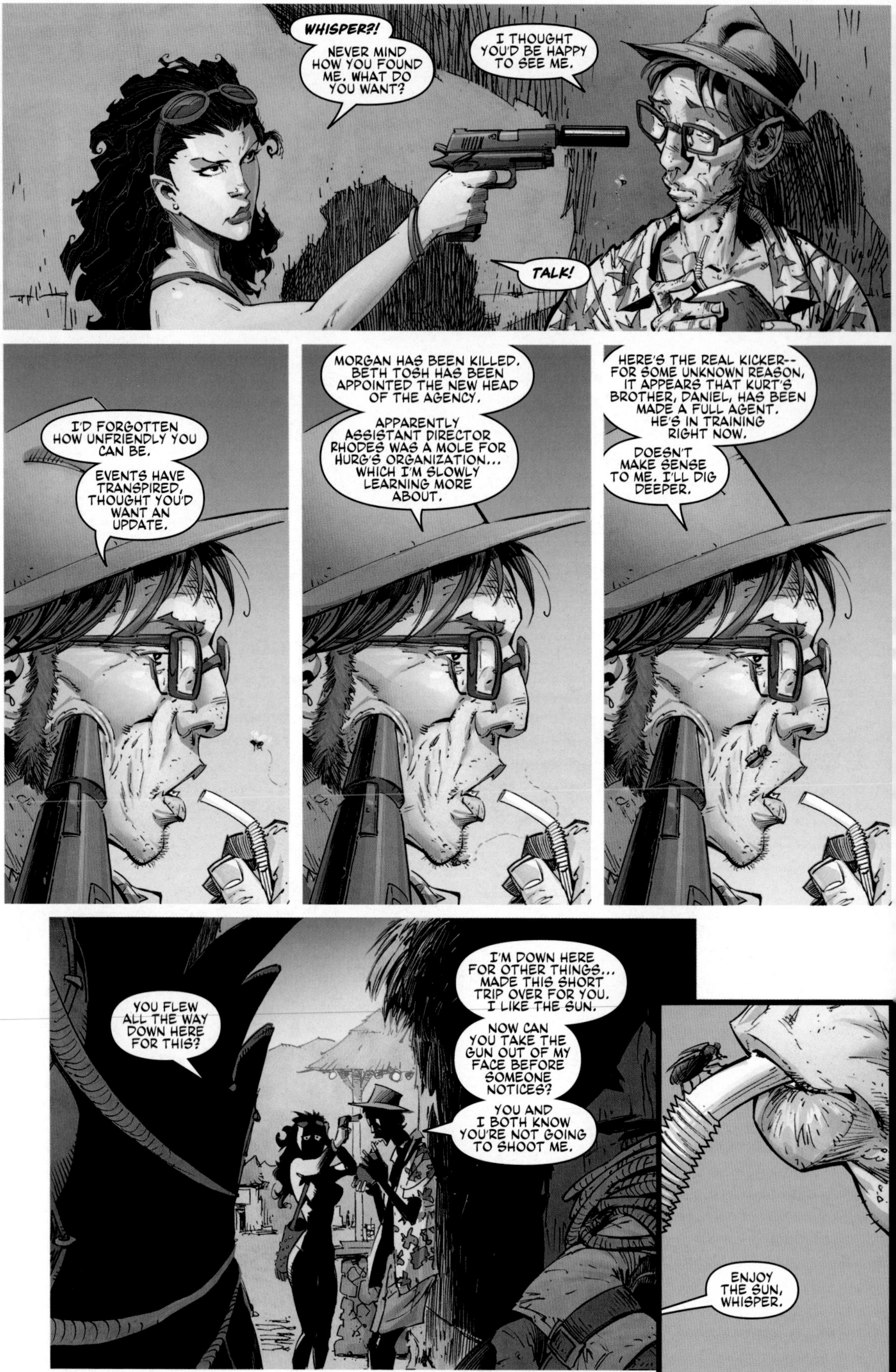
WHISPER?!
NEVER MIND HOW YOU FOUND ME. WHAT DO YOU WANT?
I THOUGHT YOU'D BE HAPPY TO SEE ME.
TALK!
I'D FORGOTTEN HOW UNFRIENDLY YOU CAN BE.
EVENTS HAVE TRANSPIRED, THOUGHT YOU'D WANT AN UPDATE.
MORGAN HAS BEEN KILLED. BETH TOSH HAS BEEN APPOINTED THE NEW HEAD OF THE AGENCY.
APPARENTLY ASSISTANT DIRECTOR RHODES WAS A MOLE FOR HURG'S ORGANIZATION... WHICH I'M SLOWLY LEARNING MORE ABOUT.
HERE'S THE REAL KICKER--FOR SOME UNKNOWN REASON, IT APPEARS THAT KURT'S BROTHER, DANIEL, HAS BEEN MADE A FULL AGENT. HE'S IN TRAINING RIGHT NOW.
DOESN'T MAKE SENSE TO ME. I'LL DIG DEEPER.
YOU FLEW ALL THE WAY DOWN HERE FOR THIS?
I'M DOWN HERE FOR OTHER THINGS... MADE THIS SHORT TRIP OVER FOR YOU. I LIKE THE SUN.
NOW CAN YOU TAKE THE GUN OUT OF MY FACE BEFORE SOMEONE NOTICES?
YOU AND I BOTH KNOW YOU'RE NOT GOING TO SHOOT ME.
ENJOY THE SUN, WHISPER.

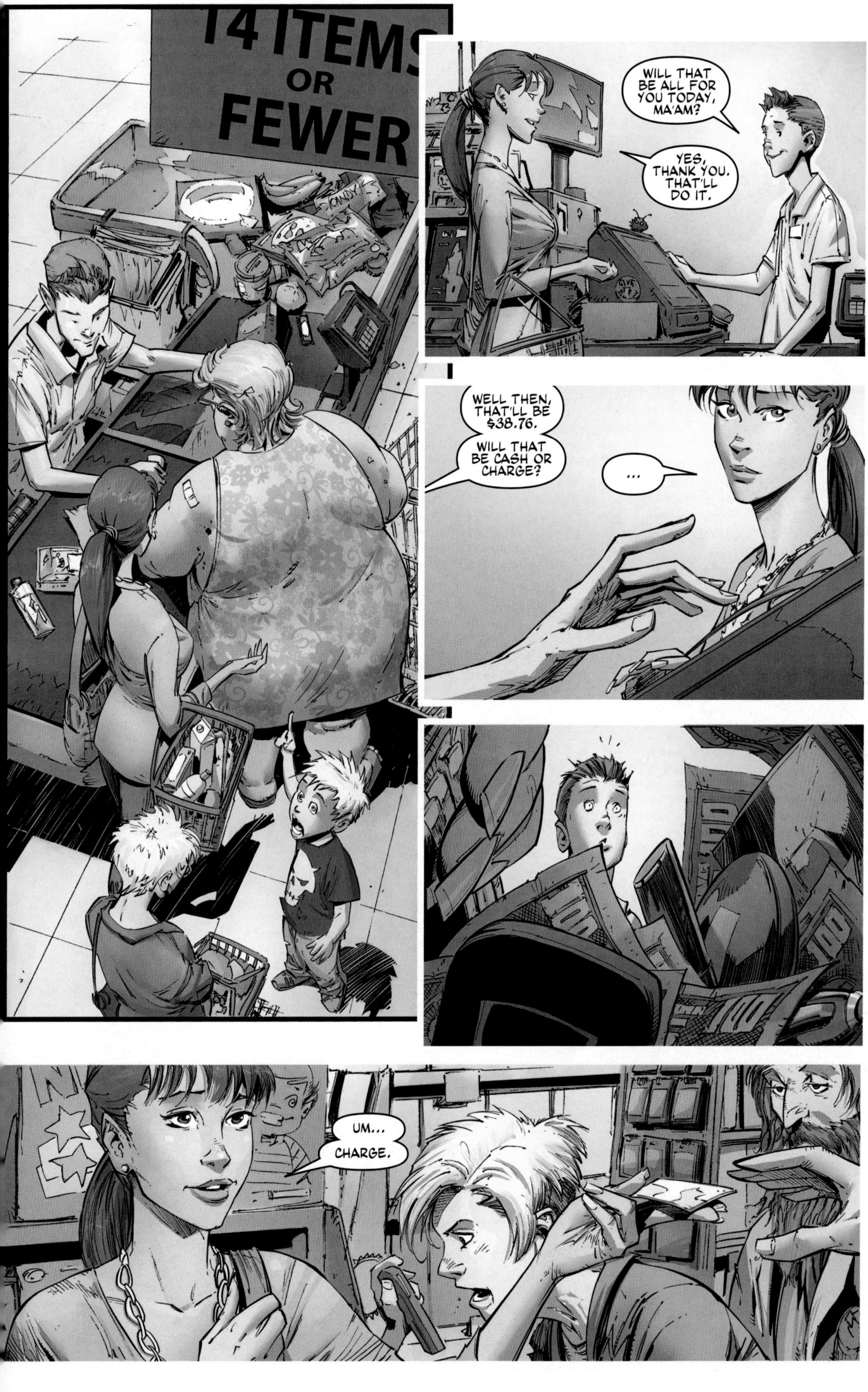
14 ITEMS OR FEWER
CANDY
WILL THAT BE ALL FOR YOU TODAY, MA'AM?
YES, THANK YOU. THAT'LL DO IT.
WELL THEN, THAT'LL BE $38.76.
WILL THAT BE CASH OR CHARGE?
...
UM... CHARGE.

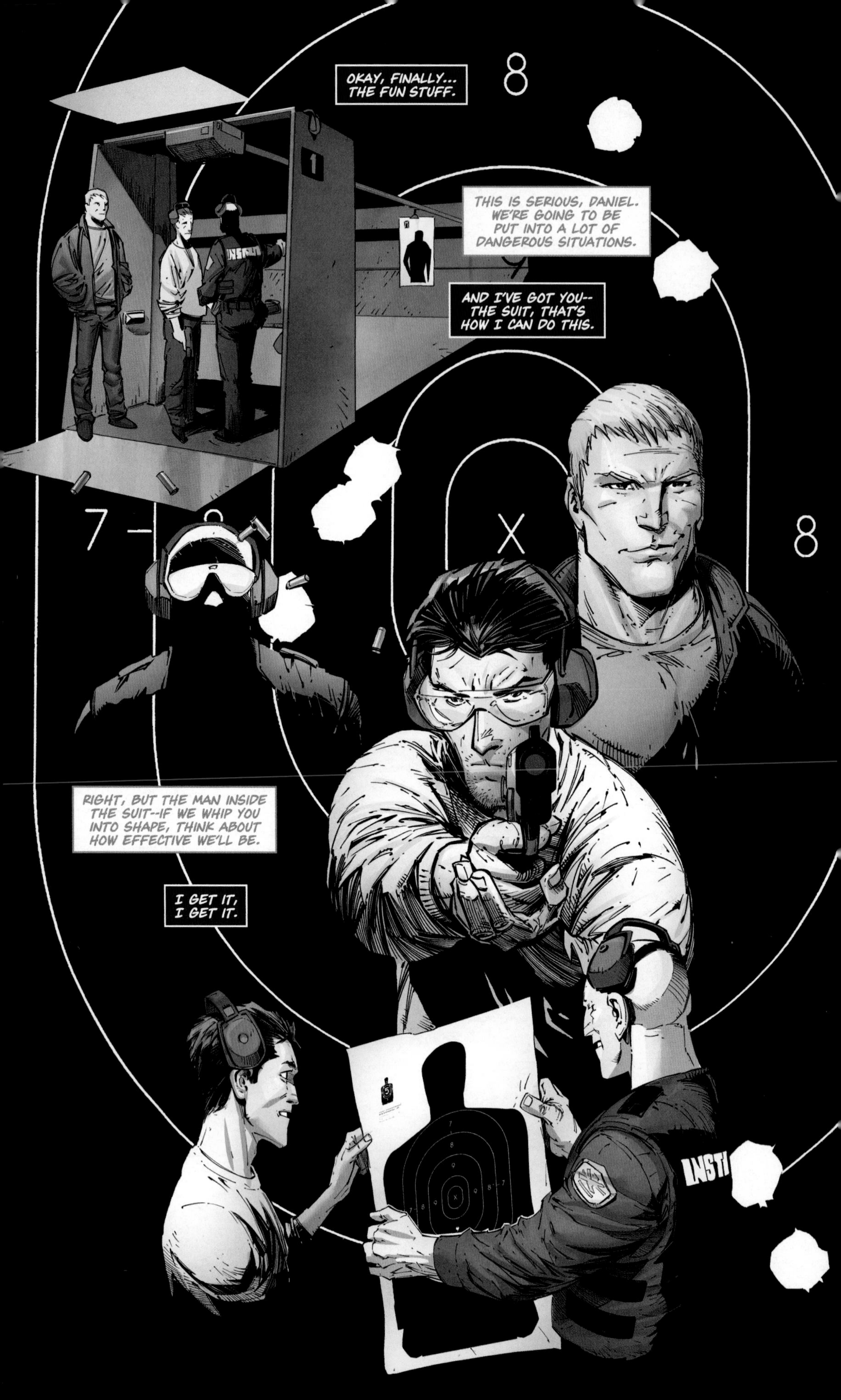
OKAY, FINALLY... THE FUN STUFF.
THIS IS SERIOUS, DANIEL. WE'RE GOING TO BE PUT INTO A LOT OF DANGEROUS SITUATIONS.
AND I'VE GOT YOU-- THE SUIT, THAT'S HOW I CAN DO THIS.
RIGHT, BUT THE MAN INSIDE THE SUIT--IF WE WHIP YOU INTO SHAPE, THINK ABOUT HOW EFFECTIVE WE'LL BE.
I GET IT, I GET IT.

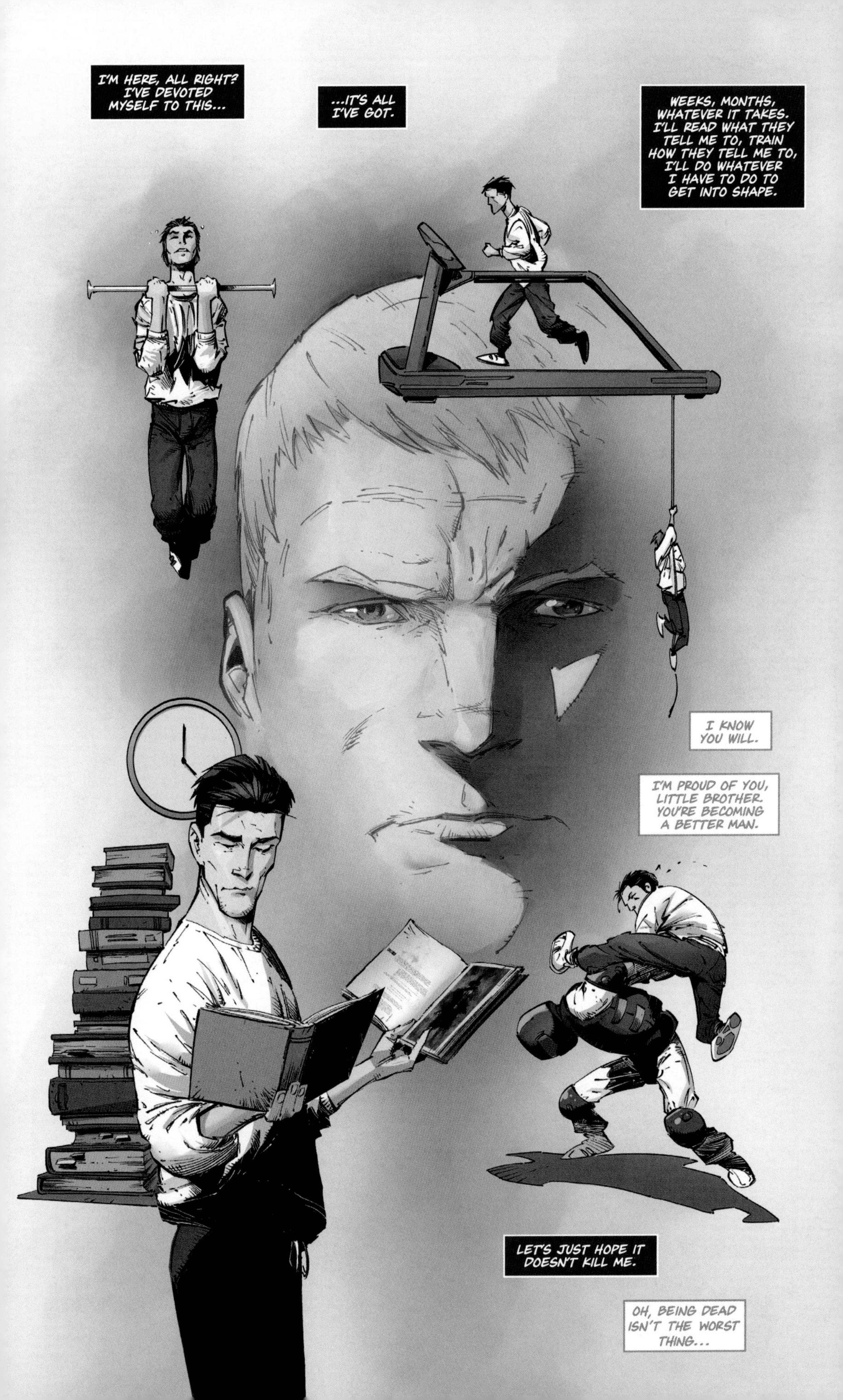
I'M HERE, ALL RIGHT? I'VE DEVOTED MYSELF TO THIS...
...IT'S ALL I'VE GOT.
WEEKS, MONTHS, WHATEVER IT TAKES. I'LL READ WHAT THEY TELL ME TO, TRAIN HOW THEY TELL ME TO, I'LL DO WHATEVER I HAVE TO DO TO GET INTO SHAPE.
I KNOW YOU WILL.
I'M PROUD OF YOU, LITTLE BROTHER. YOU'RE BECOMING A BETTER MAN.
LET'S JUST HOPE IT DOESN'T KILL ME.
OH, BEING DEAD ISN'T THE WORST THING...

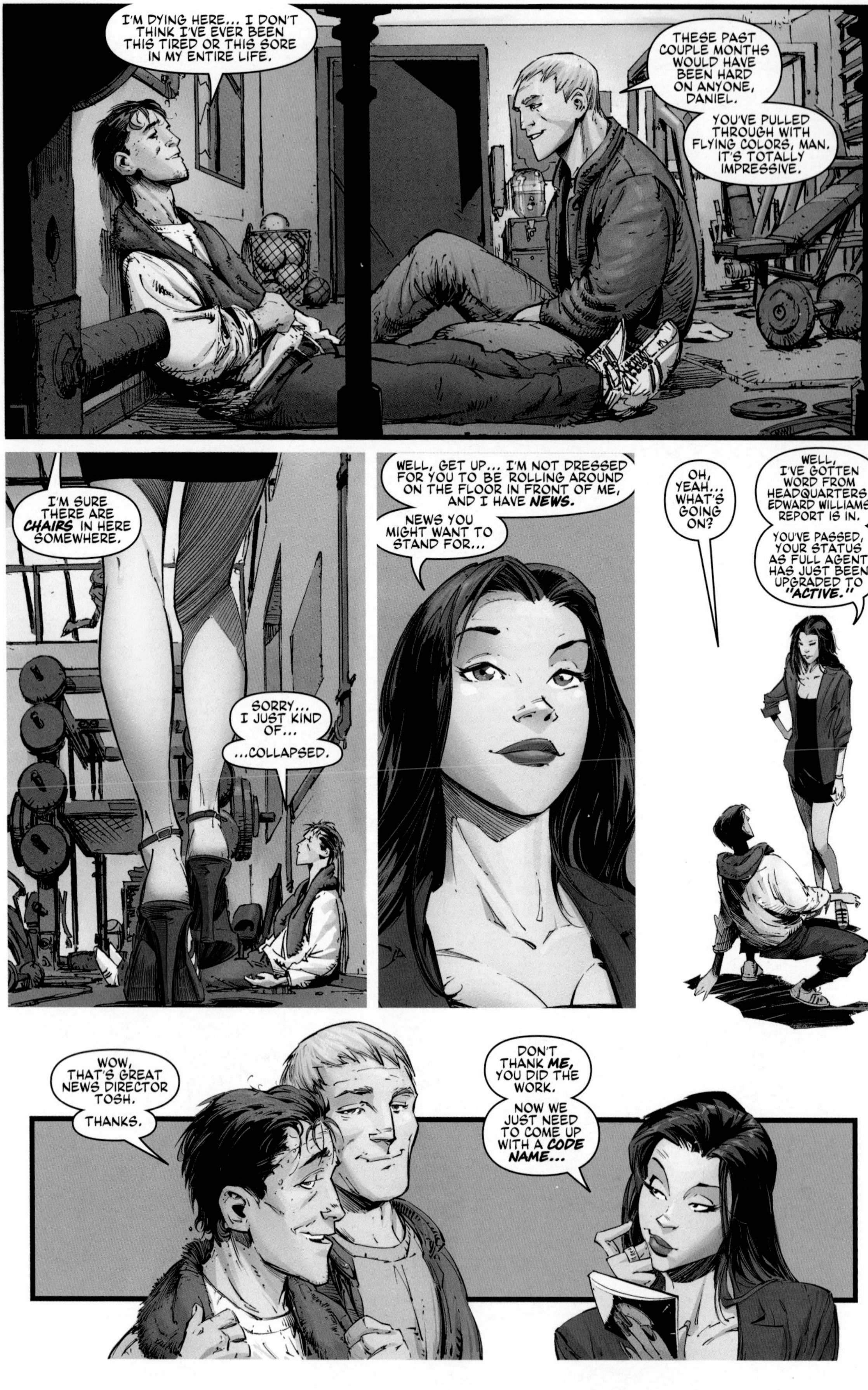
I'M DYING HERE... I DON'T THINK I'VE EVER BEEN THIS TIRED OR THIS SORE IN MY ENTIRE LIFE.
THESE PAST COUPLE MONTHS WOULD HAVE BEEN HARD ON ANYONE, DANIEL.
YOU'VE PULLED THROUGH WITH FLYING COLORS, MAN. IT'S TOTALLY IMPRESSIVE.
I'M SURE THERE ARE CHAIRS IN HERE SOMEWHERE.
SORRY... I JUST KIND OF...
...COLLAPSED.
WELL, GET UP... I'M NOT DRESSED FOR YOU TO BE ROLLING AROUND ON THE FLOOR IN FRONT OF ME, AND I HAVE NEWS.
NEWS YOU MIGHT WANT TO STAND FOR...
OH, YEAH... WHAT'S GOING ON?
WELL, I'VE GOTTEN WORD FROM HEADQUARTERS. EDWARD WILLIAMS' REPORT IS IN.
YOU'VE PASSED, YOUR STATUS AS FULL AGENT HAS JUST BEEN UPGRADED TO "ACTIVE."
WOW, THAT'S GREAT NEWS DIRECTOR TOSH.
THANKS.
DON'T THANK ME, YOU DID THE WORK.
NOW WE JUST NEED TO COME UP WITH A CODE NAME...

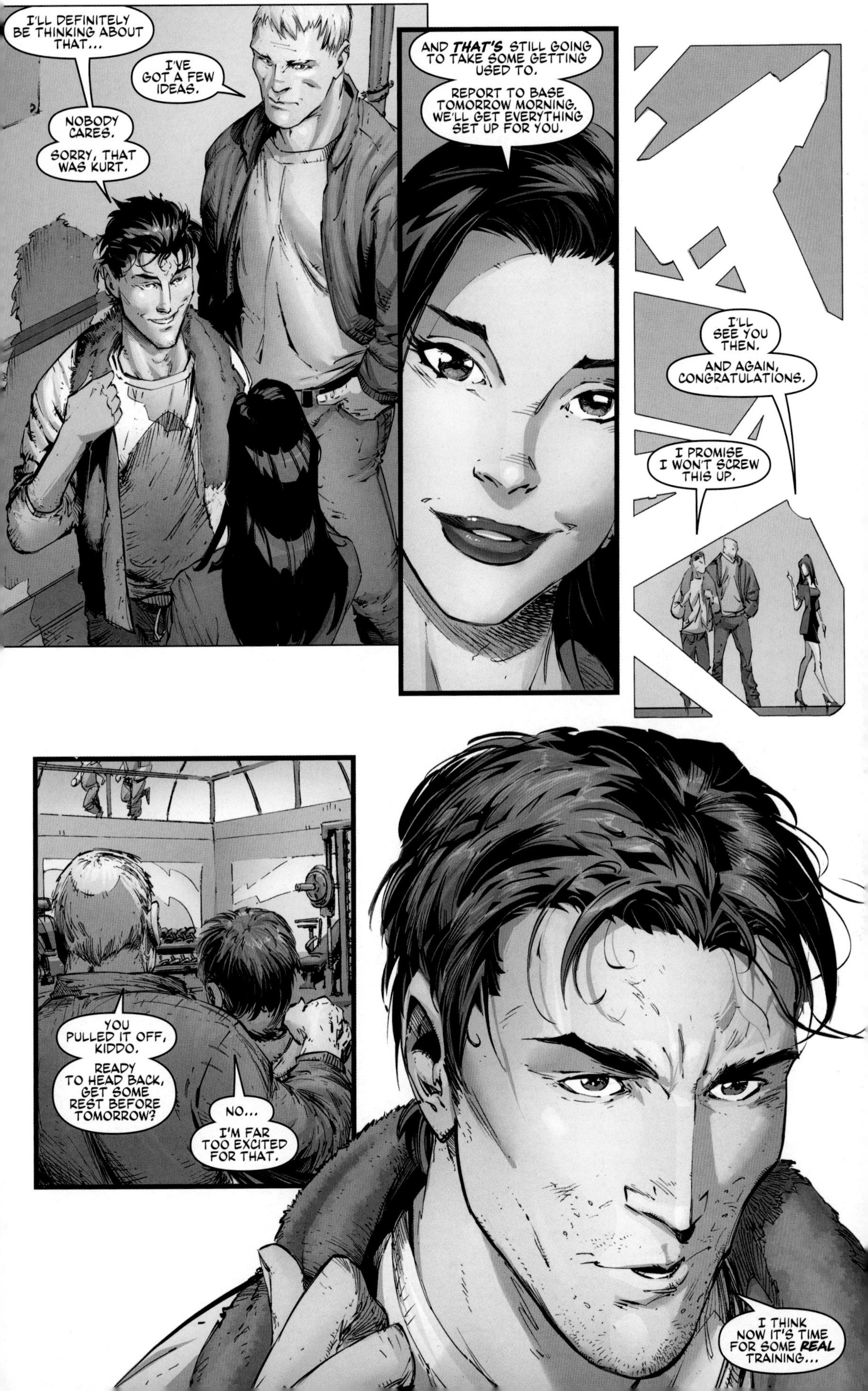

I'LL DEFINITELY BE THINKING ABOUT THAT...
I'VE GOT A FEW IDEAS.
NOBODY CARES.
SORRY, THAT WAS KURT.
AND ***THAT'S*** STILL GOING TO TAKE SOME GETTING USED TO.
REPORT TO BASE TOMORROW MORNING. WE'LL GET EVERYTHING SET UP FOR YOU.
I'LL SEE YOU THEN.
AND AGAIN, CONGRATULATIONS.
I PROMISE I WON'T SCREW THIS UP.
YOU PULLED IT OFF, KIDDO.
READY TO HEAD BACK, GET SOME REST BEFORE TOMORROW?
NO...
I'M FAR TOO EXCITED FOR THAT.
I THINK NOW IT'S TIME FOR SOME ***REAL*** TRAINING...

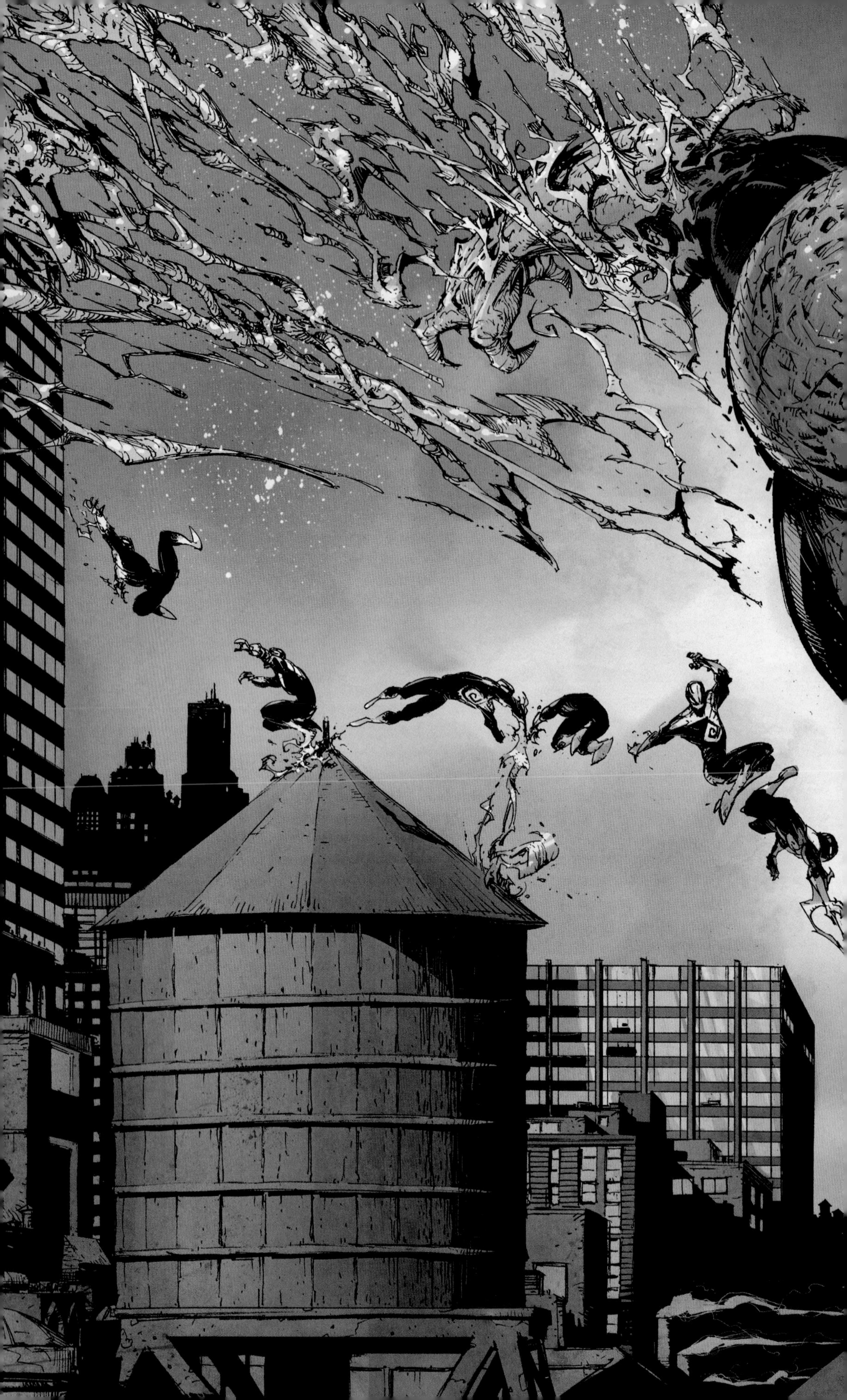

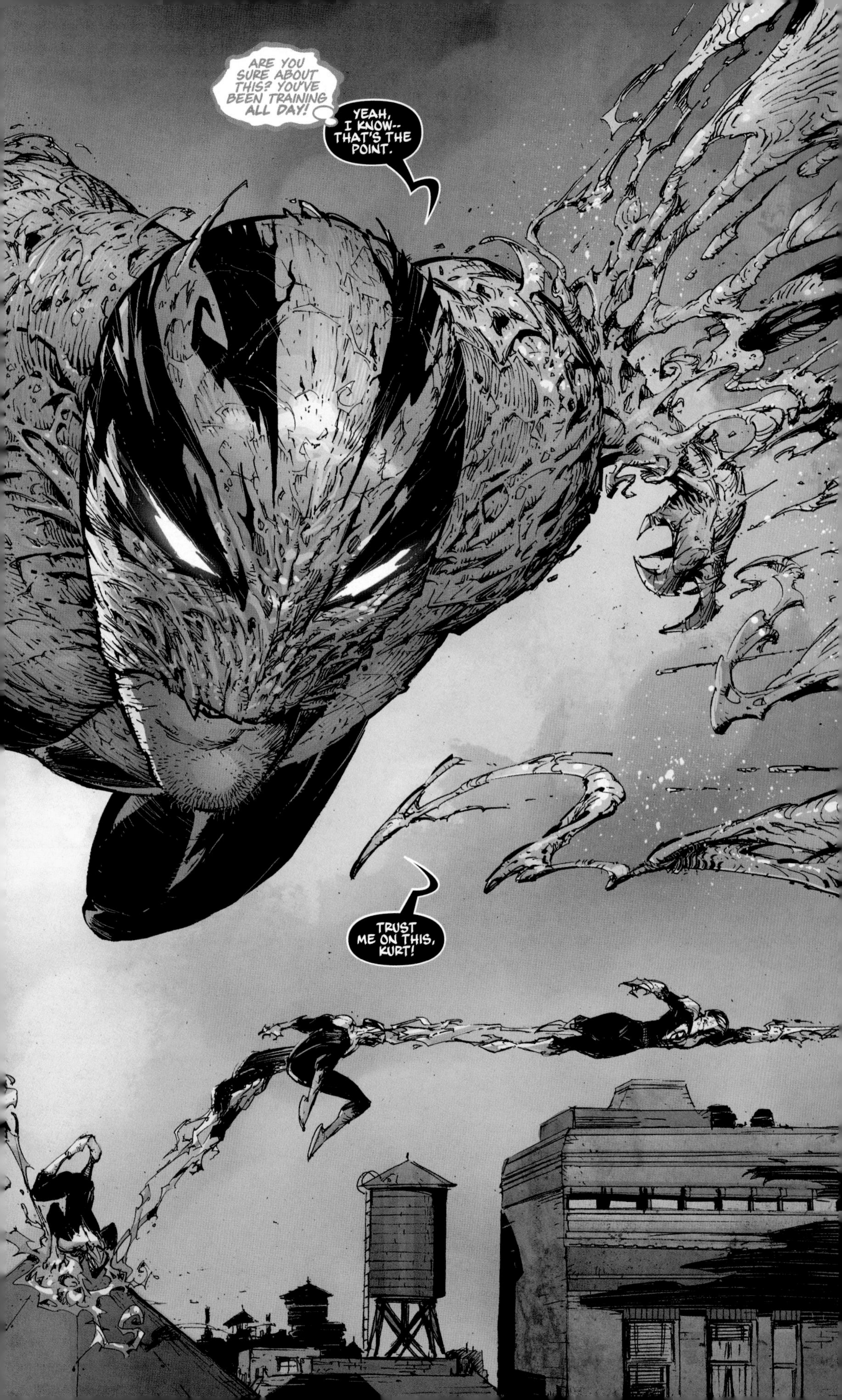
ARE YOU SURE ABOUT THIS? YOU'VE BEEN TRAINING ALL DAY!
YEAH, I KNOW-- THAT'S THE POINT.
TRUST ME ON THIS, KURT!

OKAY, TIME TO CALL IT A NIGHT. WE'VE BEEN AT THIS A WHILE, LET'S NOT PUSH IT. WE'RE ALMOST THERE, WORKING TOGETHER AS ONE, WE'VE JUST ABOUT GOT IT DOWN TO A SCIENCE.

THEN WHY ARE WE OUT HERE?

I GET THAT, THAT'S NOT WHAT I'M WORRIED ABOUT.

OUR LIMIT--THE ENERGY YOU DRAIN FROM ME, WHEN WE PUSH OURSELVES... WHEN YOU STAY ATTACHED TOO LONG.

THAT'S DANGEROUS--IT'S A WEAKNESS THAT WE CAN'T LEAVE UNCHECKED.

SO YOU'RE TRYING TO WEAR US DOWN? SEE HOW MUCH WE CAN HANDLE?

GOOD JOB, YOU'VE DONE IT.

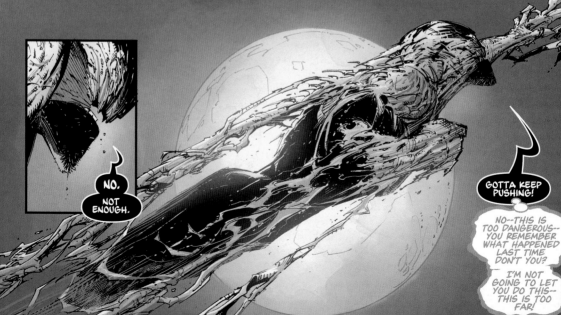

NO. NOT ENOUGH.

GOTTA KEEP PUSHING!

NO--THIS IS TOO DANGEROUS-- YOU REMEMBER WHAT HAPPENED LAST TIME DON'T YOU?

I'M NOT GOING TO LET YOU DO THIS-- THIS IS TOO FAR!

NO. IT'S NOT.

I'M GOING TO BE OUT THERE RISKING MY LIFE WITH YOU--I HAVE TO KNOW THE LIMIT.

I NEED TO KNOW WHAT IT FEELS LIKE TO COME RIGHT TO THE EDGE OF IT--TO FEEL MY BODY SUCCUMB TO IT--TO FEEL MYSELF DRIFT OFF.

I NEED TO KNOW THE EXACT--POINT--WHERE I'VE PUSHED HARD ENOUGH--

THE EXACT--

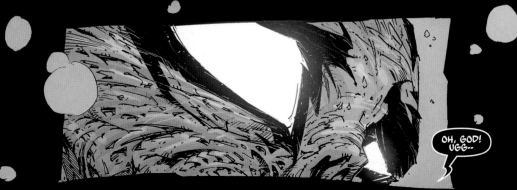

OH, GOD! UGG--

THUNK

...

HUNH?

NOT GOOD!

DANIEL!

WAKE UP!!

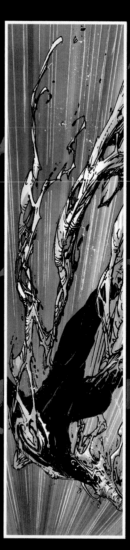

SKKRRGGG

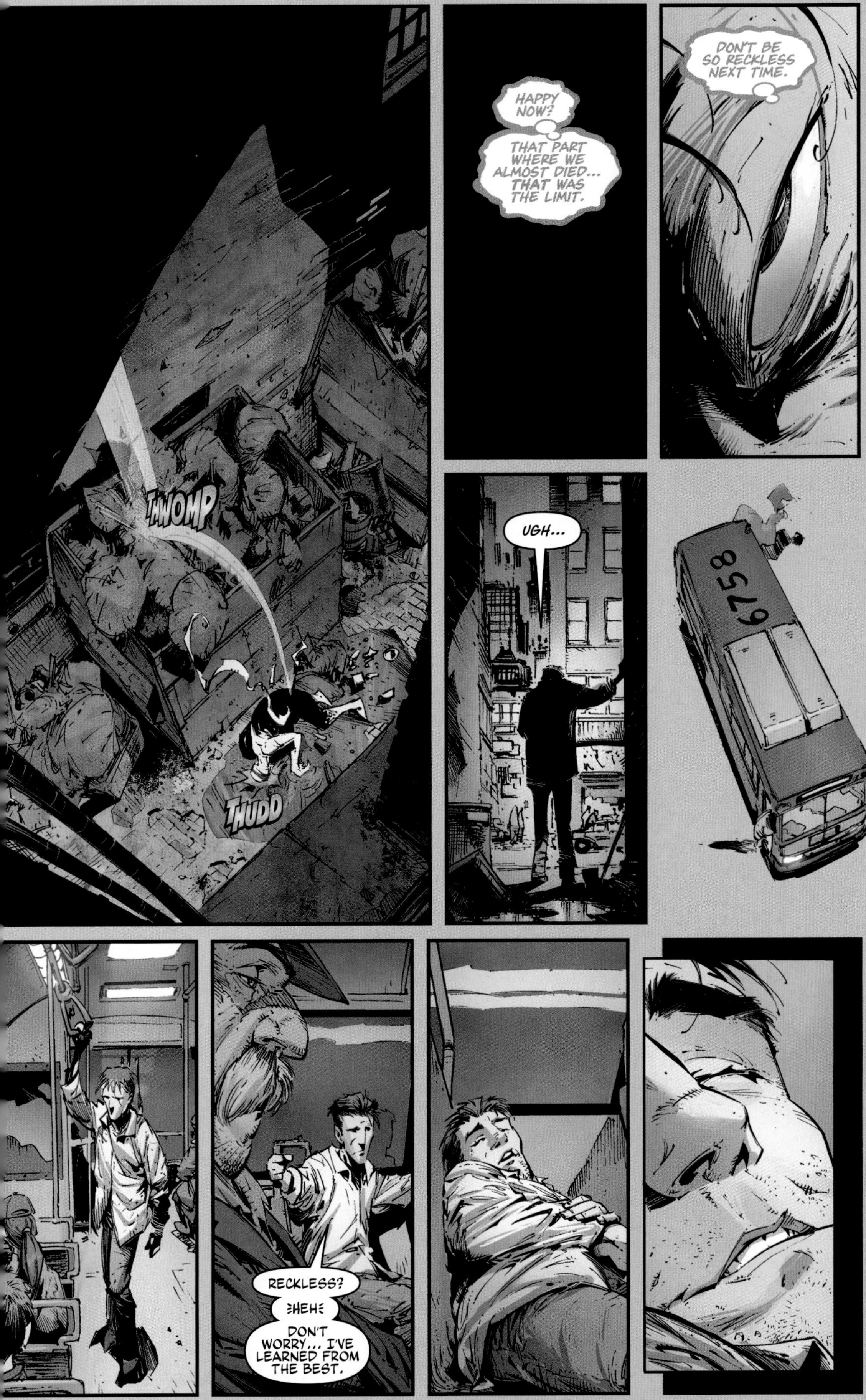

THWOMP
THUDD
HAPPY NOW?
THAT PART WHERE WE ALMOST DIED... THAT WAS THE LIMIT.
DON'T BE SO RECKLESS NEXT TIME.
UGH...
6758
RECKLESS?
HEH
DON'T WORRY... I'VE LEARNED FROM THE BEST.

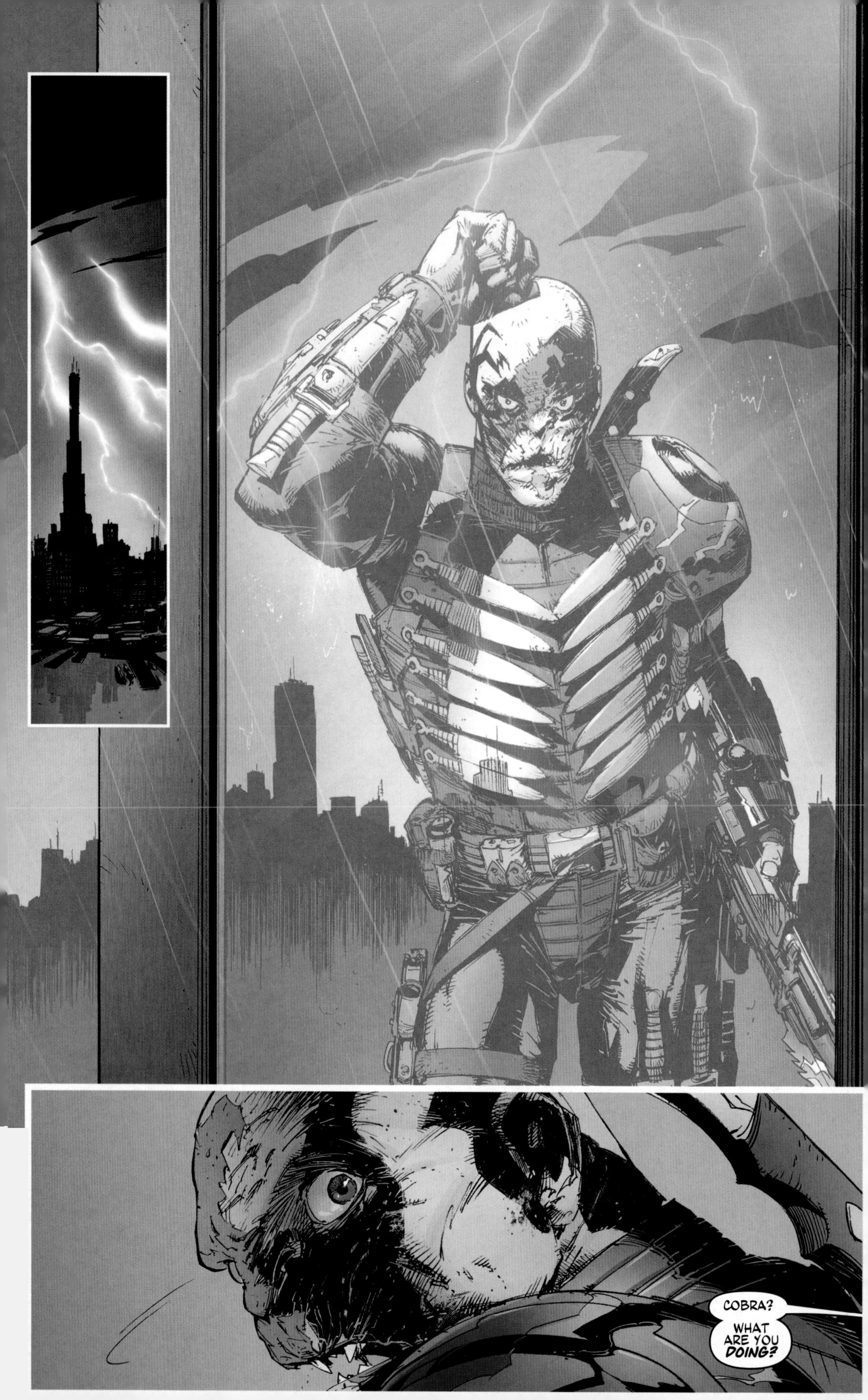
COBRA?
WHAT ARE YOU *DOING?*

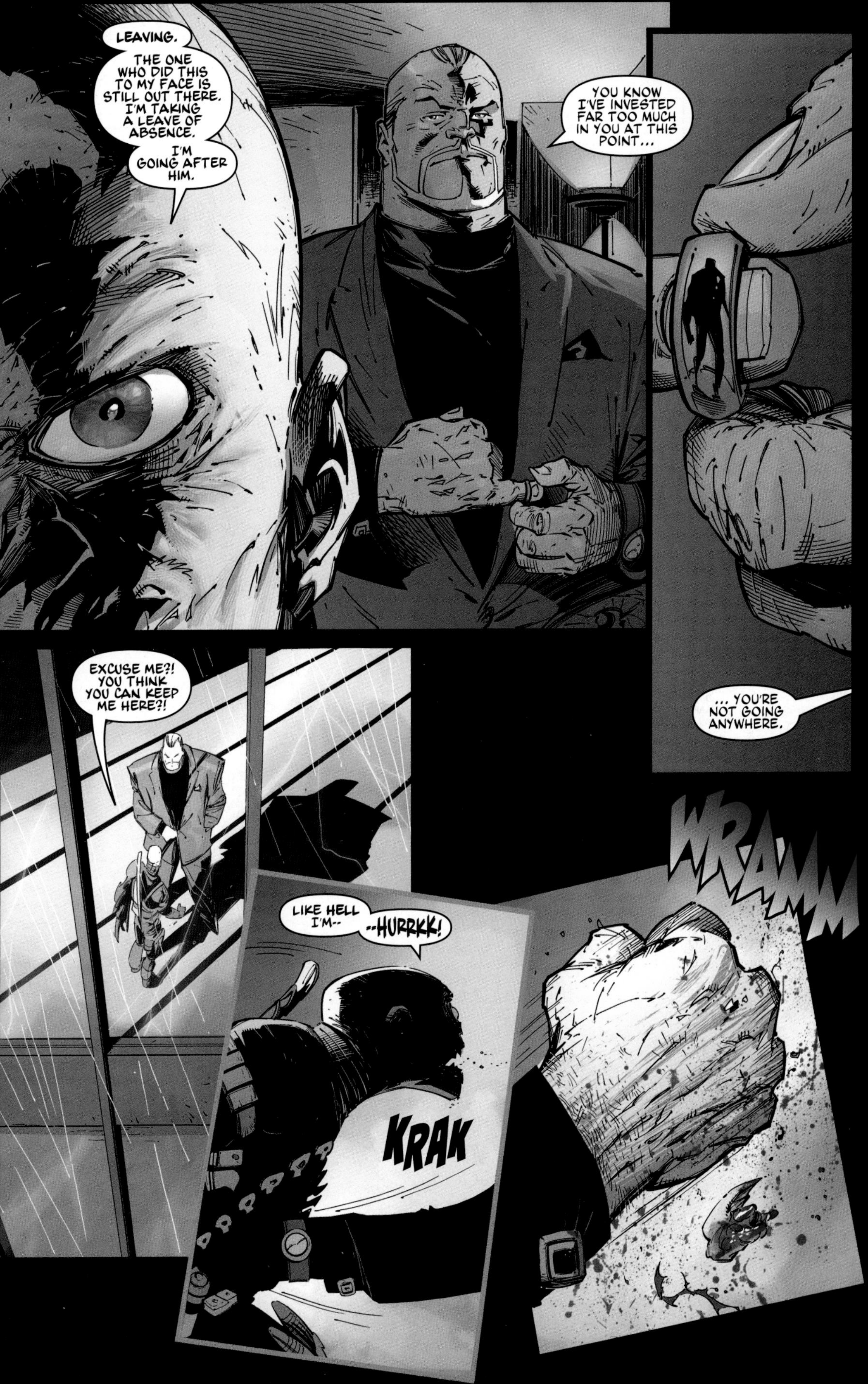
LEAVING.
THE ONE WHO DID THIS TO MY FACE IS STILL OUT THERE. I'M TAKING A LEAVE OF ABSENCE.
I'M GOING AFTER HIM.
YOU KNOW I'VE INVESTED FAR TOO MUCH IN YOU AT THIS POINT...
...YOU'RE NOT GOING ANYWHERE.
EXCUSE ME?! YOU THINK YOU CAN KEEP ME HERE?!
WRAMM
LIKE HELL I'M--
--HURRKK!
KRAK

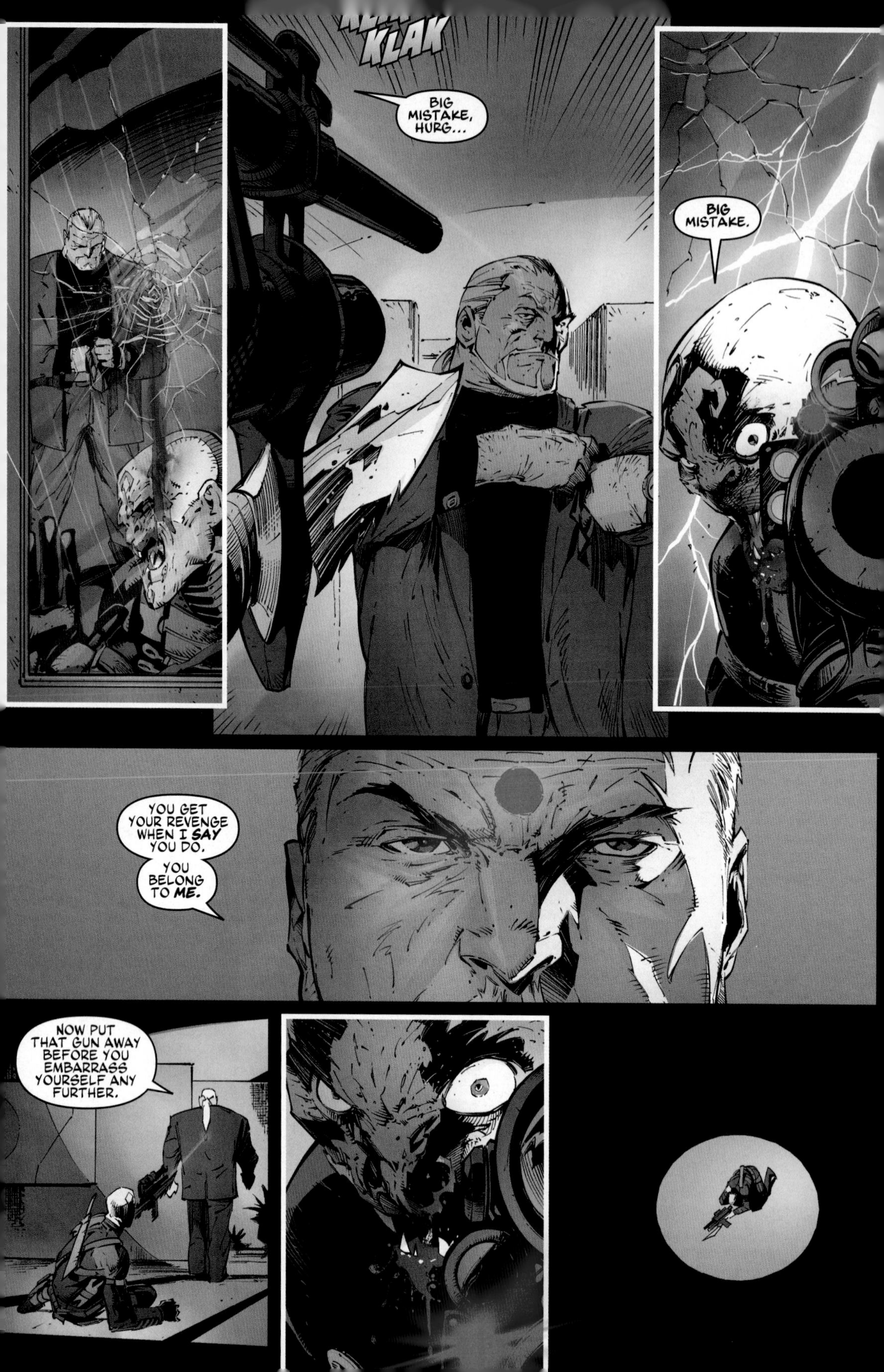
KLAK
BIG MISTAKE, HURG...
BIG MISTAKE.
YOU GET YOUR REVENGE WHEN I SAY YOU DO.
YOU BELONG TO ME.
NOW PUT THAT GUN AWAY BEFORE YOU EMBARRASS YOURSELF ANY FURTHER.

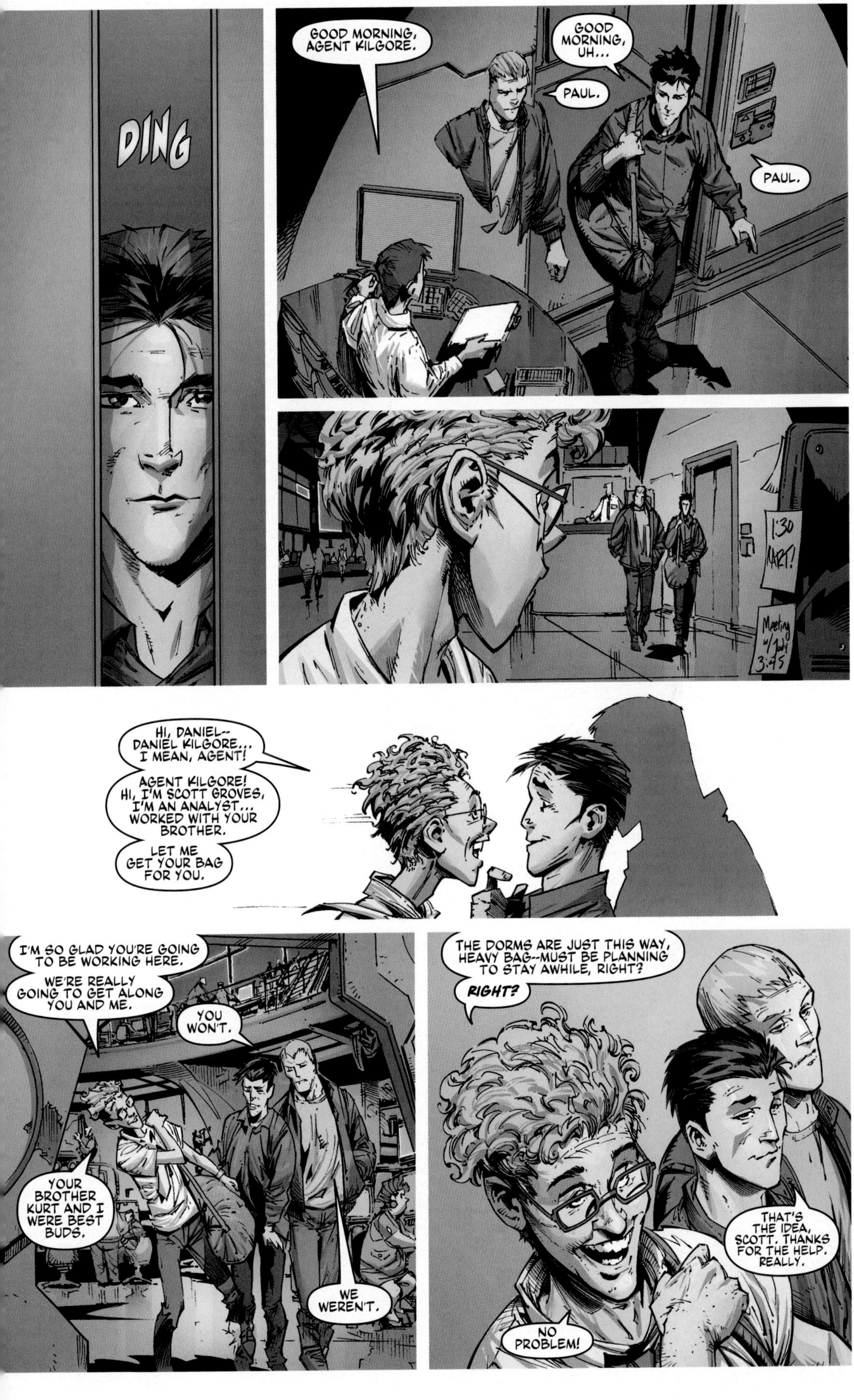
DING
GOOD MORNING, AGENT KILGORE.
GOOD MORNING, UH...
PAUL.
PAUL.
1:30 KART!
Meeting w/Jodi 3:45
HI, DANIEL-- DANIEL KILGORE... I MEAN, AGENT!
AGENT KILGORE! HI, I'M SCOTT GROVES, I'M AN ANALYST... WORKED WITH YOUR BROTHER.
LET ME GET YOUR BAG FOR YOU.
I'M SO GLAD YOU'RE GOING TO BE WORKING HERE.
WE'RE REALLY GOING TO GET ALONG YOU AND ME.
YOU WON'T.
YOUR BROTHER KURT AND I WERE BEST BUDS.
WE WEREN'T.
THE DORMS ARE JUST THIS WAY, HEAVY BAG--MUST BE PLANNING TO STAY AWHILE, RIGHT?
RIGHT?
THAT'S THE IDEA, SCOTT. THANKS FOR THE HELP. REALLY.
NO PROBLEM!

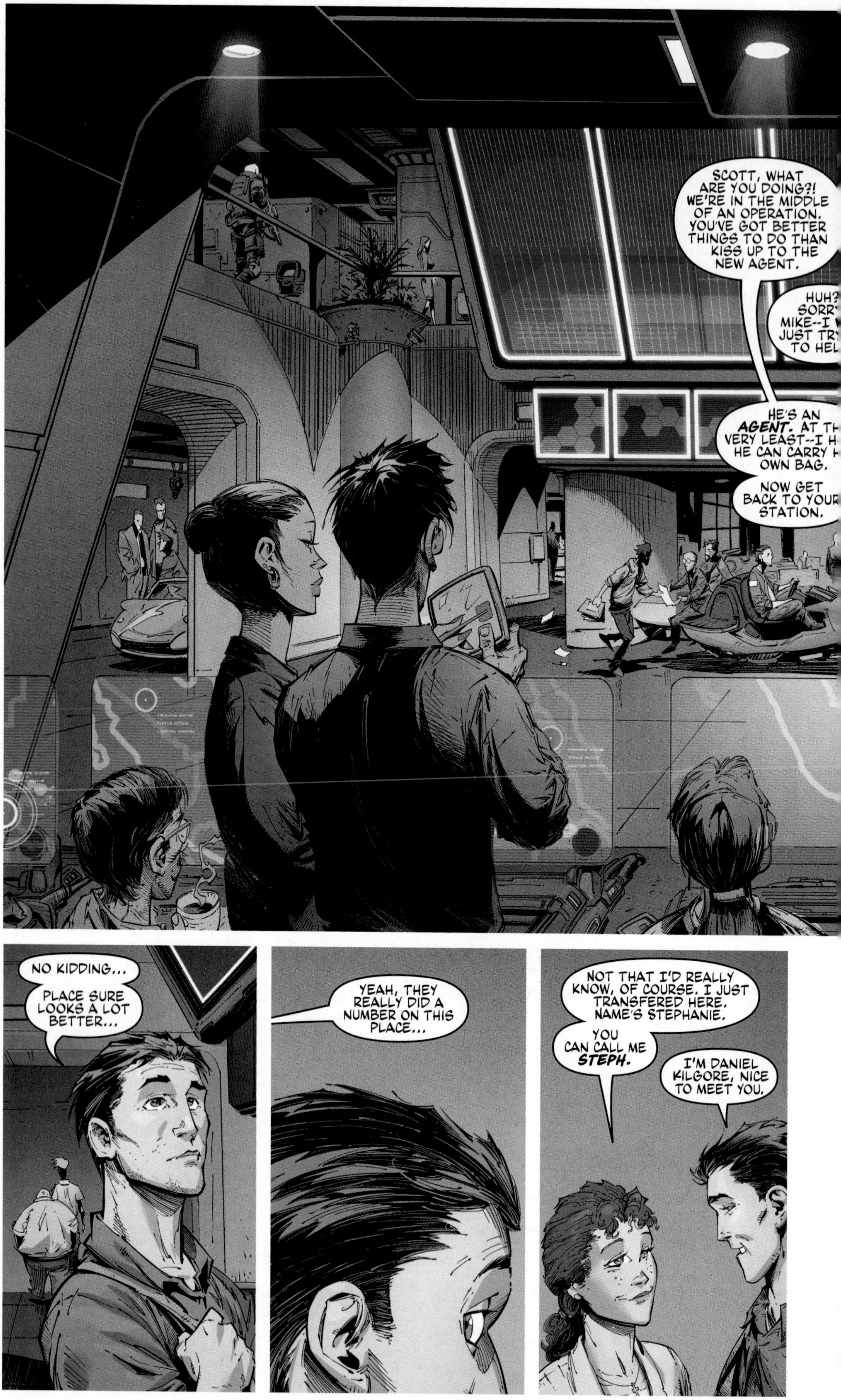

SCOTT, WHAT ARE YOU DOING?! WE'RE IN THE MIDDLE OF AN OPERATION. YOU'VE GOT BETTER THINGS TO DO THAN KISS UP TO THE NEW AGENT.
HUH? SORR MIKE--I JUST TR TO HEL
HE'S AN AGENT. AT T VERY LEAST--I H HE CAN CARRY OWN BAG.
NOW GET BACK TO YOUR STATION.
NO KIDDING...
PLACE SURE LOOKS A LOT BETTER...
YEAH, THEY REALLY DID A NUMBER ON THIS PLACE...
NOT THAT I'D REALLY KNOW, OF COURSE. I JUST TRANSFERED HERE. NAME'S STEPHANIE.
YOU CAN CALL ME STEPH.
I'M DANIEL KILGORE, NICE TO MEET YOU.

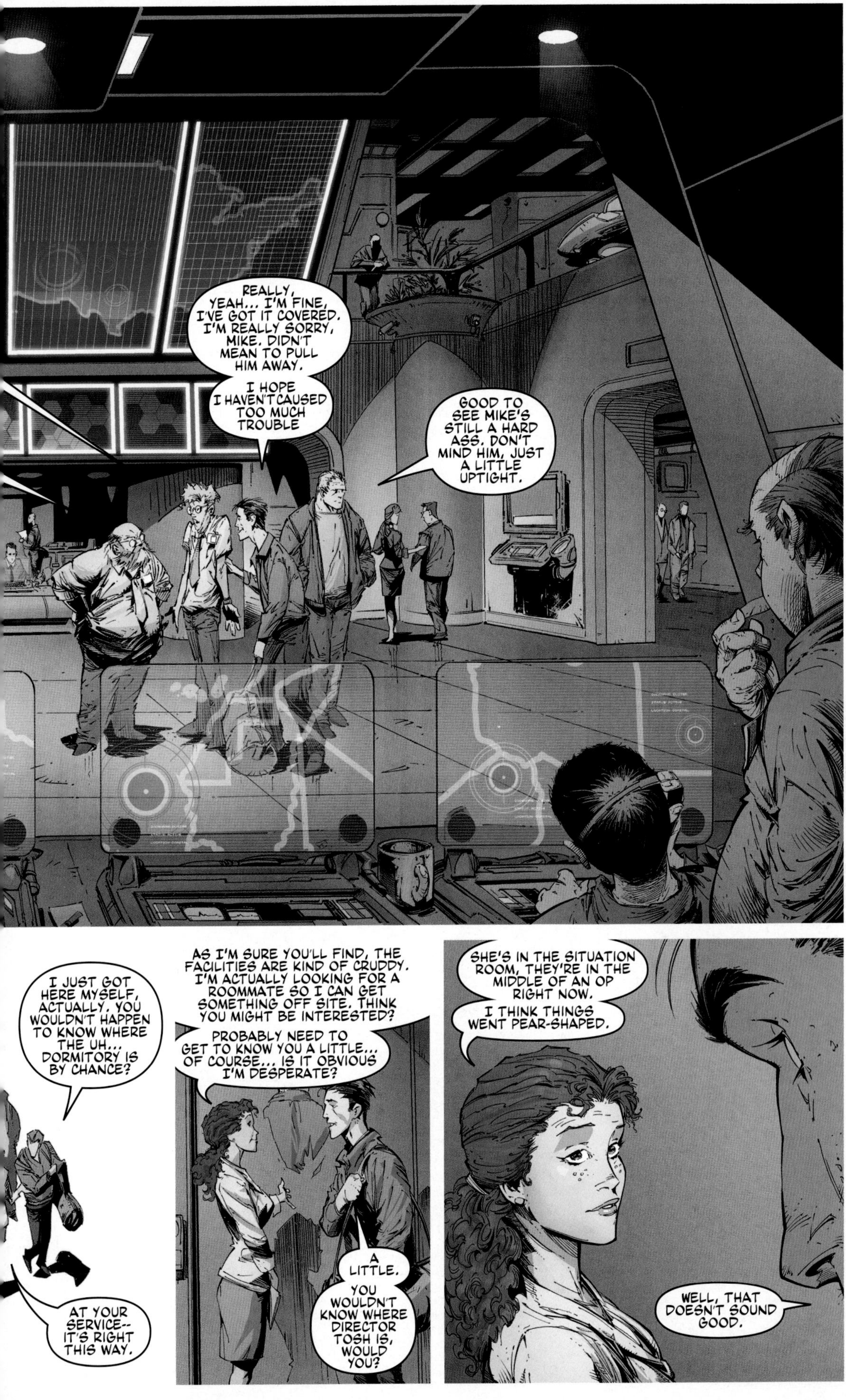
REALLY, YEAH... I'M FINE, I'VE GOT IT COVERED. I'M REALLY SORRY, MIKE. DIDN'T MEAN TO PULL HIM AWAY.
I HOPE I HAVEN'T CAUSED TOO MUCH TROUBLE
GOOD TO SEE MIKE'S STILL A HARD ASS. DON'T MIND HIM, JUST A LITTLE UPTIGHT.
I JUST GOT HERE MYSELF, ACTUALLY. YOU WOULDN'T HAPPEN TO KNOW WHERE THE UH... DORMITORY IS BY CHANCE?
AT YOUR SERVICE-- IT'S RIGHT THIS WAY.
AS I'M SURE YOU'LL FIND, THE FACILITIES ARE KIND OF CRUDDY. I'M ACTUALLY LOOKING FOR A ROOMMATE SO I CAN GET SOMETHING OFF SITE. THINK YOU MIGHT BE INTERESTED?
PROBABLY NEED TO GET TO KNOW YOU A LITTLE... OF COURSE... IS IT OBVIOUS I'M DESPERATE?
A LITTLE.
YOU WOULDN'T KNOW WHERE DIRECTOR TOSH IS, WOULD YOU?
SHE'S IN THE SITUATION ROOM, THEY'RE IN THE MIDDLE OF AN OP RIGHT NOW.
I THINK THINGS WENT PEAR-SHAPED.
WELL, THAT DOESN'T SOUND GOOD.

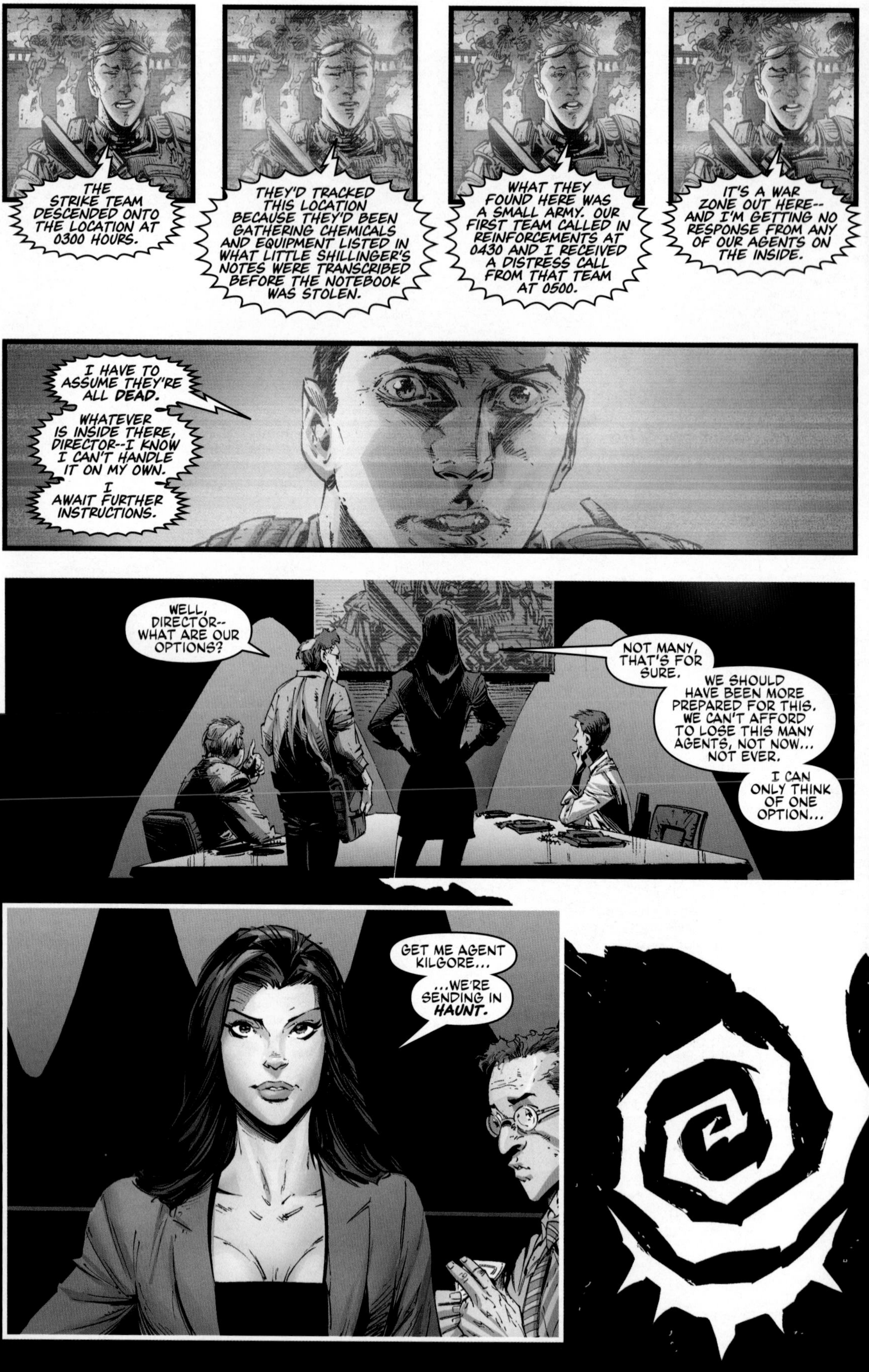
THE STRIKE TEAM DESCENDED ONTO THE LOCATION AT 0300 HOURS.
THEY'D TRACKED THIS LOCATION BECAUSE THEY'D BEEN GATHERING CHEMICALS AND EQUIPMENT LISTED IN WHAT LITTLE SHILLINGER'S NOTES WERE TRANSCRIBED BEFORE THE NOTEBOOK WAS STOLEN.
WHAT THEY FOUND HERE WAS A SMALL ARMY. OUR FIRST TEAM CALLED IN REINFORCEMENTS AT 0430 AND I RECEIVED A DISTRESS CALL FROM THAT TEAM AT 0500.
IT'S A WAR ZONE OUT HERE--AND I'M GETTING NO RESPONSE FROM ANY OF OUR AGENTS ON THE INSIDE.
I HAVE TO ASSUME THEY'RE ALL DEAD.
WHATEVER IS INSIDE THERE, DIRECTOR--I KNOW I CAN'T HANDLE IT ON MY OWN.
I AWAIT FURTHER INSTRUCTIONS.
WELL, DIRECTOR--WHAT ARE OUR OPTIONS?
NOT MANY, THAT'S FOR SURE.
WE SHOULD HAVE BEEN MORE PREPARED FOR THIS. WE CAN'T AFFORD TO LOSE THIS MANY AGENTS, NOT NOW... NOT EVER.
I CAN ONLY THINK OF ONE OPTION...
GET ME AGENT KILGORE...
...WE'RE SENDING IN HAUNT.

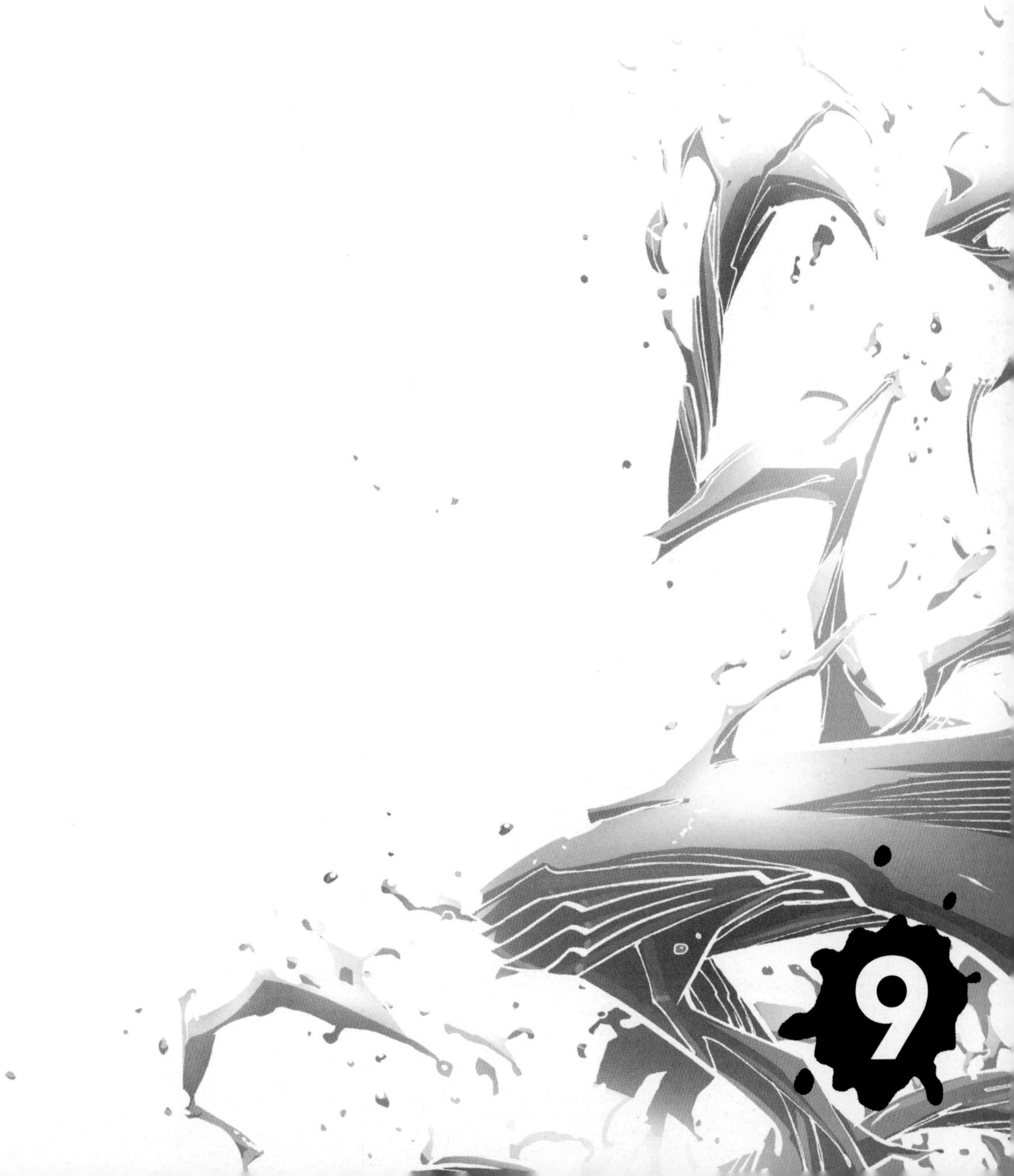
9

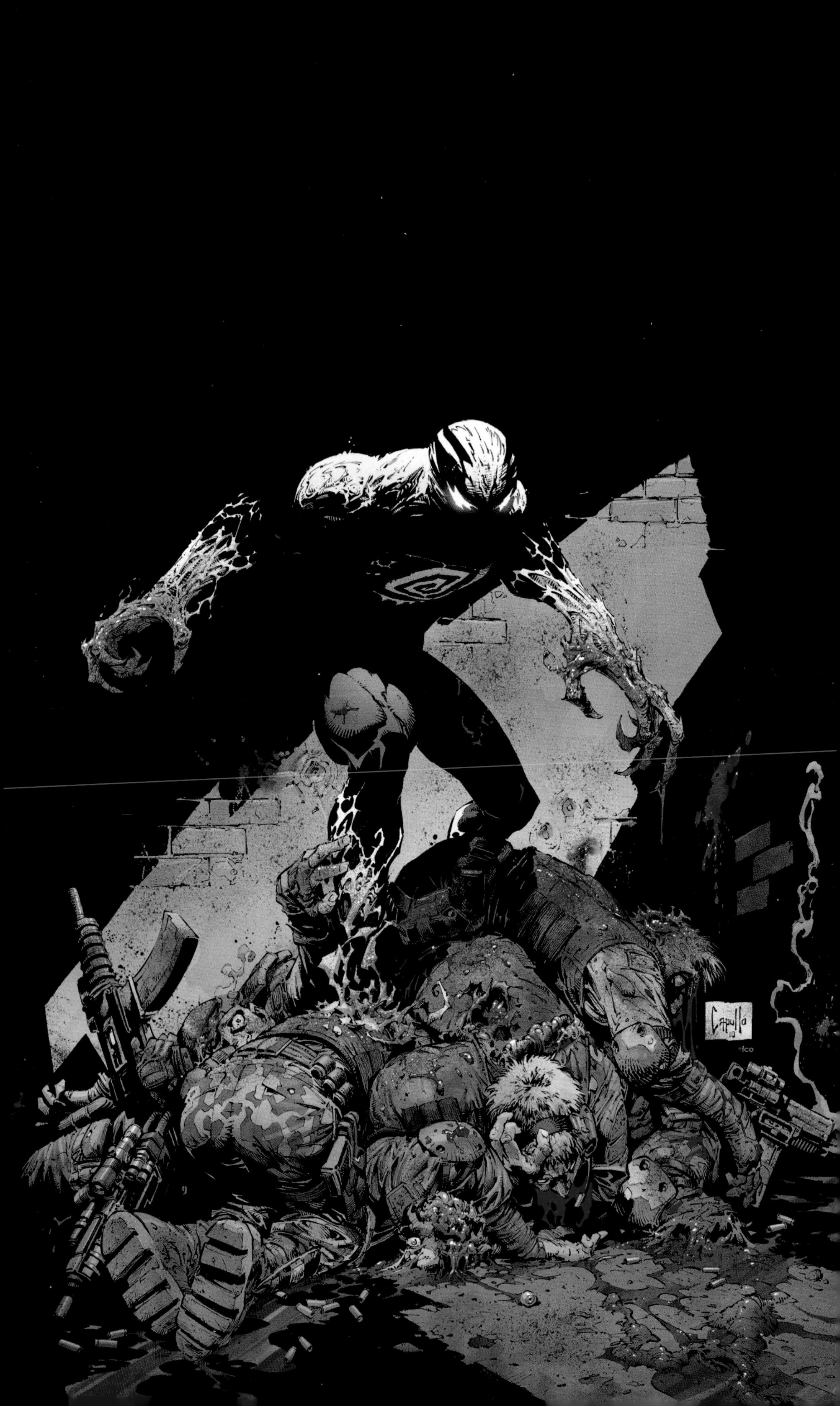

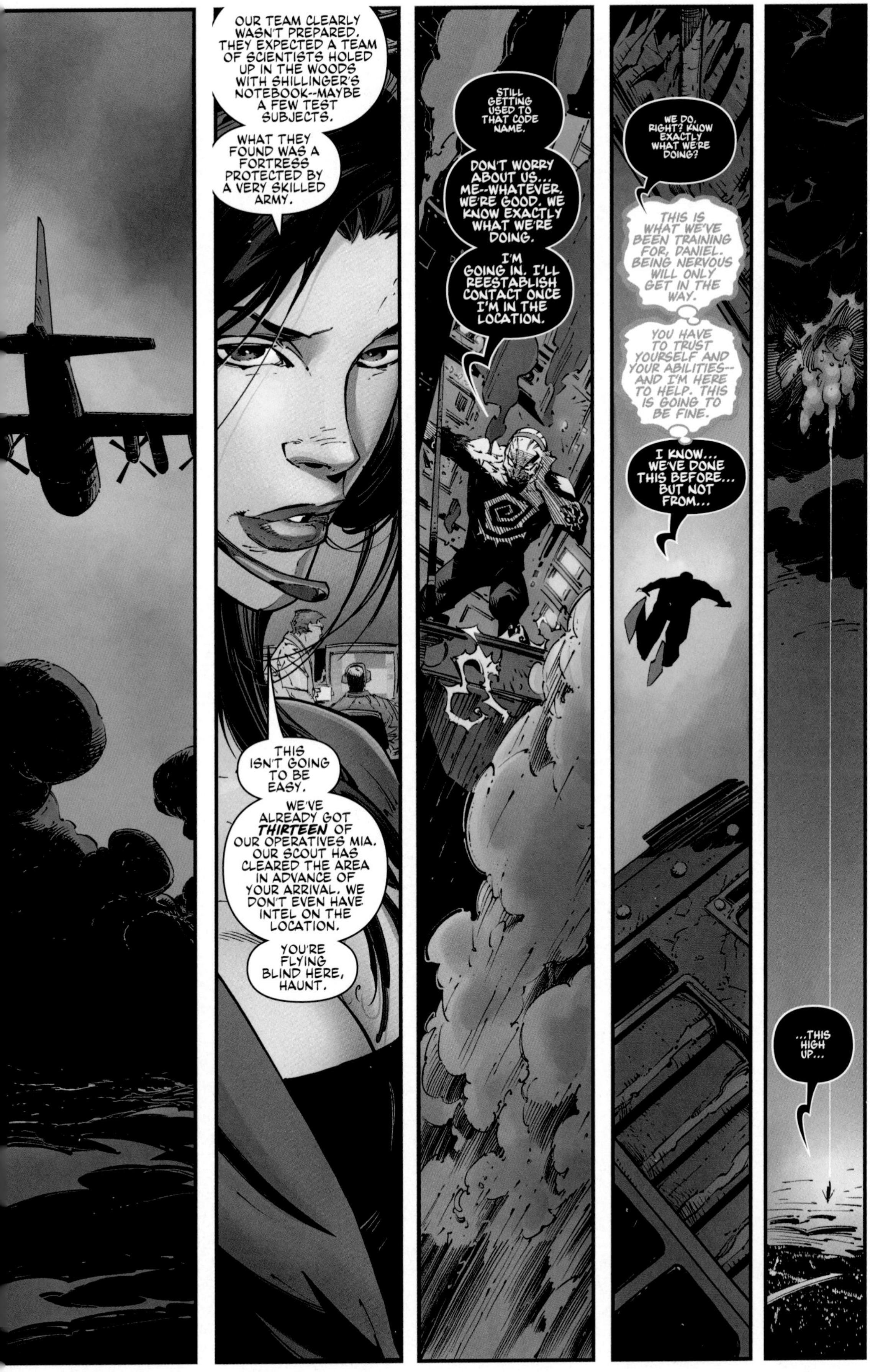

OUR TEAM CLEARLY WASN'T PREPARED. THEY EXPECTED A TEAM OF SCIENTISTS HOLED UP IN THE WOODS WITH SHILLINGER'S NOTEBOOK--MAYBE A FEW TEST SUBJECTS.
WHAT THEY FOUND WAS A FORTRESS PROTECTED BY A VERY SKILLED ARMY.
THIS ISN'T GOING TO BE EASY.
WE'VE ALREADY GOT THIRTEEN OF OUR OPERATIVES MIA. OUR SCOUT HAS CLEARED THE AREA IN ADVANCE OF YOUR ARRIVAL. WE DON'T EVEN HAVE INTEL ON THE LOCATION.
YOU'RE FLYING BLIND HERE, HAUNT.
STILL GETTING USED TO THAT CODE NAME.
DON'T WORRY ABOUT US... ME--WHATEVER. WE'RE GOOD. WE KNOW EXACTLY WHAT WE'RE DOING.
I'M GOING IN. I'LL REESTABLISH CONTACT ONCE I'M IN THE LOCATION.
WE DO, RIGHT? KNOW EXACTLY WHAT WE'RE DOING?
THIS IS WHAT WE'VE BEEN TRAINING FOR, DANIEL. BEING NERVOUS WILL ONLY GET IN THE WAY.
YOU HAVE TO TRUST YOURSELF AND YOUR ABILITIES--AND I'M HERE TO HELP. THIS IS GOING TO BE FINE.
I KNOW... WE'VE DONE THIS BEFORE... BUT NOT FROM...
...THIS HIGH UP...

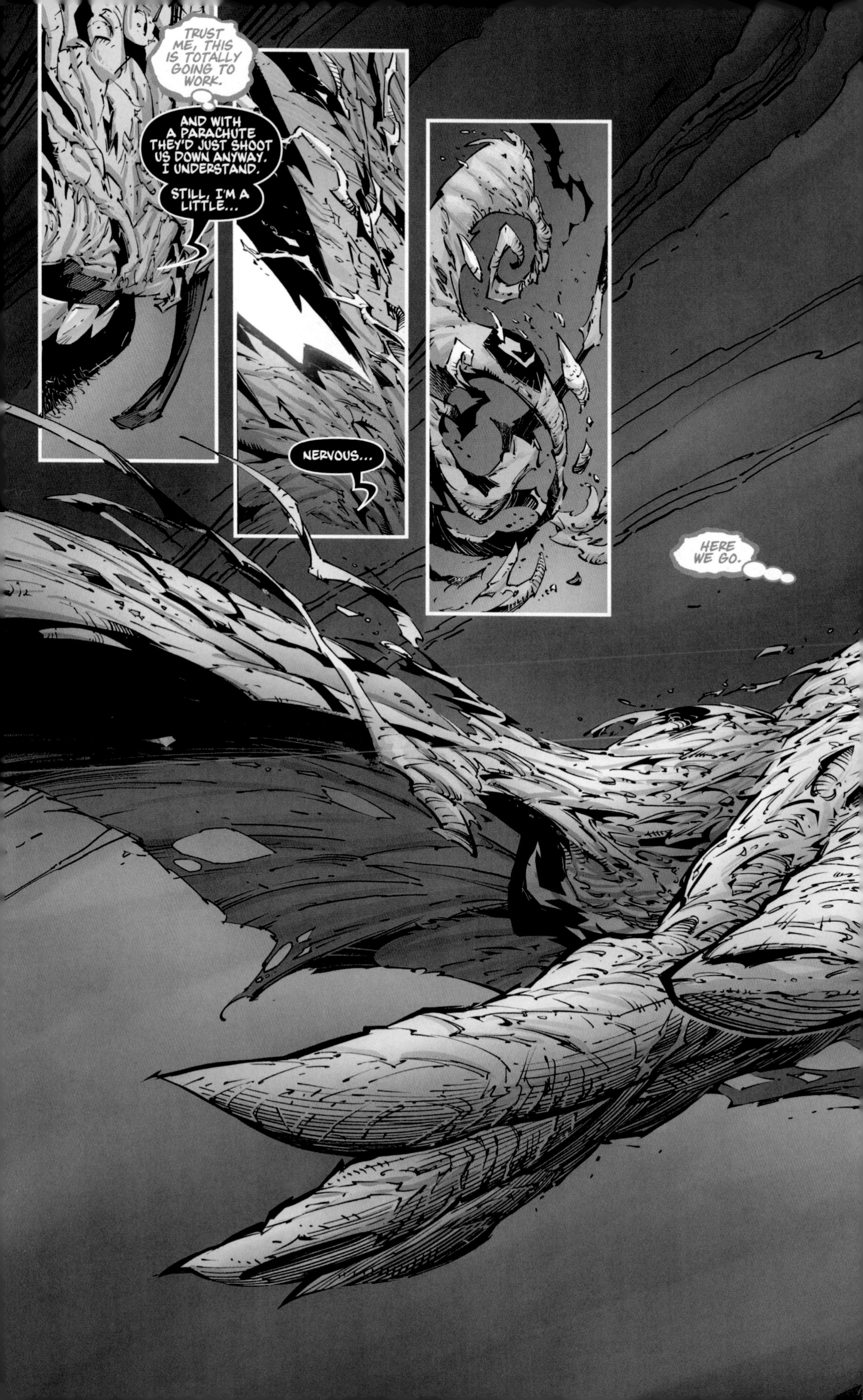
TRUST ME, THIS IS TOTALLY GOING TO WORK.
AND WITH A PARACHUTE THEY'D JUST SHOOT US DOWN ANYWAY. I UNDERSTAND.
STILL, I'M A LITTLE...
NERVOUS...
HERE WE GO.

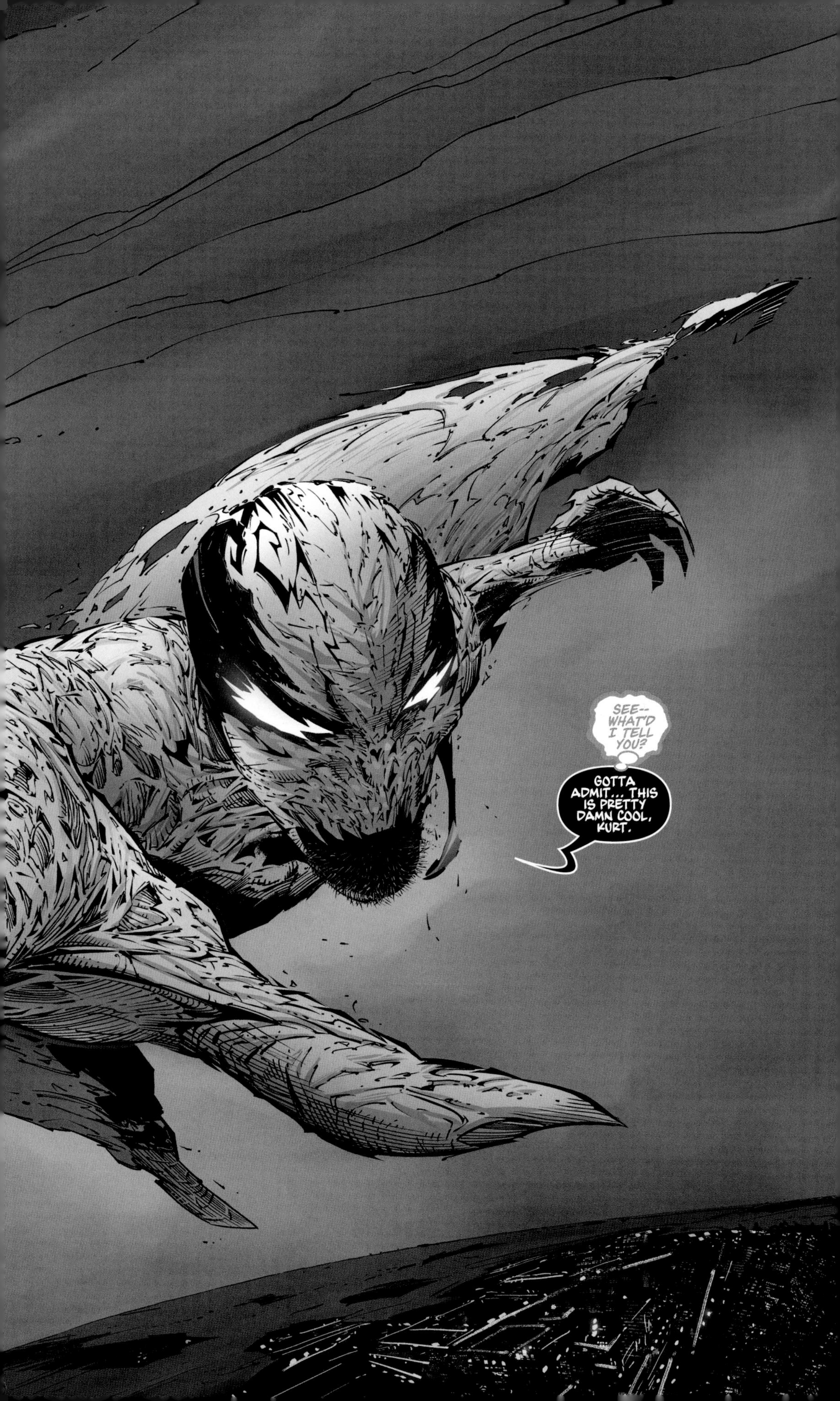
SEE--
WHAT'D I TELL YOU?
GOTTA ADMIT... THIS IS PRETTY DAMN COOL, KURT.

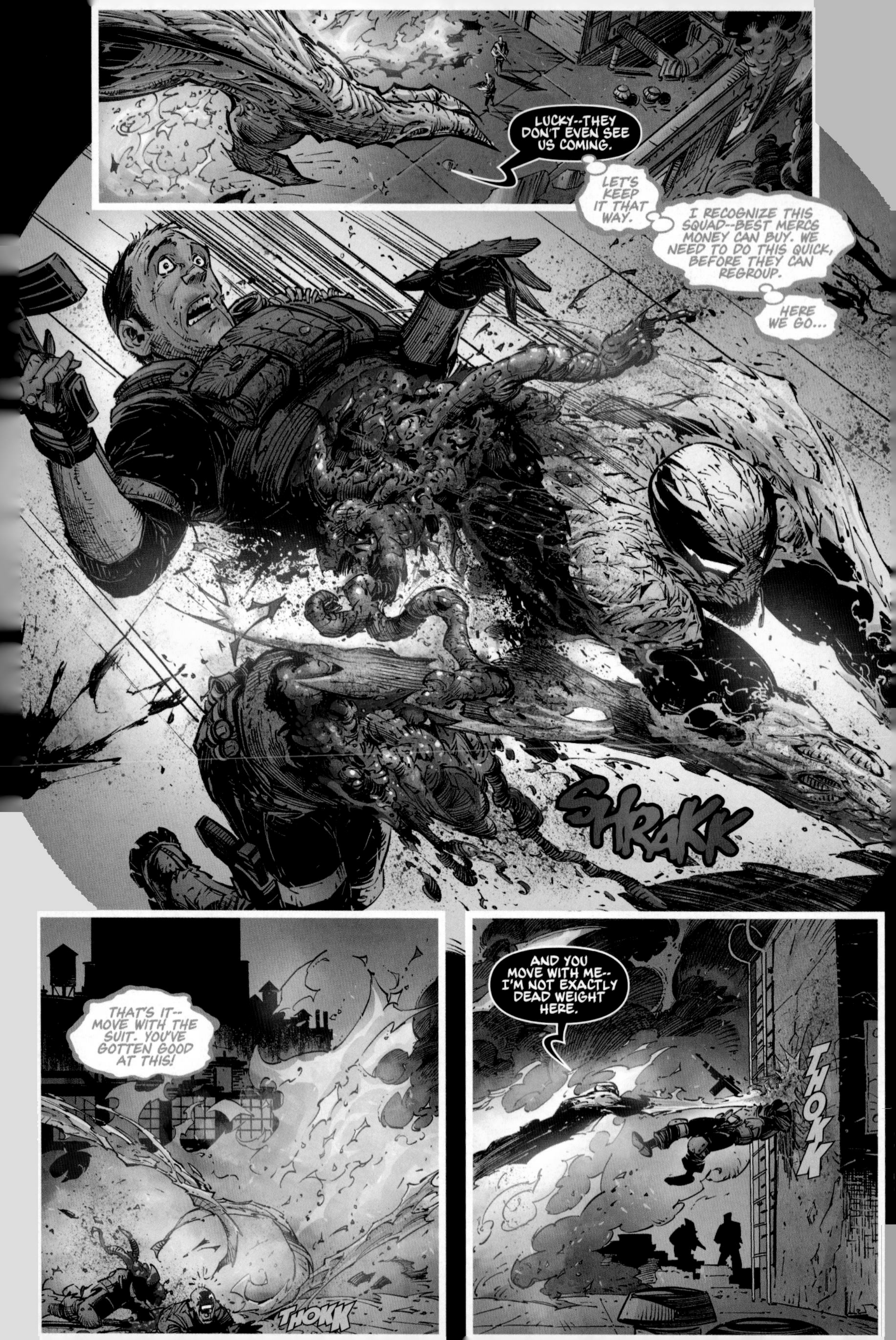
LUCKY--THEY DON'T EVEN SEE US COMING.
LET'S KEEP IT THAT WAY.
I RECOGNIZE THIS SQUAD--BEST MERCS MONEY CAN BUY. WE NEED TO DO THIS QUICK, BEFORE THEY CAN REGROUP.
HERE WE GO...
SHRAKK
THAT'S IT--MOVE WITH THE SUIT. YOU'VE GOTTEN GOOD AT THIS!
THOKK
AND YOU MOVE WITH ME--I'M NOT EXACTLY DEAD WEIGHT HERE.
THOKK

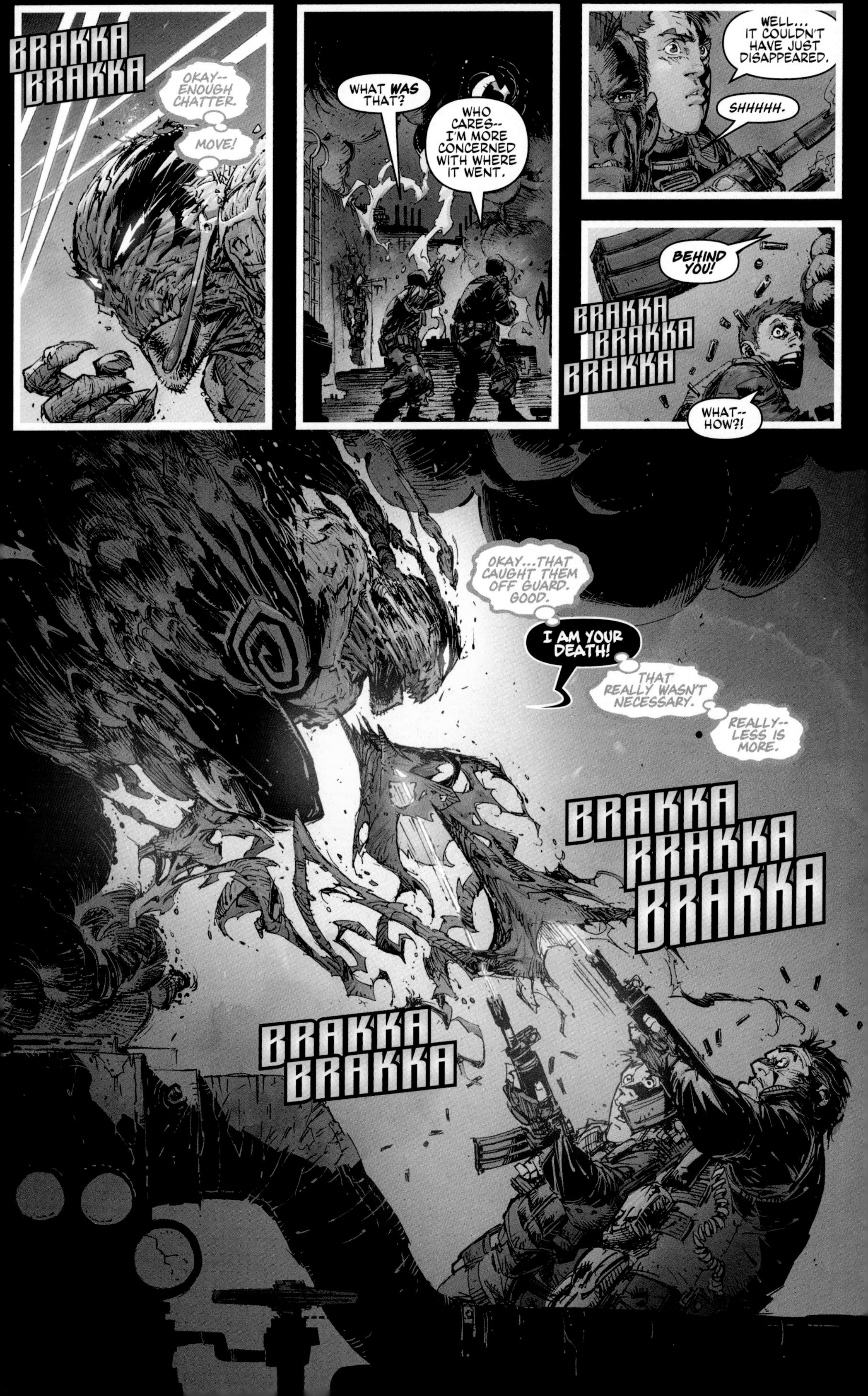
BRAKKA BRAKKA
OKAY-- ENOUGH CHATTER.
MOVE!
WHAT WAS THAT?
WHO CARES-- I'M MORE CONCERNED WITH WHERE IT WENT.
WELL... IT COULDN'T HAVE JUST DISAPPEARED.
SHHHHH.
BEHIND YOU!
BRAKKA BRAKKA BRAKKA
WHAT-- HOW?!
OKAY...THAT CAUGHT THEM OFF GUARD. GOOD.
I AM YOUR DEATH!
THAT REALLY WASN'T NECESSARY.
REALLY-- LESS IS MORE.
BRAKKA RRAKKA BRAKKA
BRAKKA BRAKKA

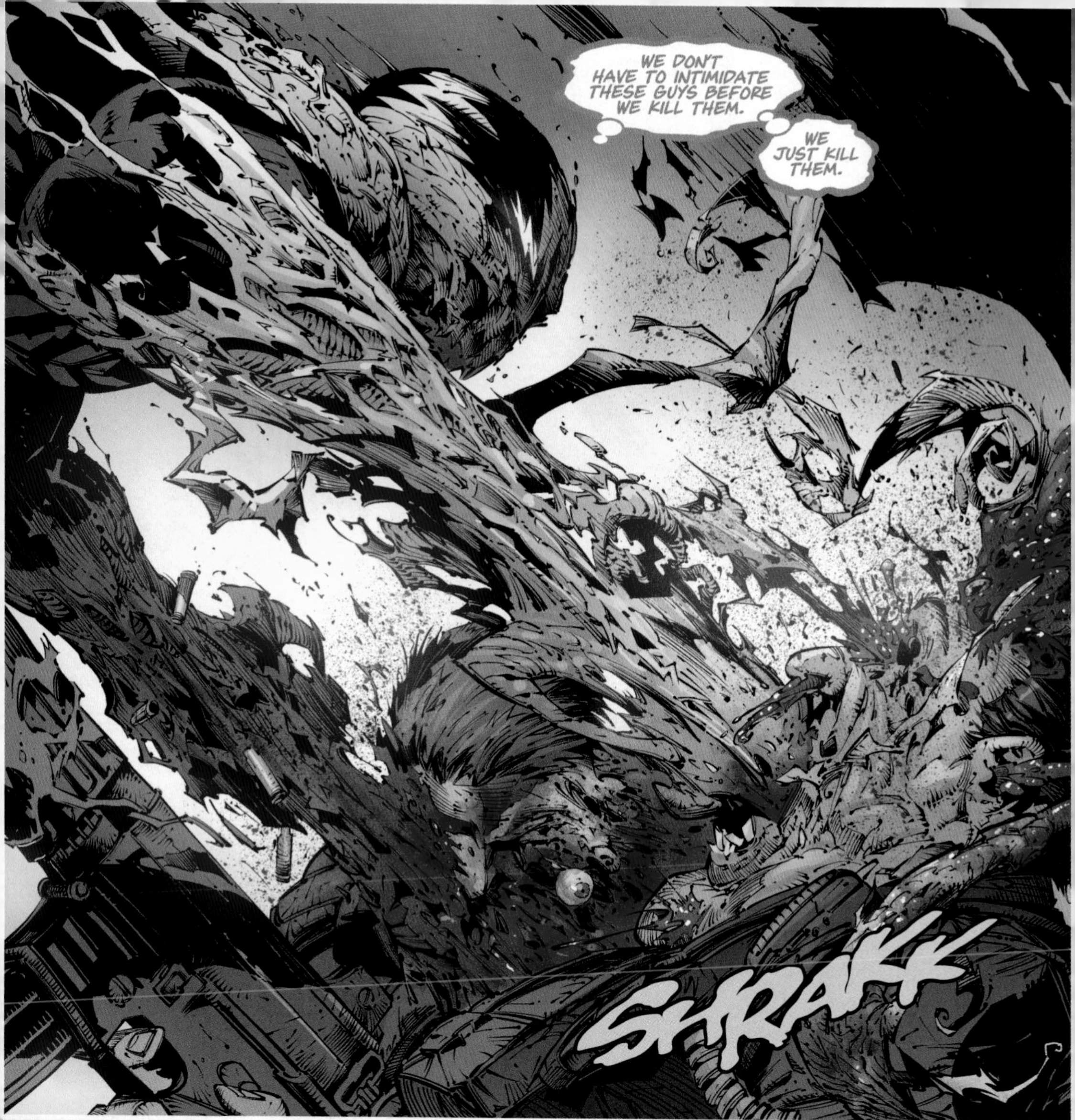
WE DON'T HAVE TO INTIMIDATE THESE GUYS BEFORE WE KILL THEM.
WE JUST KILL THEM.
SHRAKK

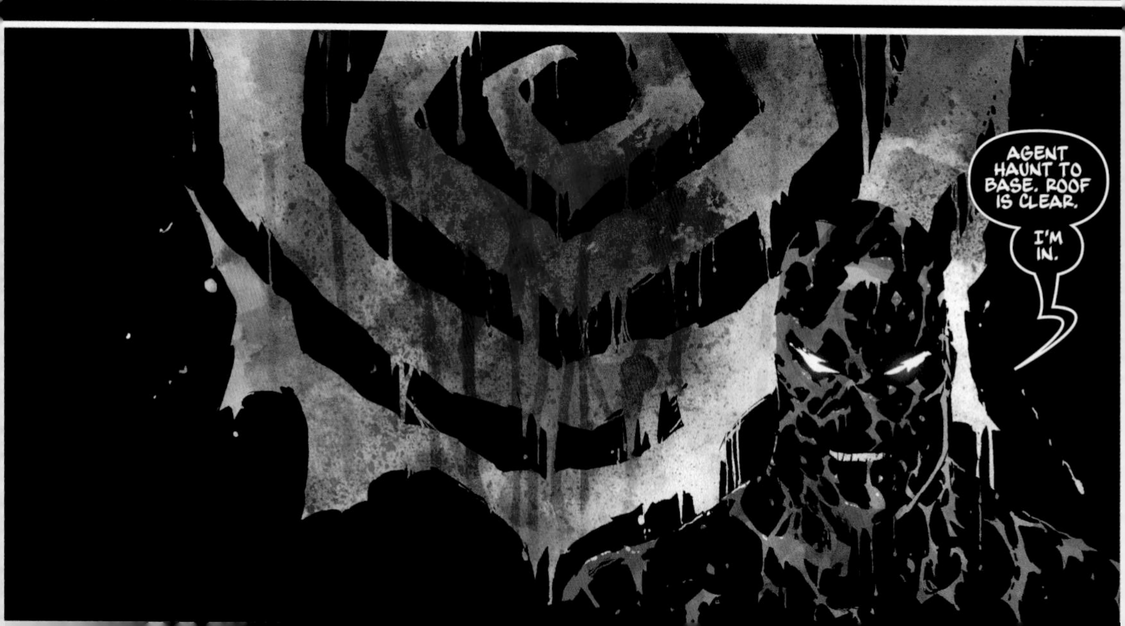
AGENT HAUNT TO BASE. ROOF IS CLEAR.
I'M IN.

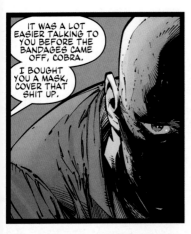

IT WAS A LOT EASIER TALKING TO YOU BEFORE THE BANDAGES CAME OFF, COBRA.

I BOUGHT YOU A MASK, COVER THAT SHIT UP.

YES, DEAR.

I DON'T WANT TO HEAR YOU COMPLAINING. THAT THING IS ONE-HUNDRED PERCENT CASHMERE, HAND SEWN BY ANTONIO BUSCHELLI.

HE HAD ALL HIS MODELS WEAR THEM WHEN HE DEBUTED HIS NEWEST LINE LAST WEEK--LET ME KEEP MINE.

I DIDN'T THINK YOU'D BE HERE WHEN I RETURNED. I THOUGHT YOU WERE THROUGH WITH HURG?

AND NOW WITH THIS INJURY--WHY DO YOU STAY WITH HIM? I REALLY JUST DON'T UNDERSTAND IT.

THE MONEY IS GOOD.

MONEY? YOU KNOW I HAVE MORE THAN ENOUGH MONEY FOR THE BOTH OF US. DON'T TRY TO LIE TO ME.

IT'S THE STABBING. HURG PAYS YOU TO MURDER PEOPLE--THAT'S HOW YOU GET YOUR KICKS.

OH, I USED TO THINK THAT WAS SO HOT-- *THAT'S* WHY I FELL IN LOVE WITH YOU.

BUT NOW IT'S LIKE YOU'RE HIS SERVANT--AND THAT FACE... UGH...

IT MAKES ME WANT TO CHEAT ON YOU AGAIN...

OH, *RELAX!* I HAVEN'T DONE ANYTHING... YET.

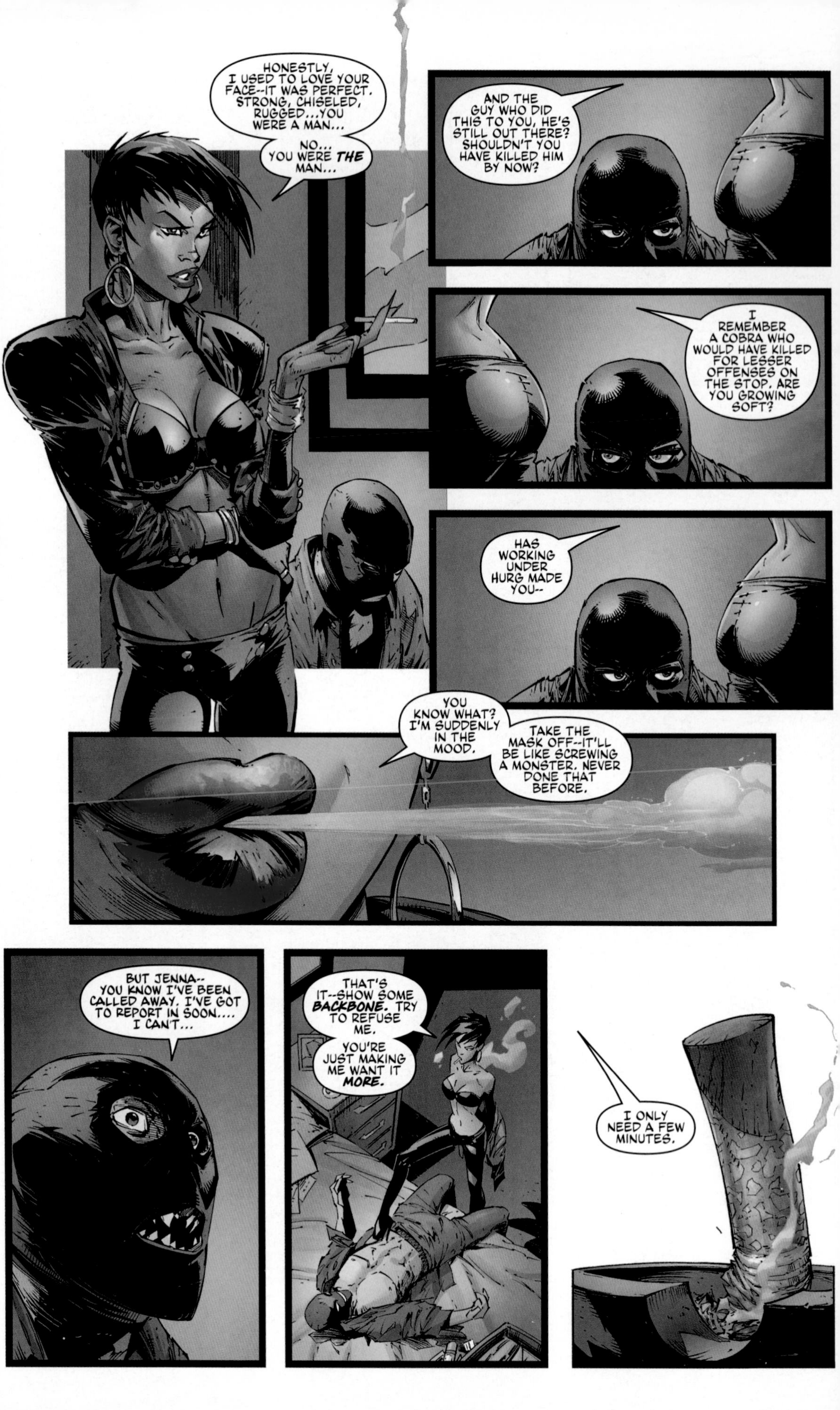
HONESTLY, I USED TO LOVE YOUR FACE--IT WAS PERFECT. STRONG, CHISELED, RUGGED...YOU WERE A MAN...
NO... YOU WERE *THE* MAN...
AND THE GUY WHO DID THIS TO YOU, HE'S STILL OUT THERE? SHOULDN'T YOU HAVE KILLED HIM BY NOW?
I REMEMBER A COBRA WHO WOULD HAVE KILLED FOR LESSER OFFENSES ON THE STOP. ARE YOU GROWING SOFT?
HAS WORKING UNDER HURG MADE YOU--
YOU KNOW WHAT? I'M SUDDENLY IN THE MOOD.
TAKE THE MASK OFF--IT'LL BE LIKE SCREWING A MONSTER. NEVER DONE THAT BEFORE.
BUT JENNA-- YOU KNOW I'VE BEEN CALLED AWAY. I'VE GOT TO REPORT IN SOON.... I CAN'T...
THAT'S IT--SHOW SOME **BACKBONE.** TRY TO REFUSE ME.
YOU'RE JUST MAKING ME WANT IT **MORE.**
I ONLY NEED A FEW MINUTES.

IT'S A WARZONE IN HERE... I SEE EVIDENCE OF A HUGE FIREFIGHT.

MULTIPLE ASSAILANTS-- LOTS OF SPENT AMMUNITION.

MUST HAVE BEEN AT LEAST TWO-DOZEN GUYS GOING AT IT FROM THE LOOKS OF IT.

I DON'T SEE HOW ANYBODY WALKED AWAY FROM THIS ONE...

BUT THERE ARE NO BODIES... I DON'T SEE ANY SIGN OF OUR SQUADRON.

I DON'T LIKE THIS AT ALL... THERE'S NO WAY THIS PLACE IS THIS EMPTY.

STAY ALERT, DANIEL.

WILL DO.

UH... SORRY. I WAS TALKING TO--

CARRYING ON-- I'VE COVERED THE ENTIRE SOUTHEAST QUADRANT OF THE BUILDING... NO SIGN OF ANYONE LIVING OR DEAD--BUT IF THERE ARE LAB FACILITIES HERE, I HAVEN'T FOUND THEM YET.

AT THIS POINT I'M MORE CONCERNED WITH FINDING ANY SIGN OF OUR TWO MISSING SQUADRONS. I DON'T WANT THEIR STATUS TO BE AN UNKNOWN.

WITH THESE EXPERIMENTS BEING DONE--I CAN'T LIVE WITH THE POSSIBILITY THAT OUR MEN HAVE BECOME THEIR LAB RATS.

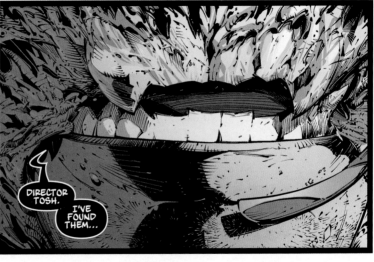

DIRECTOR TOSH.

I'VE FOUND THEM...

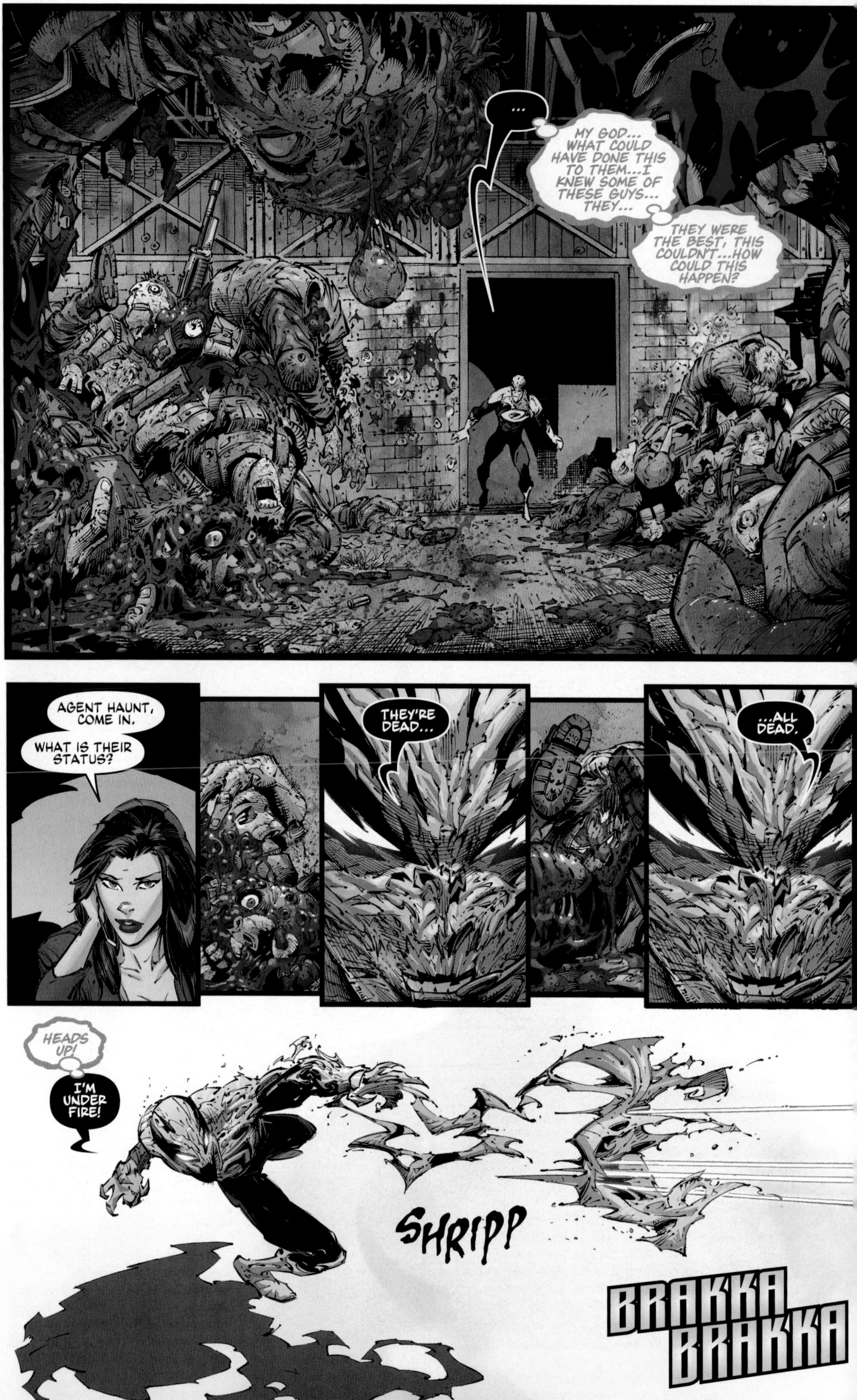
...
MY GOD... WHAT COULD HAVE DONE THIS TO THEM...I KNEW SOME OF THESE GUYS... THEY...
THEY WERE THE BEST, THIS COULDN'T...HOW COULD THIS HAPPEN?
AGENT HAUNT, COME IN.
WHAT IS THEIR STATUS?
THEY'RE DEAD...
...ALL DEAD.
HEADS UP!
I'M UNDER FIRE!
SHRIPP
BRAKKA BRAKKA

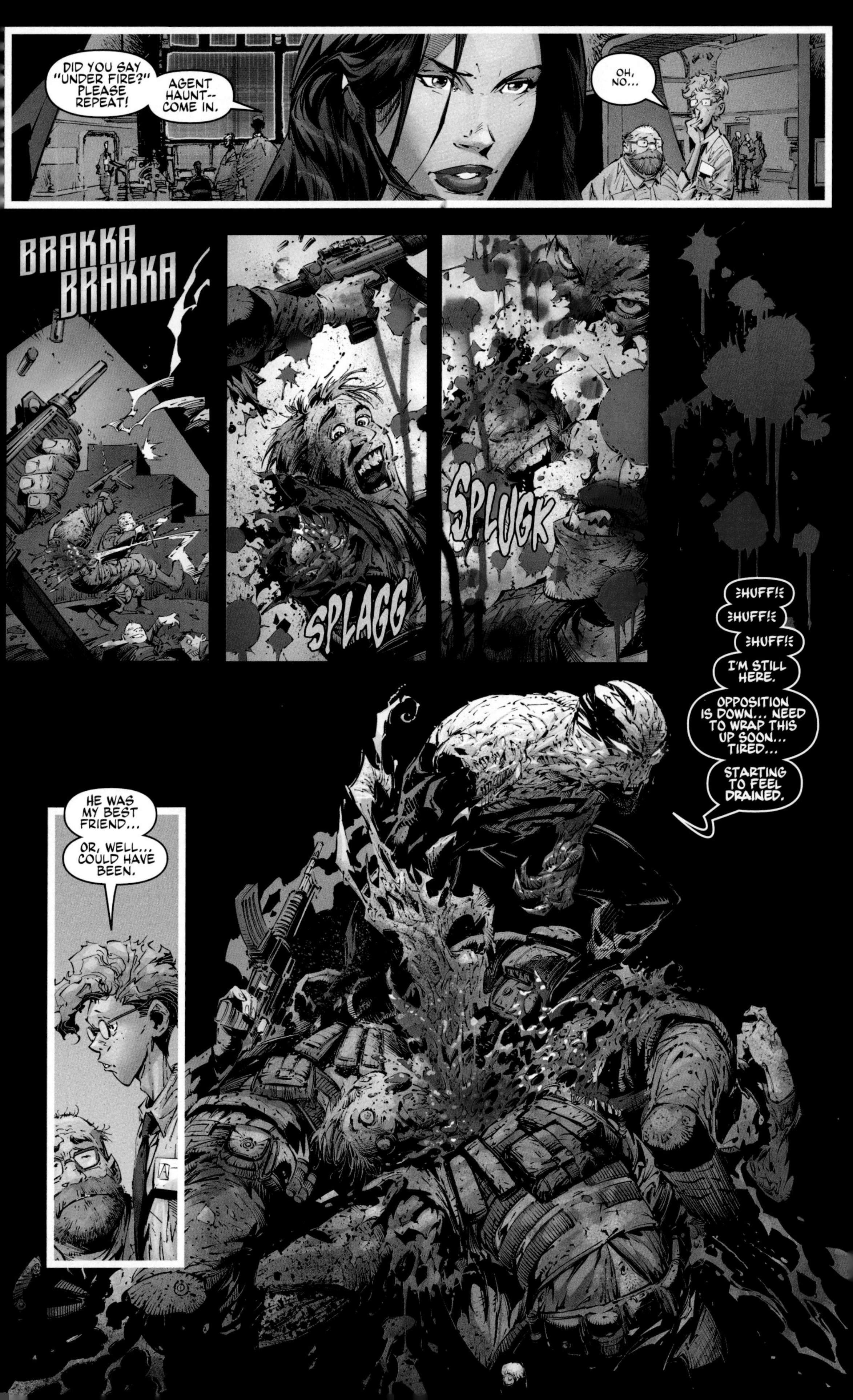
DID YOU SAY "UNDER FIRE?" PLEASE REPEAT!
AGENT HAUNT-- COME IN.
OH, NO...
BRAKKA BRAKKA
SPLAGG
SPLUGK
HUFF!
HUFF!
HUFF!
I'M STILL HERE.
OPPOSITION IS DOWN... NEED TO WRAP THIS UP SOON... TIRED...
STARTING TO FEEL DRAINED.
HE WAS MY BEST FRIEND...
OR, WELL... COULD HAVE BEEN.

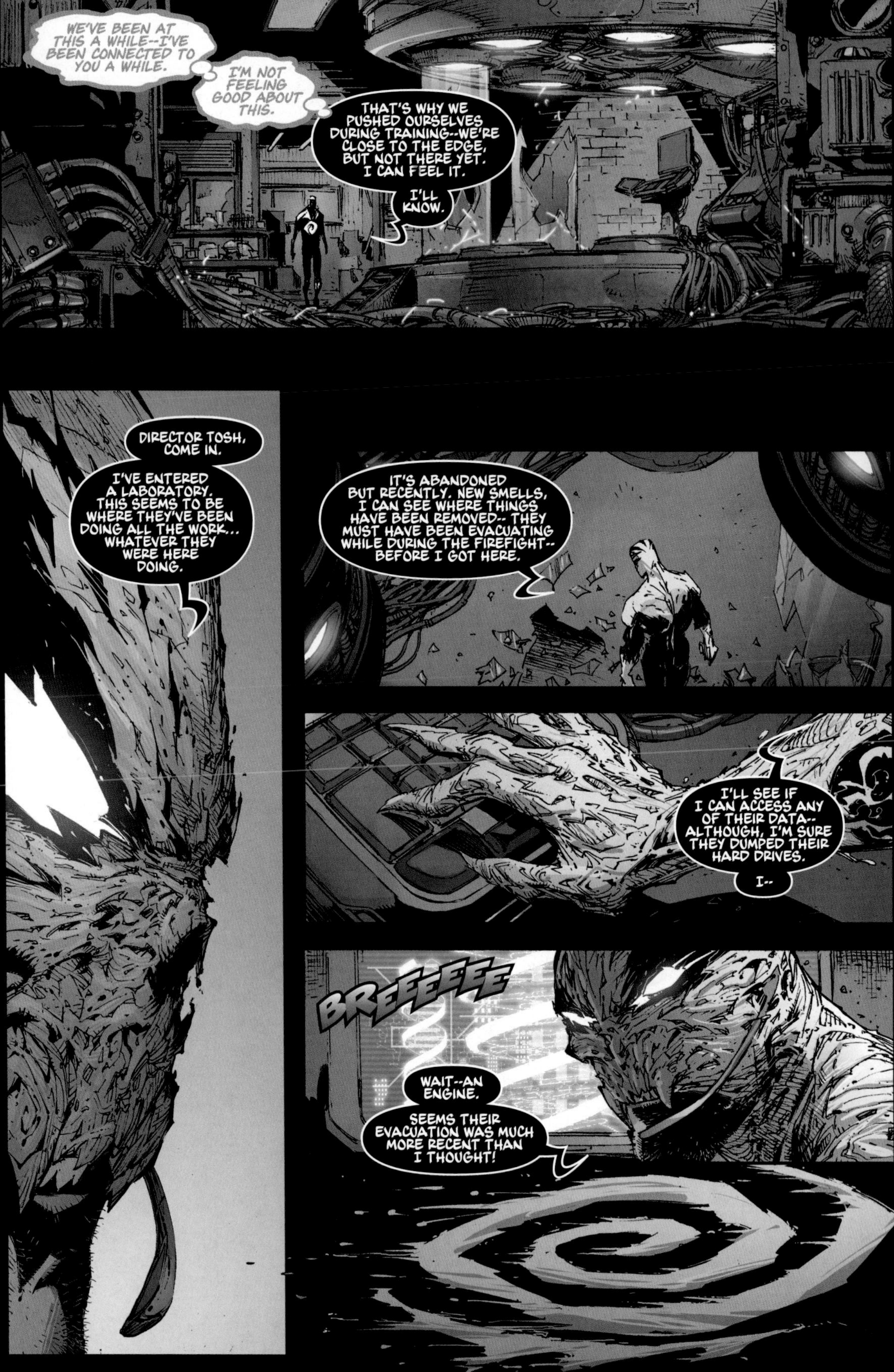
WE'VE BEEN AT THIS A WHILE--I'VE BEEN CONNECTED TO YOU A WHILE.
I'M NOT FEELING GOOD ABOUT THIS.
THAT'S WHY WE PUSHED OURSELVES DURING TRAINING--WE'RE CLOSE TO THE EDGE, BUT NOT THERE YET. I CAN FEEL IT.
I'LL KNOW.
DIRECTOR TOSH, COME IN.
I'VE ENTERED A LABORATORY. THIS SEEMS TO BE WHERE THEY'VE BEEN DOING ALL THE WORK... WHATEVER THEY WERE HERE DOING.
IT'S ABANDONED BUT RECENTLY. NEW SMELLS, I CAN SEE WHERE THINGS HAVE BEEN REMOVED-- THEY MUST HAVE BEEN EVACUATING WHILE DURING THE FIREFIGHT-- BEFORE I GOT HERE.
I'LL SEE IF I CAN ACCESS ANY OF THEIR DATA-- ALTHOUGH, I'M SURE THEY DUMPED THEIR HARD DRIVES.
I--
BREEEEEE
WAIT--AN ENGINE.
SEEMS THEIR EVACUATION WAS MUCH MORE RECENT THAN I THOUGHT!

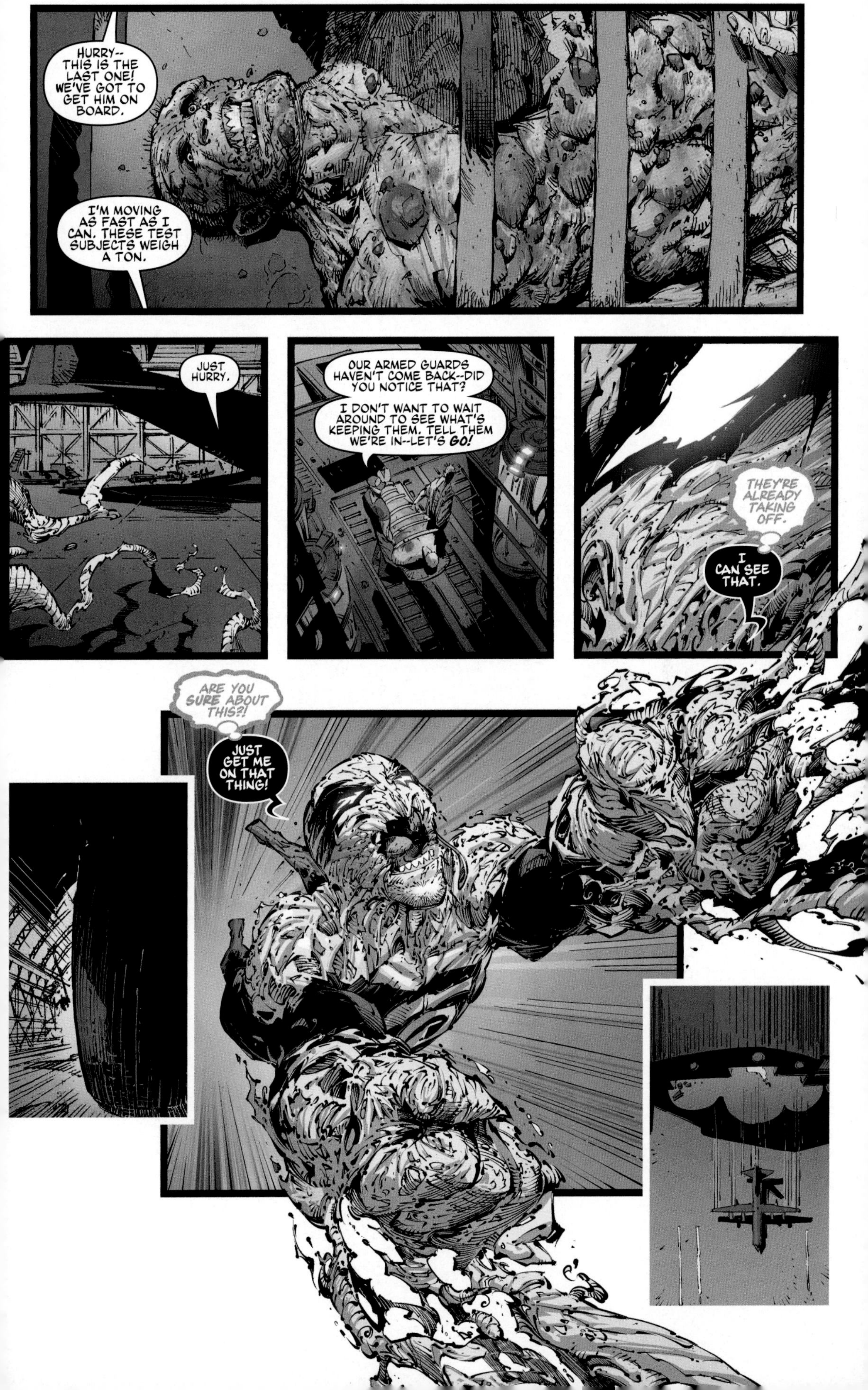
HURRY-- THIS IS THE LAST ONE! WE'VE GOT TO GET HIM ON BOARD.
I'M MOVING AS FAST AS I CAN. THESE TEST SUBJECTS WEIGH A TON.
JUST HURRY.
OUR ARMED GUARDS HAVEN'T COME BACK--DID YOU NOTICE THAT?
I DON'T WANT TO WAIT AROUND TO SEE WHAT'S KEEPING THEM. TELL THEM WE'RE IN--LET'S GO!
THEY'RE ALREADY TAKING OFF.
I CAN SEE THAT.
ARE YOU SURE ABOUT THIS?!
JUST GET ME ON THAT THING!

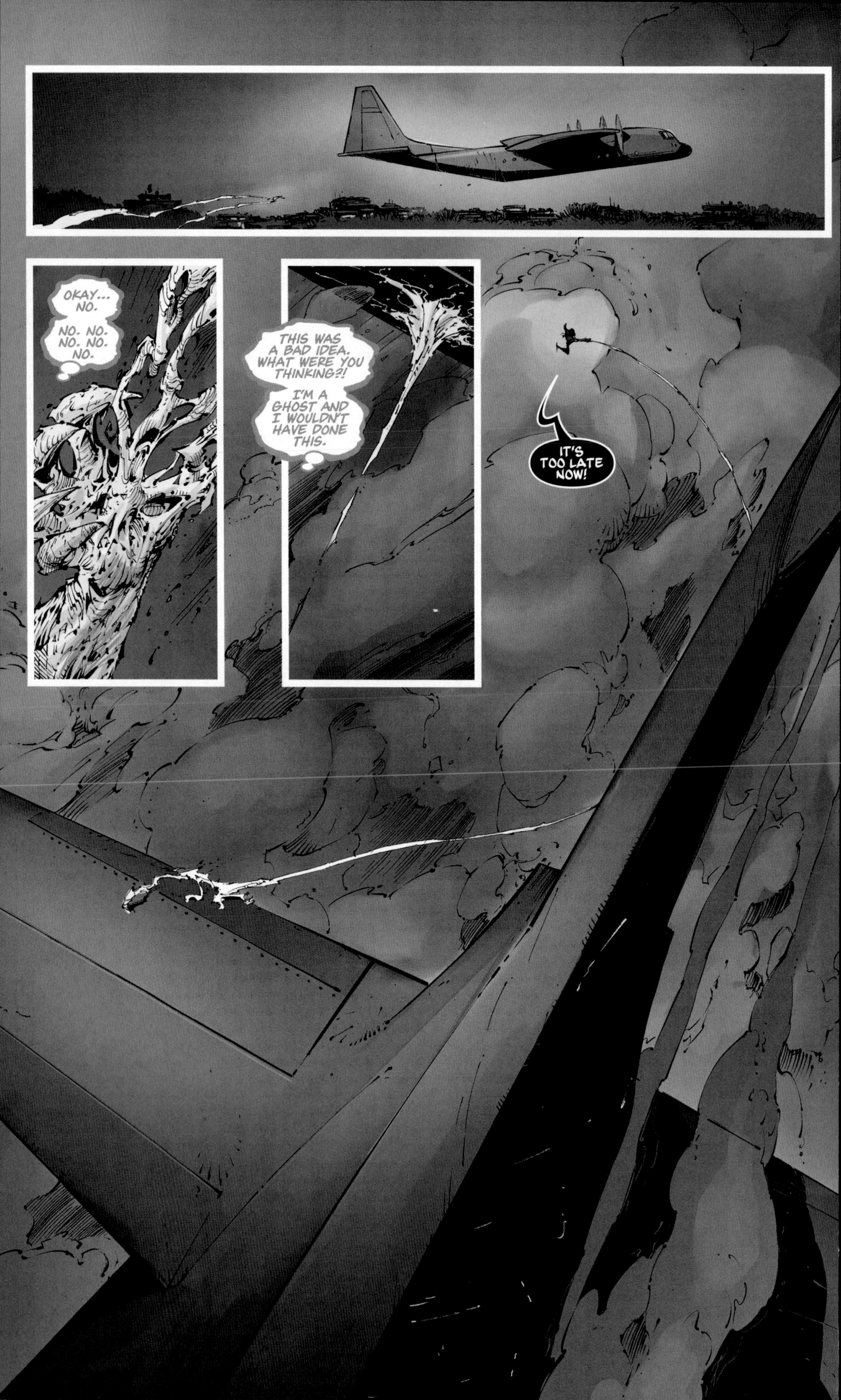

OKAY... NO.
NO. NO. NO. NO. NO.
THIS WAS A BAD IDEA. WHAT WERE YOU THINKING?!
I'M A GHOST AND I WOULDN'T HAVE DONE THIS.
IT'S TOO LATE NOW!

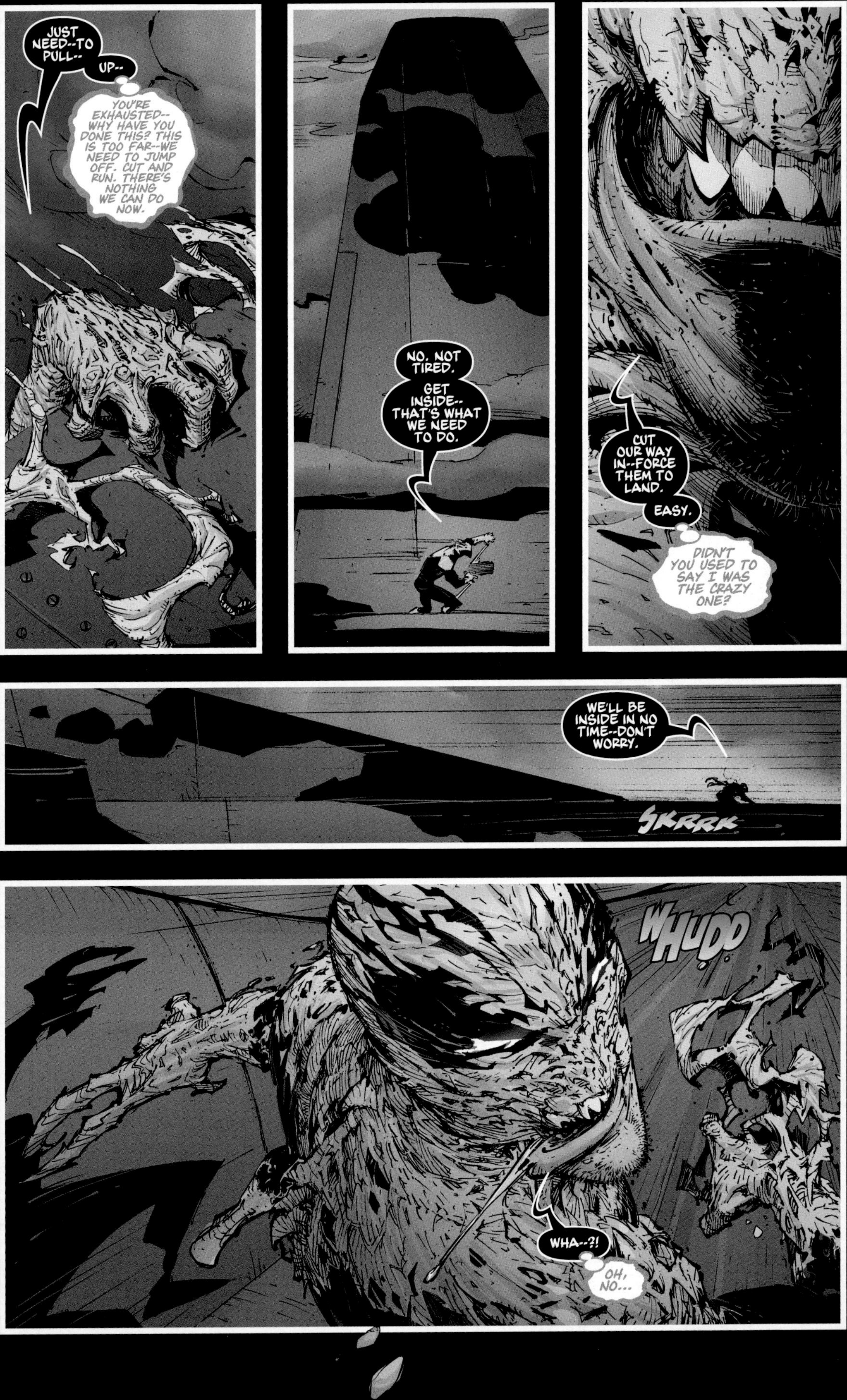
JUST NEED--TO PULL--
UP--
YOU'RE EXHAUSTED--WHY HAVE YOU DONE THIS? THIS IS TOO FAR--WE NEED TO JUMP OFF. CUT AND RUN. THERE'S NOTHING WE CAN DO NOW.
NO. NOT TIRED.
GET INSIDE--THAT'S WHAT WE NEED TO DO.
CUT OUR WAY IN--FORCE THEM TO LAND.
EASY.
DIDN'T YOU USED TO SAY I WAS THE CRAZY ONE?
WE'LL BE INSIDE IN NO TIME--DON'T WORRY.
SKRRK
WHUDD
WHA--?!
OH, NO...

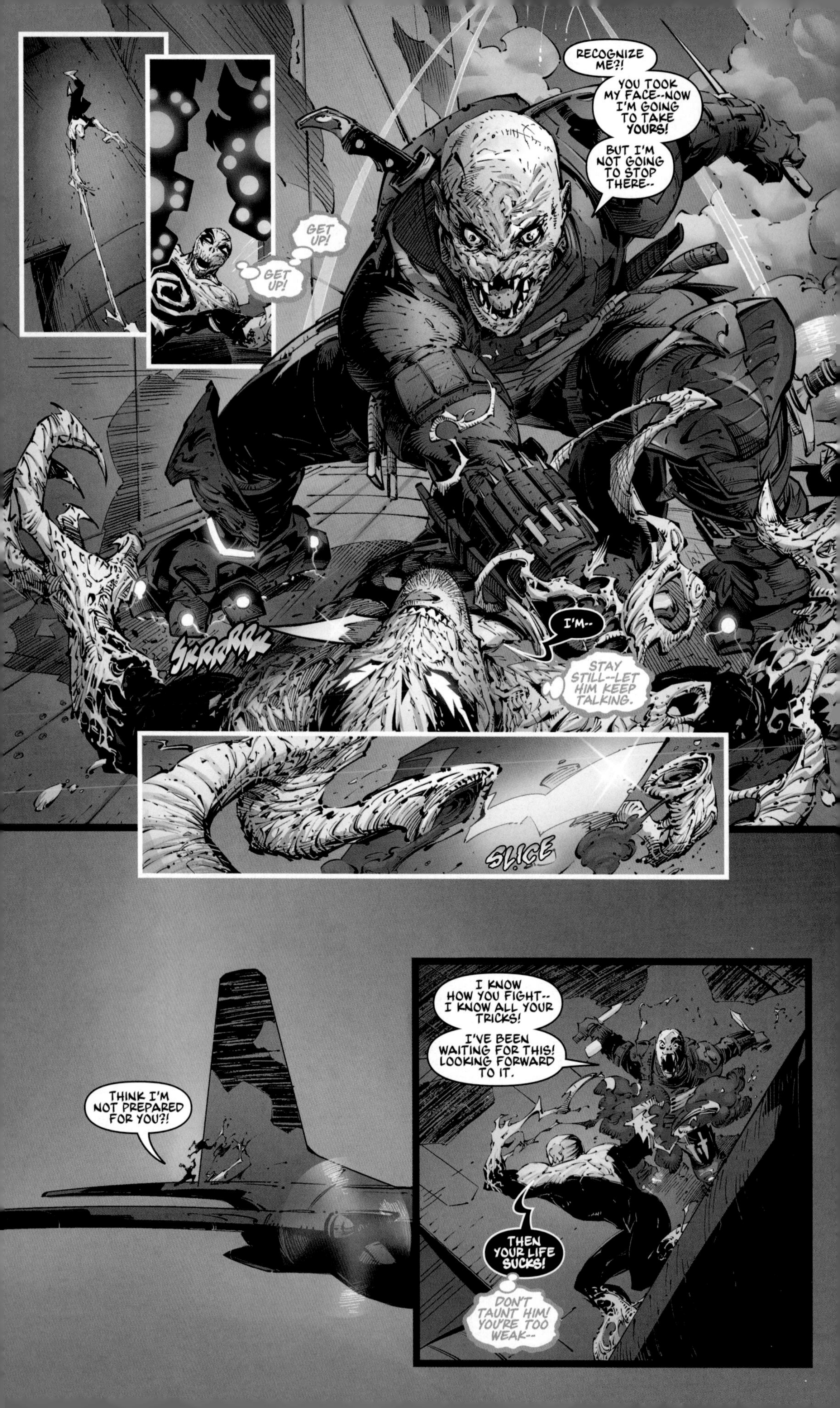
GET UP!
GET UP!
RECOGNIZE ME?!
YOU TOOK MY FACE--NOW I'M GOING TO TAKE YOURS!
BUT I'M NOT GOING TO STOP THERE--
SKRRRRK
I'M--
STAY STILL--LET HIM KEEP TALKING.
SLICE
THINK I'M NOT PREPARED FOR YOU?!
I KNOW HOW YOU FIGHT-- I KNOW ALL YOUR TRICKS!
I'VE BEEN WAITING FOR THIS! LOOKING FORWARD TO IT.
THEN YOUR LIFE SUCKS!
DON'T TAUNT HIM! YOU'RE TOO WEAK--

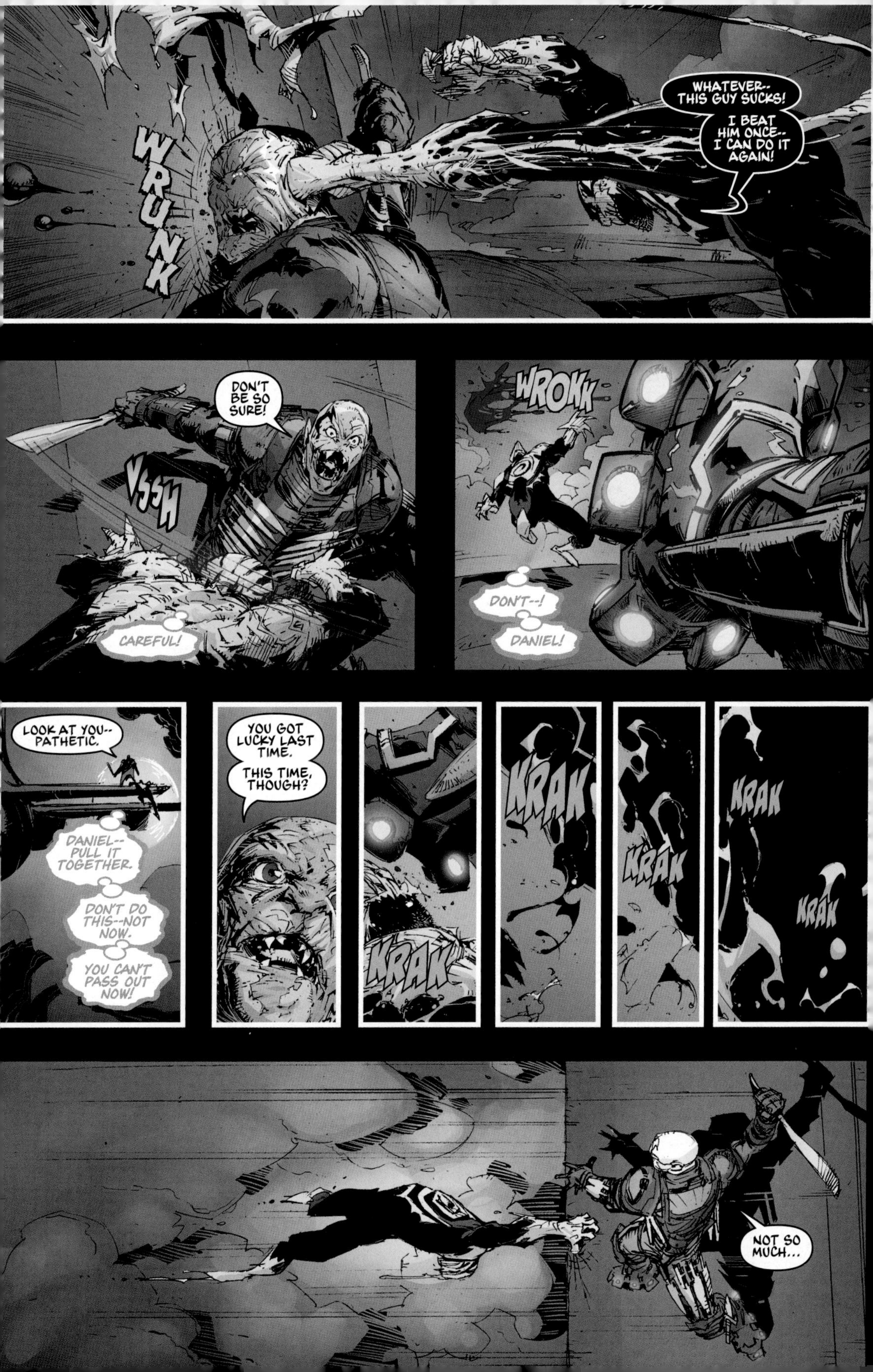
WRUNK
WHATEVER-- THIS GUY SUCKS!
I BEAT HIM ONCE-- I CAN DO IT AGAIN!
DON'T BE SO SURE!
VSSH
CAREFUL!
WROKK
DON'T--!
DANIEL!
LOOK AT YOU-- PATHETIC.
DANIEL-- PULL IT TOGETHER.
DON'T DO THIS--NOT NOW.
YOU CAN'T PASS OUT NOW!
YOU GOT LUCKY LAST TIME.
THIS TIME, THOUGH?
KRAK
KRAK
KRAK
KRAK
KRAK
NOT SO MUCH...

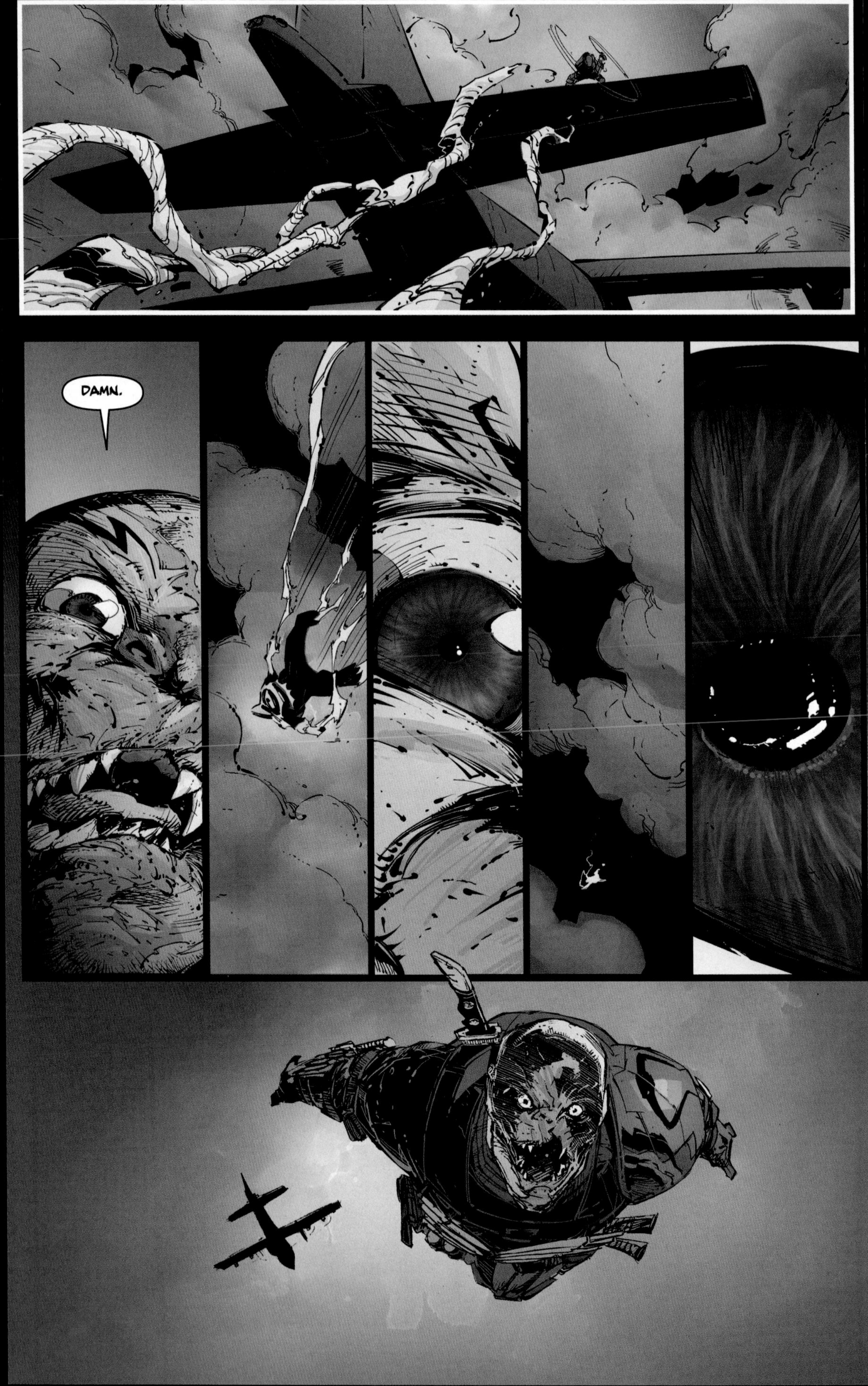
DAMN.

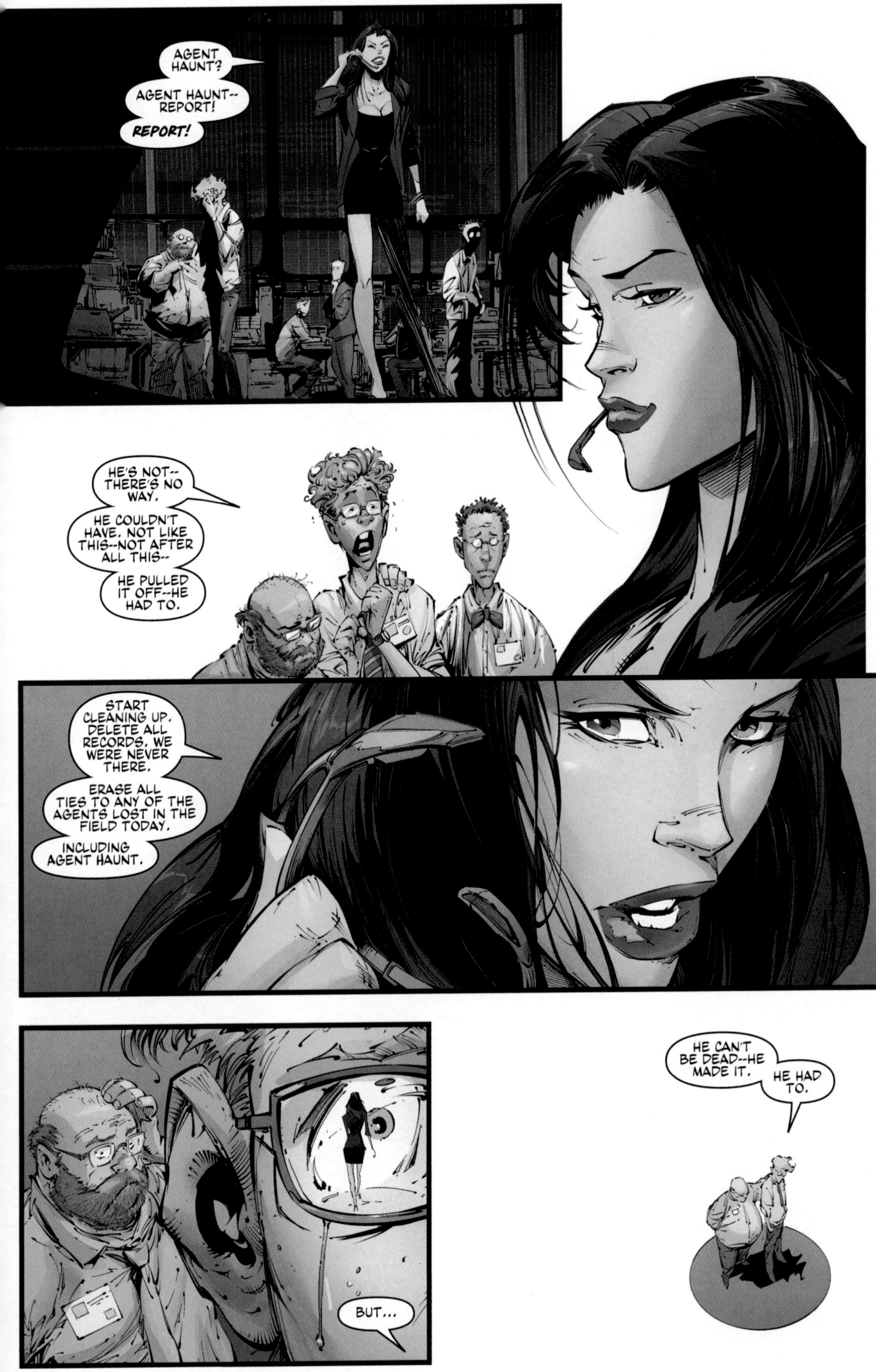
AGENT HAUNT?
AGENT HAUNT-- REPORT!
REPORT!
HE'S NOT-- THERE'S NO WAY.
HE COULDN'T HAVE. NOT LIKE THIS--NOT AFTER ALL THIS--
HE PULLED IT OFF--HE HAD TO.
START CLEANING UP. DELETE ALL RECORDS. WE WERE NEVER THERE.
ERASE ALL TIES TO ANY OF THE AGENTS LOST IN THE FIELD TODAY.
INCLUDING AGENT HAUNT.
BUT...
HE CAN'T BE DEAD--HE MADE IT.
HE HAD TO.

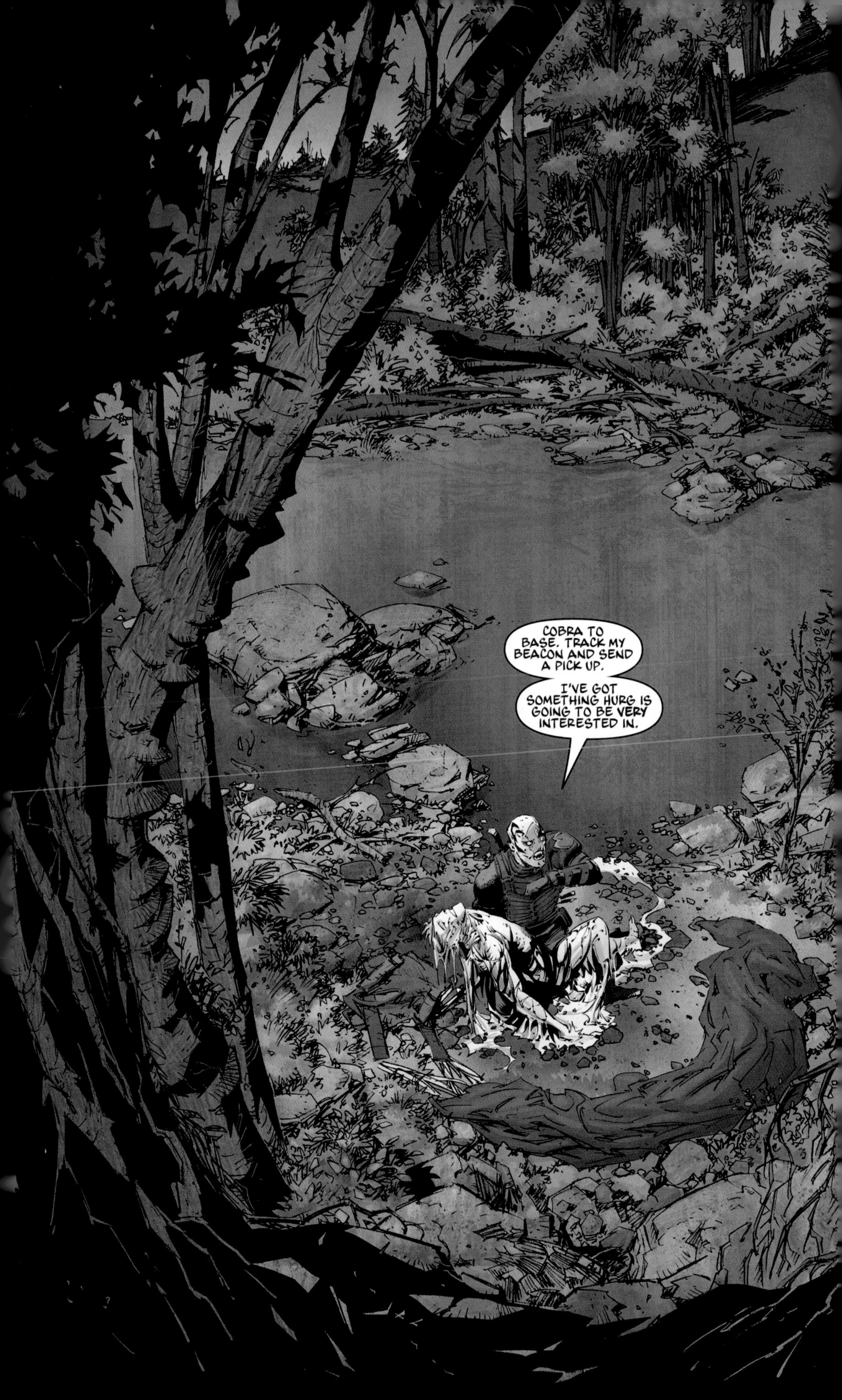
COBRA TO BASE. TRACK MY BEACON AND SEND A PICK UP.
I'VE GOT SOMETHING HURG IS GOING TO BE VERY INTERESTED IN.

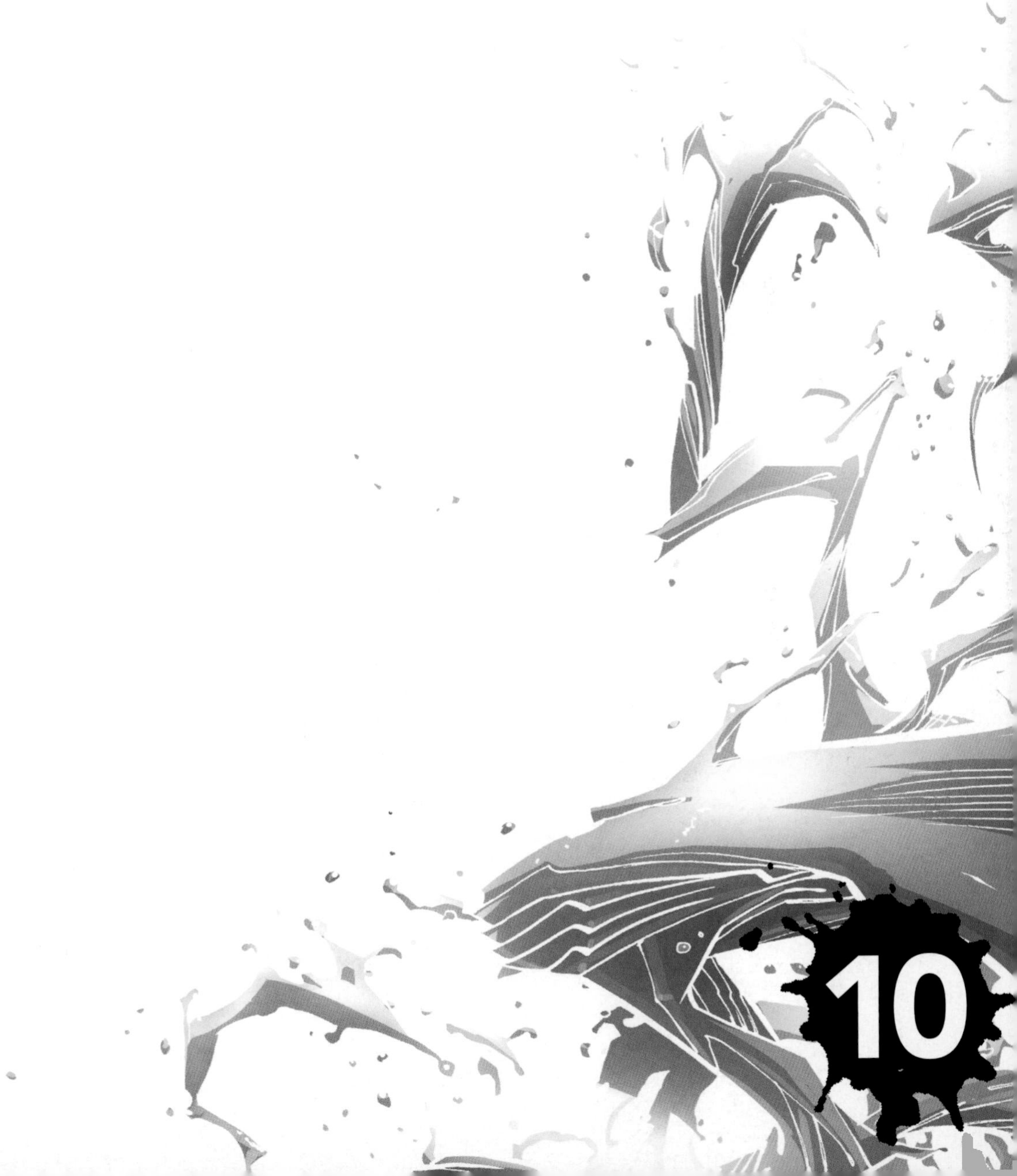
10

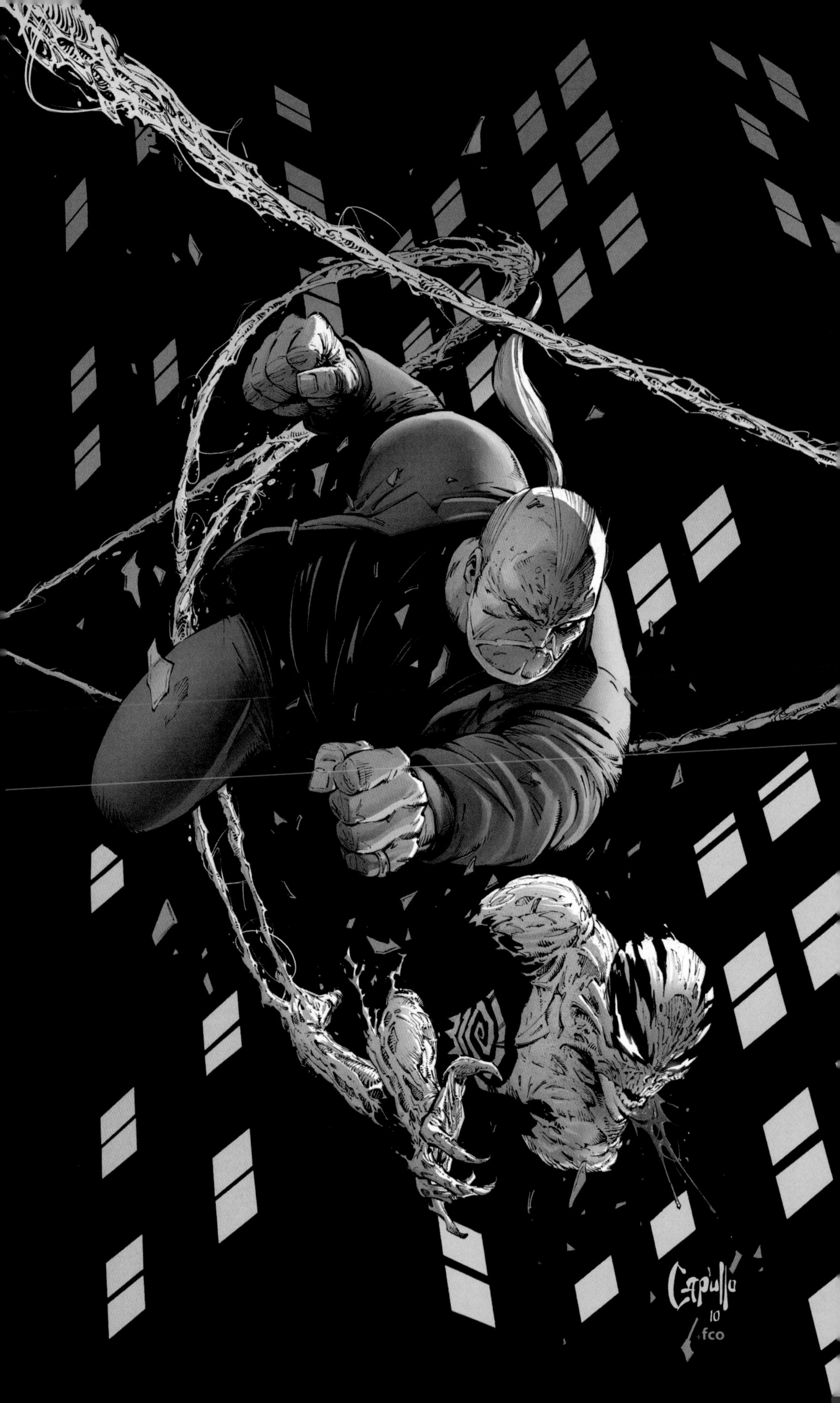
Capullo
10
fco

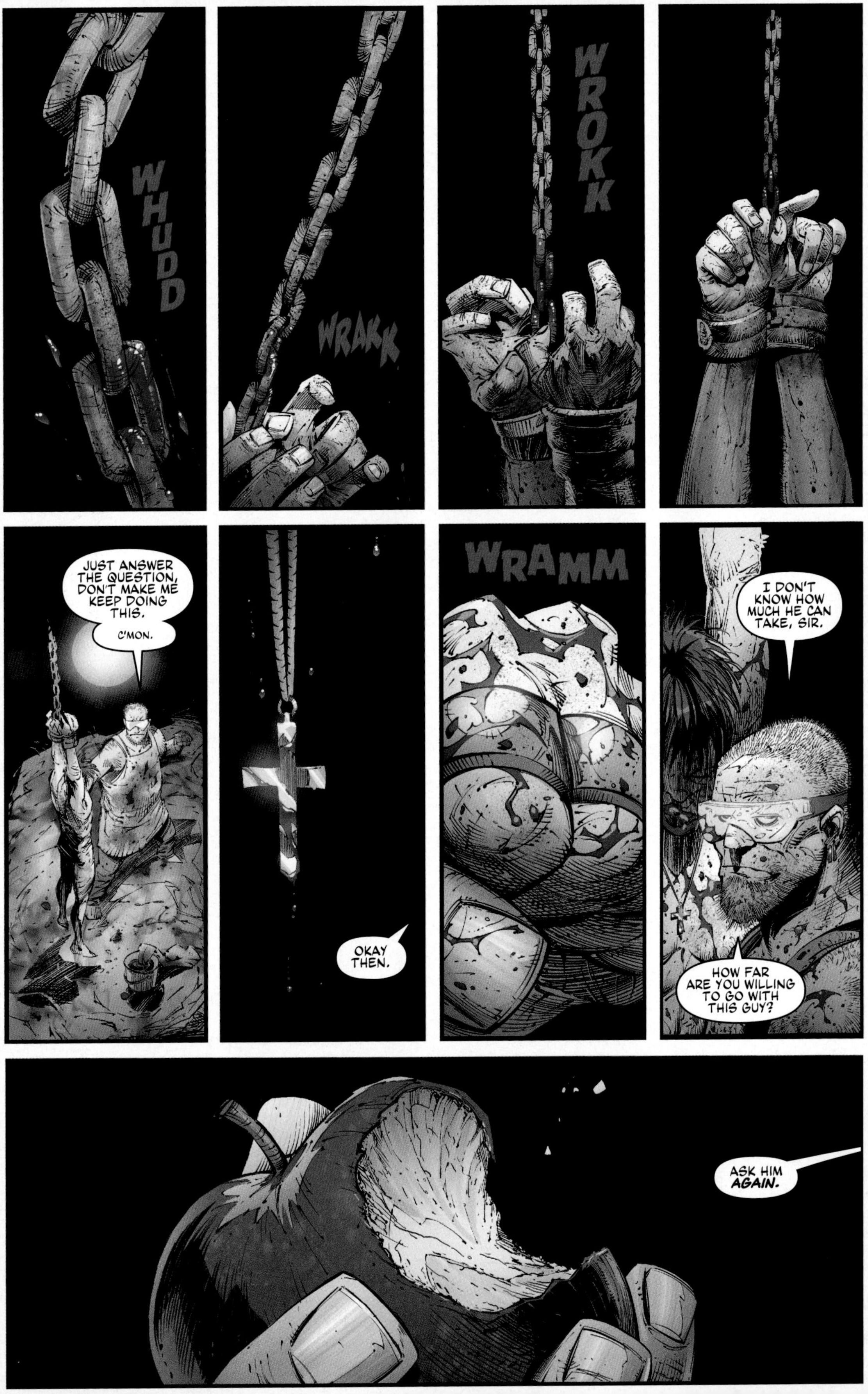

WHUDD
WRAKK
WROKK
JUST ANSWER THE QUESTION, DON'T MAKE ME KEEP DOING THIS.
C'MON.
OKAY THEN.
WRAMM
I DON'T KNOW HOW MUCH HE CAN TAKE, SIR.
HOW FAR ARE YOU WILLING TO GO WITH THIS GUY?
ASK HIM **AGAIN.**

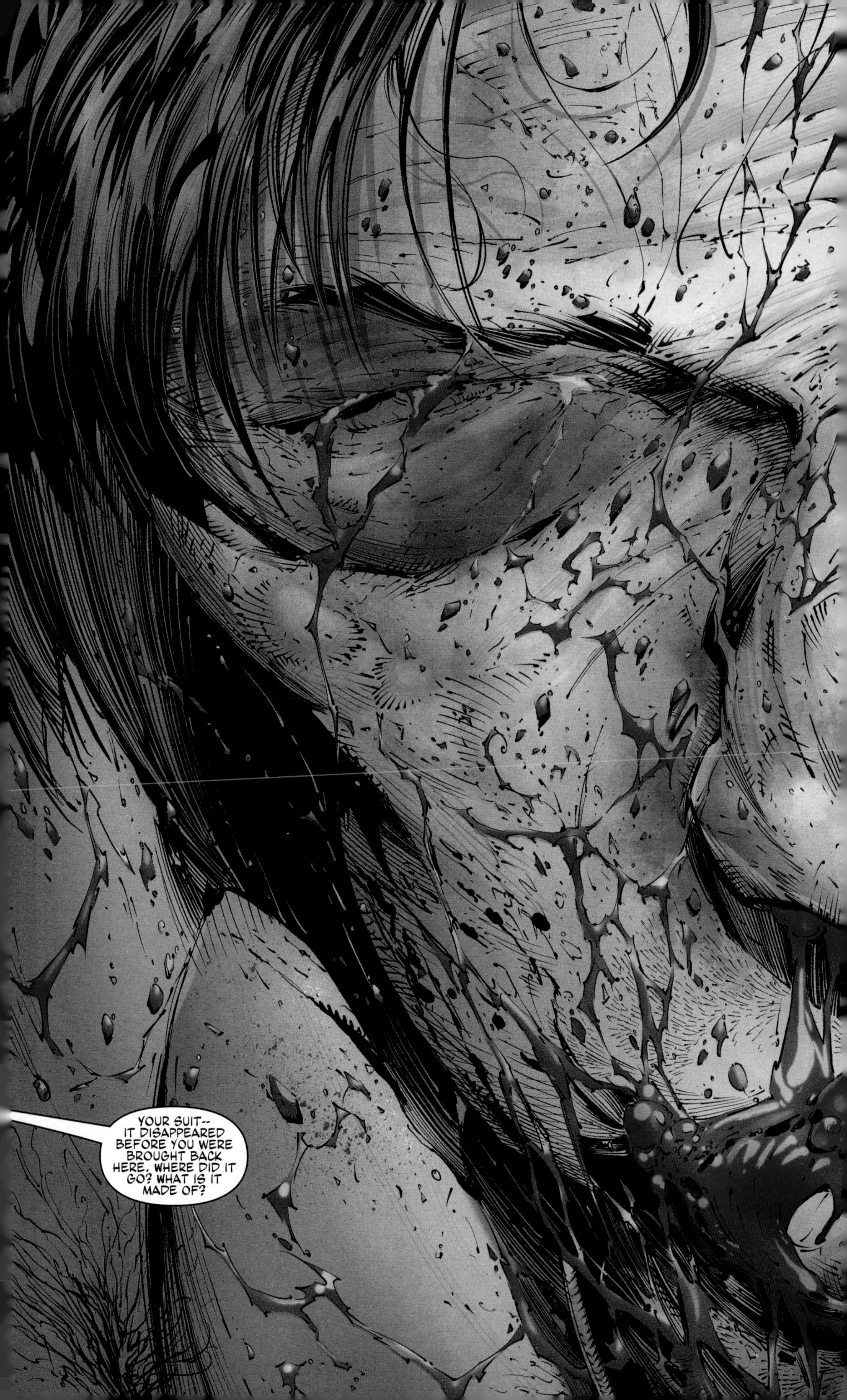
YOUR SUIT-- IT DISAPPEARED BEFORE YOU WERE BROUGHT BACK HERE. WHERE DID IT GO? WHAT IS IT MADE OF?

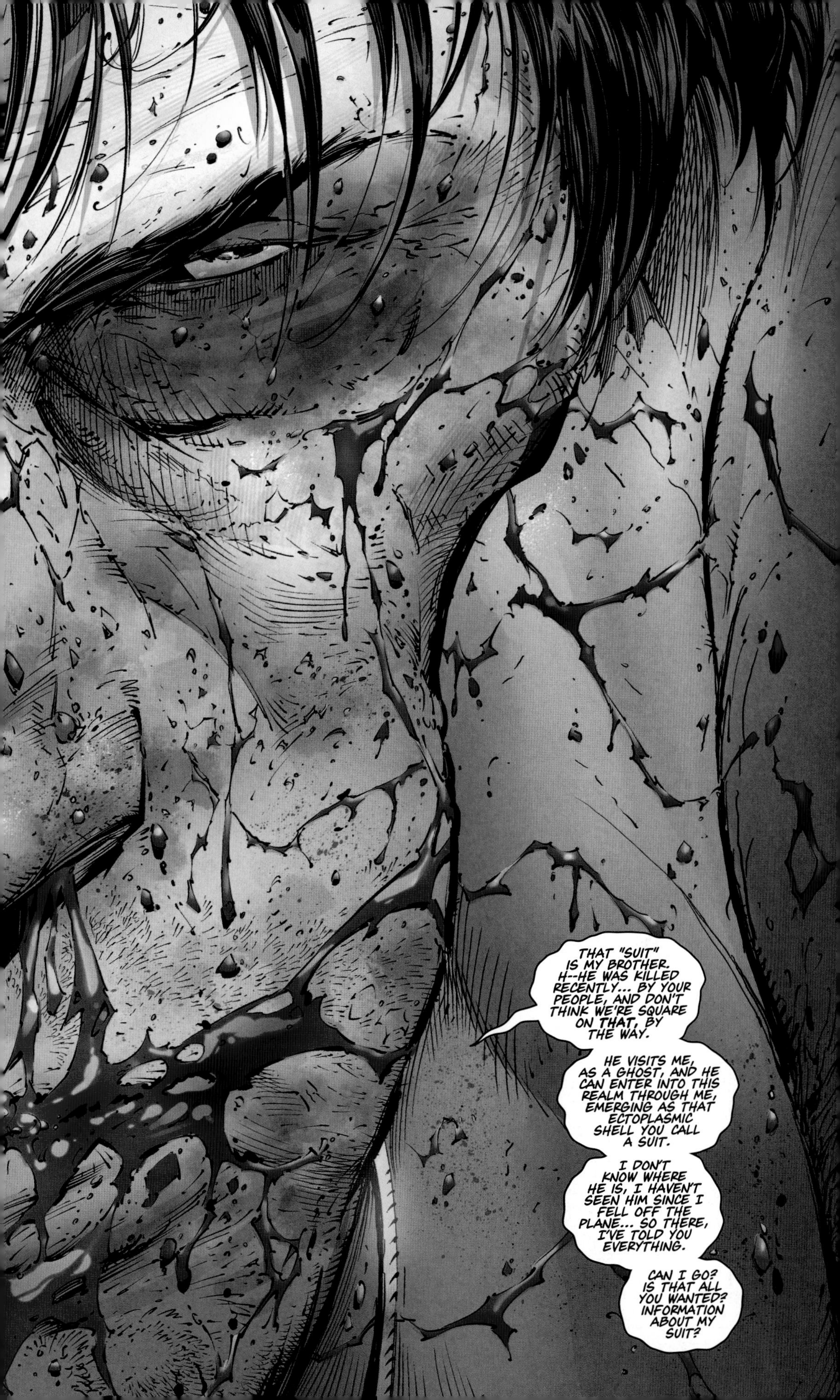
THAT "SUIT" IS MY BROTHER. H--HE WAS KILLED RECENTLY... BY YOUR PEOPLE, AND DON'T THINK WE'RE SQUARE ON THAT, BY THE WAY.
HE VISITS ME, AS A GHOST, AND HE CAN ENTER INTO THIS REALM THROUGH ME, EMERGING AS THAT ECTOPLASMIC SHELL YOU CALL A SUIT.
I DON'T KNOW WHERE HE IS, I HAVEN'T SEEN HIM SINCE I FELL OFF THE PLANE... SO THERE, I'VE TOLD YOU EVERYTHING.
CAN I GO? IS THAT ALL YOU WANTED? INFORMATION ABOUT MY SUIT?

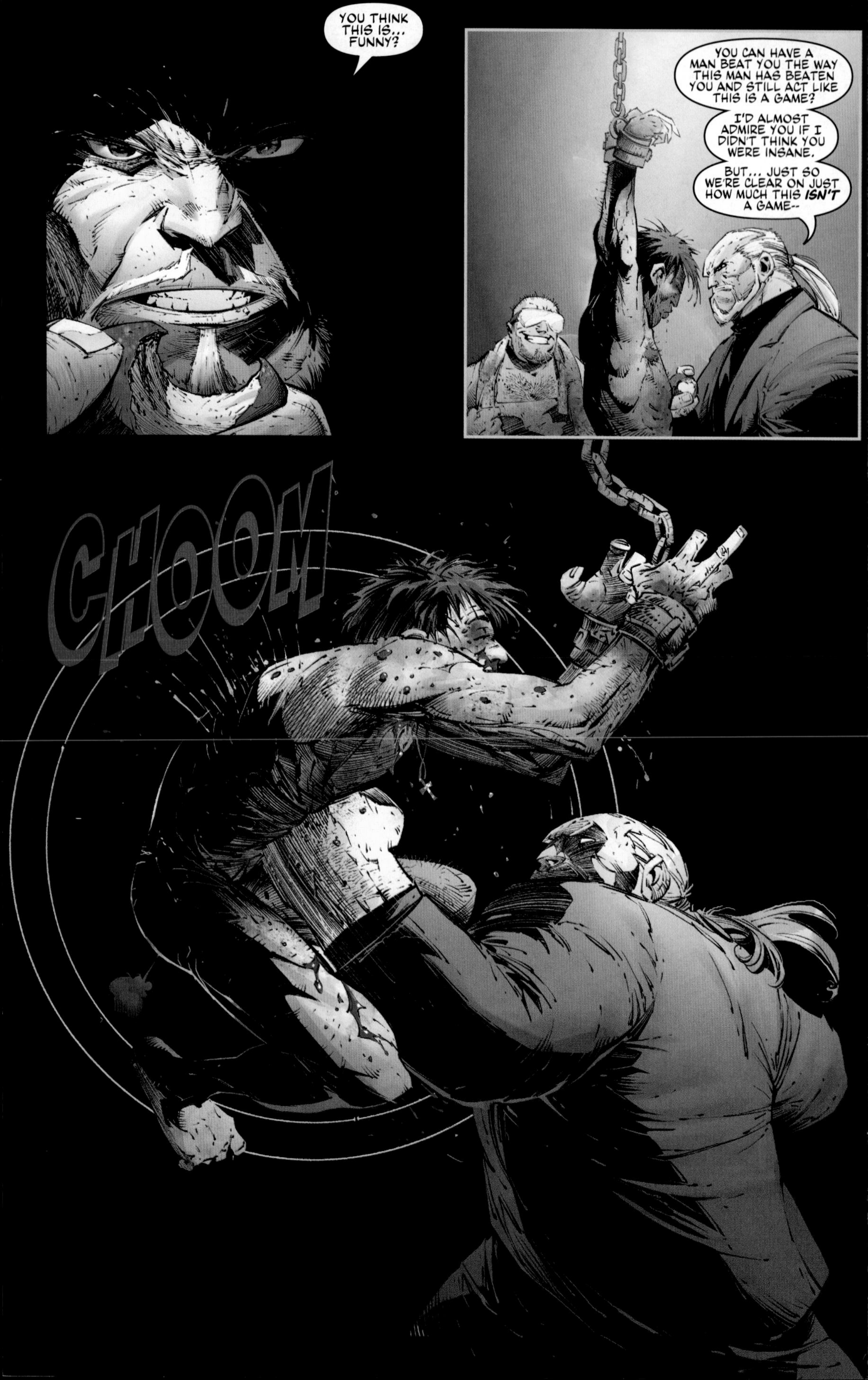
YOU THINK THIS IS... FUNNY?
YOU CAN HAVE A MAN BEAT YOU THE WAY THIS MAN HAS BEATEN YOU AND STILL ACT LIKE THIS IS A GAME?
I'D ALMOST ADMIRE YOU IF I DIDN'T THINK YOU WERE INSANE.
BUT... JUST SO WE'RE CLEAR ON JUST HOW MUCH THIS ISN'T A GAME--
CHOOM

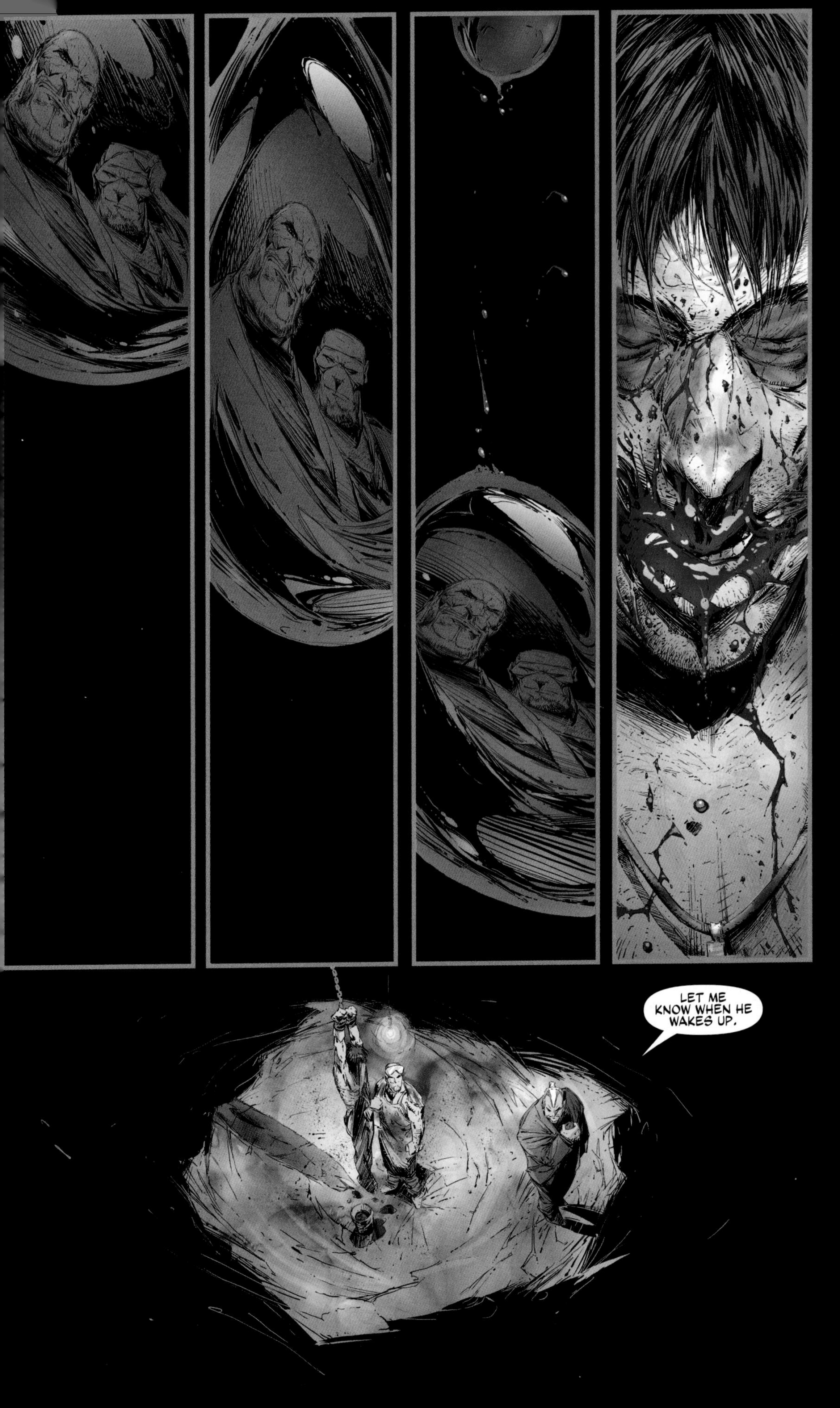
LET ME KNOW WHEN HE WAKES UP.

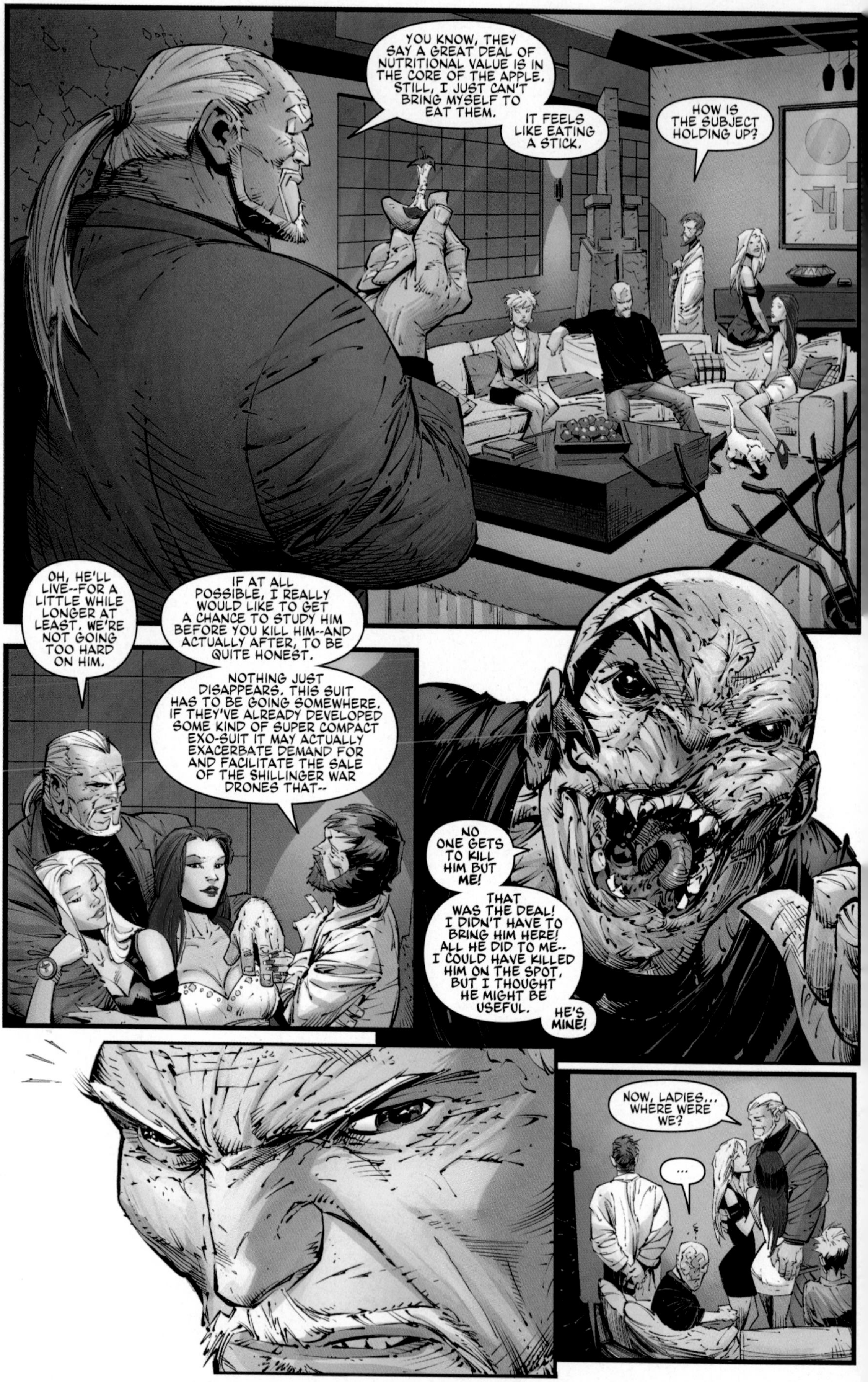
YOU KNOW, THEY SAY A GREAT DEAL OF NUTRITIONAL VALUE IS IN THE CORE OF THE APPLE. STILL, I JUST CAN'T BRING MYSELF TO EAT THEM.
IT FEELS LIKE EATING A STICK.
HOW IS THE SUBJECT HOLDING UP?
OH, HE'LL LIVE--FOR A LITTLE WHILE LONGER AT LEAST. WE'RE NOT GOING TOO HARD ON HIM.
IF AT ALL POSSIBLE, I REALLY WOULD LIKE TO GET A CHANCE TO STUDY HIM BEFORE YOU KILL HIM--AND ACTUALLY AFTER, TO BE QUITE HONEST.
NOTHING JUST DISAPPEARS. THIS SUIT HAS TO BE GOING SOMEWHERE. IF THEY'VE ALREADY DEVELOPED SOME KIND OF SUPER COMPACT EXO-SUIT IT MAY ACTUALLY EXACERBATE DEMAND FOR AND FACILITATE THE SALE OF THE SHILLINGER WAR DRONES THAT--
NO ONE GETS TO KILL HIM BUT ME!
THAT WAS THE DEAL! I DIDN'T HAVE TO BRING HIM HERE! ALL HE DID TO ME-- I COULD HAVE KILLED HIM ON THE SPOT, BUT I THOUGHT HE MIGHT BE USEFUL.
HE'S MINE!
NOW, LADIES... WHERE WERE WE?
...

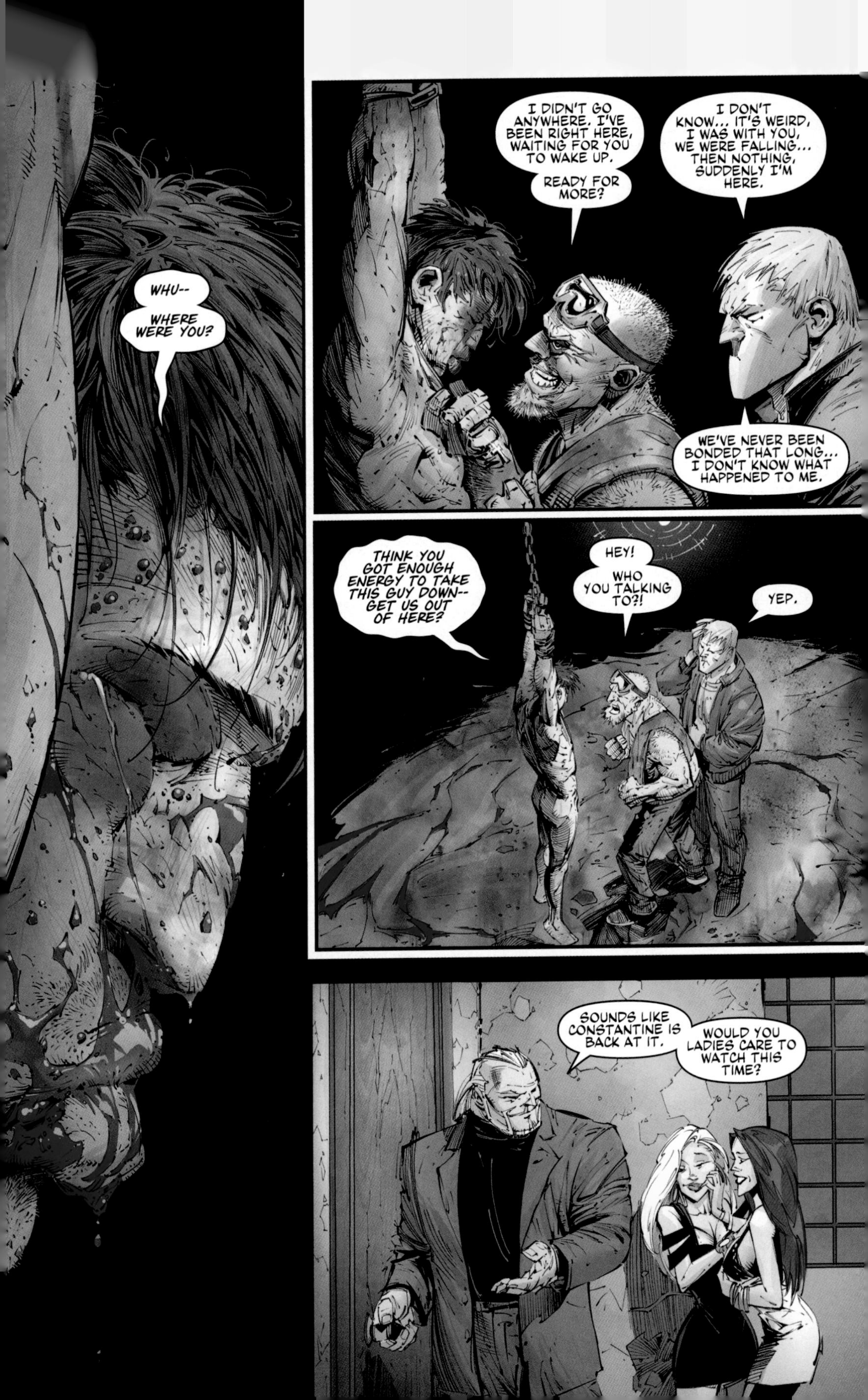
WHU--
WHERE WERE YOU?
I DIDN'T GO ANYWHERE. I'VE BEEN RIGHT HERE, WAITING FOR YOU TO WAKE UP.
READY FOR MORE?
I DON'T KNOW... IT'S WEIRD, I WAS WITH YOU, WE WERE FALLING... THEN NOTHING, SUDDENLY I'M HERE.
WE'VE NEVER BEEN BONDED THAT LONG... I DON'T KNOW WHAT HAPPENED TO ME.
THINK YOU GOT ENOUGH ENERGY TO TAKE THIS GUY DOWN-- GET US OUT OF HERE?
HEY!
WHO YOU TALKING TO?!
YEP.
SOUNDS LIKE CONSTANTINE IS BACK AT IT.
WOULD YOU LADIES CARE TO WATCH THIS TIME?

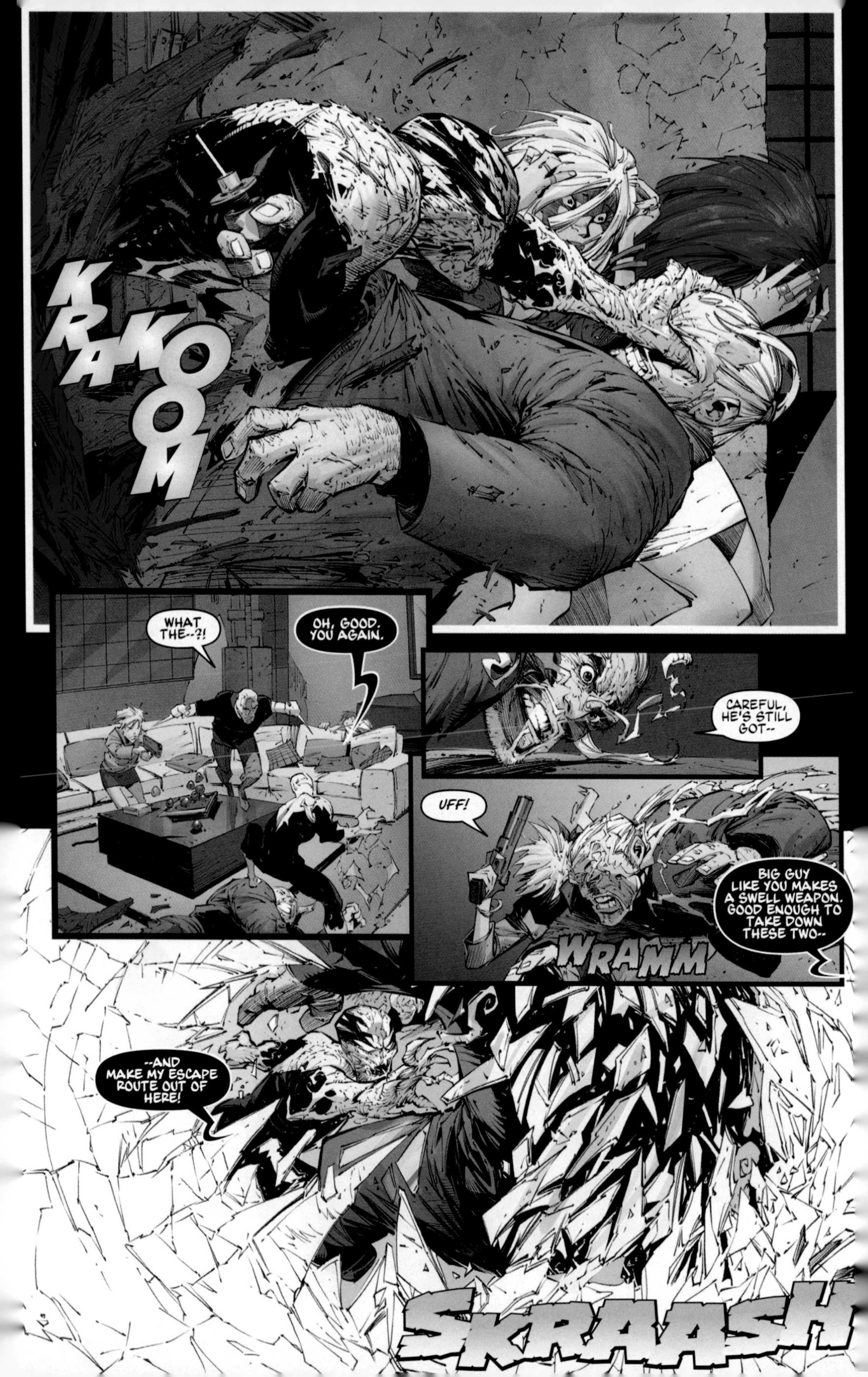
KRAKOOM
WHAT THE--?!
OH, GOOD. YOU AGAIN.
CAREFUL, HE'S STILL GOT--
UFF!
BIG GUY LIKE YOU MAKES A SWELL WEAPON. GOOD ENOUGH TO TAKE DOWN THESE TWO--
WRAMM
--AND MAKE MY ESCAPE ROUTE OUT OF HERE!
SKRAASH

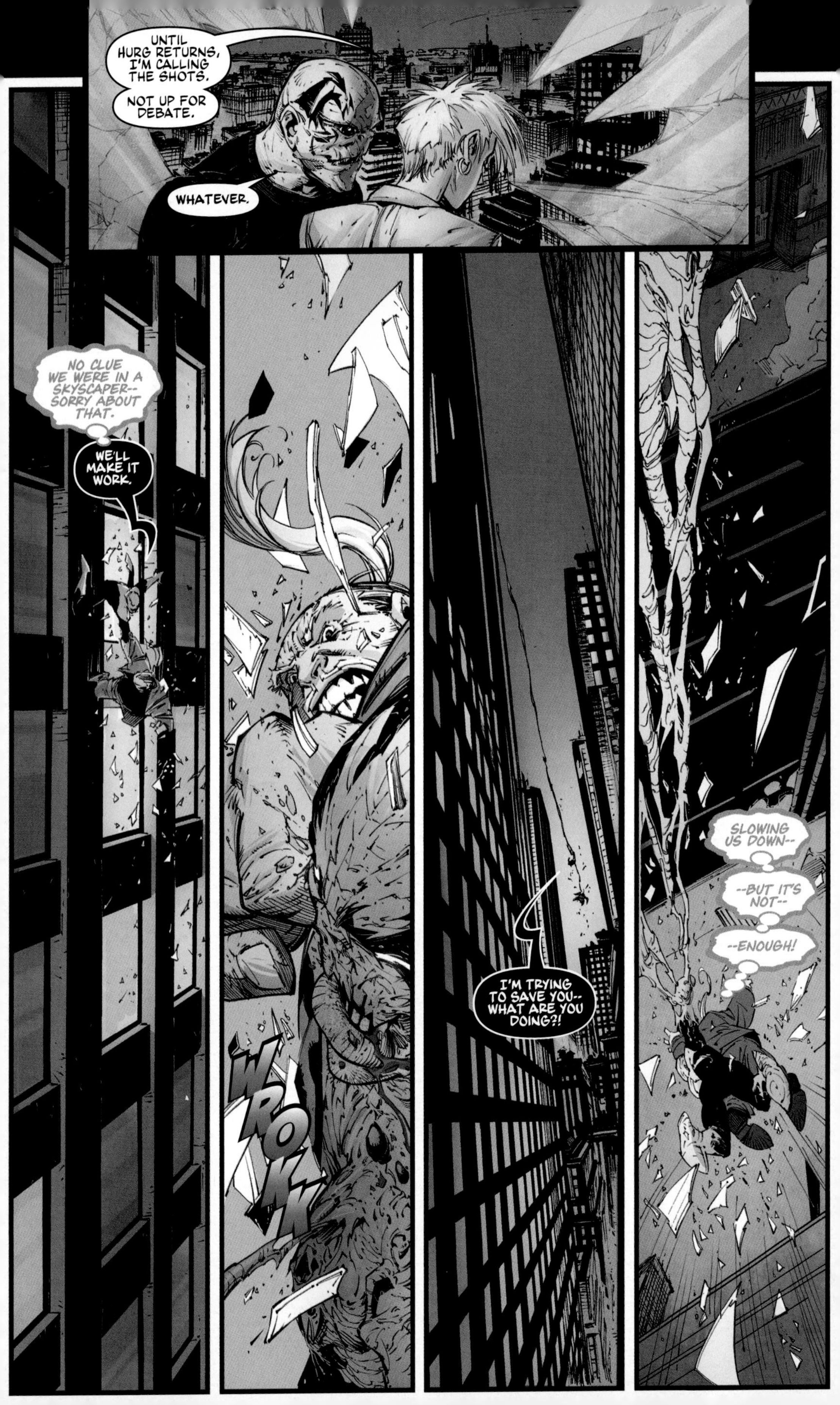

UNTIL HURG RETURNS, I'M CALLING THE SHOTS.
NOT UP FOR DEBATE.
WHATEVER.
NO CLUE WE WERE IN A SKYSCRAPER-- SORRY ABOUT THAT.
WE'LL MAKE IT WORK.
WROKK
I'M TRYING TO SAVE YOU-- WHAT ARE YOU DOING?!
SLOWING US DOWN--
--BUT IT'S NOT--
--ENOUGH!

CHOOM

DANIEL?

YOU OKAY?

UUUGGH.

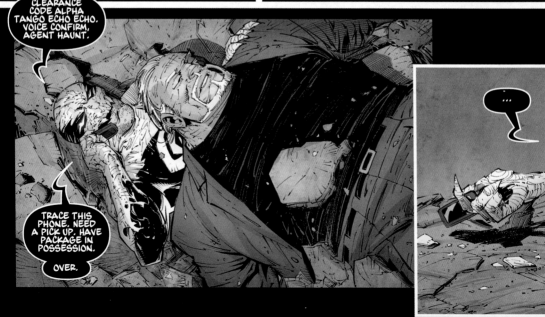

CLEARANCE CODE ALPHA TANGO ECHO ECHO. VOICE CONFIRM, AGENT HAUNT.

...

TRACE THIS PHONE. NEED A PICK UP. HAVE PACKAGE IN POSSESSION.

OVER.

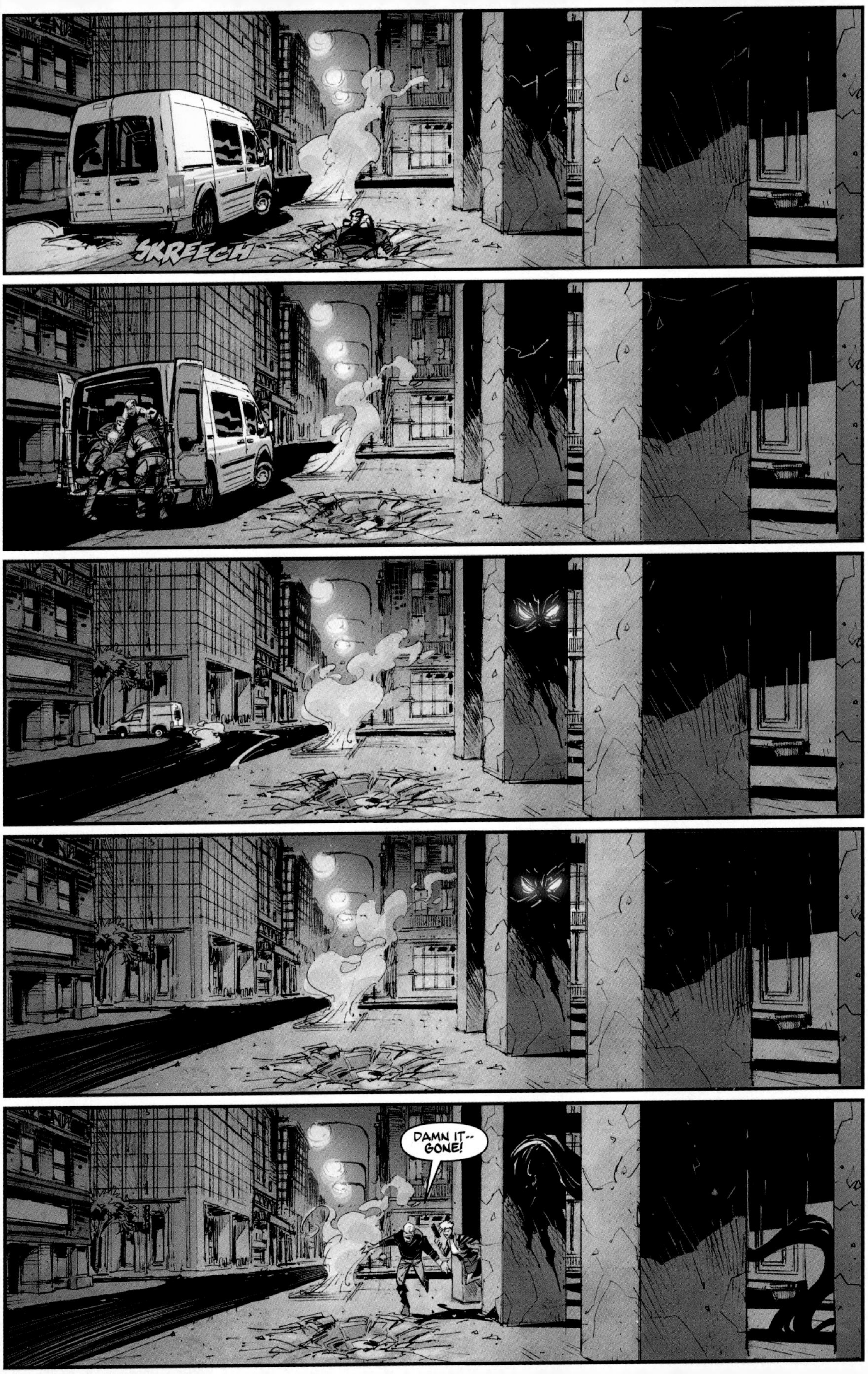
SKREECH
DAMN IT--
GONE!

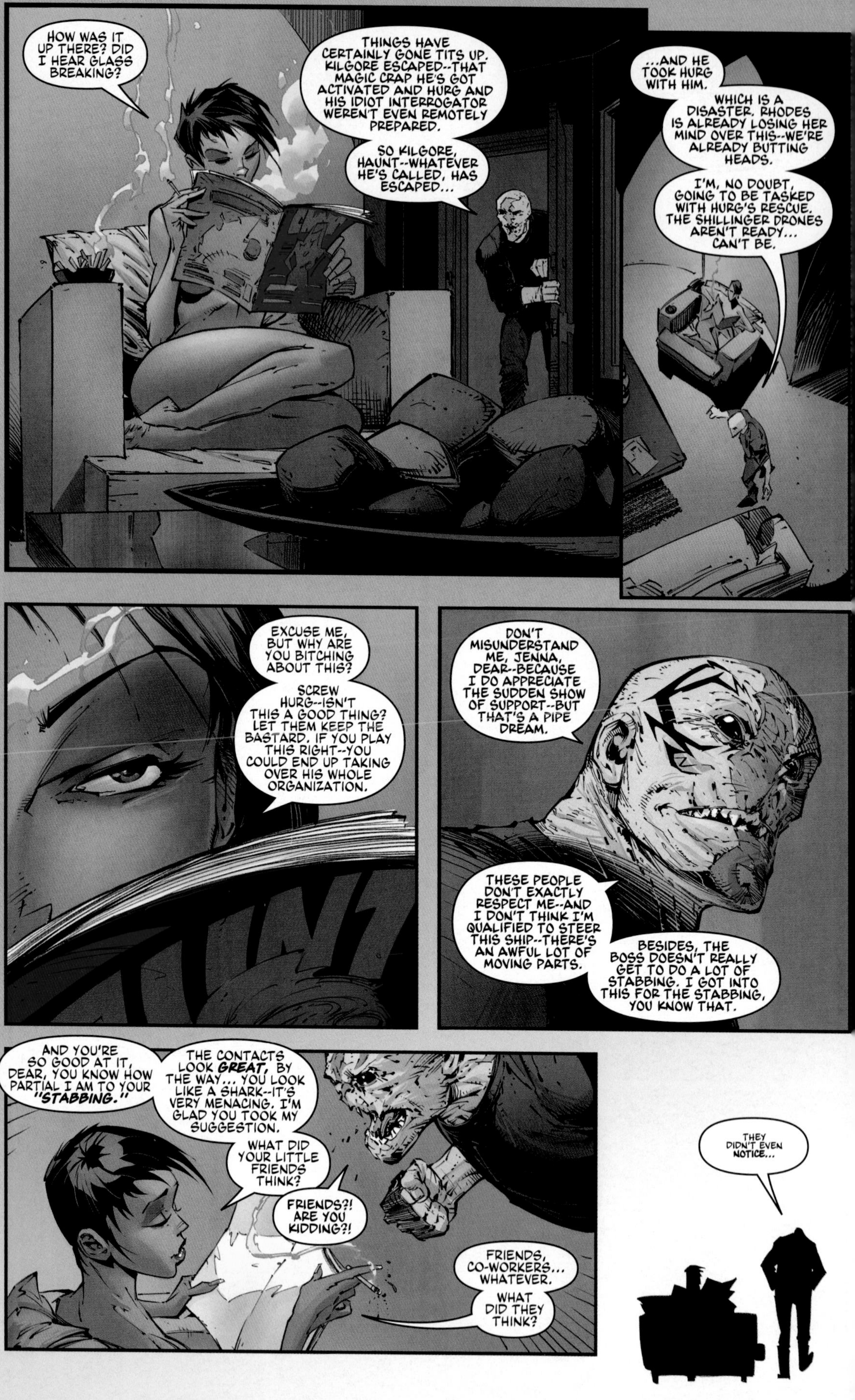

HOW WAS IT UP THERE? DID I HEAR GLASS BREAKING?
THINGS HAVE CERTAINLY GONE TITS UP. KILGORE ESCAPED--THAT MAGIC CRAP HE'S GOT ACTIVATED AND HURG AND HIS IDIOT INTERROGATOR WEREN'T EVEN REMOTELY PREPARED.
SO KILGORE, HAUNT--WHATEVER HE'S CALLED, HAS ESCAPED...
...AND HE TOOK HURG WITH HIM.
WHICH IS A DISASTER. RHODES IS ALREADY LOSING HER MIND OVER THIS--WE'RE ALREADY BUTTING HEADS.
I'M, NO DOUBT, GOING TO BE TASKED WITH HURG'S RESCUE. THE SHILLINGER DRONES AREN'T READY... CAN'T BE.
EXCUSE ME, BUT WHY ARE YOU BITCHING ABOUT THIS?
SCREW HURG--ISN'T THIS A GOOD THING? LET THEM KEEP THE BASTARD. IF YOU PLAY THIS RIGHT--YOU COULD END UP TAKING OVER HIS WHOLE ORGANIZATION.
DON'T MISUNDERSTAND ME, JENNA, DEAR--BECAUSE I DO APPRECIATE THE SUDDEN SHOW OF SUPPORT--BUT THAT'S A PIPE DREAM.
THESE PEOPLE DON'T EXACTLY RESPECT ME--AND I DON'T THINK I'M QUALIFIED TO STEER THIS SHIP--THERE'S AN AWFUL LOT OF MOVING PARTS.
BESIDES, THE BOSS DOESN'T REALLY GET TO DO A LOT OF STABBING. I GOT INTO THIS FOR THE STABBING, YOU KNOW THAT.
AND YOU'RE SO GOOD AT IT, DEAR, YOU KNOW HOW PARTIAL I AM TO YOUR "STABBING."
THE CONTACTS LOOK GREAT, BY THE WAY... YOU LOOK LIKE A SHARK--IT'S VERY MENACING. I'M GLAD YOU TOOK MY SUGGESTION.
WHAT DID YOUR LITTLE FRIENDS THINK?
FRIENDS?! ARE YOU KIDDING?!
FRIENDS, CO-WORKERS... WHATEVER.
WHAT DID THEY THINK?
THEY DIDN'T EVEN NOTICE...

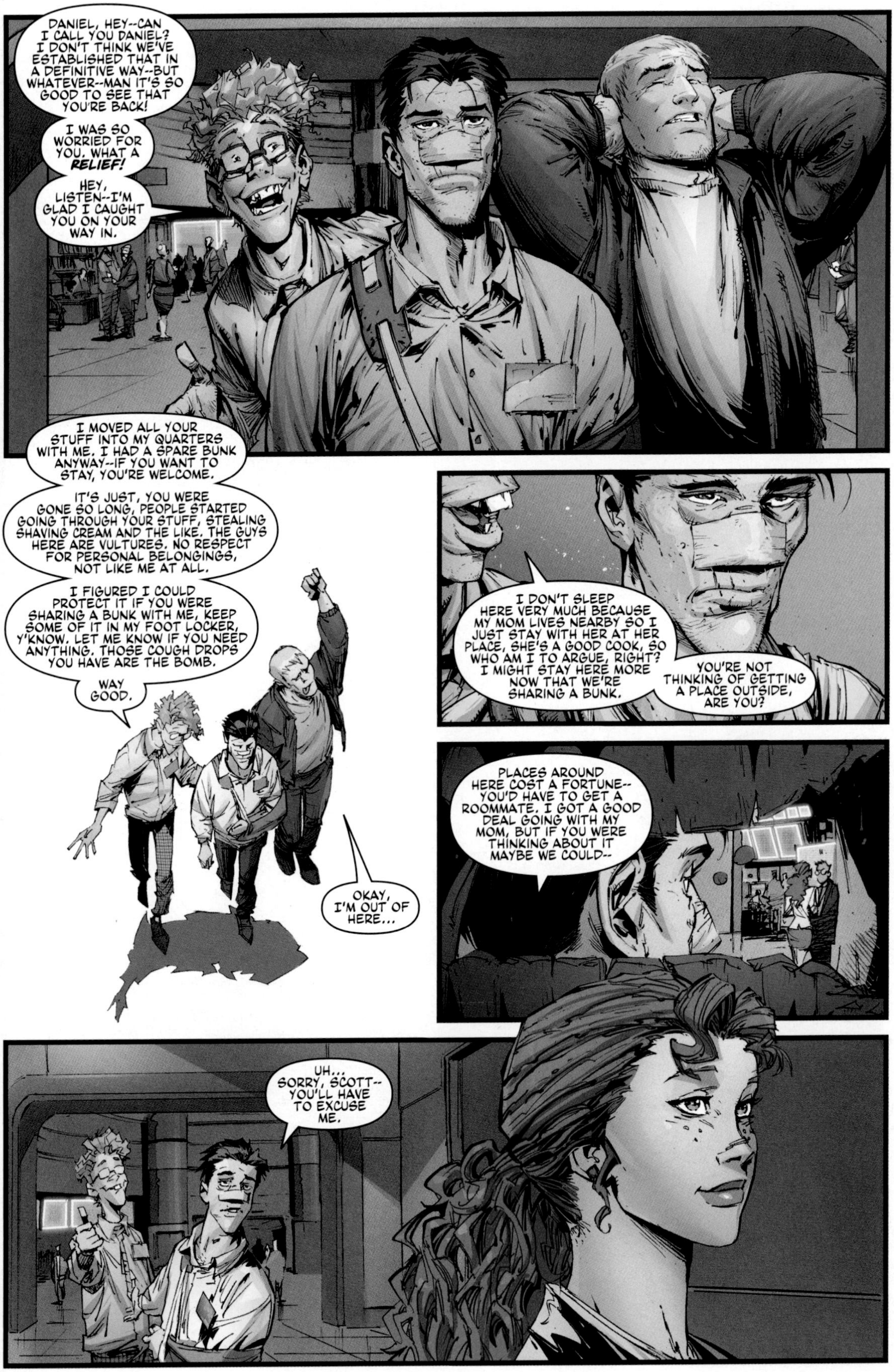
DANIEL, HEY--CAN I CALL YOU DANIEL? I DON'T THINK WE'VE ESTABLISHED THAT IN A DEFINITIVE WAY--BUT WHATEVER--MAN IT'S SO GOOD TO SEE THAT YOU'RE BACK!
I WAS SO WORRIED FOR YOU. WHAT A RELIEF!
HEY, LISTEN--I'M GLAD I CAUGHT YOU ON YOUR WAY IN.
I MOVED ALL YOUR STUFF INTO MY QUARTERS WITH ME. I HAD A SPARE BUNK ANYWAY--IF YOU WANT TO STAY, YOU'RE WELCOME.
IT'S JUST, YOU WERE GONE SO LONG, PEOPLE STARTED GOING THROUGH YOUR STUFF, STEALING SHAVING CREAM AND THE LIKE. THE GUYS HERE ARE VULTURES. NO RESPECT FOR PERSONAL BELONGINGS, NOT LIKE ME AT ALL.
I FIGURED I COULD PROTECT IT IF YOU WERE SHARING A BUNK WITH ME, KEEP SOME OF IT IN MY FOOT LOCKER, Y'KNOW. LET ME KNOW IF YOU NEED ANYTHING. THOSE COUGH DROPS YOU HAVE ARE THE BOMB.
WAY GOOD.
OKAY, I'M OUT OF HERE...
I DON'T SLEEP HERE VERY MUCH BECAUSE MY MOM LIVES NEARBY SO I JUST STAY WITH HER AT HER PLACE, SHE'S A GOOD COOK, SO WHO AM I TO ARGUE, RIGHT? I MIGHT STAY HERE MORE NOW THAT WE'RE SHARING A BUNK.
YOU'RE NOT THINKING OF GETTING A PLACE OUTSIDE, ARE YOU?
PLACES AROUND HERE COST A FORTUNE--YOU'D HAVE TO GET A ROOMMATE. I GOT A GOOD DEAL GOING WITH MY MOM, BUT IF YOU WERE THINKING ABOUT IT MAYBE WE COULD--
UH... SORRY, SCOTT--YOU'LL HAVE TO EXCUSE ME.

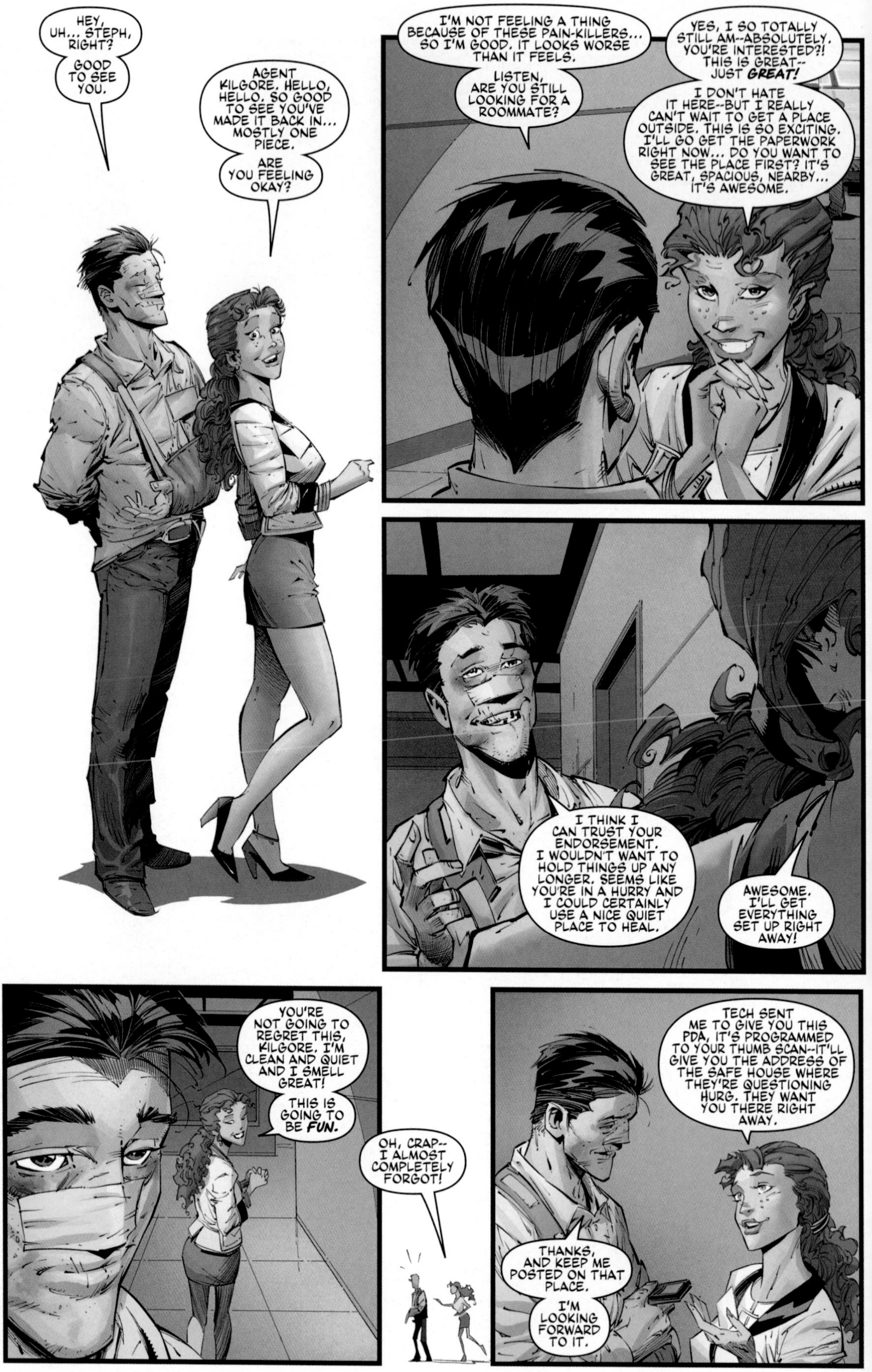

HEY, UH... STEPH, RIGHT?
GOOD TO SEE YOU.
AGENT KILGORE. HELLO, HELLO. SO GOOD TO SEE YOU'VE MADE IT BACK IN... MOSTLY ONE PIECE.
ARE YOU FEELING OKAY?
I'M NOT FEELING A THING BECAUSE OF THESE PAIN-KILLERS... SO I'M GOOD. IT LOOKS WORSE THAN IT FEELS.
LISTEN, ARE YOU STILL LOOKING FOR A ROOMMATE?
YES, I SO TOTALLY STILL AM--ABSOLUTELY. YOU'RE INTERESTED?! THIS IS GREAT-- JUST **GREAT!**
I DON'T HATE IT HERE--BUT I REALLY CAN'T WAIT TO GET A PLACE OUTSIDE. THIS IS SO EXCITING. I'LL GO GET THE PAPERWORK RIGHT NOW... DO YOU WANT TO SEE THE PLACE FIRST? IT'S GREAT, SPACIOUS, NEARBY... IT'S AWESOME.
I THINK I CAN TRUST YOUR ENDORSEMENT. I WOULDN'T WANT TO HOLD THINGS UP ANY LONGER. SEEMS LIKE YOU'RE IN A HURRY AND I COULD CERTAINLY USE A NICE QUIET PLACE TO HEAL.
AWESOME. I'LL GET EVERYTHING SET UP RIGHT AWAY!
YOU'RE NOT GOING TO REGRET THIS, KILGORE. I'M CLEAN AND QUIET AND I SMELL GREAT!
THIS IS GOING TO BE **FUN.**
OH, CRAP-- I ALMOST COMPLETELY FORGOT!
TECH SENT ME TO GIVE YOU THIS PDA, IT'S PROGRAMMED TO YOUR THUMB SCAN--IT'LL GIVE YOU THE ADDRESS OF THE SAFE HOUSE WHERE THEY'RE QUESTIONING HURG. THEY WANT YOU THERE RIGHT AWAY.
THANKS, AND KEEP ME POSTED ON THAT PLACE.
I'M LOOKING FORWARD TO IT.

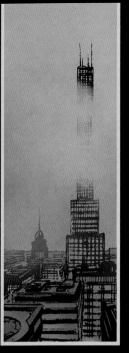

WE DO NOT LIKE TO BE KEPT WAITING, MISS RHODES.

NOR DO WE, GENTLEMEN. I SAY WE GO AHEAD AND START WITHOUT MY ESTEEMED EMPLOYER, MISTER HURG. I ASSURE YOU IT MUST BE SOMETHING EXTREMELY SERIOUS THAT IS KEEPING HIM.

THIS IS *UNACCEPTABLE.* WE WILL HAVE OUR TERMS MET AND WE EXPECT DELIVERY OF THE SOLDIER DRONES IN *THREE DAYS.*

NO EXCUSES.

THAT WORKS PERFECTLY FOR US, WE'RE CONDUCTING OUR FIRST FIELD TEST TONIGHT.

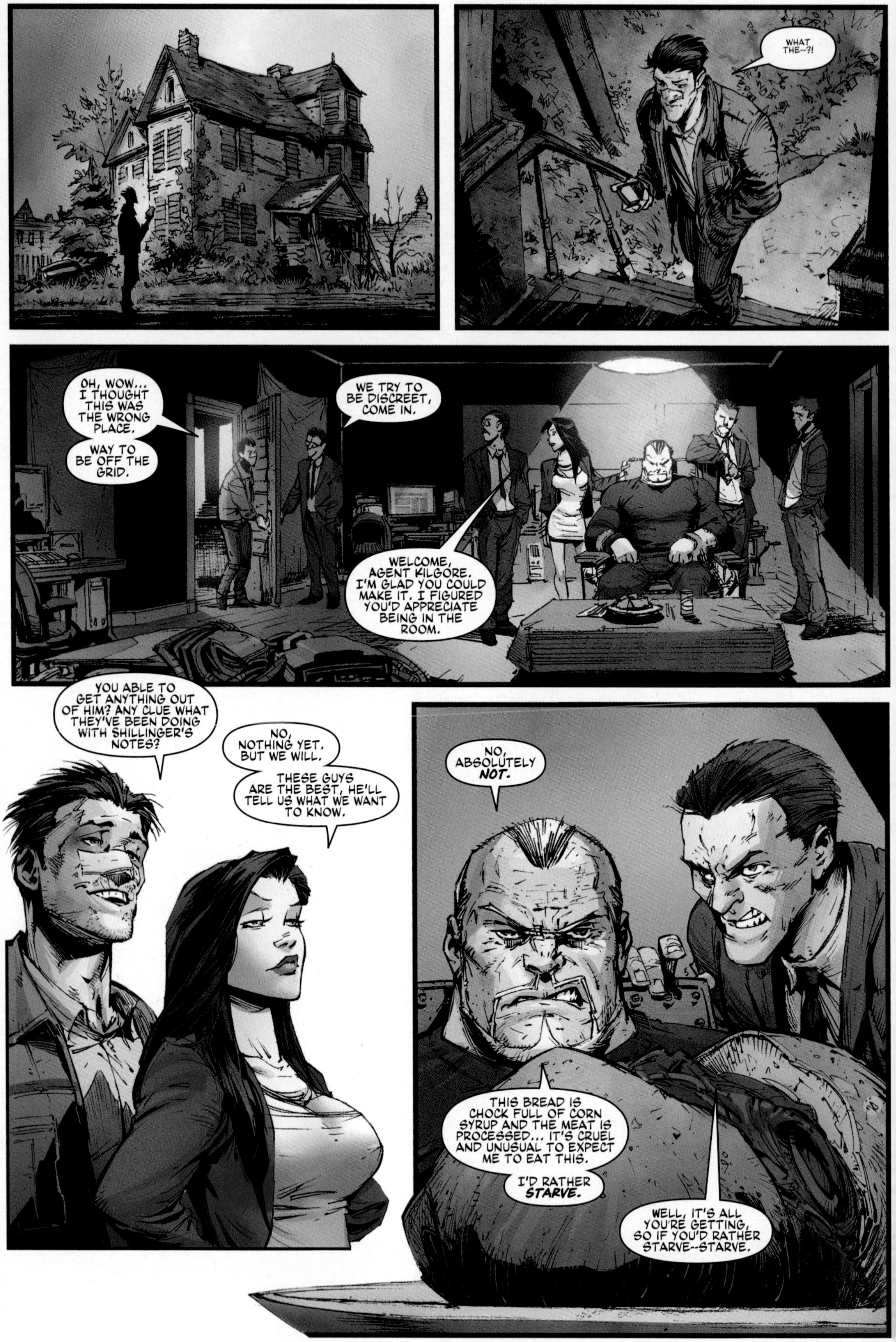
WHAT THE--?!
OH, WOW... I THOUGHT THIS WAS THE WRONG PLACE.
WAY TO BE OFF THE GRID.
WE TRY TO BE DISCREET, COME IN.
WELCOME, AGENT KILGORE. I'M GLAD YOU COULD MAKE IT. I FIGURED YOU'D APPRECIATE BEING IN THE ROOM.
YOU ABLE TO GET ANYTHING OUT OF HIM? ANY CLUE WHAT THEY'VE BEEN DOING WITH SHILLINGER'S NOTES?
NO, NOTHING YET. BUT WE WILL.
THESE GUYS ARE THE BEST, HE'LL TELL US WHAT WE WANT TO KNOW.
NO, ABSOLUTELY NOT.
THIS BREAD IS CHOCK FULL OF CORN SYRUP AND THE MEAT IS PROCESSED... IT'S CRUEL AND UNUSUAL TO EXPECT ME TO EAT THIS.
I'D RATHER STARVE.
WELL, IT'S ALL YOU'RE GETTING, SO IF YOU'D RATHER STARVE--STARVE.

WELL, SINCE WE'RE NOT BREAKING FOR DINNER, LET'S GET BACK TO IT. DO YOURSELF A FAVOR, BEFORE WE START INJECTING YOU WITH GOD KNOWS WHAT... TELL US WHAT YOU'RE DOING WITH SHILLINGER'S NOTES.

WHAT WERE YOU DOING AT THE LAB WE FOUND?

FIRST OF ALL, I DON'T KNOW THAT I HAVE ANY TIES TO THIS LAB THAT YOU SPEAK OF. CERTAINLY NONE THAT CAN BE PROVEN. SO I'M AT A BIT OF A LOSS ON THAT SUBJECT.

SECOND, DEAR LADY, DON'T FORCE ME TO BE RUDE. PLEASE ALLOW ME TO GREET OUR NEW GUEST.

AGENT KILGORE, IT'S GOOD TO SEE YOU AGAIN.

YOU'RE LOOKING... WELL. SORRY ABOUT THE TEETH.

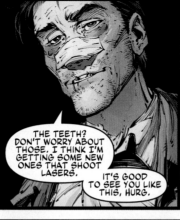

THE TEETH? DON'T WORRY ABOUT THOSE. I THINK I'M GETTING SOME NEW ONES THAT SHOOT LASERS.

IT'S GOOD TO SEE YOU LIKE THIS, HURG.

DON'T GET USED TO IT. YOU WON'T SEE ME LIKE THIS FOR MUCH LONGER. I ASSURE YOU.

GET COMFORTABLE, YOU'RE NOT GOING ANYWHERE FOR A LONG TIME. YOU'LL BE BEGGING FOR THAT SANDWICH BEFORE YOU'RE OUT OF THAT CHAIR.

I WILL DO NO SUCH THING. YOU PEOPLE ARE *ADORABLE* WITH YOUR NERVE AGENTS AND YOUR WATER TORTURE.

IT'S LIKE BEGINNER'S CLASS AT TORTURE HIGH.

YOU'RE COMPLETELY OUT OF YOUR LEAGUE HERE. YOU COULD FEED ME MY EARS AND YOU WOULDN'T GET ANY INFORMATION FROM ME. I WOULD SIT QUIETLY AS YOU REMOVE FINGERS.

YOU COULD BURN THE FLESH FROM MY BONES AND I WOULDN'T EVEN GIVE YOU THE SATISFACTION OF A SCREAM.

BUT YOU WON'T EVEN GET A CHANCE TO TRY ANY OF THAT.

SUCH A SHAME, I DID SO LOOK FORWARD TO IMPRESSING YOU ALL.

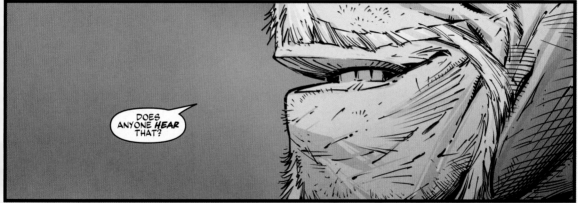

DOES ANYONE *HEAR* THAT?

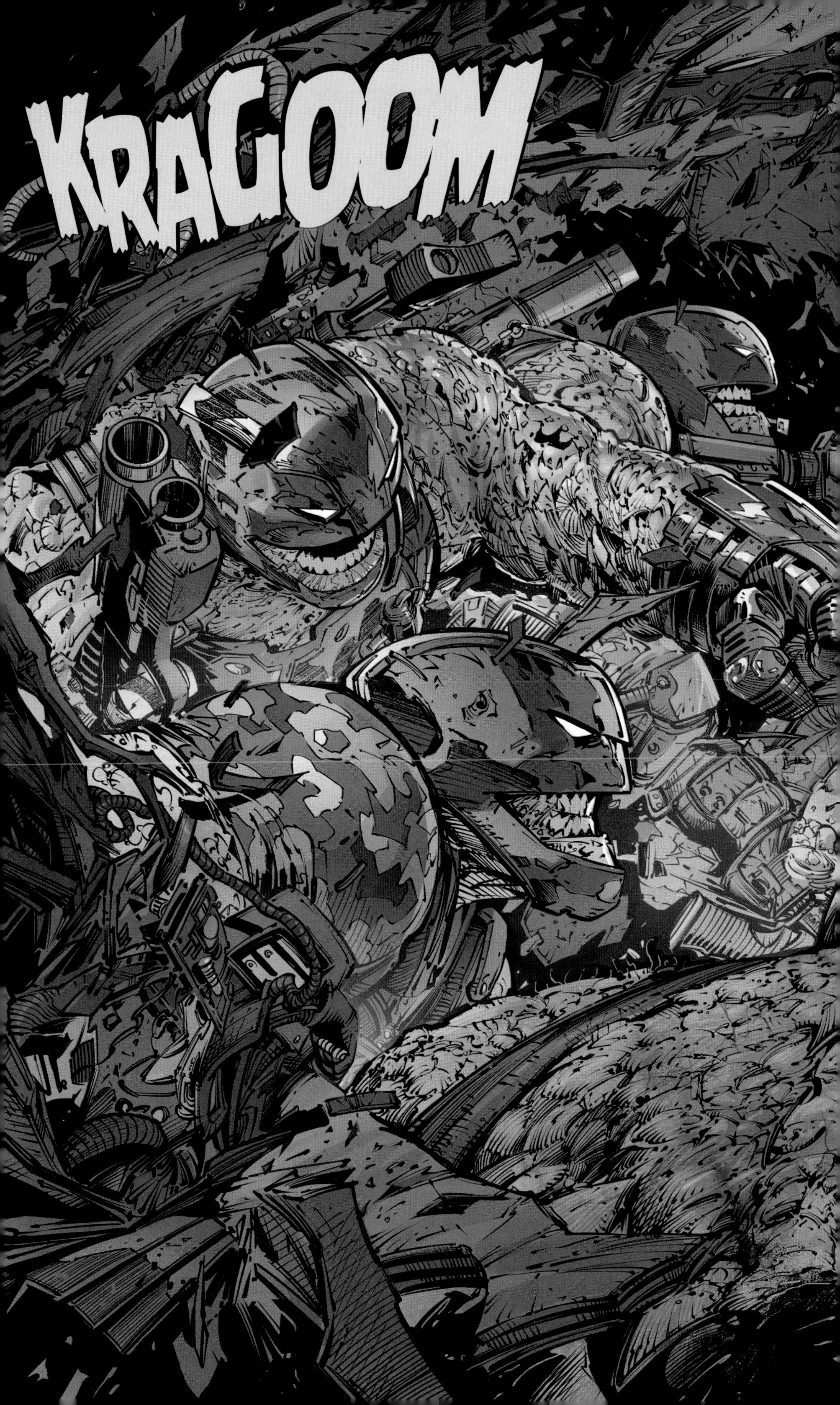
KRAGOOM

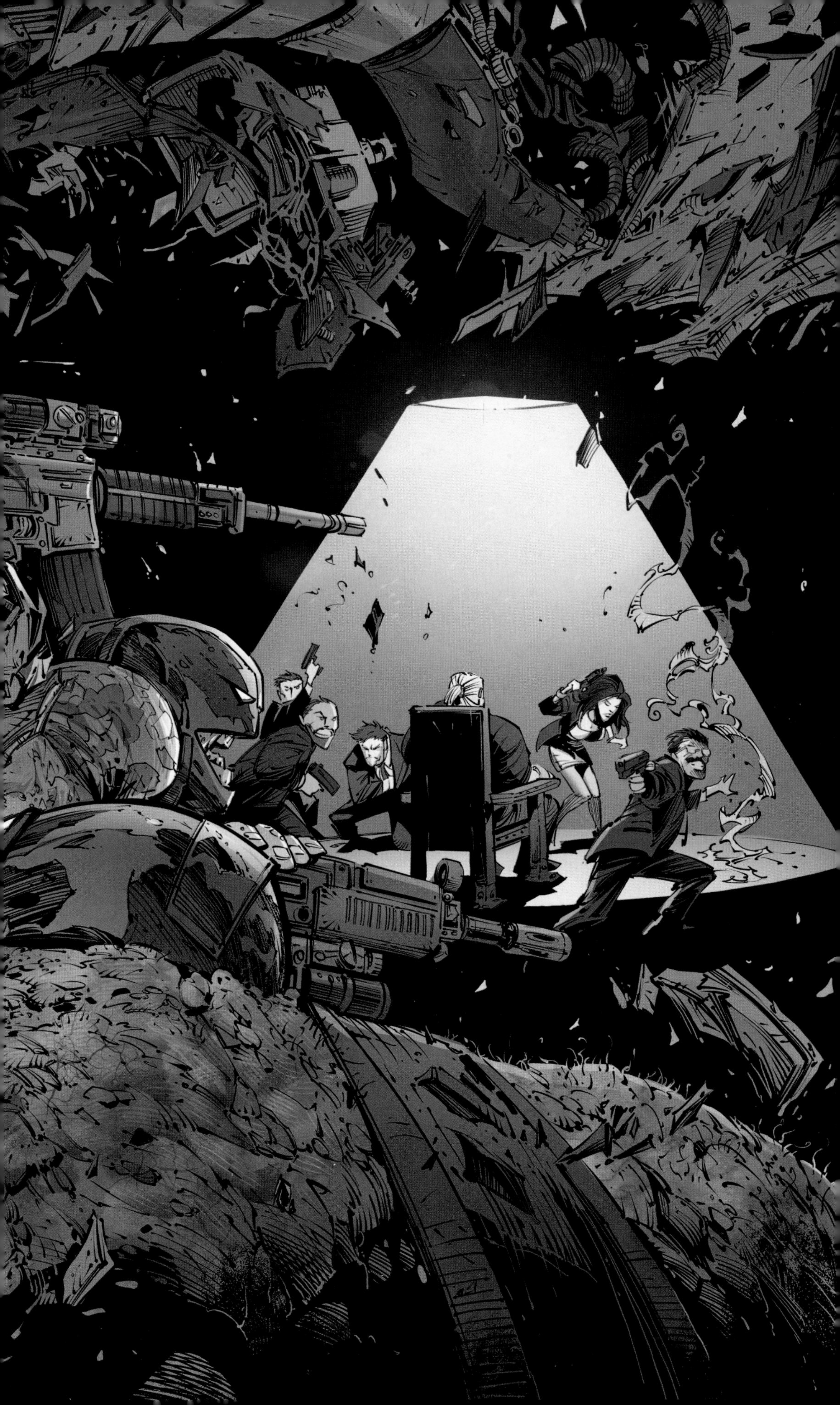

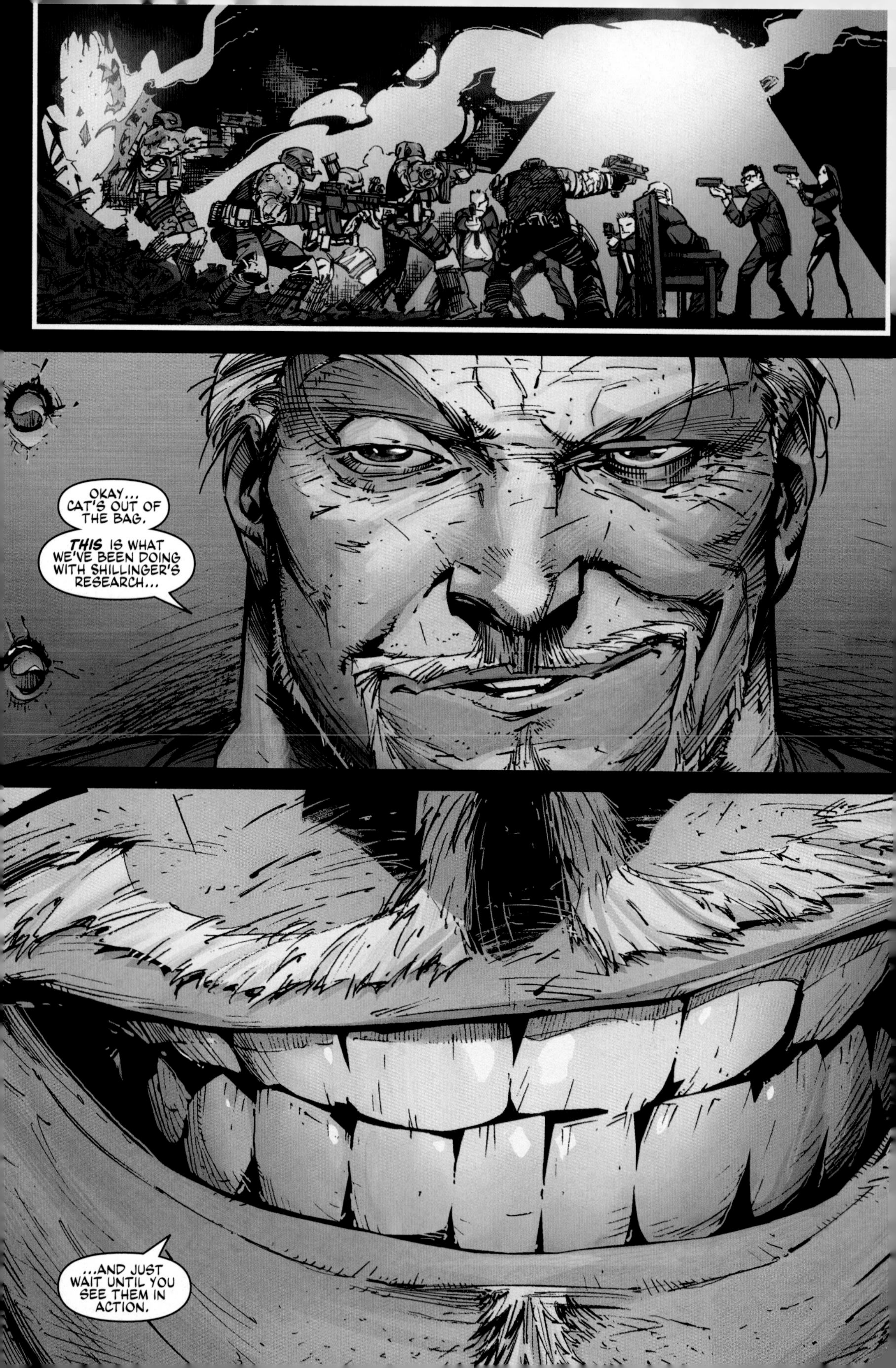
OKAY... CAT'S OUT OF THE BAG.
THIS IS WHAT WE'VE BEEN DOING WITH SHILLINGER'S RESEARCH...
...AND JUST WAIT UNTIL YOU SEE THEM IN ACTION.

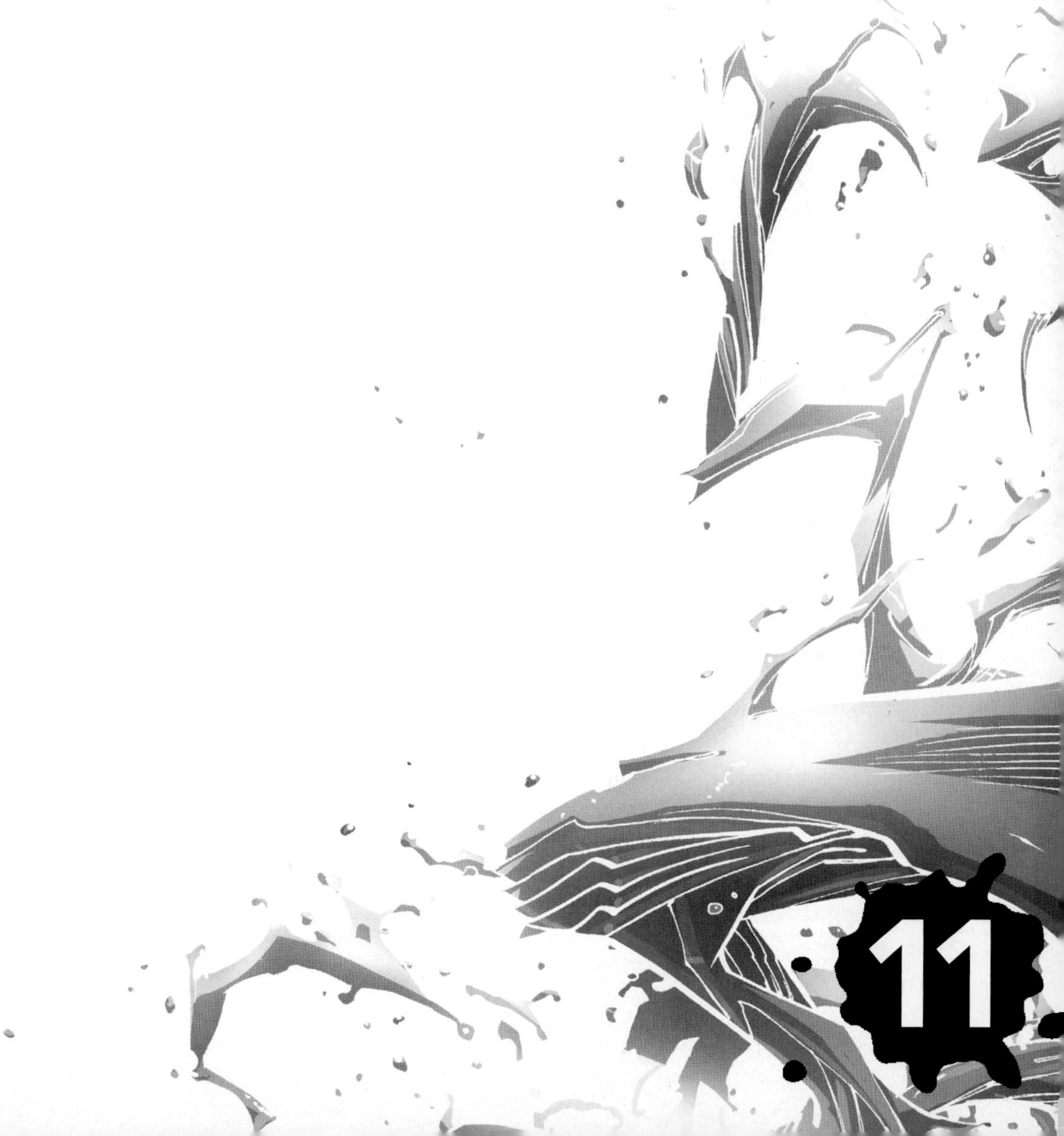
11

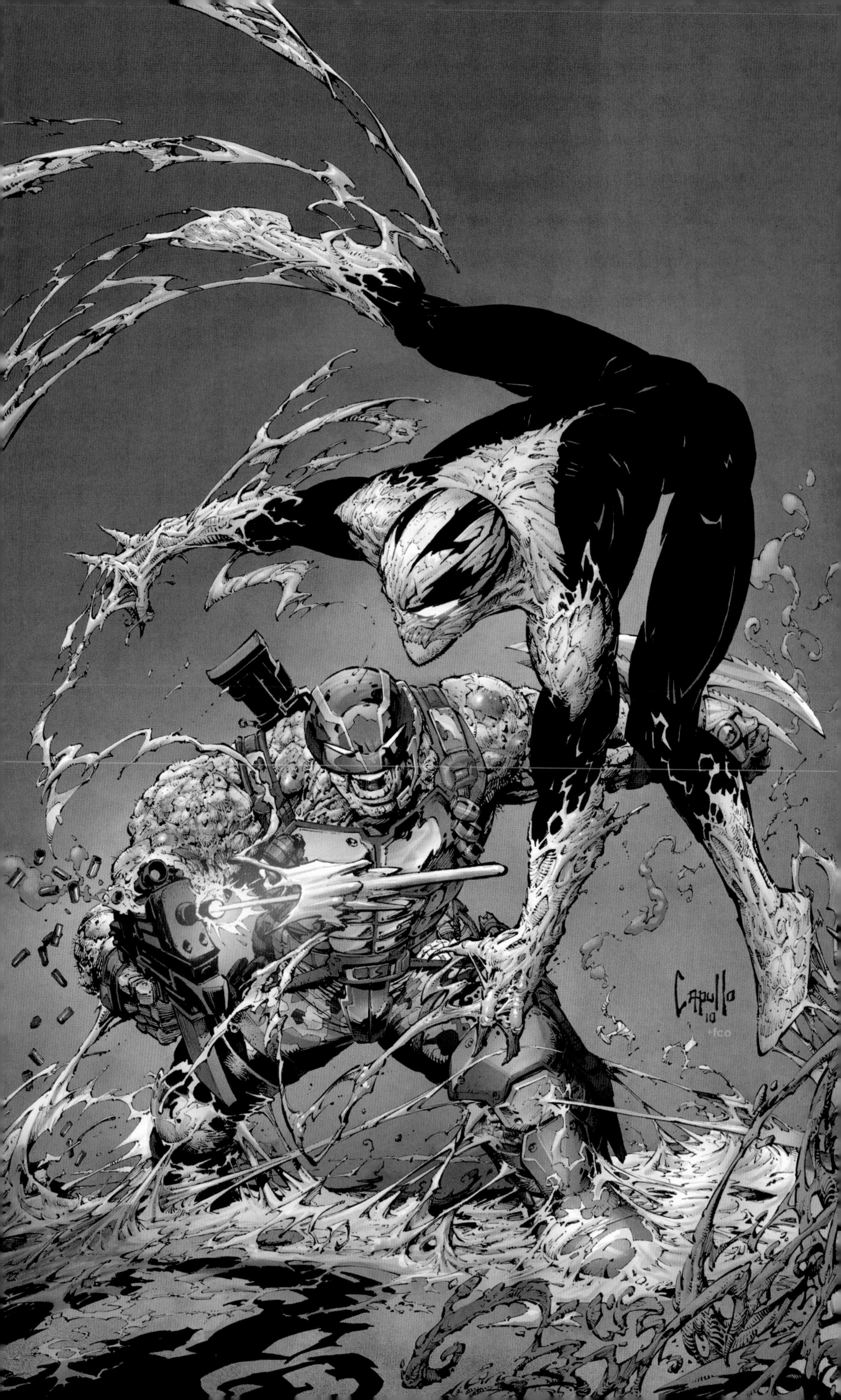
Capullo 10
+fco

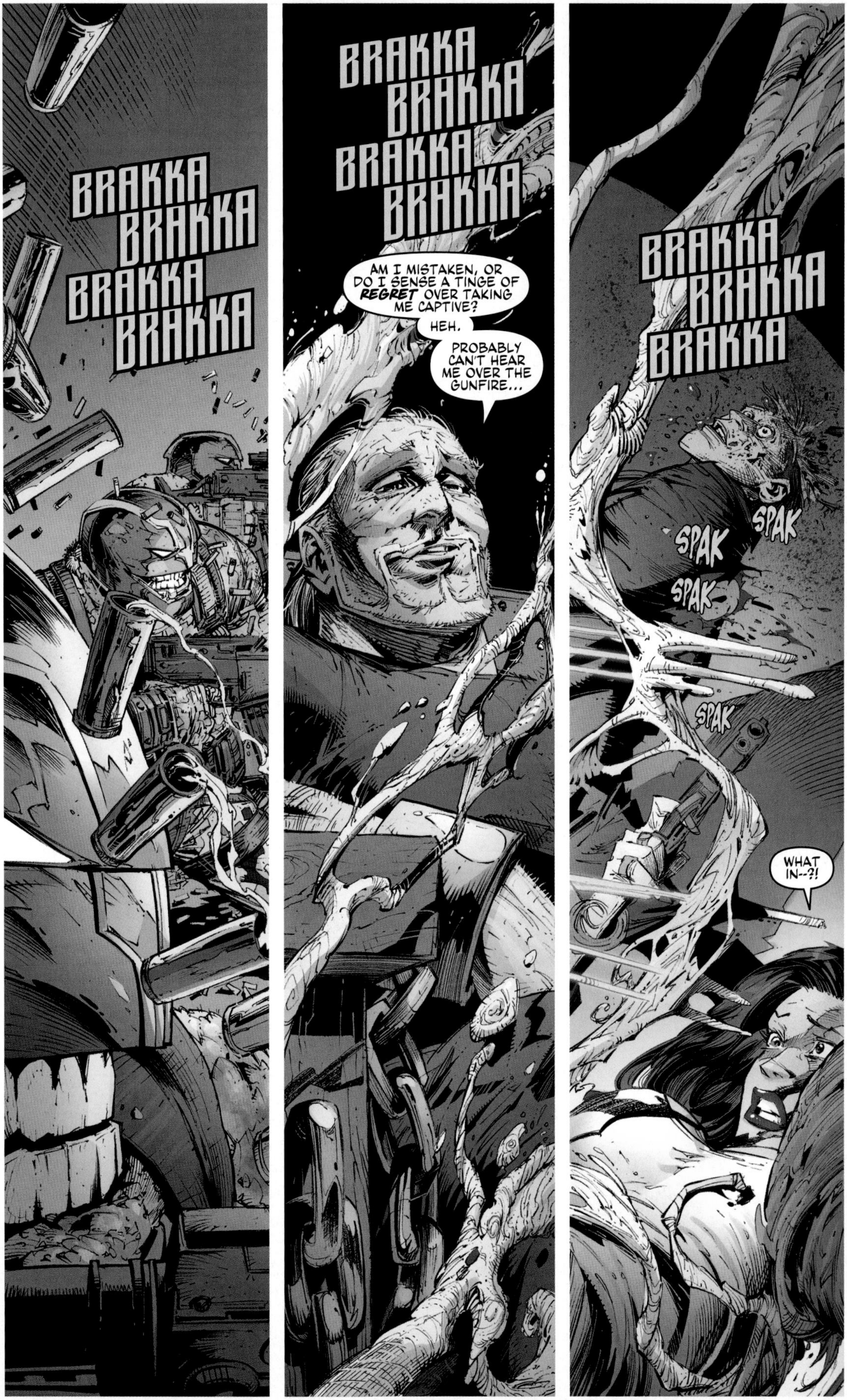
BRAKKA BRAKKA BRAKKA BRAKKA
BRAKKA BRAKKA BRAKKA BRAKKA
AM I MISTAKEN, OR DO I SENSE A TINGE OF REGRET OVER TAKING ME CAPTIVE?
HEH.
PROBABLY CAN'T HEAR ME OVER THE GUNFIRE...
BRAKKA BRAKKA BRAKKA
SPAK
SPAK
SPAK
SPAK
WHAT IN--?!

BETH TOSH, I'M STARTING TO GET THE SENSE THAT YOU'RE NOT QUALIFIED FOR THIS POSITION.

MORGAN STANTZ WOULD HAVE KNOWN YOU'D NEED FAR MORE AGENTS TO SECURE ME. THERE WOULD HAVE BEEN A SWAT TEAM DOWN THE STREET WITH NO CLUE WHY THEY WERE THERE--JUST IN CASE.

OH, GOD.

OH, GOD.

CAN YOU DO THIS?

I'M FINE. I CAN PROTECT MY ARM, JUST NEED TO MAKE SURE YOU'RE SAFE.

HOW TOUGH COULD THESE THINGS BE?

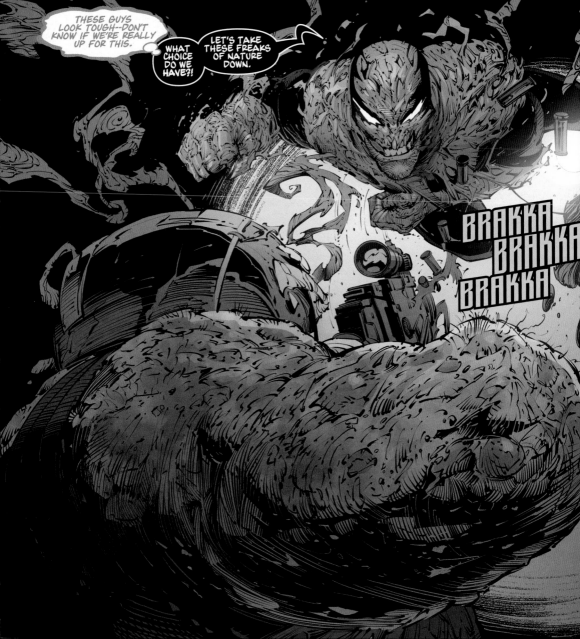

THESE GUYS LOOK TOUGH--DON'T KNOW IF WE'RE REALLY UP FOR THIS.

WHAT CHOICE DO WE HAVE?!

LET'S TAKE THESE FREAKS OF NATURE DOWN.

BRAKKA
BRAKKA
BRAKKA

SPLAGG

CHRIST.

NO TIME FOR THAT. OUR OBJECTIVE IS TO REACQUIRE HURG AND RETREAT-- DON'T WORRY ABOUT THESE MONSTERS.

THIS LOCATION IS CLEAN. WE WALK AWAY, NO EVIDENCE OF HAVING BEEN HERE.

THE SANDWICH, TOO. I HOPE YOU'RE REGRETTING THAT AWFUL SANDWICH YOU TRIED TO MAKE ME EAT, AS WELL.

IF YOU'RE CONSUMED BY GUILT, DON'T WORRY-- IT'LL ALL BE OVER SOON.

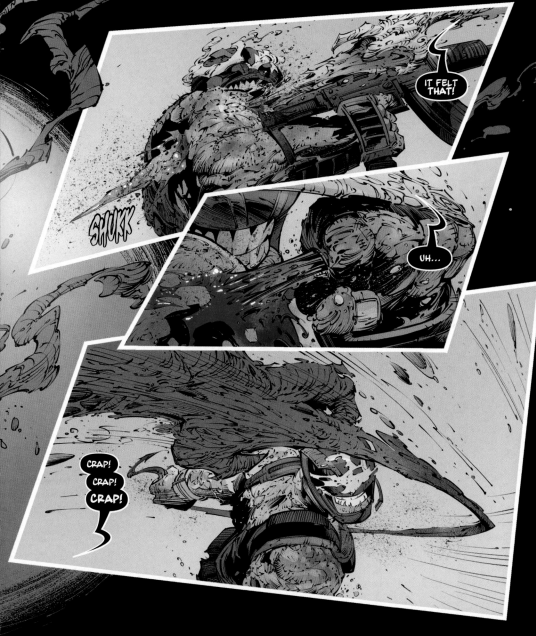

IT FELT THAT!

SHUKK

UH...

CRAP!
CRAP!
CRAP!

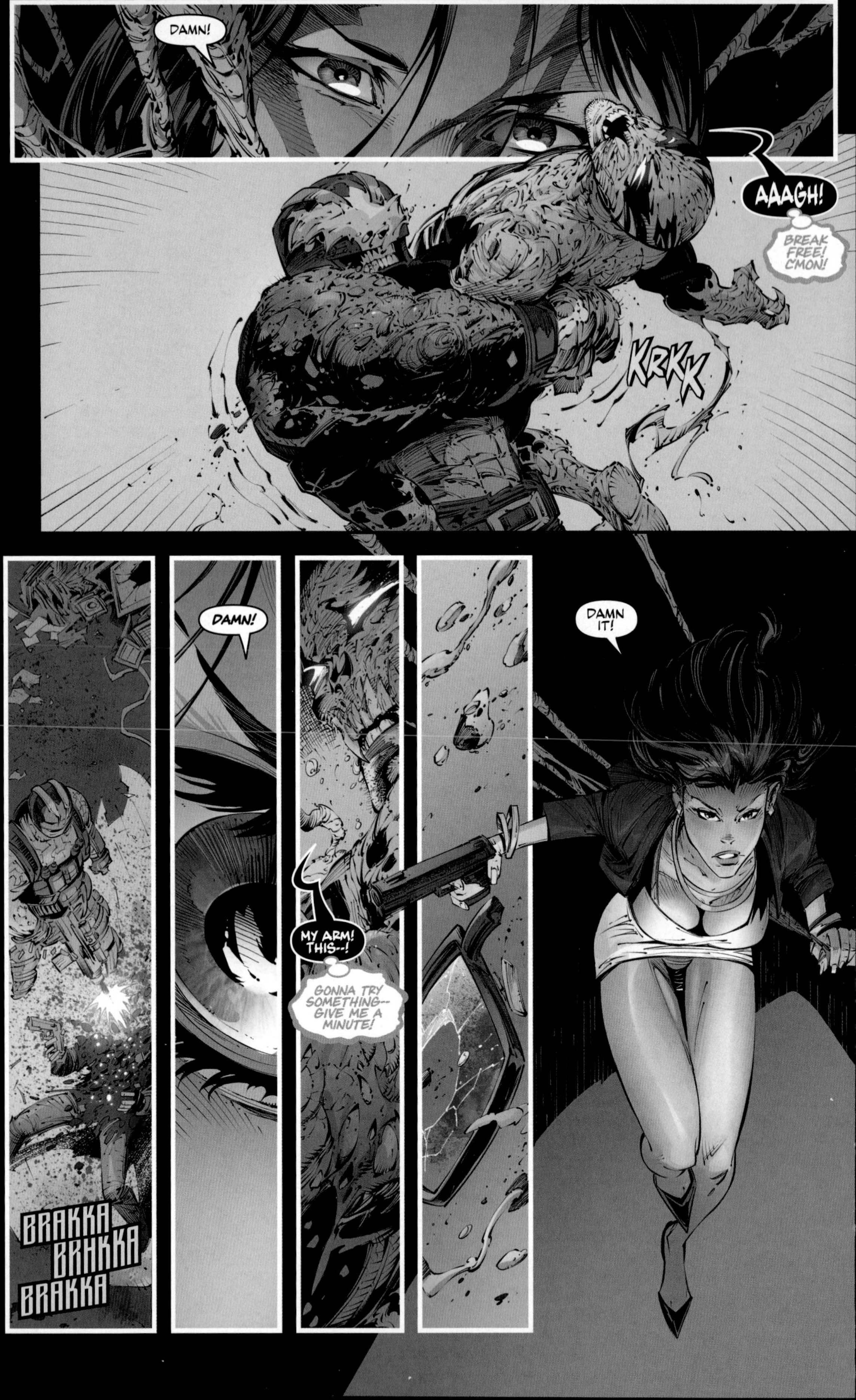
DAMN!
AAAGH!
BREAK FREE! C'MON!
KRKK
BRAKKA BRAKKA BRAKKA
DAMN!
MY ARM! THIS--!
GONNA TRY SOMETHING-- GIVE ME A MINUTE!
DAMN IT!

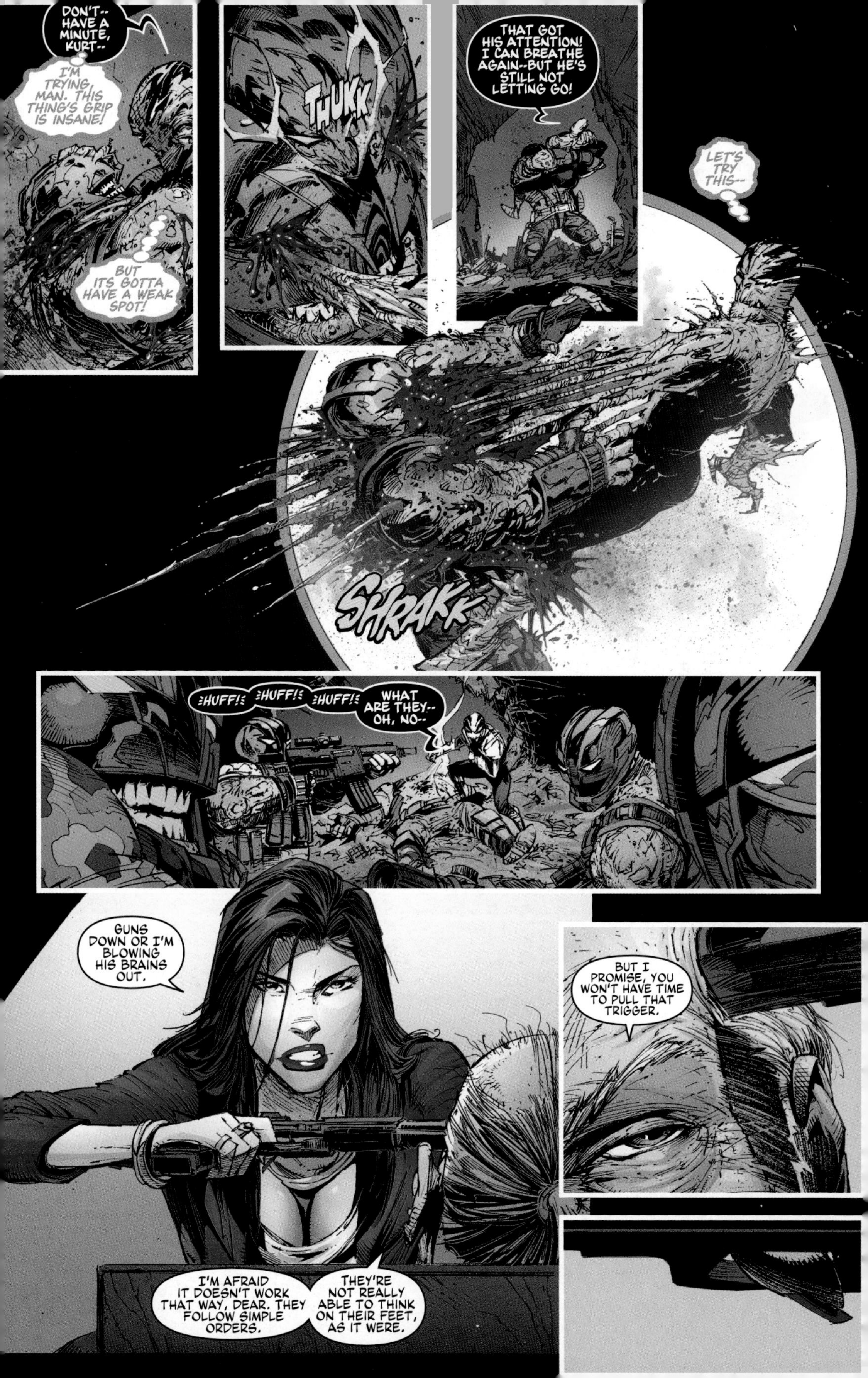

DON'T-- HAVE A MINUTE, KURT--
I'M TRYING, MAN. THIS THING'S GRIP IS INSANE!
BUT ITS GOTTA HAVE A WEAK SPOT!
THUKK
THAT GOT HIS ATTENTION! I CAN BREATHE AGAIN--BUT HE'S STILL NOT LETTING GO!
LET'S TRY THIS--
SHRAKK
HUFF!
HUFF!
HUFF!
WHAT ARE THEY-- OH, NO--
GUNS DOWN OR I'M BLOWING HIS BRAINS OUT.
BUT I PROMISE, YOU WON'T HAVE TIME TO PULL THAT TRIGGER.
I'M AFRAID IT DOESN'T WORK THAT WAY, DEAR. THEY FOLLOW SIMPLE ORDERS.
THEY'RE NOT REALLY ABLE TO THINK ON THEIR FEET, AS IT WERE.

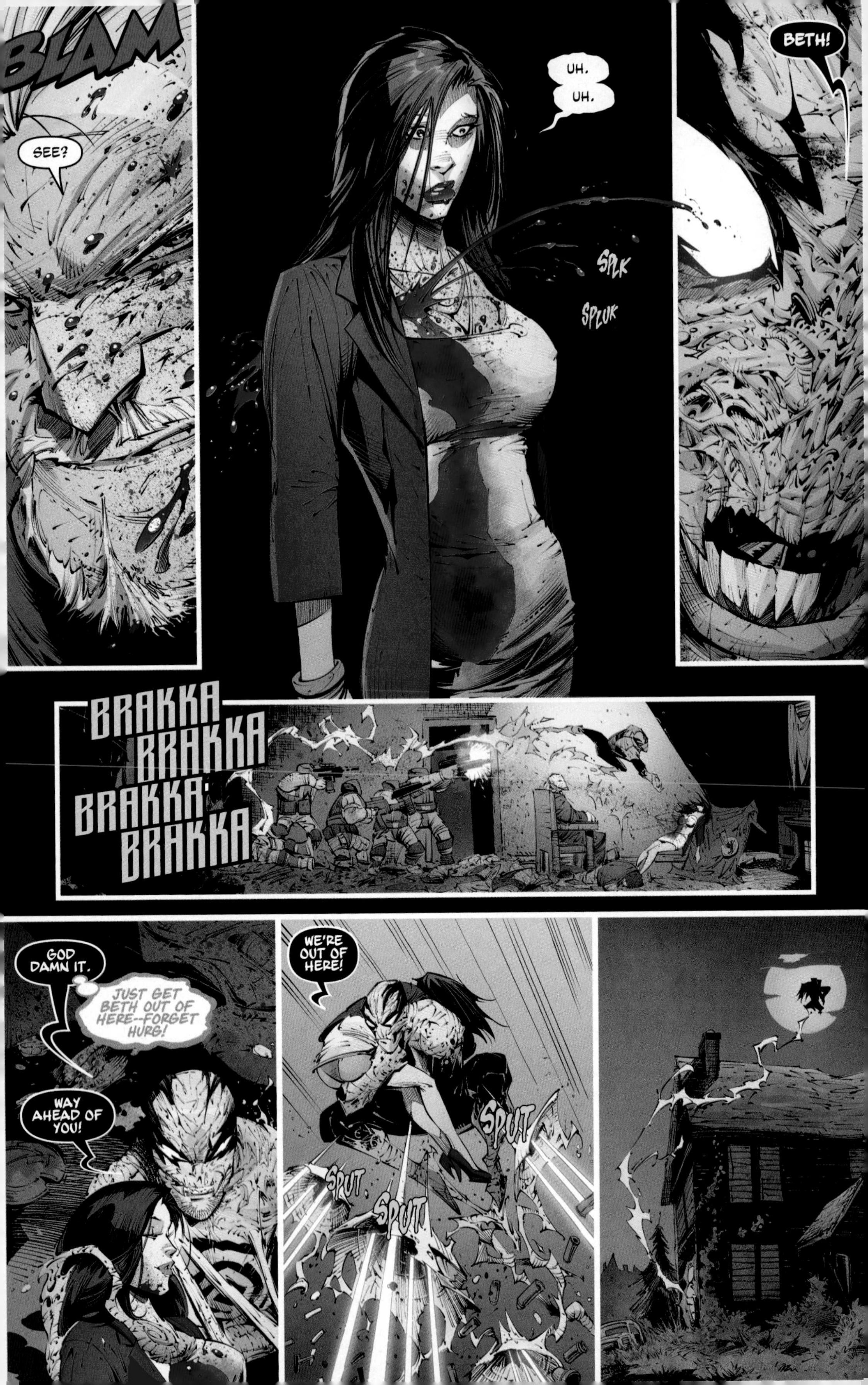
BLAM
SEE?
UH. UH.
SPLK
SPLUK
BETH!
BRAKKA BRAKKA BRAKKA BRAKKA
GOD DAMN IT.
JUST GET BETH OUT OF HERE--FORGET HURG!
WAY AHEAD OF YOU!
WE'RE OUT OF HERE!
SPUT
SPUT
SPUT

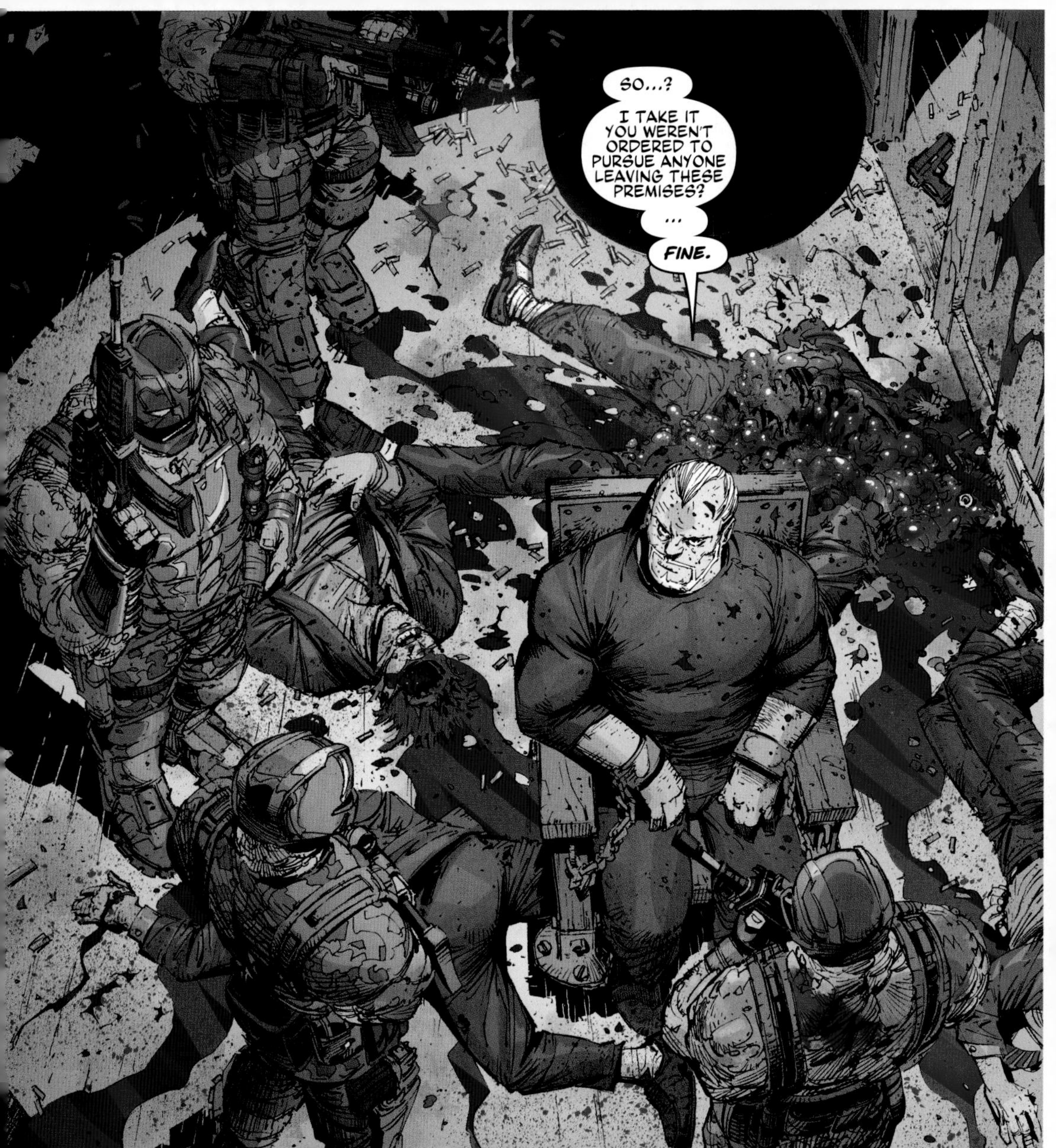
SO...?
I TAKE IT YOU WEREN'T ORDERED TO PURSUE ANYONE LEAVING THESE PREMISES?
...
FINE.

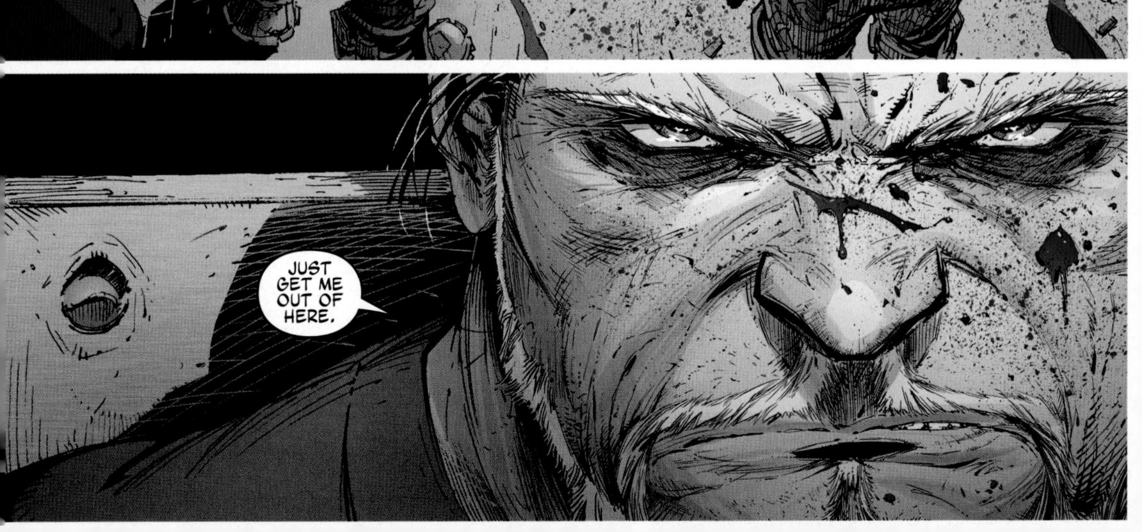
JUST GET ME OUT OF HERE.

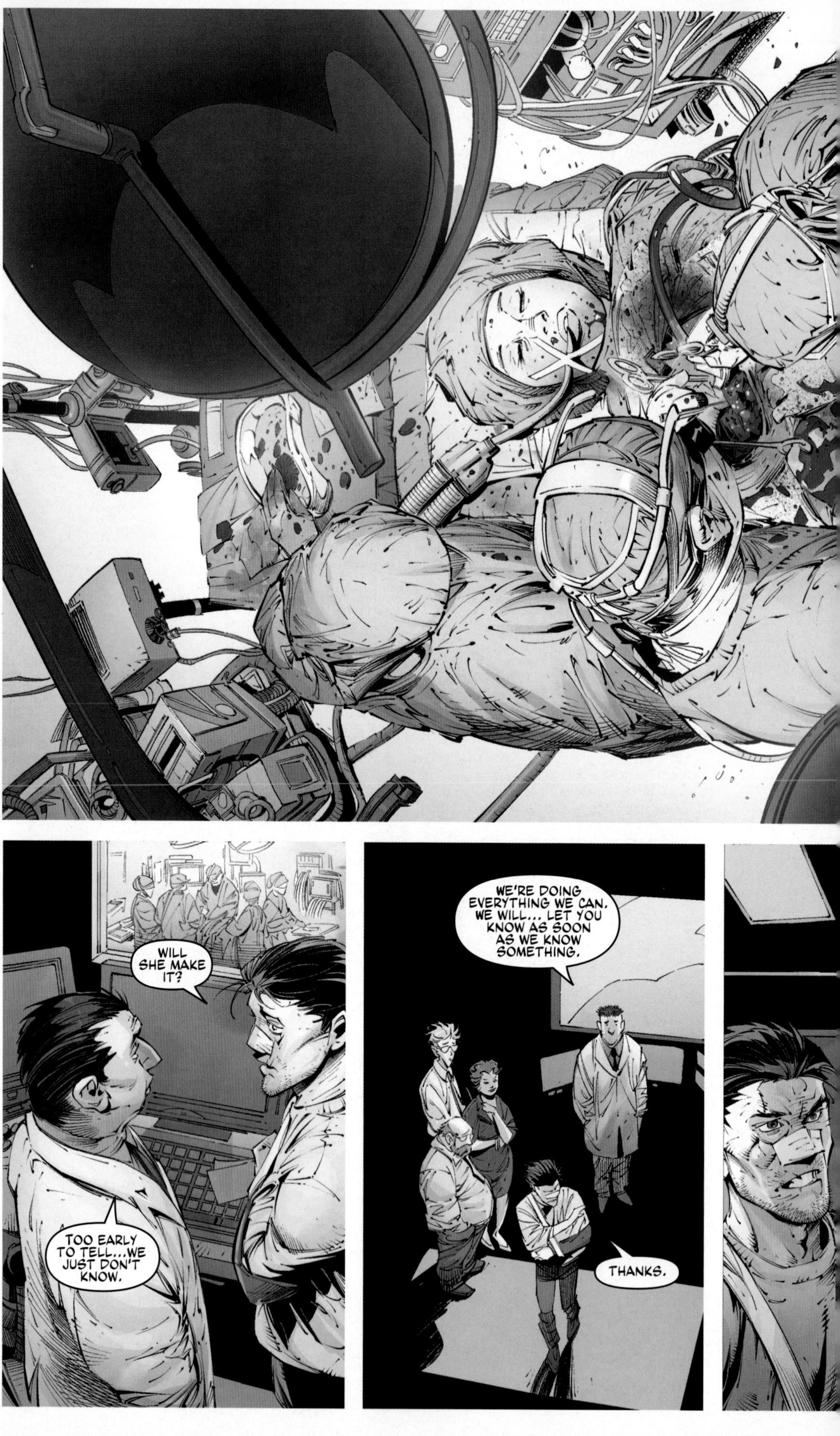
WILL SHE MAKE IT?
TOO EARLY TO TELL...WE JUST DON'T KNOW.
WE'RE DOING EVERYTHING WE CAN. WE WILL... LET YOU KNOW AS SOON AS WE KNOW SOMETHING.
THANKS.

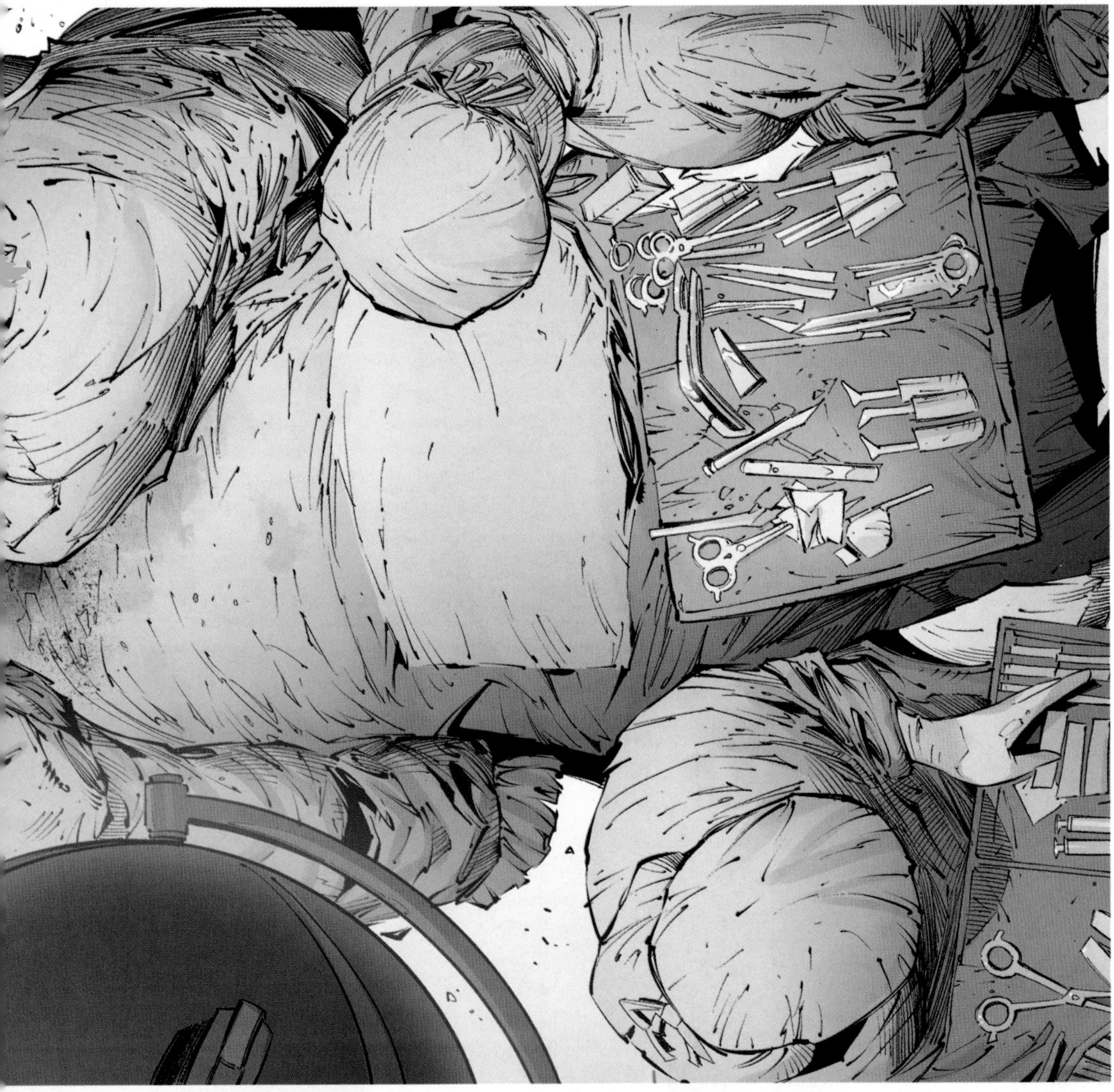

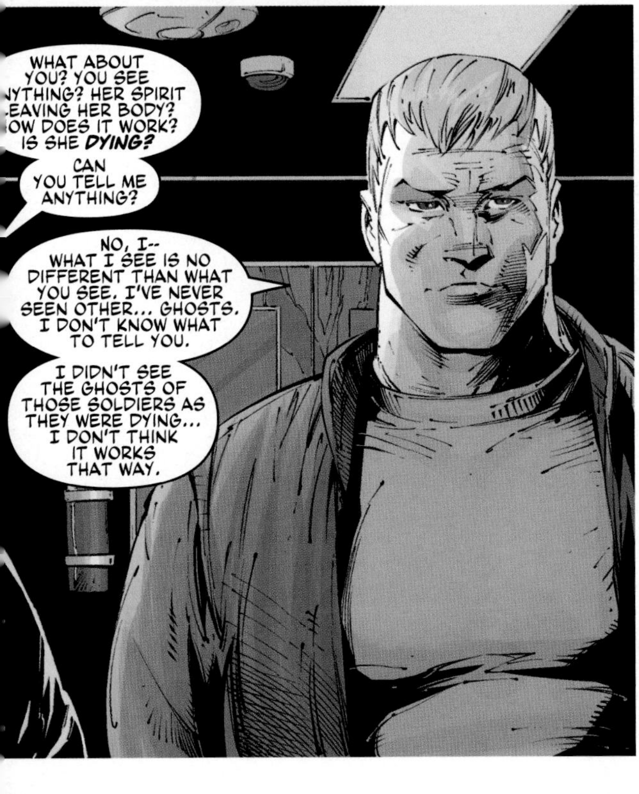
WHAT ABOUT YOU? YOU SEE ANYTHING? HER SPIRIT LEAVING HER BODY? HOW DOES IT WORK? IS SHE *DYING?*
CAN YOU TELL ME ANYTHING?
NO, I-- WHAT I SEE IS NO DIFFERENT THAN WHAT YOU SEE. I'VE NEVER SEEN OTHER... GHOSTS. I DON'T KNOW WHAT TO TELL YOU.
I DIDN'T SEE THE GHOSTS OF THOSE SOLDIERS AS THEY WERE DYING... I DON'T THINK IT WORKS THAT WAY.

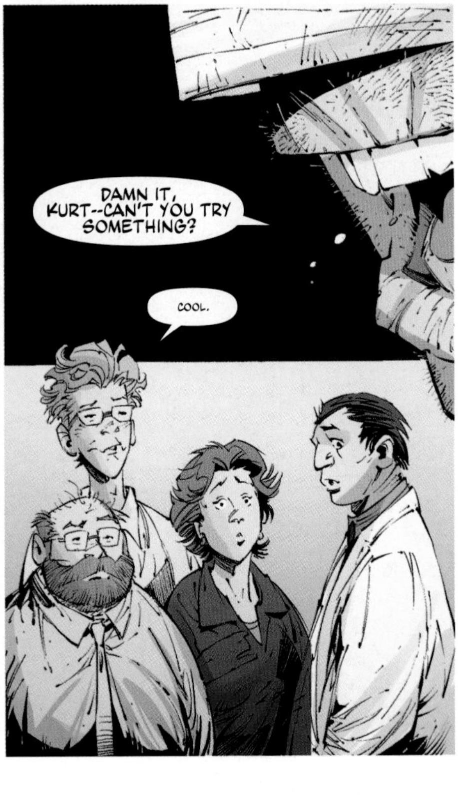
DAMN IT, KURT--CAN'T YOU TRY SOMETHING?
COOL.

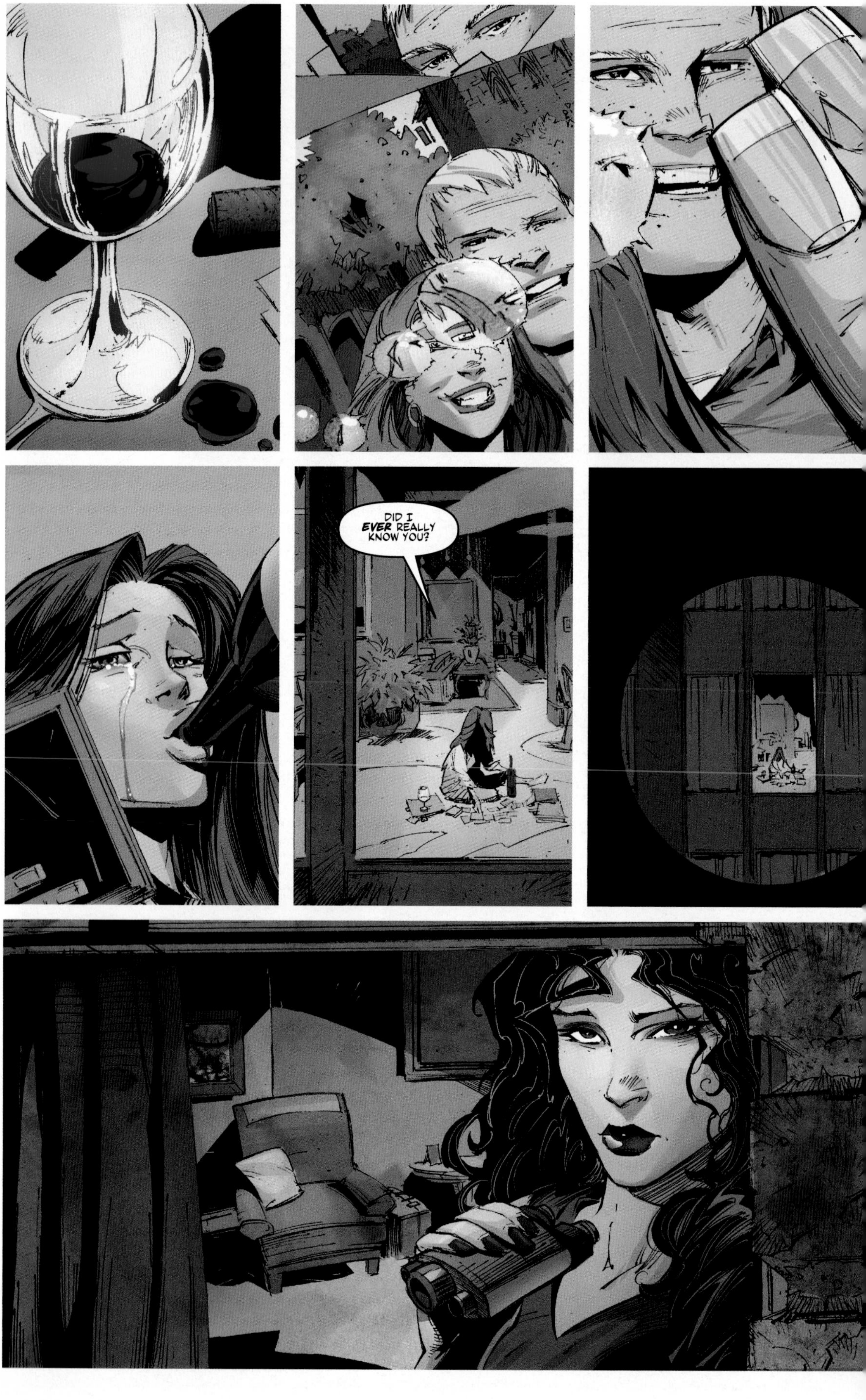
DID I
EVER REALLY
KNOW YOU?

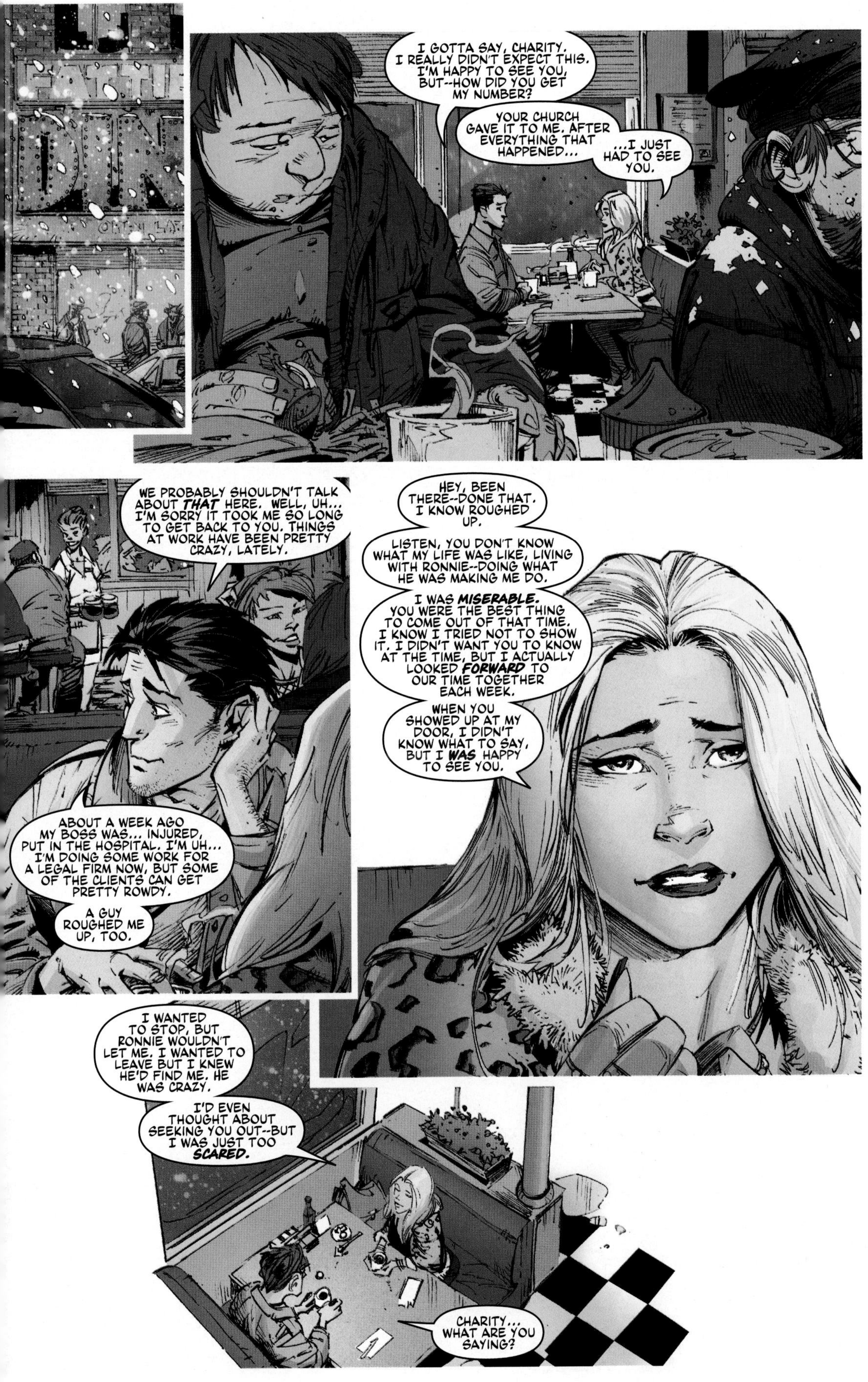
I GOTTA SAY, CHARITY. I REALLY DIDN'T EXPECT THIS. I'M HAPPY TO SEE YOU, BUT--HOW DID YOU GET MY NUMBER?
YOUR CHURCH GAVE IT TO ME. AFTER EVERYTHING THAT HAPPENED...
...I JUST HAD TO SEE YOU.
WE PROBABLY SHOULDN'T TALK ABOUT THAT HERE. WELL, UH... I'M SORRY IT TOOK ME SO LONG TO GET BACK TO YOU. THINGS AT WORK HAVE BEEN PRETTY CRAZY, LATELY.
ABOUT A WEEK AGO MY BOSS WAS... INJURED, PUT IN THE HOSPITAL. I'M UH... I'M DOING SOME WORK FOR A LEGAL FIRM NOW, BUT SOME OF THE CLIENTS CAN GET PRETTY ROWDY.
A GUY ROUGHED ME UP, TOO.
HEY, BEEN THERE--DONE THAT. I KNOW ROUGHED UP.
LISTEN, YOU DON'T KNOW WHAT MY LIFE WAS LIKE, LIVING WITH RONNIE--DOING WHAT HE WAS MAKING ME DO.
I WAS MISERABLE. YOU WERE THE BEST THING TO COME OUT OF THAT TIME. I KNOW I TRIED NOT TO SHOW IT. I DIDN'T WANT YOU TO KNOW AT THE TIME, BUT I ACTUALLY LOOKED FORWARD TO OUR TIME TOGETHER EACH WEEK.
WHEN YOU SHOWED UP AT MY DOOR, I DIDN'T KNOW WHAT TO SAY, BUT I WAS HAPPY TO SEE YOU.
I WANTED TO STOP, BUT RONNIE WOULDN'T LET ME. I WANTED TO LEAVE BUT I KNEW HE'D FIND ME. HE WAS CRAZY.
I'D EVEN THOUGHT ABOUT SEEKING YOU OUT--BUT I WAS JUST TOO SCARED.
CHARITY... WHAT ARE YOU SAYING?

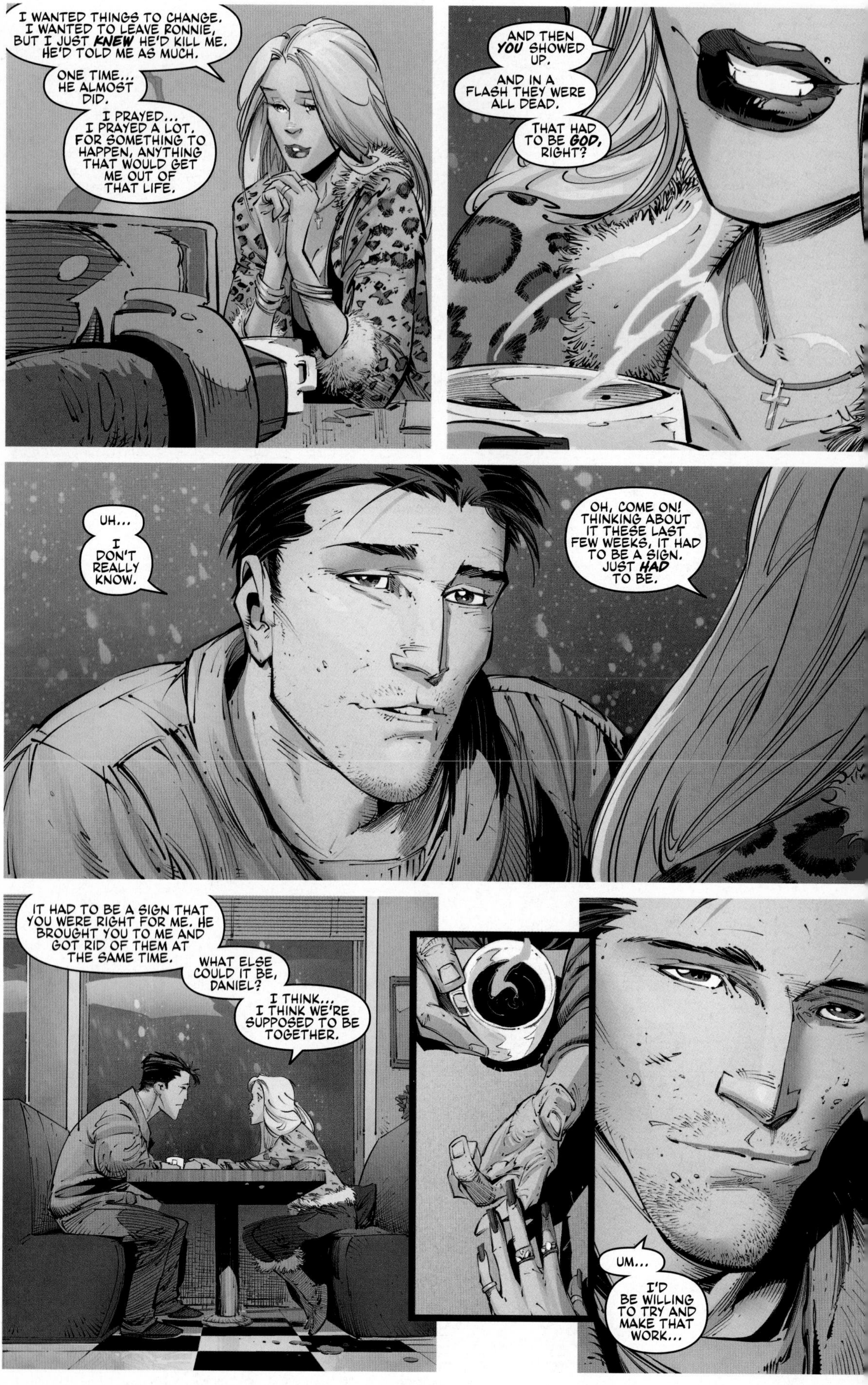
I WANTED THINGS TO CHANGE. I WANTED TO LEAVE RONNIE, BUT I JUST KNEW HE'D KILL ME. HE'D TOLD ME AS MUCH.
ONE TIME... HE ALMOST DID.
I PRAYED... I PRAYED A LOT. FOR SOMETHING TO HAPPEN, ANYTHING THAT WOULD GET ME OUT OF THAT LIFE.
AND THEN YOU SHOWED UP.
AND IN A FLASH THEY WERE ALL DEAD.
THAT HAD TO BE GOD, RIGHT?
UH... I DON'T REALLY KNOW.
OH, COME ON! THINKING ABOUT IT THESE LAST FEW WEEKS, IT HAD TO BE A SIGN. JUST HAD TO BE.
IT HAD TO BE A SIGN THAT YOU WERE RIGHT FOR ME. HE BROUGHT YOU TO ME AND GOT RID OF THEM AT THE SAME TIME.
WHAT ELSE COULD IT BE, DANIEL?
I THINK... I THINK WE'RE SUPPOSED TO BE TOGETHER.
UM...
I'D BE WILLING TO TRY AND MAKE THAT WORK...

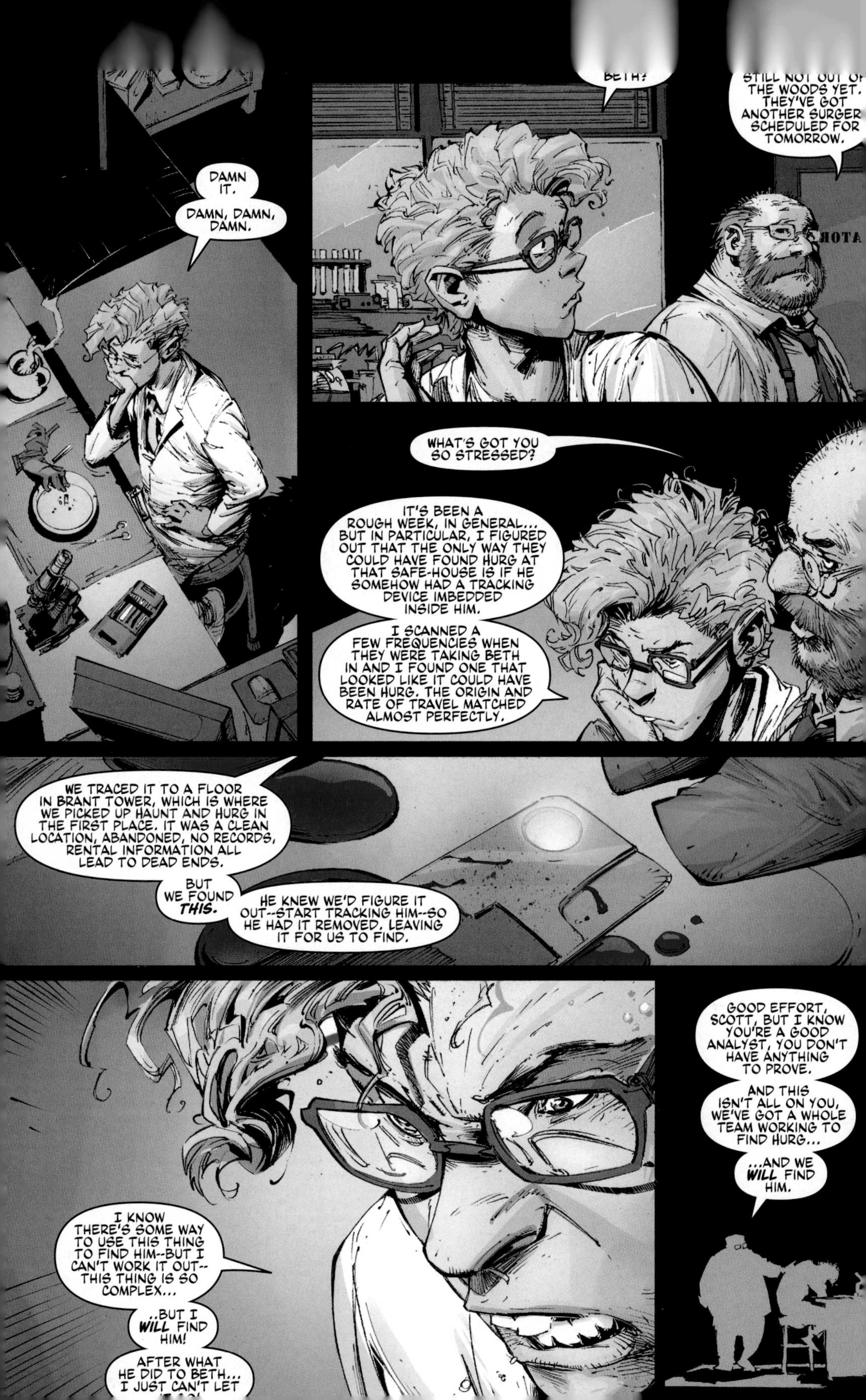
DAMN IT.
DAMN, DAMN, DAMN.
BETH?
STILL NOT OUT OF THE WOODS YET. THEY'VE GOT ANOTHER SURGER SCHEDULED FOR TOMORROW.
WHAT'S GOT YOU SO STRESSED?
IT'S BEEN A ROUGH WEEK, IN GENERAL... BUT IN PARTICULAR, I FIGURED OUT THAT THE ONLY WAY THEY COULD HAVE FOUND HURG AT THAT SAFE-HOUSE IS IF HE SOMEHOW HAD A TRACKING DEVICE IMBEDDED INSIDE HIM.
I SCANNED A FEW FREQUENCIES WHEN THEY WERE TAKING BETH IN AND I FOUND ONE THAT LOOKED LIKE IT COULD HAVE BEEN HURG. THE ORIGIN AND RATE OF TRAVEL MATCHED ALMOST PERFECTLY.
WE TRACED IT TO A FLOOR IN BRANT TOWER, WHICH IS WHERE WE PICKED UP HAUNT AND HURG IN THE FIRST PLACE. IT WAS A CLEAN LOCATION, ABANDONED, NO RECORDS, RENTAL INFORMATION ALL LEAD TO DEAD ENDS.
BUT WE FOUND *THIS.*
HE KNEW WE'D FIGURE IT OUT--START TRACKING HIM--SO HE HAD IT REMOVED. LEAVING IT FOR US TO FIND.
I KNOW THERE'S SOME WAY TO USE THIS THING TO FIND HIM--BUT I CAN'T WORK IT OUT-- THIS THING IS SO COMPLEX...
..BUT I *WILL* FIND HIM!
AFTER WHAT HE DID TO BETH... I JUST CAN'T LET
GOOD EFFORT, SCOTT, BUT I KNOW YOU'RE A GOOD ANALYST, YOU DON'T HAVE ANYTHING TO PROVE.
AND THIS ISN'T ALL ON YOU, WE'VE GOT A WHOLE TEAM WORKING TO FIND HURG...
...AND WE *WILL* FIND HIM.

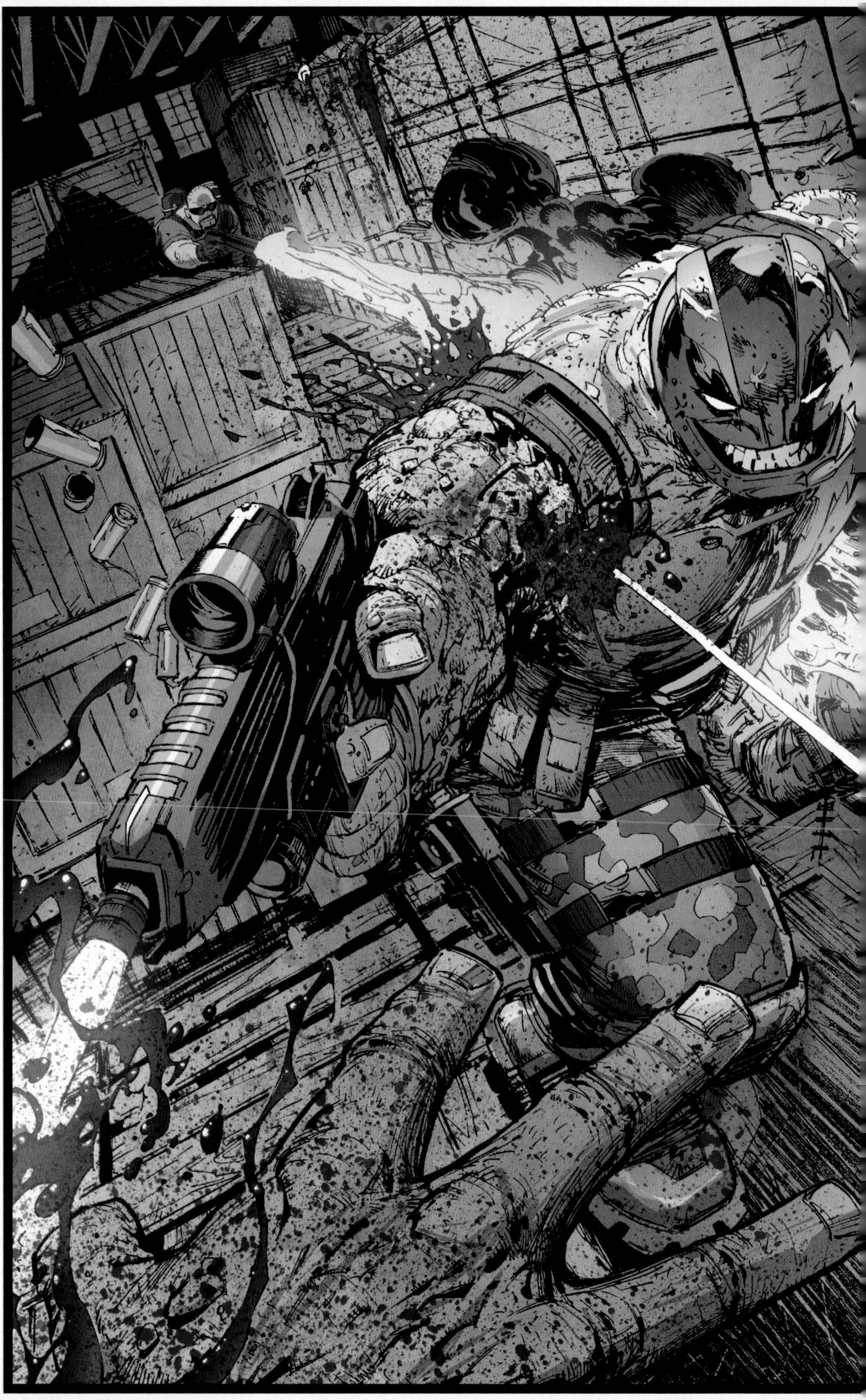

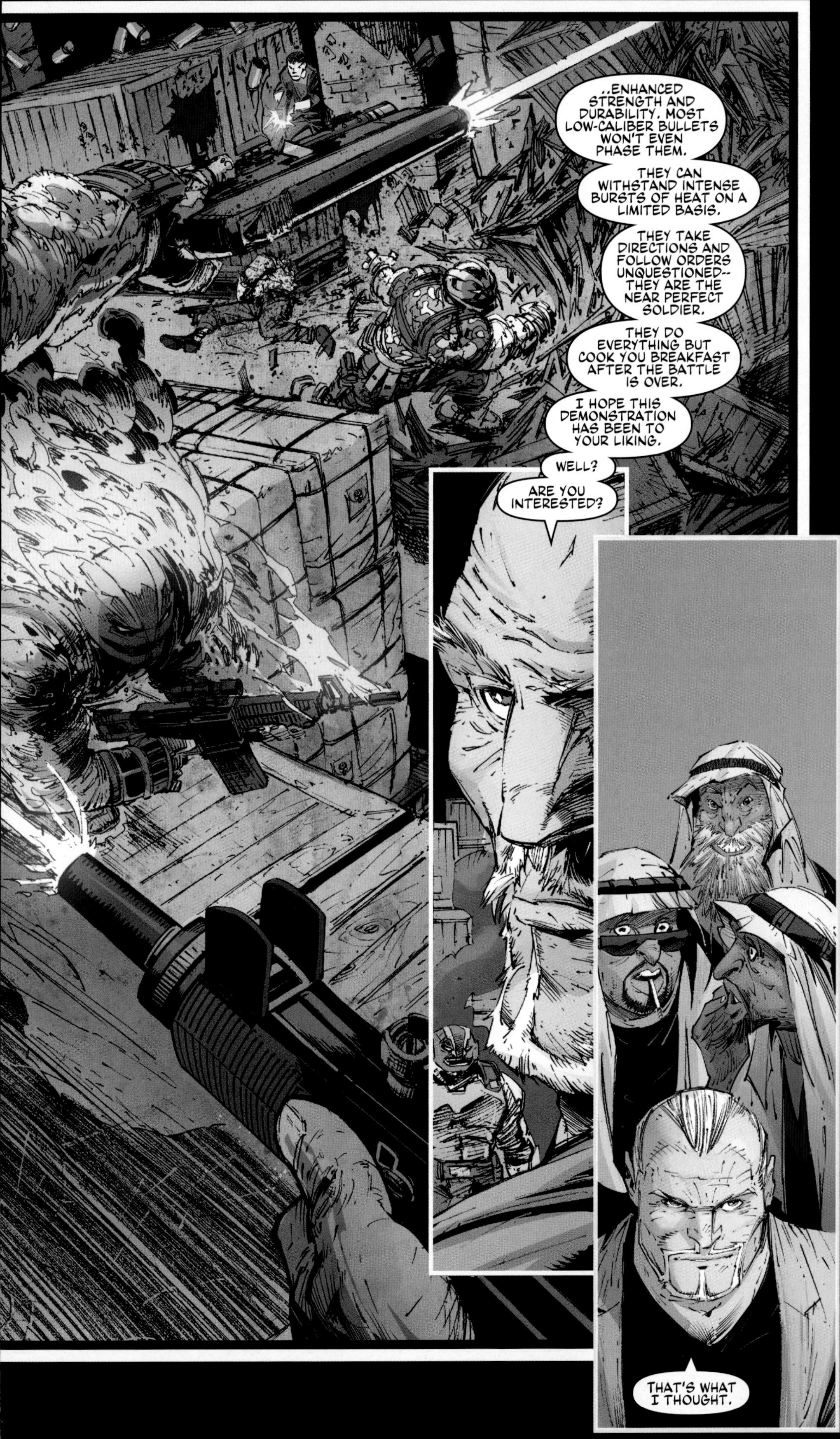
..ENHANCED STRENGTH AND DURABILITY. MOST LOW-CALIBER BULLETS WON'T EVEN PHASE THEM.
THEY CAN WITHSTAND INTENSE BURSTS OF HEAT ON A LIMITED BASIS.
THEY TAKE DIRECTIONS AND FOLLOW ORDERS UNQUESTIONED-- THEY ARE THE NEAR PERFECT SOLDIER.
THEY DO EVERYTHING BUT COOK YOU BREAKFAST AFTER THE BATTLE IS OVER.
I HOPE THIS DEMONSTRATION HAS BEEN TO YOUR LIKING.
WELL?
ARE YOU INTERESTED?
THAT'S WHAT I THOUGHT.

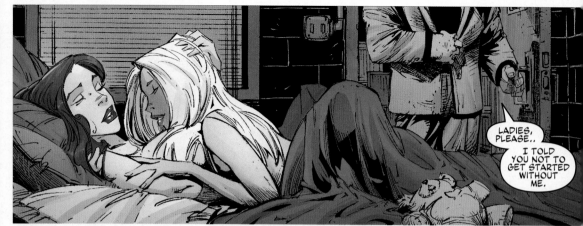

LADIES, PLEASE... I TOLD YOU NOT TO GET STARTED WITHOUT ME.

WELL, HOW DID IT GO?

THE SHILLINGER DRONES ARE NOW *OFFICIALLY* SOLD OUT.

BUT WHAT ABOUT TOSHIMA AND HIS SON?

THEY'RE NOT GOING TO BE HAPPY WHEN THEY FIND OUT THEY DON'T HAVE THE EXCLUSIVE.

IT'S PURE BUSINESS...

WHY SELL TO ONE GROUP IN A CONFLICT WHEN YOU CAN SELL TO *BOTH* OF THEM?

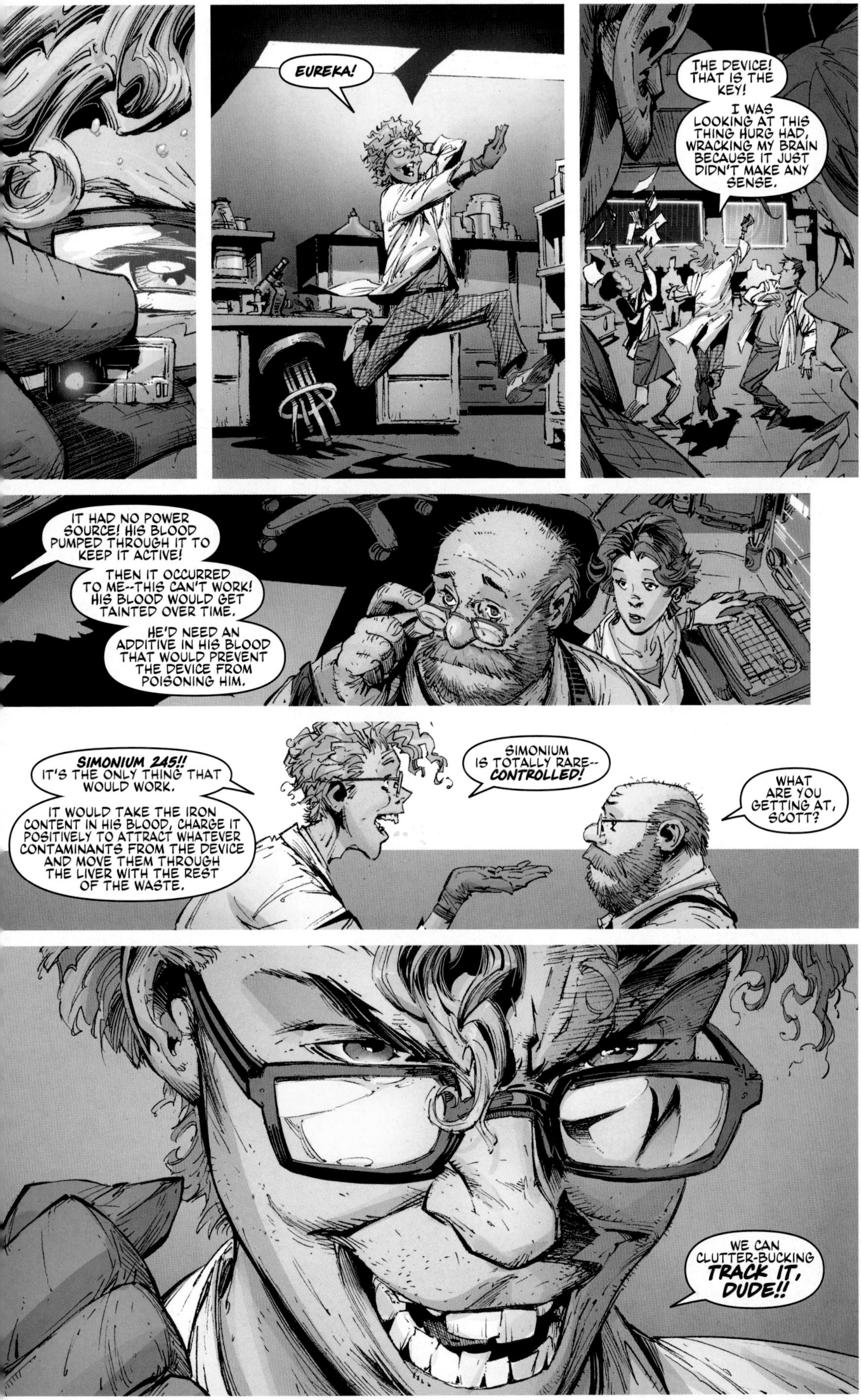
EUREKA!
THE DEVICE! THAT IS THE KEY!
I WAS LOOKING AT THIS THING HURG HAD, WRACKING MY BRAIN BECAUSE IT JUST DIDN'T MAKE ANY SENSE.
IT HAD NO POWER SOURCE! HIS BLOOD PUMPED THROUGH IT TO KEEP IT ACTIVE!
THEN IT OCCURRED TO ME--THIS CAN'T WORK! HIS BLOOD WOULD GET TAINTED OVER TIME.
HE'D NEED AN ADDITIVE IN HIS BLOOD THAT WOULD PREVENT THE DEVICE FROM POISONING HIM.
SIMONIUM 245!! IT'S THE ONLY THING THAT WOULD WORK.
IT WOULD TAKE THE IRON CONTENT IN HIS BLOOD, CHARGE IT POSITIVELY TO ATTRACT WHATEVER CONTAMINANTS FROM THE DEVICE AND MOVE THEM THROUGH THE LIVER WITH THE REST OF THE WASTE.
SIMONIUM IS TOTALLY RARE--CONTROLLED!
WHAT ARE YOU GETTING AT, SCOTT?
WE CAN CLUTTER-BUCKING TRACK IT, DUDE!!

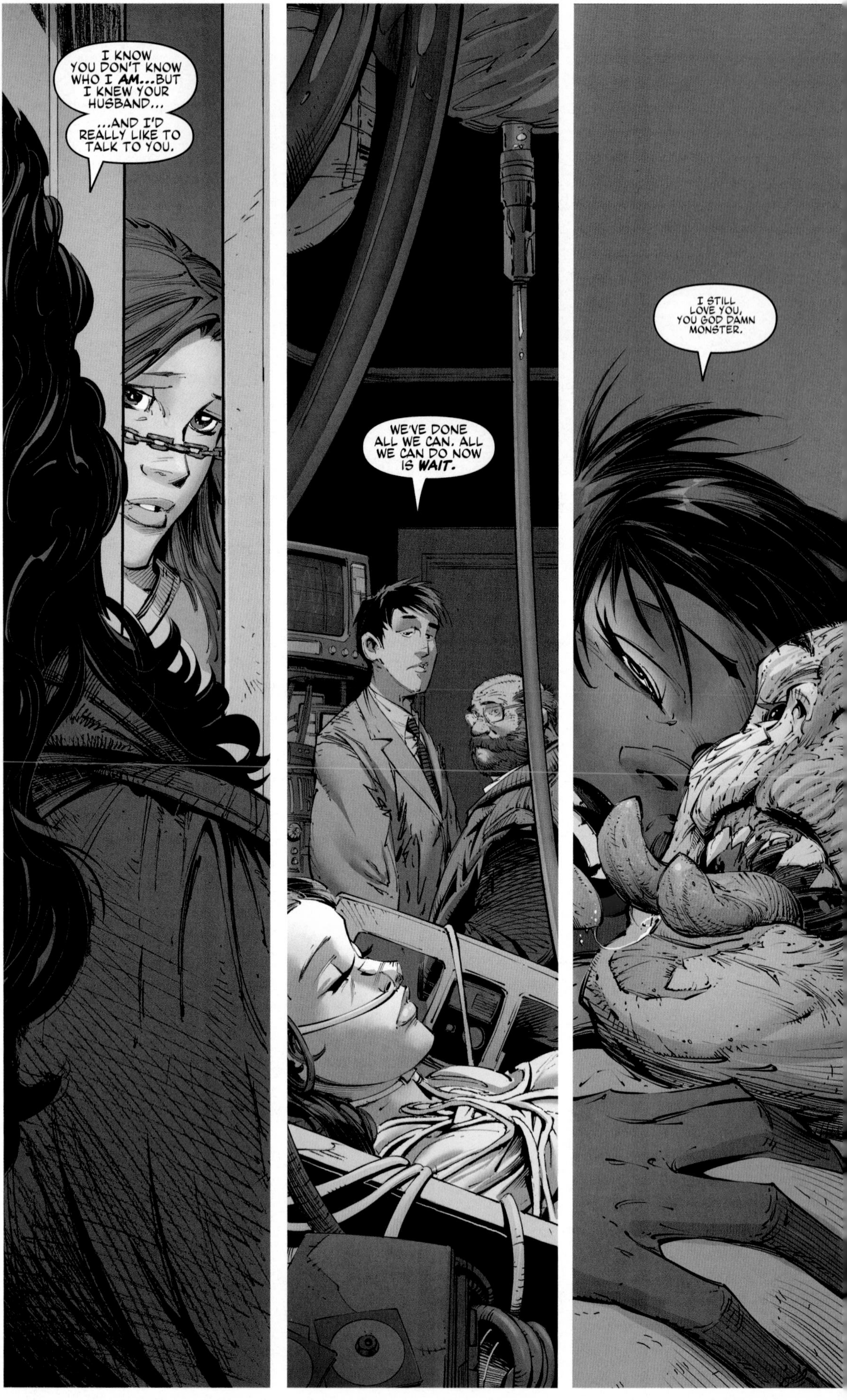
I KNOW YOU DON'T KNOW WHO I AM...BUT I KNEW YOUR HUSBAND...
...AND I'D REALLY LIKE TO TALK TO YOU.
WE'VE DONE ALL WE CAN. ALL WE CAN DO NOW IS WAIT.
I STILL LOVE YOU, YOU GOD DAMN MONSTER.

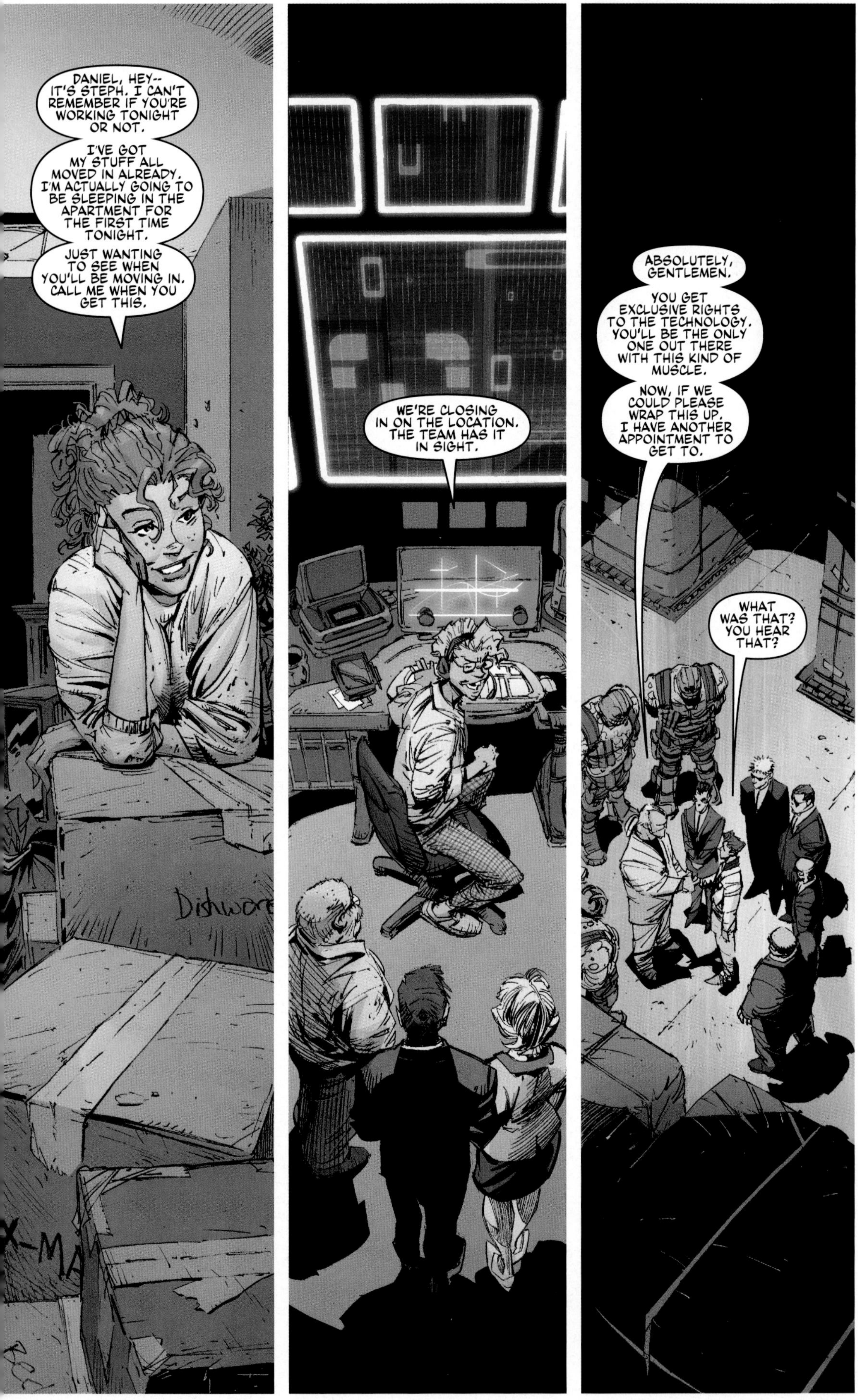
DANIEL, HEY-- IT'S STEPH. I CAN'T REMEMBER IF YOU'RE WORKING TONIGHT OR NOT.
I'VE GOT MY STUFF ALL MOVED IN ALREADY. I'M ACTUALLY GOING TO BE SLEEPING IN THE APARTMENT FOR THE FIRST TIME TONIGHT.
JUST WANTING TO SEE WHEN YOU'LL BE MOVING IN. CALL ME WHEN YOU GET THIS.
Dishware
X-MA
WE'RE CLOSING IN ON THE LOCATION. THE TEAM HAS IT IN SIGHT.
ABSOLUTELY, GENTLEMEN.
YOU GET EXCLUSIVE RIGHTS TO THE TECHNOLOGY. YOU'LL BE THE ONLY ONE OUT THERE WITH THIS KIND OF MUSCLE.
NOW, IF WE COULD PLEASE WRAP THIS UP. I HAVE ANOTHER APPOINTMENT TO GET TO.
WHAT WAS THAT? YOU HEAR THAT?

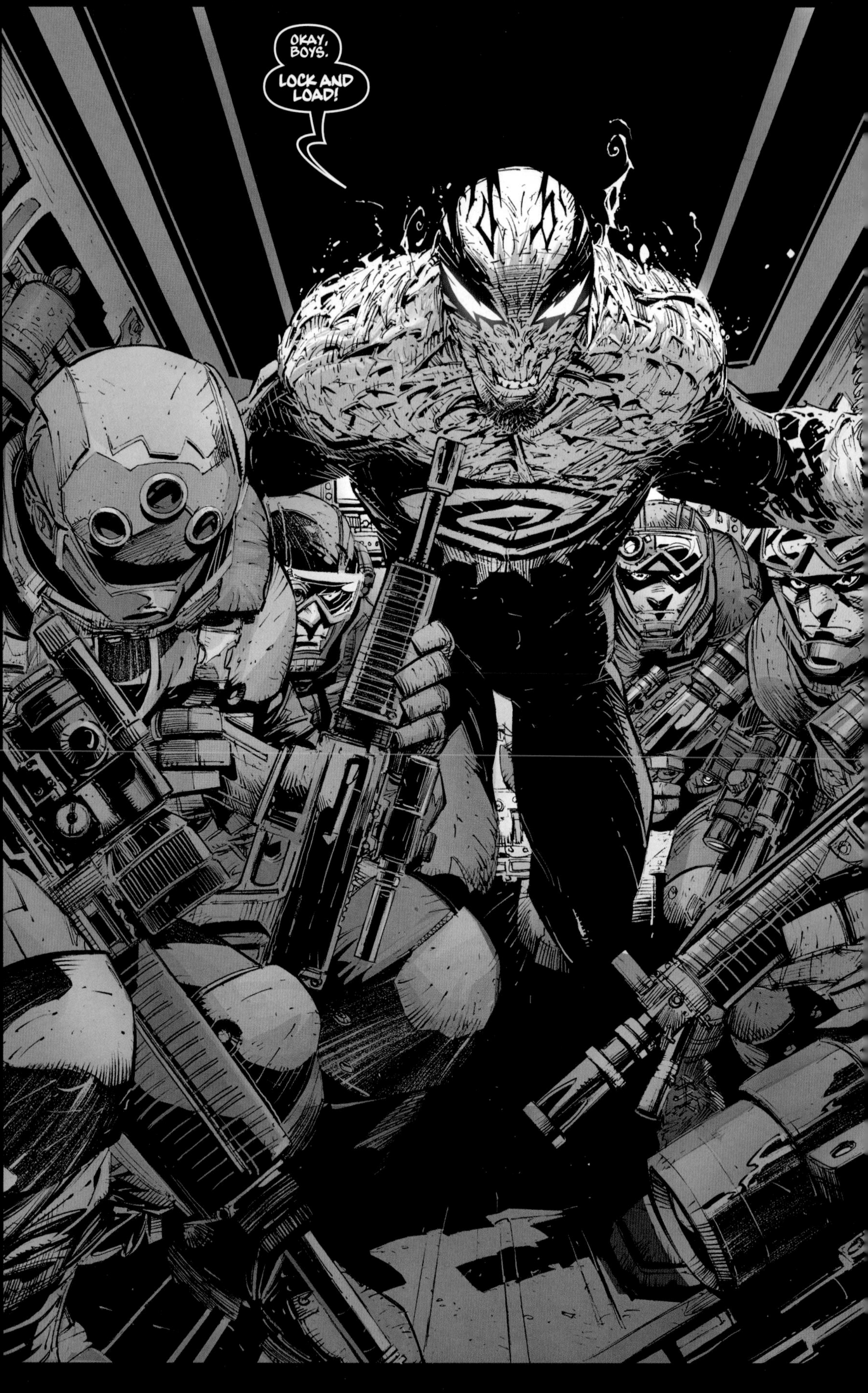
OKAY, BOYS.
LOCK AND LOAD!

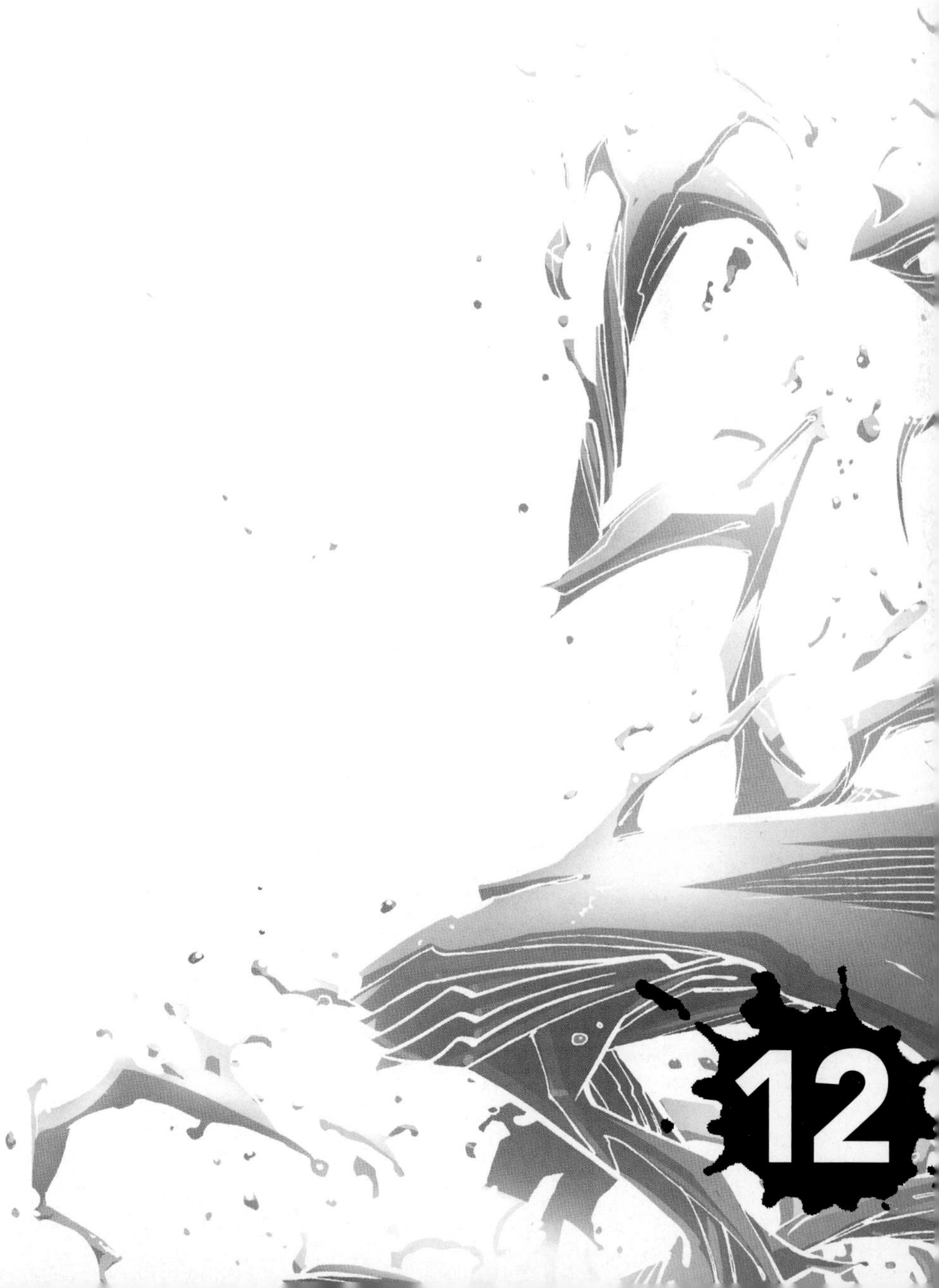
12

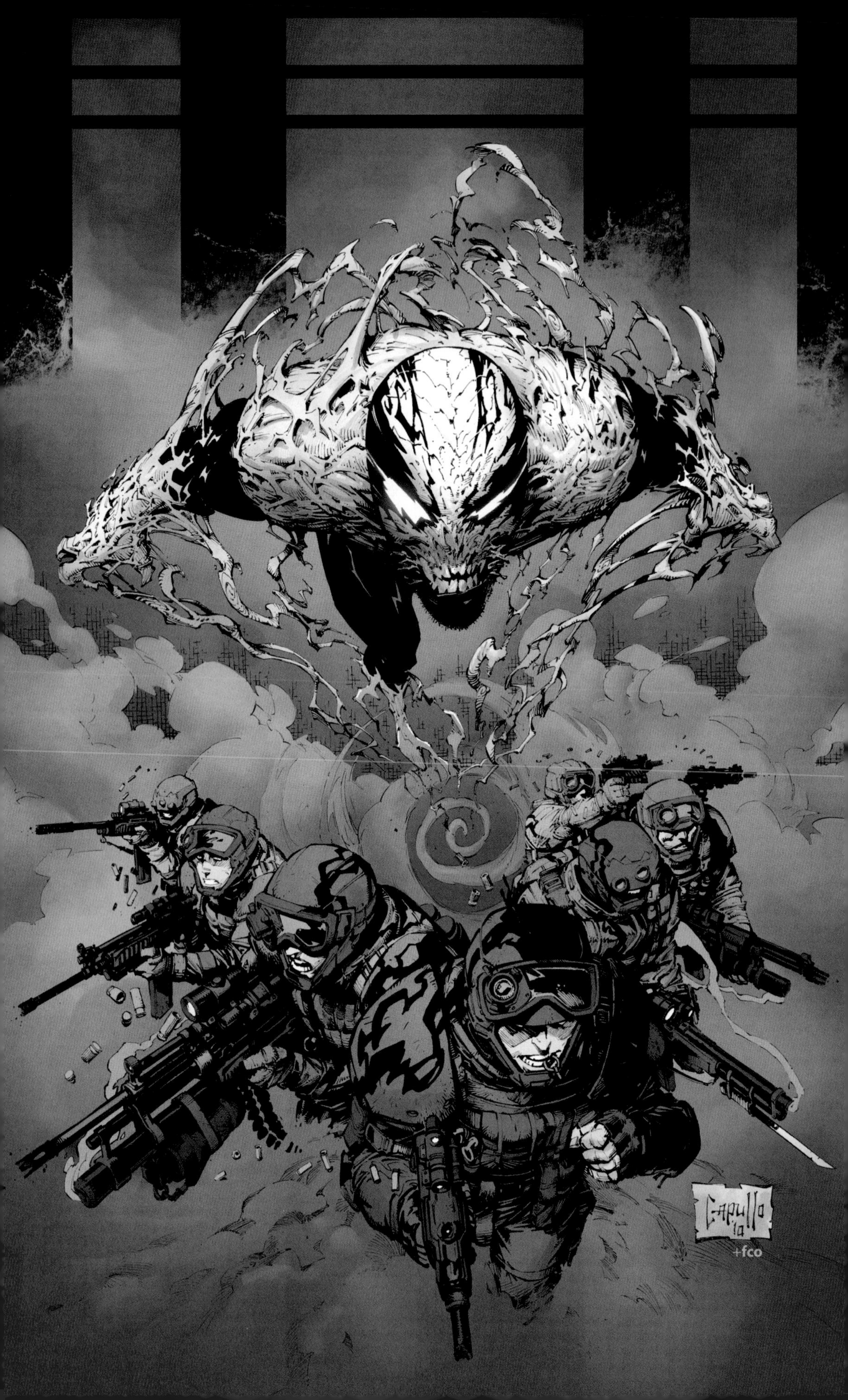

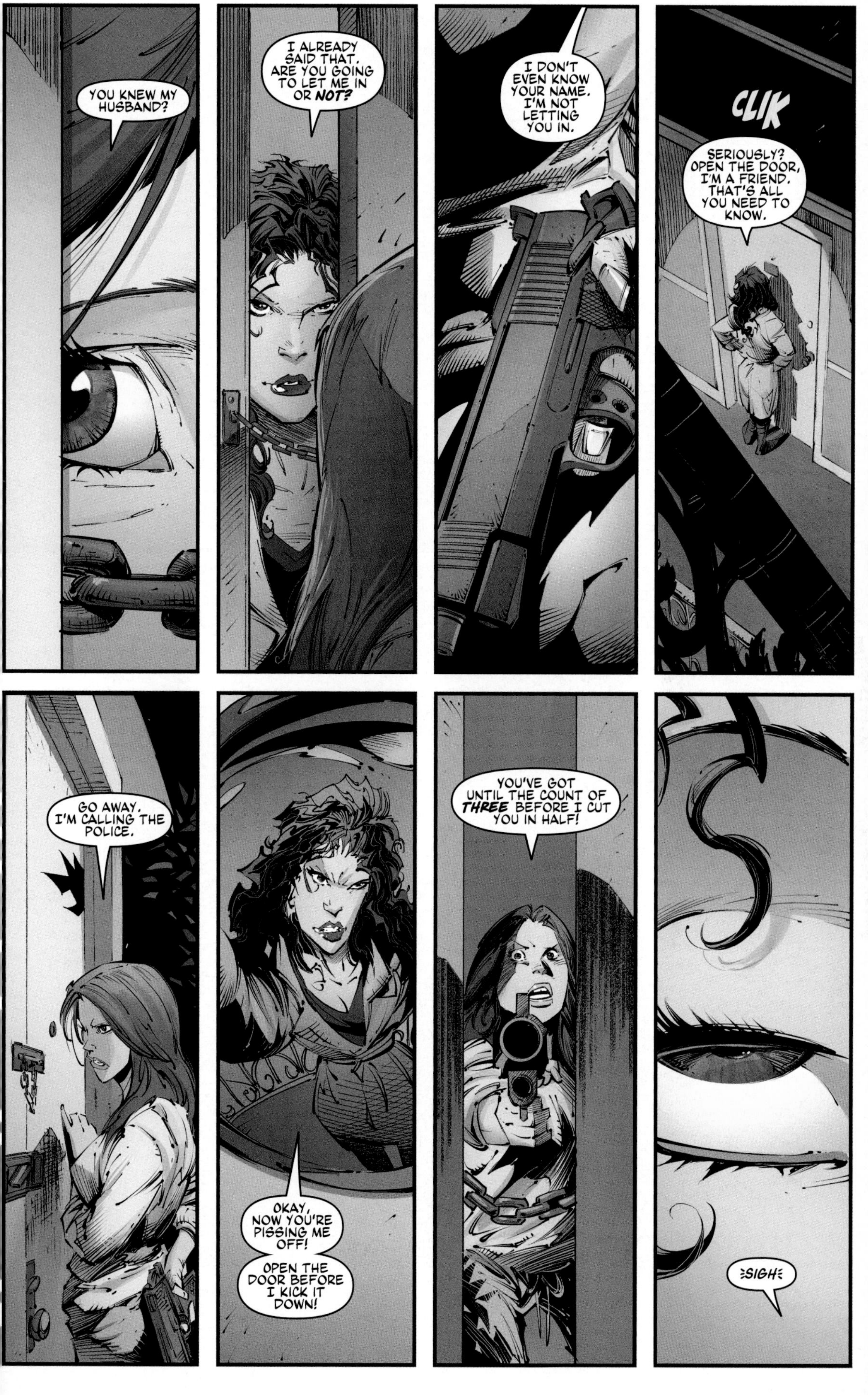
YOU KNEW MY HUSBAND?
I ALREADY SAID THAT. ARE YOU GOING TO LET ME IN OR NOT?
I DON'T EVEN KNOW YOUR NAME. I'M NOT LETTING YOU IN.
CLIK
SERIOUSLY? OPEN THE DOOR, I'M A FRIEND. THAT'S ALL YOU NEED TO KNOW.
GO AWAY. I'M CALLING THE POLICE.
OKAY, NOW YOU'RE PISSING ME OFF!
OPEN THE DOOR BEFORE I KICK IT DOWN!
YOU'VE GOT UNTIL THE COUNT OF THREE BEFORE I CUT YOU IN HALF!
SIGH

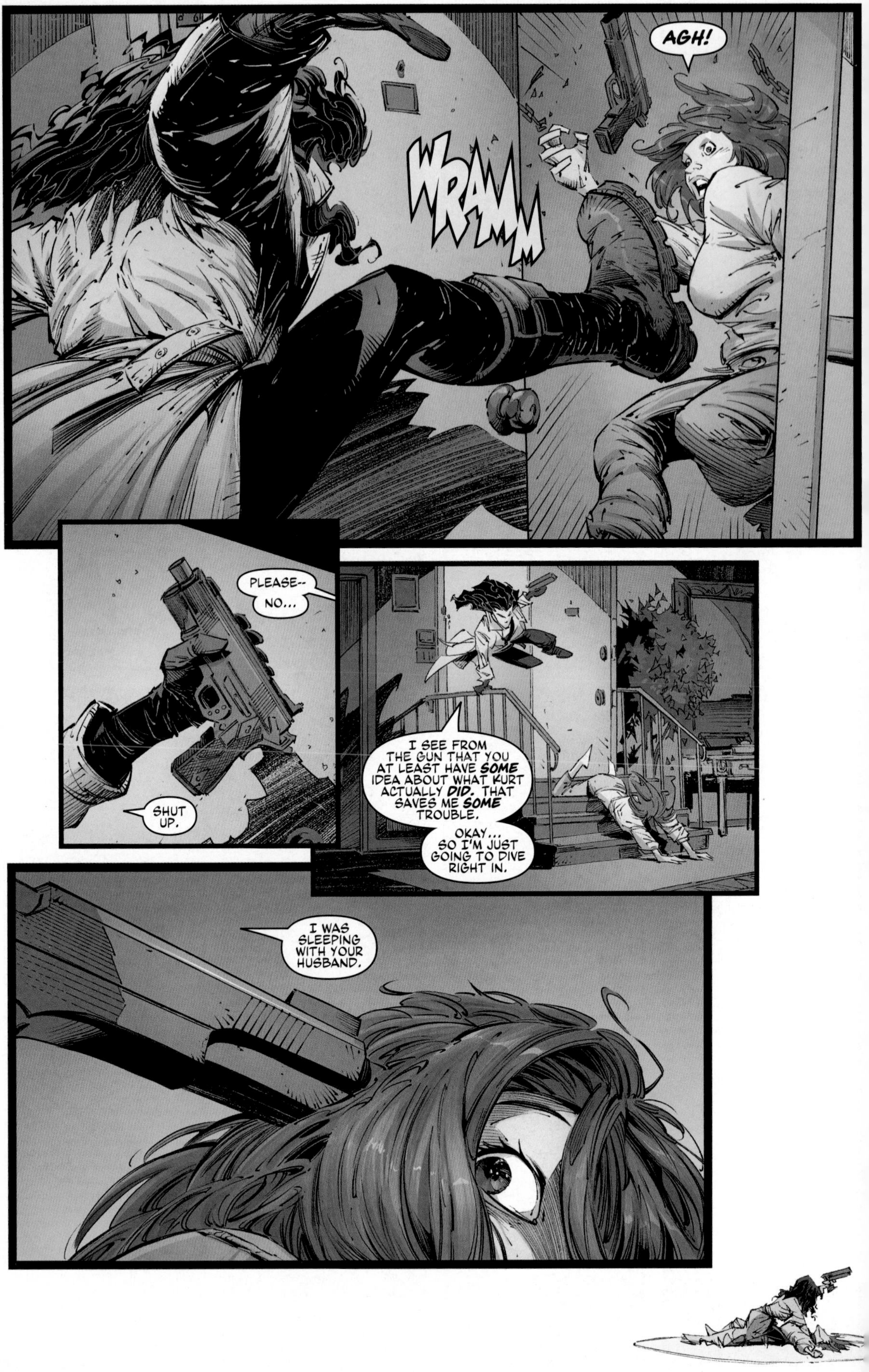
AGH!
WRAMM
PLEASE--
NO...
SHUT UP.
I SEE FROM THE GUN THAT YOU AT LEAST HAVE *SOME* IDEA ABOUT WHAT KURT ACTUALLY *DID*. THAT SAVES ME *SOME* TROUBLE.
OKAY... SO I'M JUST GOING TO DIVE RIGHT IN.
I WAS SLEEPING WITH YOUR HUSBAND.

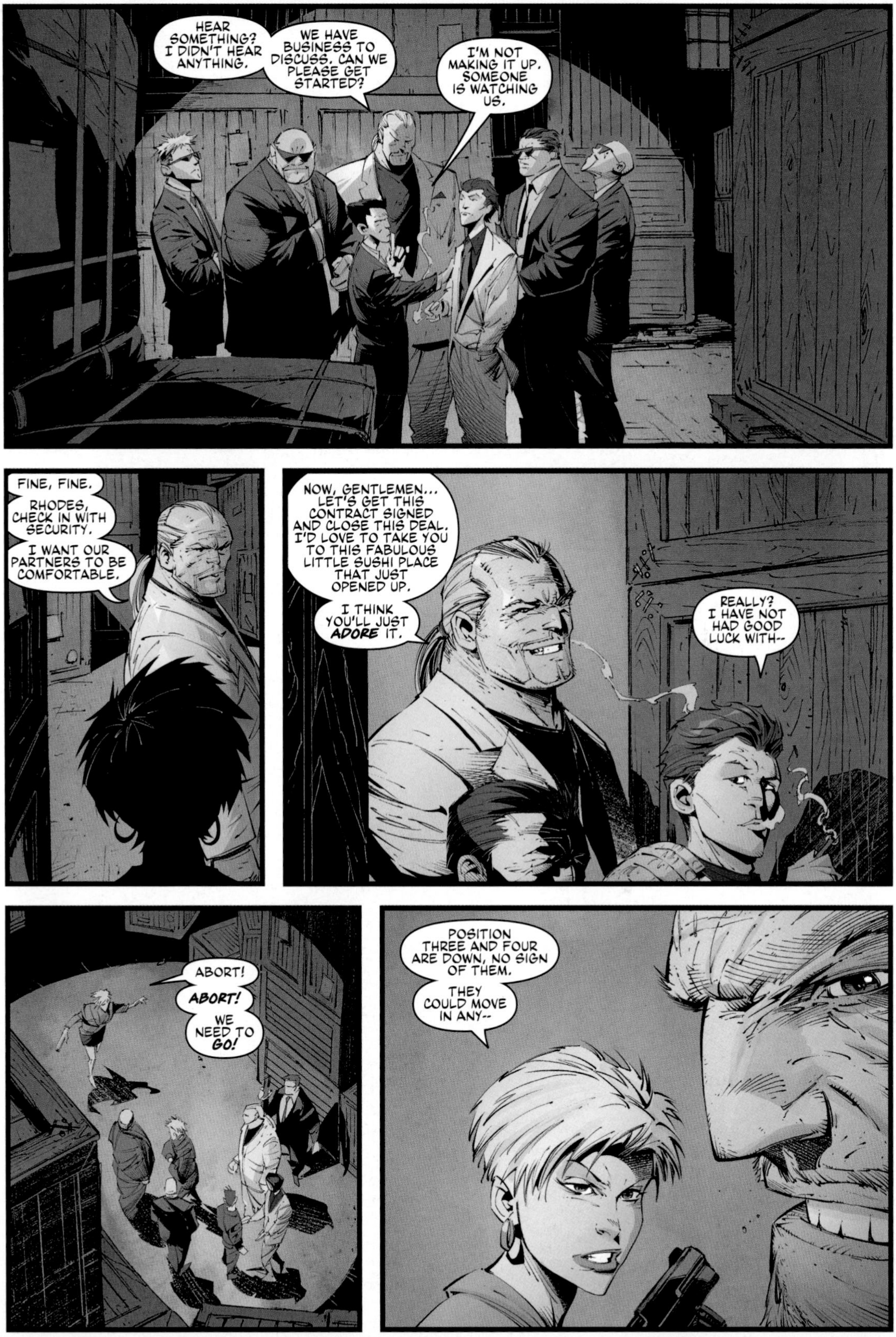
HEAR SOMETHING? I DIDN'T HEAR ANYTHING.
WE HAVE BUSINESS TO DISCUSS. CAN WE PLEASE GET STARTED?
I'M NOT MAKING IT UP. SOMEONE IS WATCHING US.
FINE, FINE.
RHODES, CHECK IN WITH SECURITY.
I WANT OUR PARTNERS TO BE COMFORTABLE.
NOW, GENTLEMEN... LET'S GET THIS CONTRACT SIGNED AND CLOSE THIS DEAL. I'D LOVE TO TAKE YOU TO THIS FABULOUS LITTLE SUSHI PLACE THAT JUST OPENED UP.
I THINK YOU'LL JUST ADORE IT.
REALLY? I HAVE NOT HAD GOOD LUCK WITH--
ABORT!
ABORT!
WE NEED TO GO!
POSITION THREE AND FOUR ARE DOWN, NO SIGN OF THEM.
THEY COULD MOVE IN ANY--

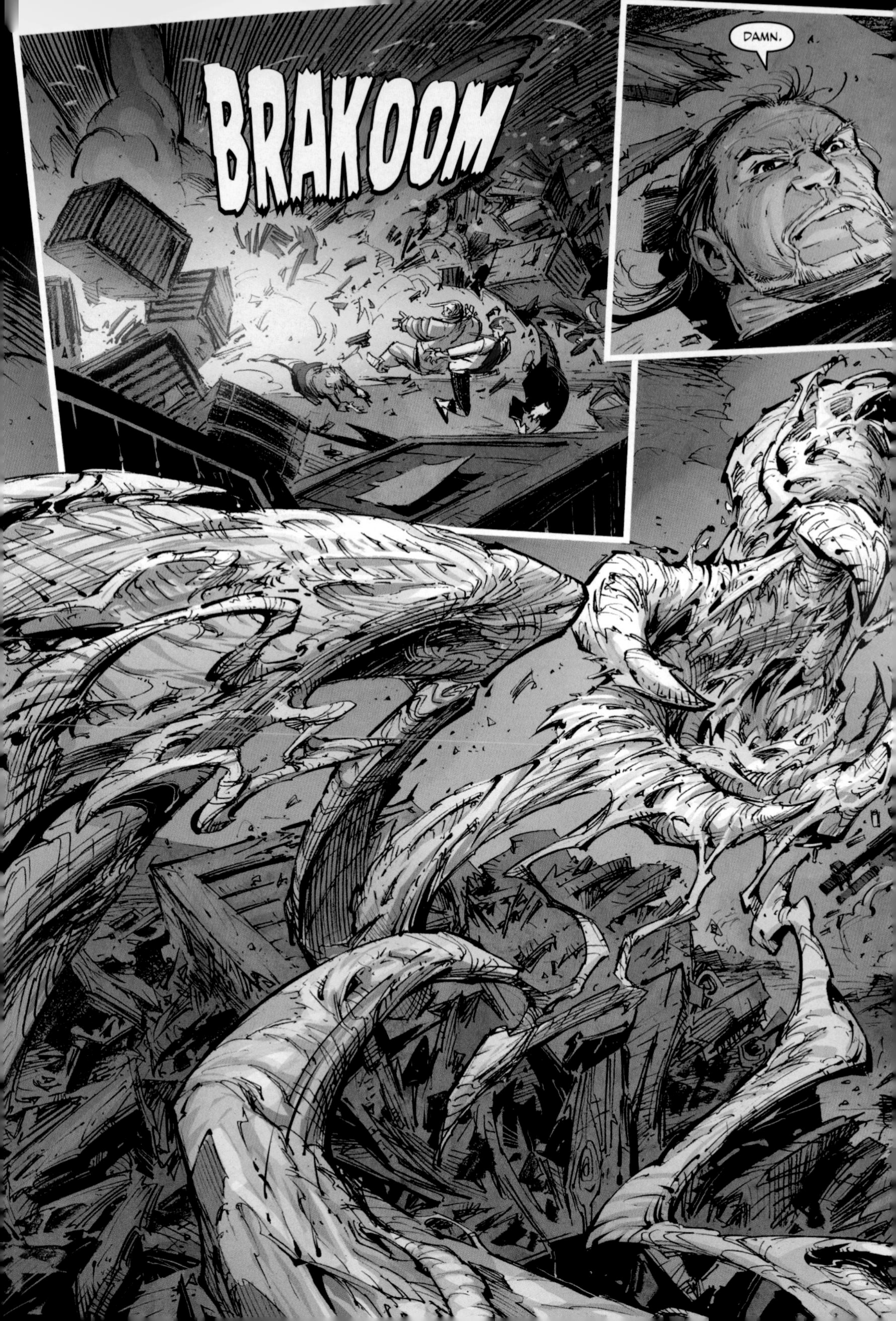
BRAKOOM
DAMN.

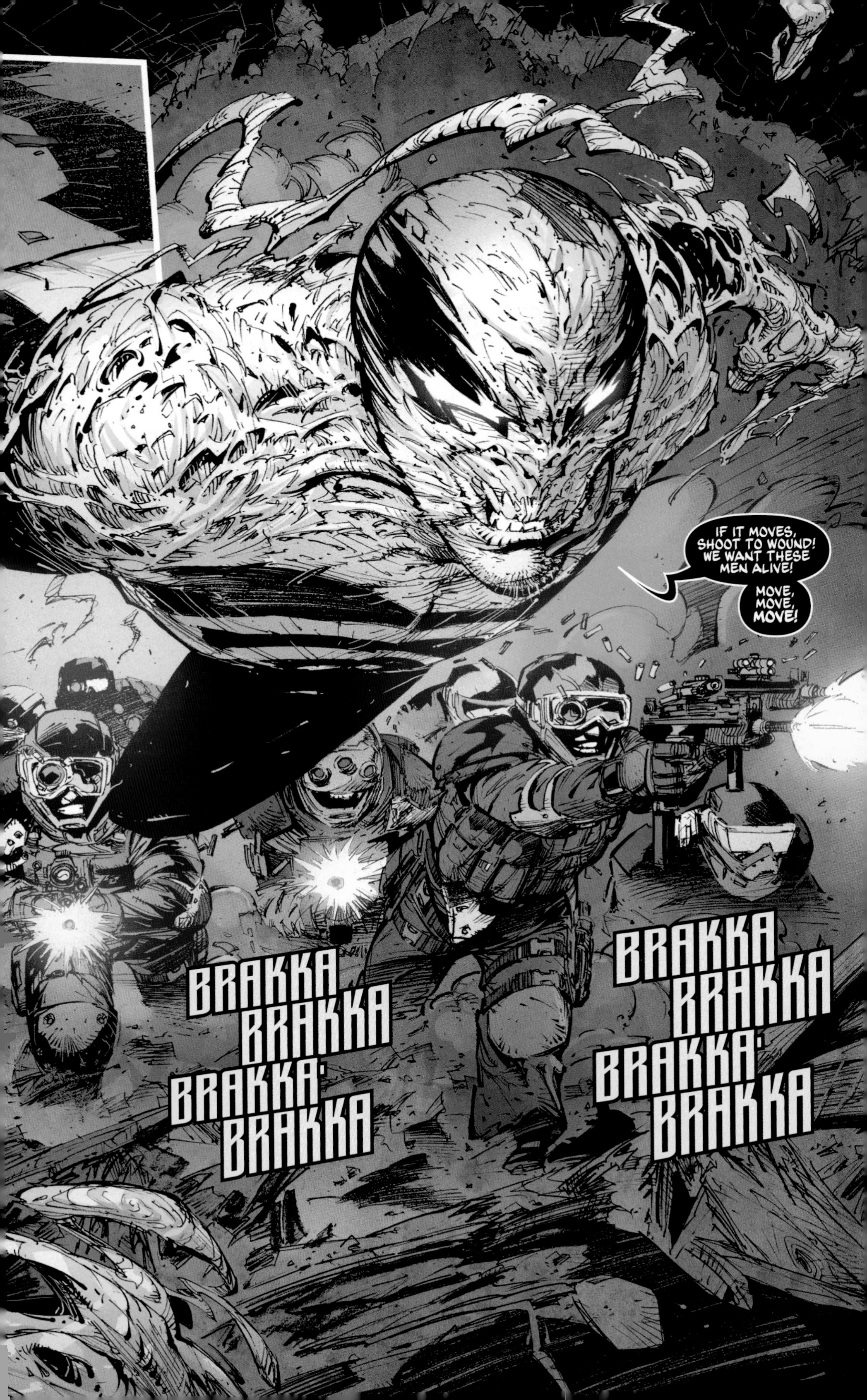
IF IT MOVES, SHOOT TO WOUND! WE WANT THESE MEN ALIVE!
MOVE, MOVE, MOVE!
BRAKKA BRAKKA BRAKKA BRAKKA
BRAKKA BRAKKA BRAKKA BRAKKA

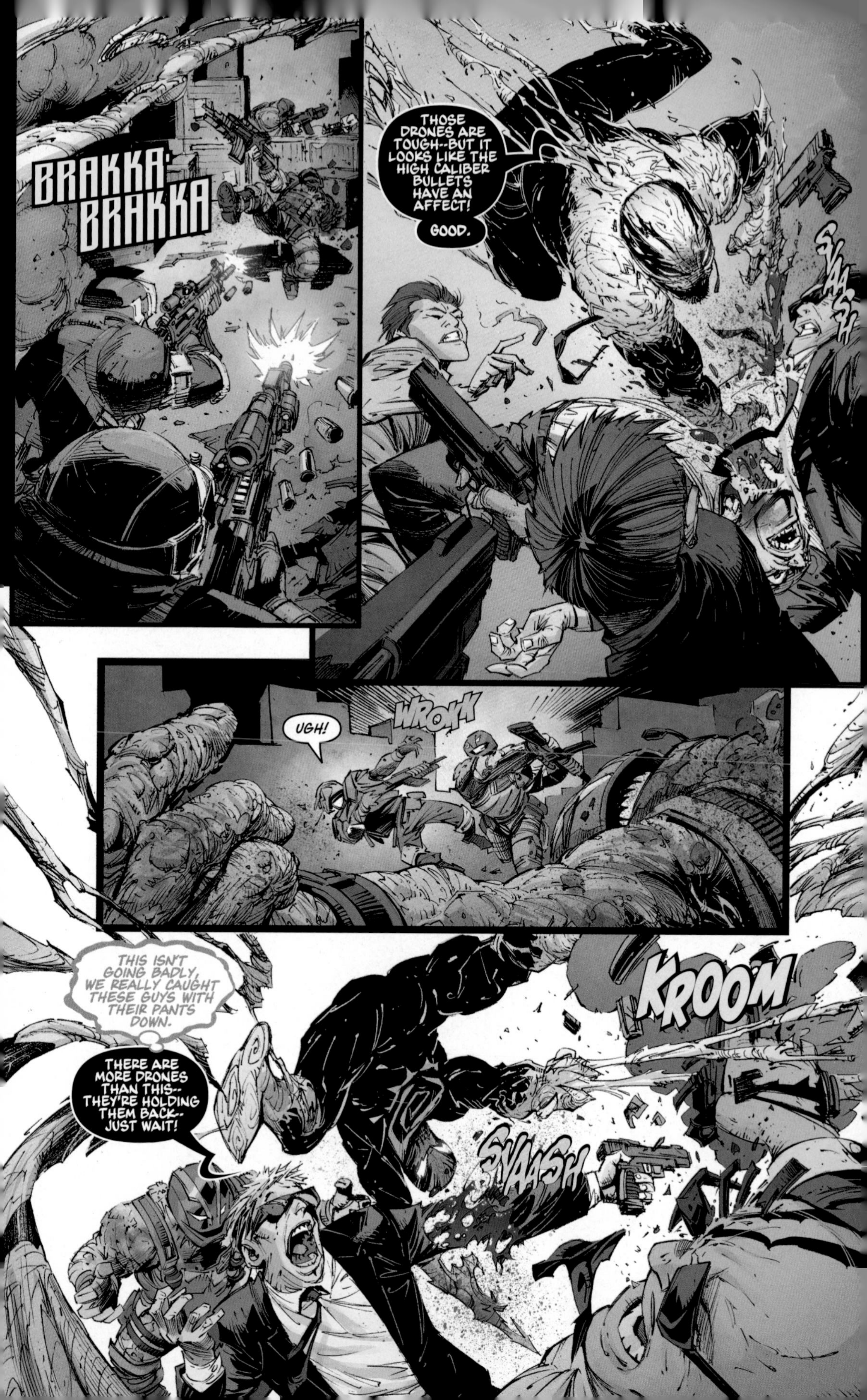
BRAKKA-BRAKKA
THOSE DRONES ARE TOUGH--BUT IT LOOKS LIKE THE HIGH CALIBER BULLETS HAVE AN AFFECT!
GOOD.
SVAASH
UGH!
WROKK
THIS ISN'T GOING BADLY, WE REALLY CAUGHT THESE GUYS WITH THEIR PANTS DOWN.
THERE ARE MORE DRONES THAN THIS-- THEY'RE HOLDING THEM BACK-- JUST WAIT!
KROOM
SVAASH

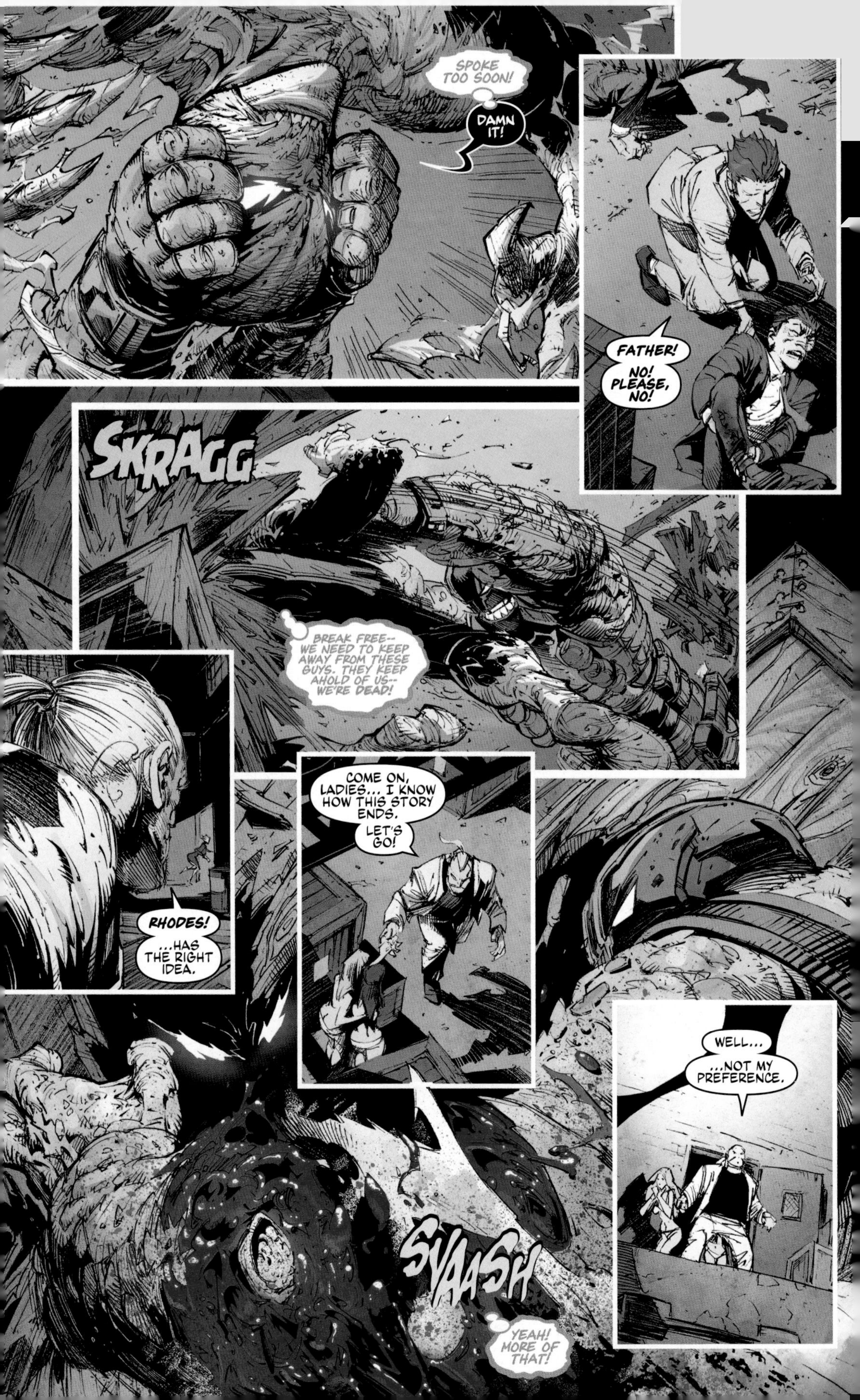
SPOKE TOO SOON!
DAMN IT!
FATHER!
NO! PLEASE, NO!
SKRAGG
BREAK FREE-- WE NEED TO KEEP AWAY FROM THESE GUYS. THEY KEEP AHOLD OF US-- WE'RE DEAD!
RHODES!
...HAS THE RIGHT IDEA.
COME ON, LADIES... I KNOW HOW THIS STORY ENDS.
LET'S GO!
WELL...
...NOT MY PREFERENCE.
SYAASH
YEAH! MORE OF THAT!

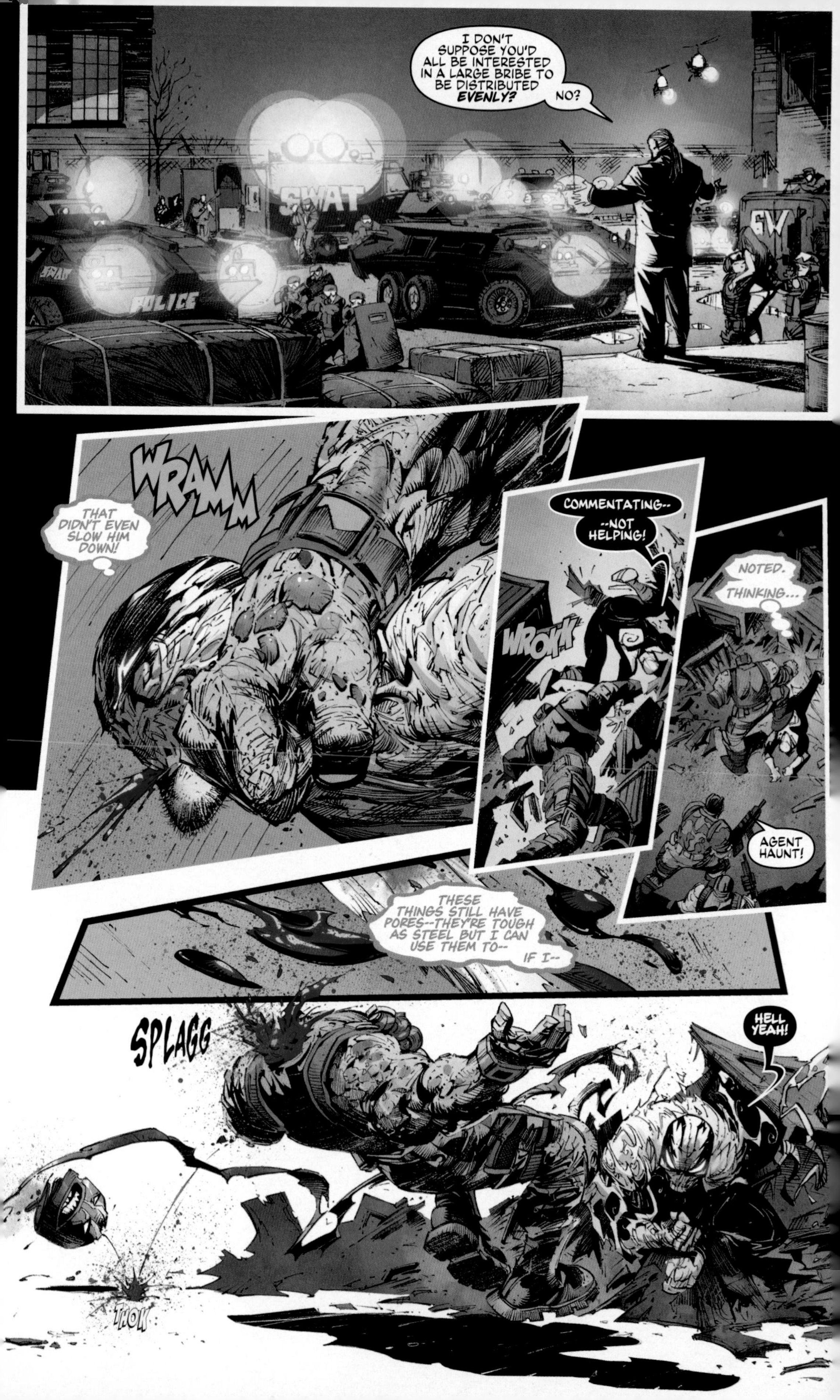

I DON'T SUPPOSE YOU'D ALL BE INTERESTED IN A LARGE BRIBE TO BE DISTRIBUTED EVENLY?
NO?
SWAT
POLICE
WRAMM
THAT DIDN'T EVEN SLOW HIM DOWN!
COMMENTATING--
--NOT HELPING!
WROKK
NOTED.
THINKING...
AGENT HAUNT!
THESE THINGS STILL HAVE PORES--THEY'RE TOUGH AS STEEL BUT I CAN USE THEM TO--
IF I--
SPLAGG
HELL YEAH!
THOK

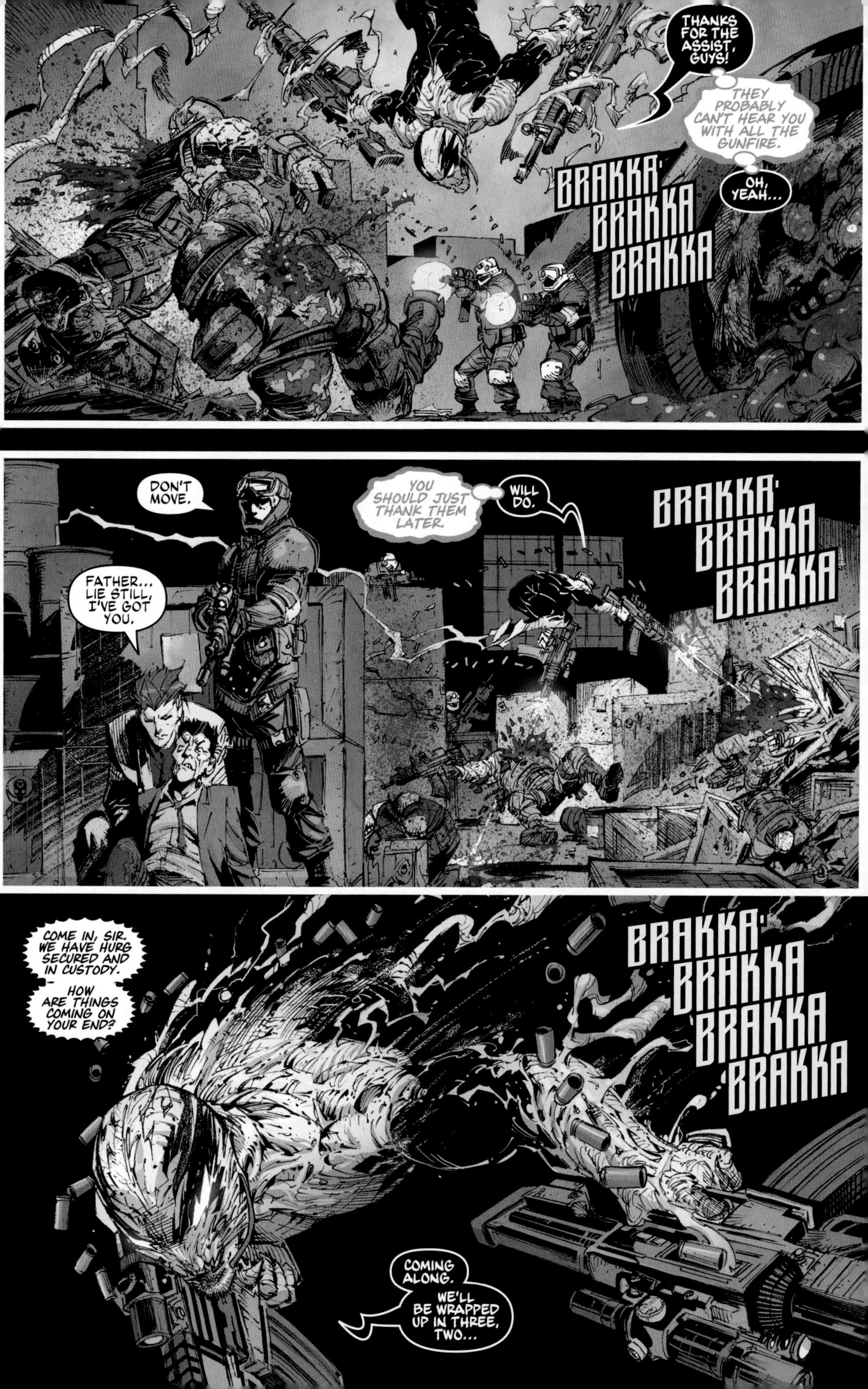

THANKS FOR THE ASSIST, GUYS!
THEY PROBABLY CAN'T HEAR YOU WITH ALL THE GUNFIRE.
OH, YEAH...
BRAKKA BRAKKA BRAKKA
DON'T MOVE.
FATHER... LIE STILL, I'VE GOT YOU.
YOU SHOULD JUST THANK THEM LATER.
WILL DO.
BRAKKA BRAKKA BRAKKA
COME IN, SIR. WE HAVE HURG SECURED AND IN CUSTODY.
HOW ARE THINGS COMING ON YOUR END?
BRAKKA BRAKKA BRAKKA BRAKKA
COMING ALONG.
WE'LL BE WRAPPED UP IN THREE, TWO...

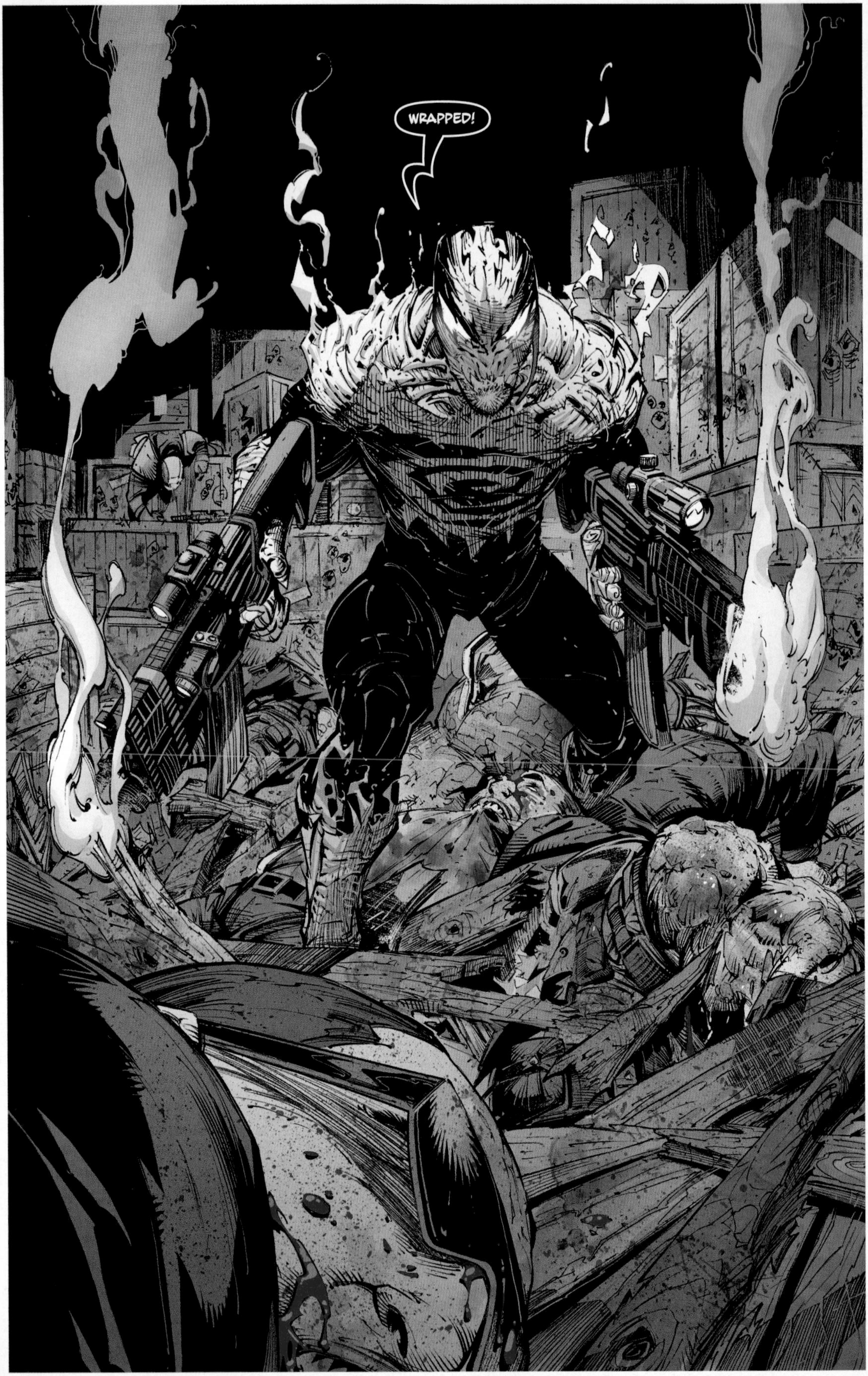
WRAPPED!

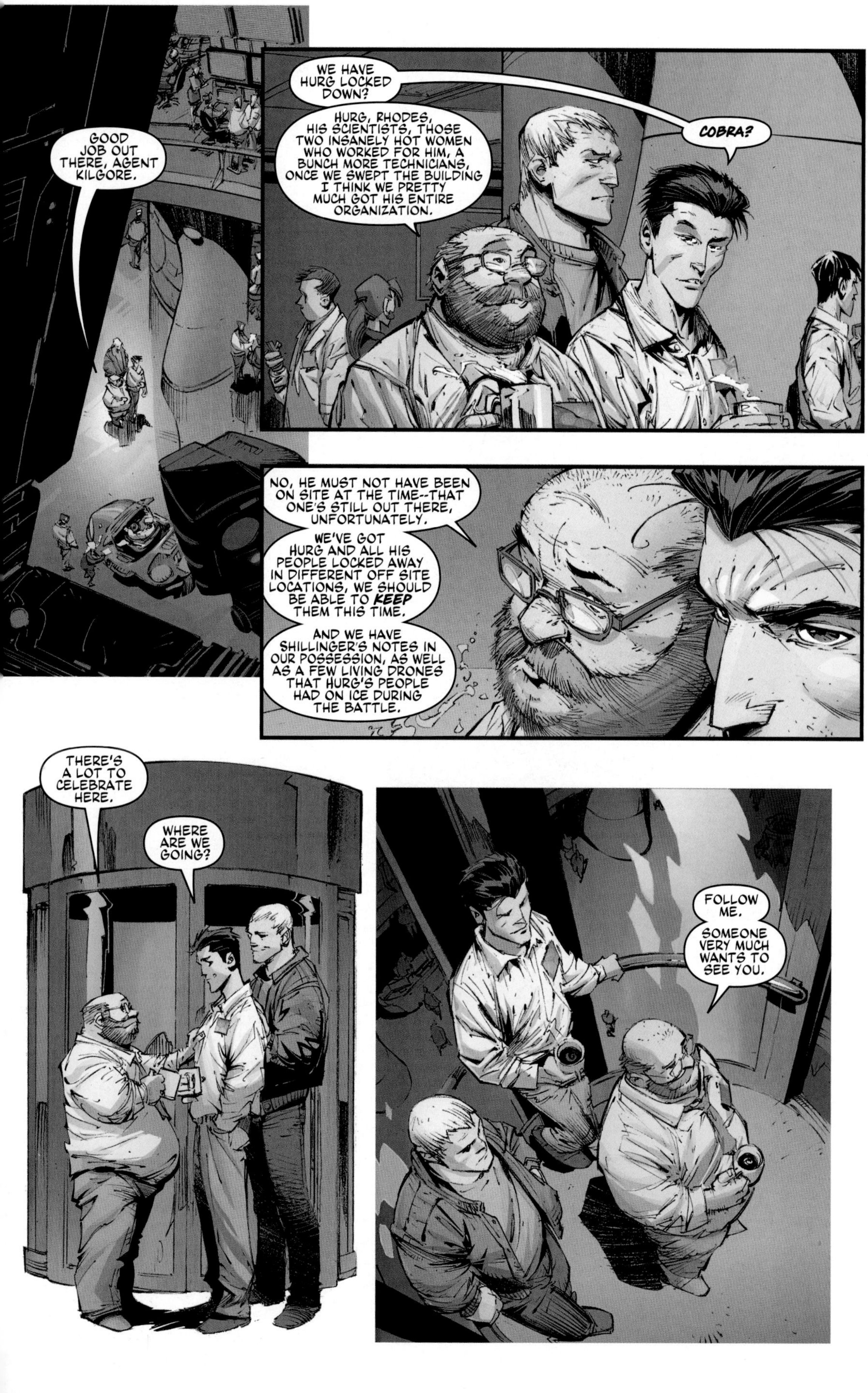
GOOD JOB OUT THERE, AGENT KILGORE.
WE HAVE HURG LOCKED DOWN?
COBRA?
HURG, RHODES, HIS SCIENTISTS, THOSE TWO INSANELY HOT WOMEN WHO WORKED FOR HIM, A BUNCH MORE TECHNICIANS, ONCE WE SWEPT THE BUILDING I THINK WE PRETTY MUCH GOT HIS ENTIRE ORGANIZATION.
NO, HE MUST NOT HAVE BEEN ON SITE AT THE TIME--THAT ONE'S STILL OUT THERE, UNFORTUNATELY.
WE'VE GOT HURG AND ALL HIS PEOPLE LOCKED AWAY IN DIFFERENT OFF SITE LOCATIONS, WE SHOULD BE ABLE TO KEEP THEM THIS TIME.
AND WE HAVE SHILLINGER'S NOTES IN OUR POSSESSION, AS WELL AS A FEW LIVING DRONES THAT HURG'S PEOPLE HAD ON ICE DURING THE BATTLE.
THERE'S A LOT TO CELEBRATE HERE.
WHERE ARE WE GOING?
FOLLOW ME.
SOMEONE VERY MUCH WANTS TO SEE YOU.

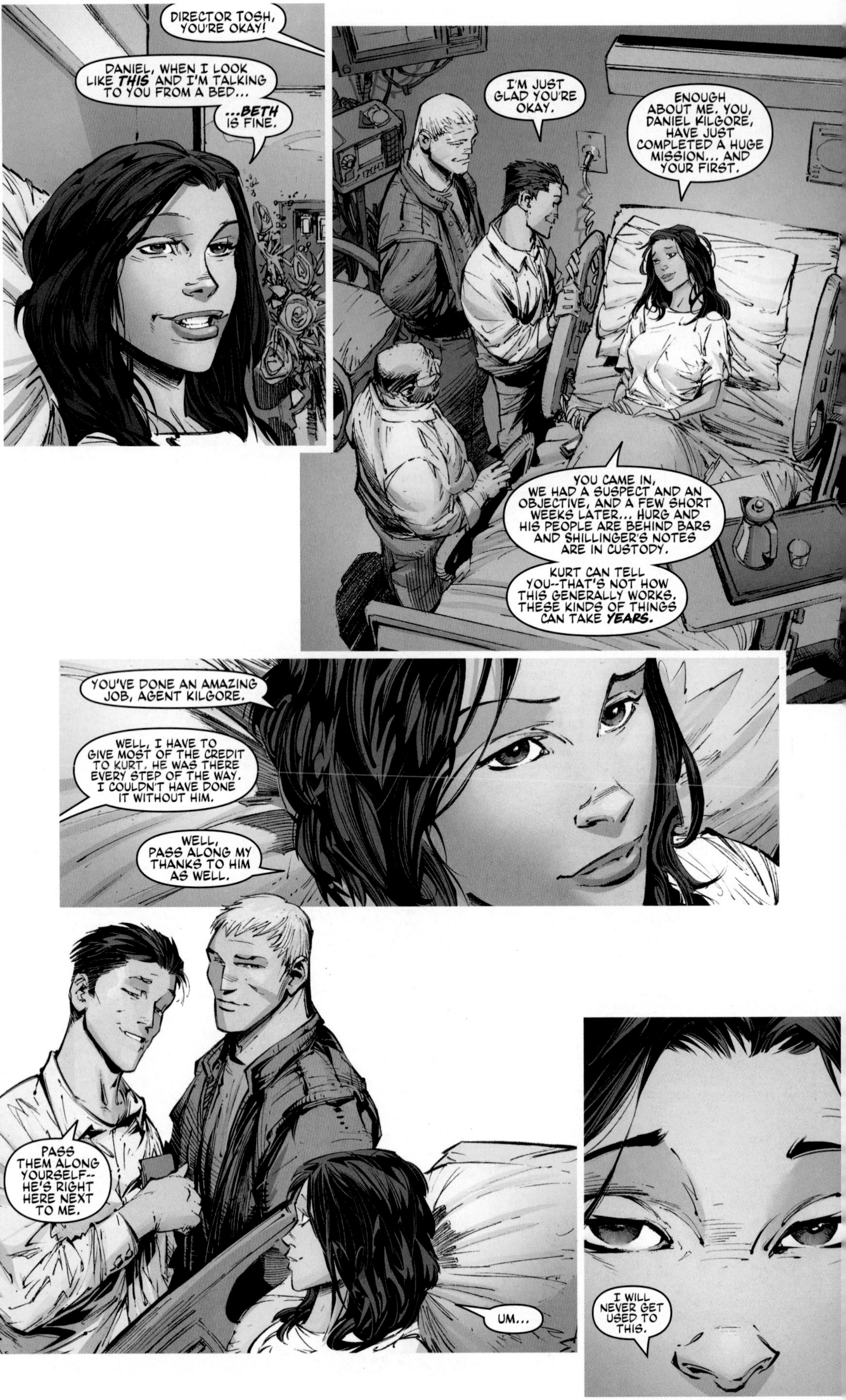

DIRECTOR TOSH, YOU'RE OKAY!
DANIEL, WHEN I LOOK LIKE ***THIS*** AND I'M TALKING TO YOU FROM A BED...
...***BETH*** IS FINE.
I'M JUST GLAD YOU'RE OKAY.
ENOUGH ABOUT ME. YOU, DANIEL KILGORE, HAVE JUST COMPLETED A HUGE MISSION... AND YOUR FIRST.
YOU CAME IN, WE HAD A SUSPECT AND AN OBJECTIVE, AND A FEW SHORT WEEKS LATER... HURG AND HIS PEOPLE ARE BEHIND BARS AND SHILLINGER'S NOTES ARE IN CUSTODY.
KURT CAN TELL YOU--THAT'S NOT HOW THIS GENERALLY WORKS. THESE KINDS OF THINGS CAN TAKE ***YEARS.***
YOU'VE DONE AN AMAZING JOB, AGENT KILGORE.
WELL, I HAVE TO GIVE MOST OF THE CREDIT TO KURT. HE WAS THERE EVERY STEP OF THE WAY. I COULDN'T HAVE DONE IT WITHOUT HIM.
WELL, PASS ALONG MY THANKS TO HIM AS WELL.
PASS THEM ALONG YOURSELF-- HE'S RIGHT HERE NEXT TO ME.
UM...
I WILL NEVER GET USED TO THIS.

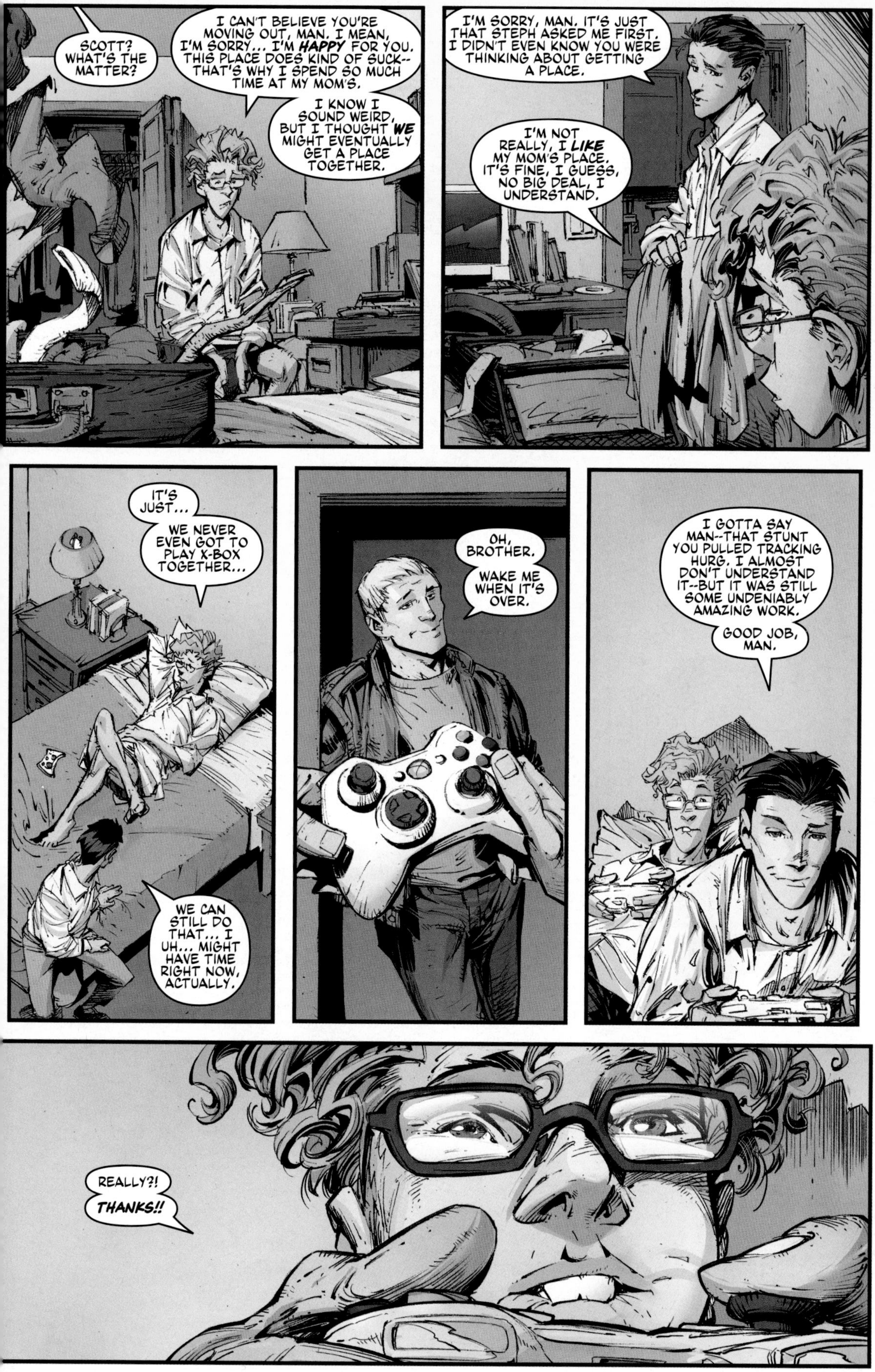
SCOTT? WHAT'S THE MATTER?
I CAN'T BELIEVE YOU'RE MOVING OUT, MAN. I MEAN, I'M SORRY... I'M HAPPY FOR YOU. THIS PLACE DOES KIND OF SUCK-- THAT'S WHY I SPEND SO MUCH TIME AT MY MOM'S.
I KNOW I SOUND WEIRD, BUT I THOUGHT WE MIGHT EVENTUALLY GET A PLACE TOGETHER.
I'M SORRY, MAN. IT'S JUST THAT STEPH ASKED ME FIRST. I DIDN'T EVEN KNOW YOU WERE THINKING ABOUT GETTING A PLACE.
I'M NOT REALLY, I LIKE MY MOM'S PLACE. IT'S FINE, I GUESS, NO BIG DEAL, I UNDERSTAND.
IT'S JUST...
WE NEVER EVEN GOT TO PLAY X-BOX TOGETHER...
WE CAN STILL DO THAT... I UH... MIGHT HAVE TIME RIGHT NOW, ACTUALLY.
OH, BROTHER.
WAKE ME WHEN IT'S OVER.
I GOTTA SAY MAN--THAT STUNT YOU PULLED TRACKING HURG. I ALMOST DON'T UNDERSTAND IT--BUT IT WAS STILL SOME UNDENIABLY AMAZING WORK.
GOOD JOB, MAN.
REALLY?! THANKS!!

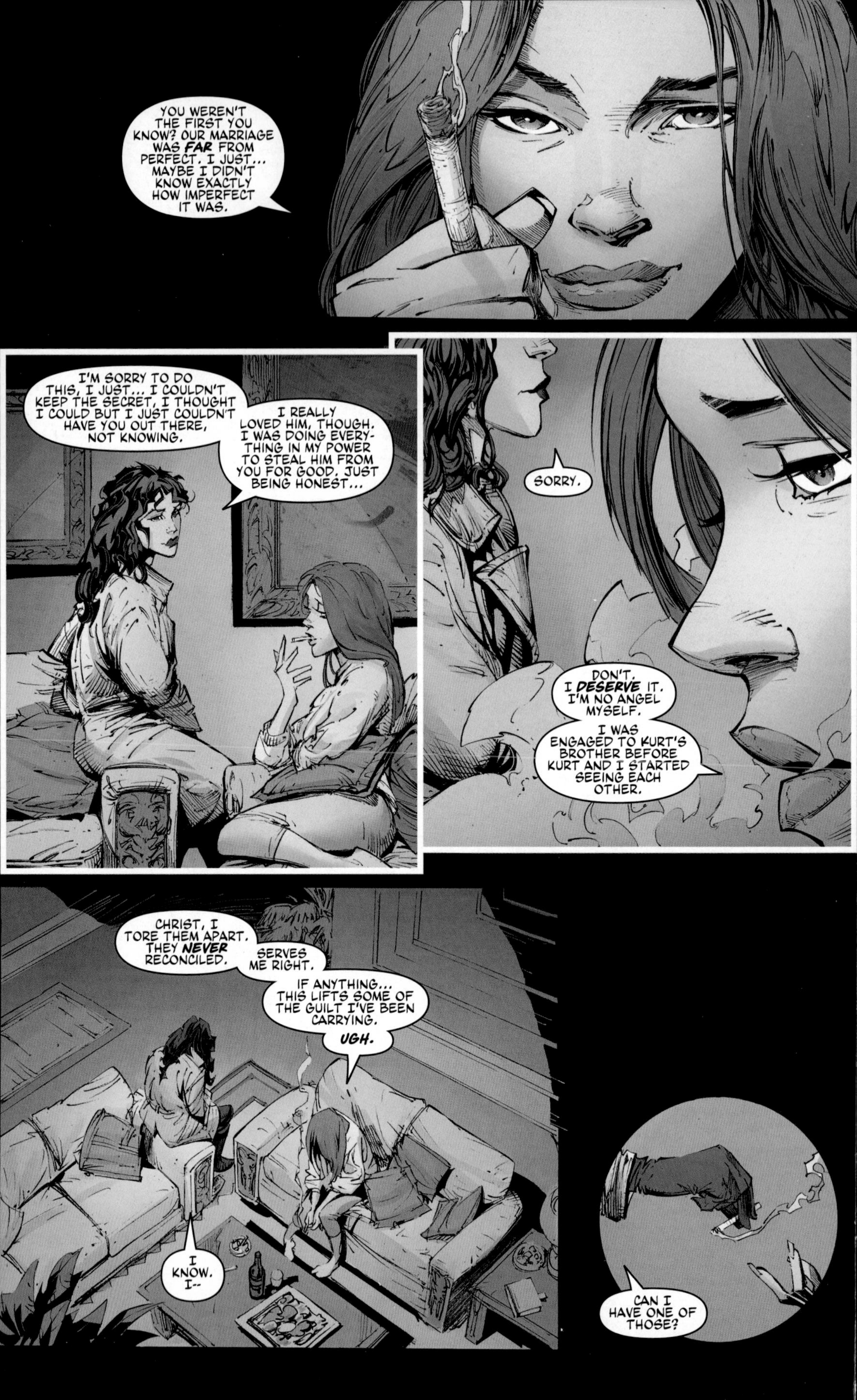
YOU WEREN'T THE FIRST YOU KNOW? OUR MARRIAGE WAS *FAR* FROM PERFECT. I JUST... MAYBE I DIDN'T KNOW EXACTLY HOW IMPERFECT IT WAS.
I'M SORRY TO DO THIS, I JUST... I COULDN'T KEEP THE SECRET, I THOUGHT I COULD BUT I JUST COULDN'T HAVE YOU OUT THERE, NOT KNOWING.
I REALLY LOVED HIM, THOUGH. I WAS DOING EVERY-THING IN MY POWER TO STEAL HIM FROM YOU FOR GOOD. JUST BEING HONEST...
SORRY.
DON'T. I *DESERVE* IT. I'M NO ANGEL MYSELF.
I WAS ENGAGED TO KURT'S BROTHER BEFORE KURT AND I STARTED SEEING EACH OTHER.
CHRIST, I TORE THEM APART. THEY *NEVER* RECONCILED.
SERVES ME RIGHT.
IF ANYTHING... THIS LIFTS SOME OF THE GUILT I'VE BEEN CARRYING.
UGH.
I KNOW. I--
CAN I HAVE ONE OF THOSE?

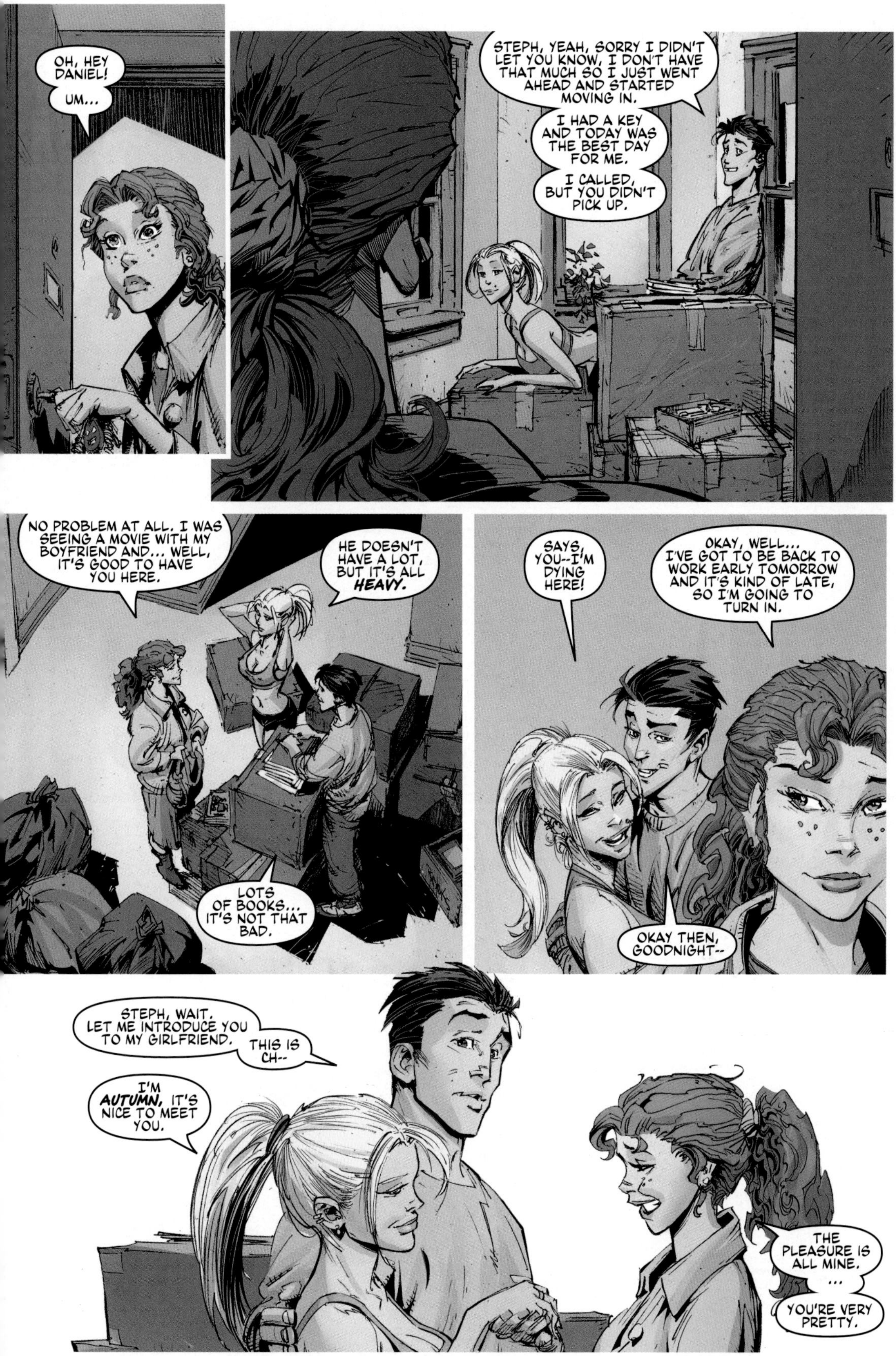
OH, HEY DANIEL!
UM...
STEPH, YEAH, SORRY I DIDN'T LET YOU KNOW, I DON'T HAVE THAT MUCH SO I JUST WENT AHEAD AND STARTED MOVING IN.
I HAD A KEY AND TODAY WAS THE BEST DAY FOR ME.
I CALLED, BUT YOU DIDN'T PICK UP.
NO PROBLEM AT ALL. I WAS SEEING A MOVIE WITH MY BOYFRIEND AND... WELL, IT'S GOOD TO HAVE YOU HERE.
HE DOESN'T HAVE A LOT, BUT IT'S ALL **HEAVY.**
LOTS OF BOOKS... IT'S NOT THAT BAD.
SAYS, YOU--I'M DYING HERE!
OKAY, WELL... I'VE GOT TO BE BACK TO WORK EARLY TOMORROW AND IT'S KIND OF LATE, SO I'M GOING TO TURN IN.
OKAY THEN, GOODNIGHT--
STEPH, WAIT. LET ME INTRODUCE YOU TO MY GIRLFRIEND.
THIS IS CH--
I'M **AUTUMN,** IT'S NICE TO MEET YOU.
THE PLEASURE IS ALL MINE.
...
YOU'RE VERY PRETTY.

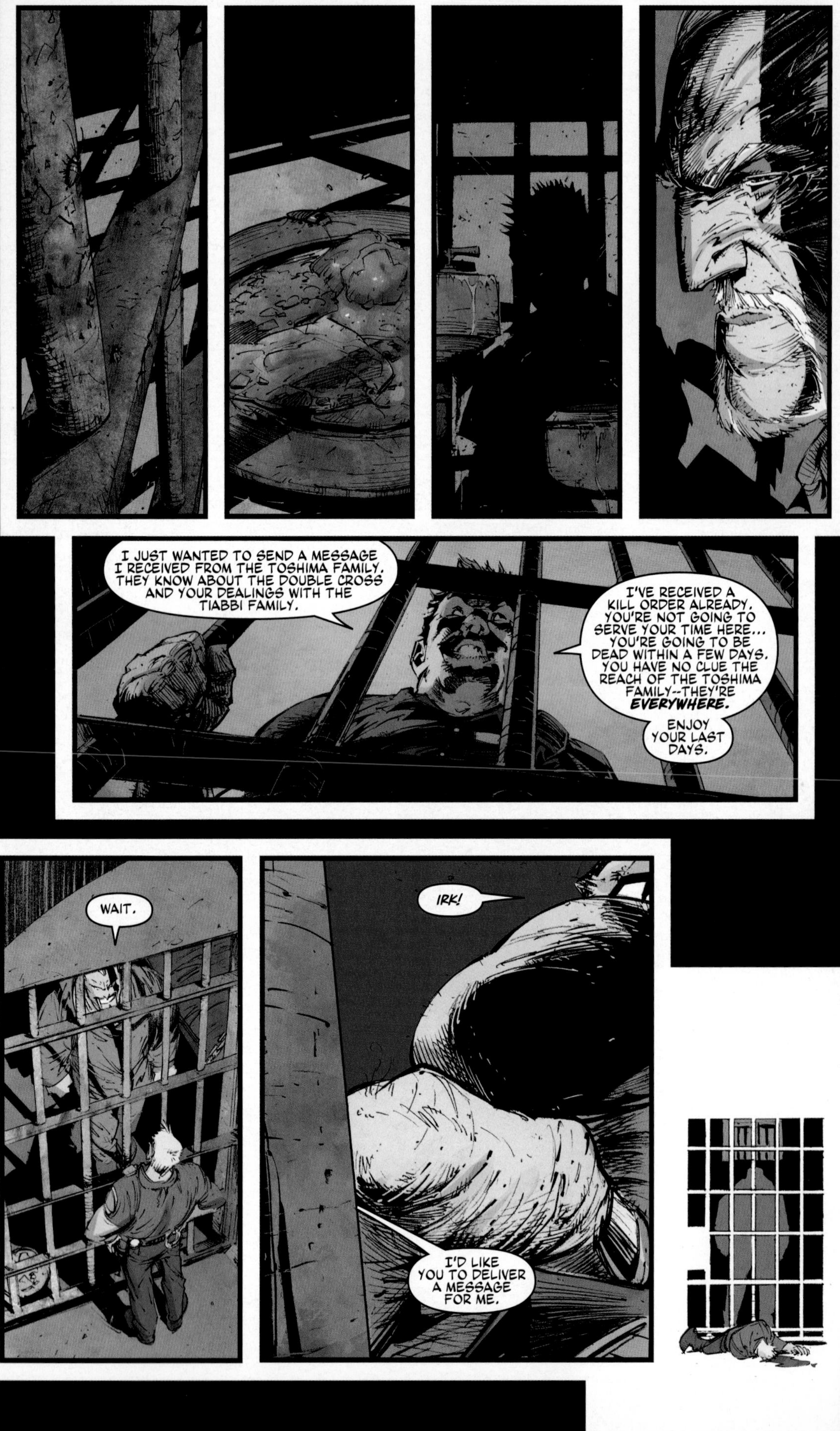
I JUST WANTED TO SEND A MESSAGE I RECEIVED FROM THE TOSHIMA FAMILY. THEY KNOW ABOUT THE DOUBLE CROSS AND YOUR DEALINGS WITH THE TIABBI FAMILY.
I'VE RECEIVED A KILL ORDER ALREADY. YOU'RE NOT GOING TO SERVE YOUR TIME HERE... YOU'RE GOING TO BE DEAD WITHIN A FEW DAYS. YOU HAVE NO CLUE THE REACH OF THE TOSHIMA FAMILY--THEY'RE ***EVERYWHERE.***
ENJOY YOUR LAST DAYS.
WAIT.
IRK!
I'D LIKE YOU TO DELIVER A MESSAGE FOR ME.

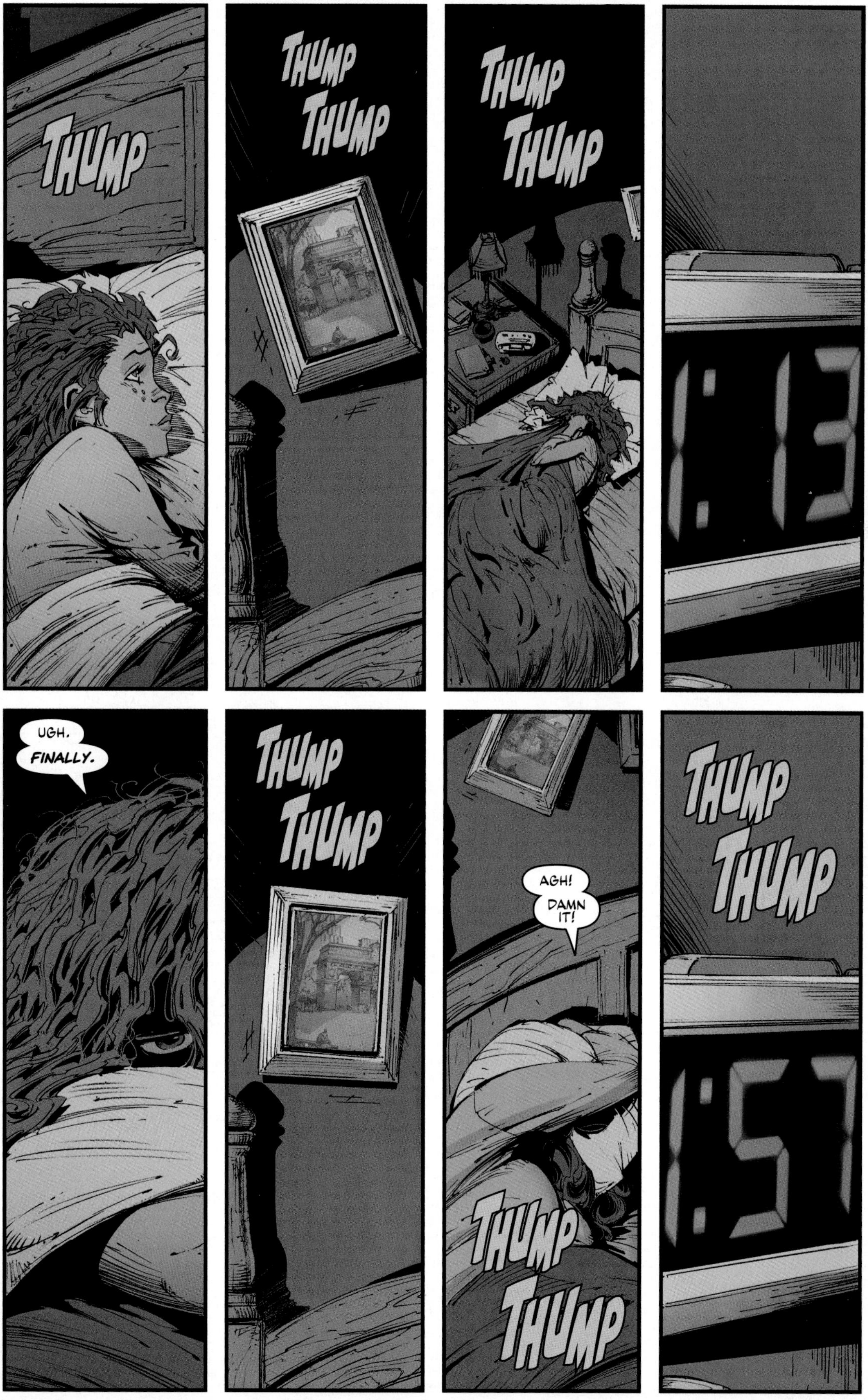
THUMP
THUMP
THUMP
THUMP
THUMP
1:13
UGH. FINALLY.
THUMP
THUMP
AGH! DAMN IT!
THUMP
THUMP
THUMP
THUMP
1:57

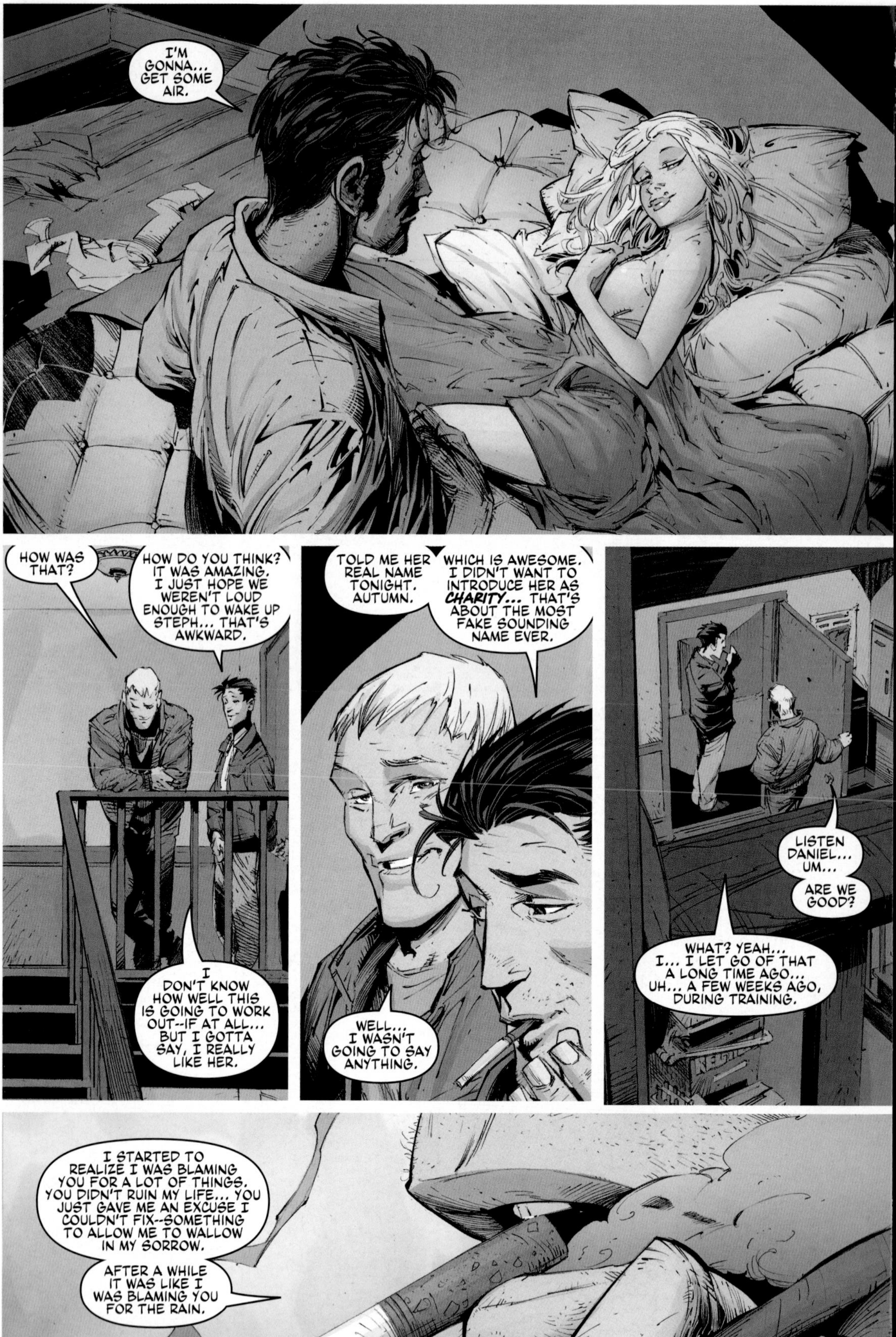
I'M GONNA... GET SOME AIR.
HOW WAS THAT?
HOW DO YOU THINK? IT WAS AMAZING. I JUST HOPE WE WEREN'T LOUD ENOUGH TO WAKE UP STEPH... THAT'S AWKWARD.
I DON'T KNOW HOW WELL THIS IS GOING TO WORK OUT--IF AT ALL... BUT I GOTTA SAY, I REALLY LIKE HER.
TOLD ME HER REAL NAME TONIGHT. AUTUMN.
WHICH IS AWESOME. I DIDN'T WANT TO INTRODUCE HER AS CHARITY... THAT'S ABOUT THE MOST FAKE SOUNDING NAME EVER.
WELL... I WASN'T GOING TO SAY ANYTHING.
LISTEN DANIEL... UM...
ARE WE GOOD?
WHAT? YEAH... I... I LET GO OF THAT A LONG TIME AGO... UH... A FEW WEEKS AGO, DURING TRAINING.
I STARTED TO REALIZE I WAS BLAMING YOU FOR A LOT OF THINGS. YOU DIDN'T RUIN MY LIFE... YOU JUST GAVE ME AN EXCUSE I COULDN'T FIX--SOMETHING TO ALLOW ME TO WALLOW IN MY SORROW.
AFTER A WHILE IT WAS LIKE I WAS BLAMING YOU FOR THE RAIN.

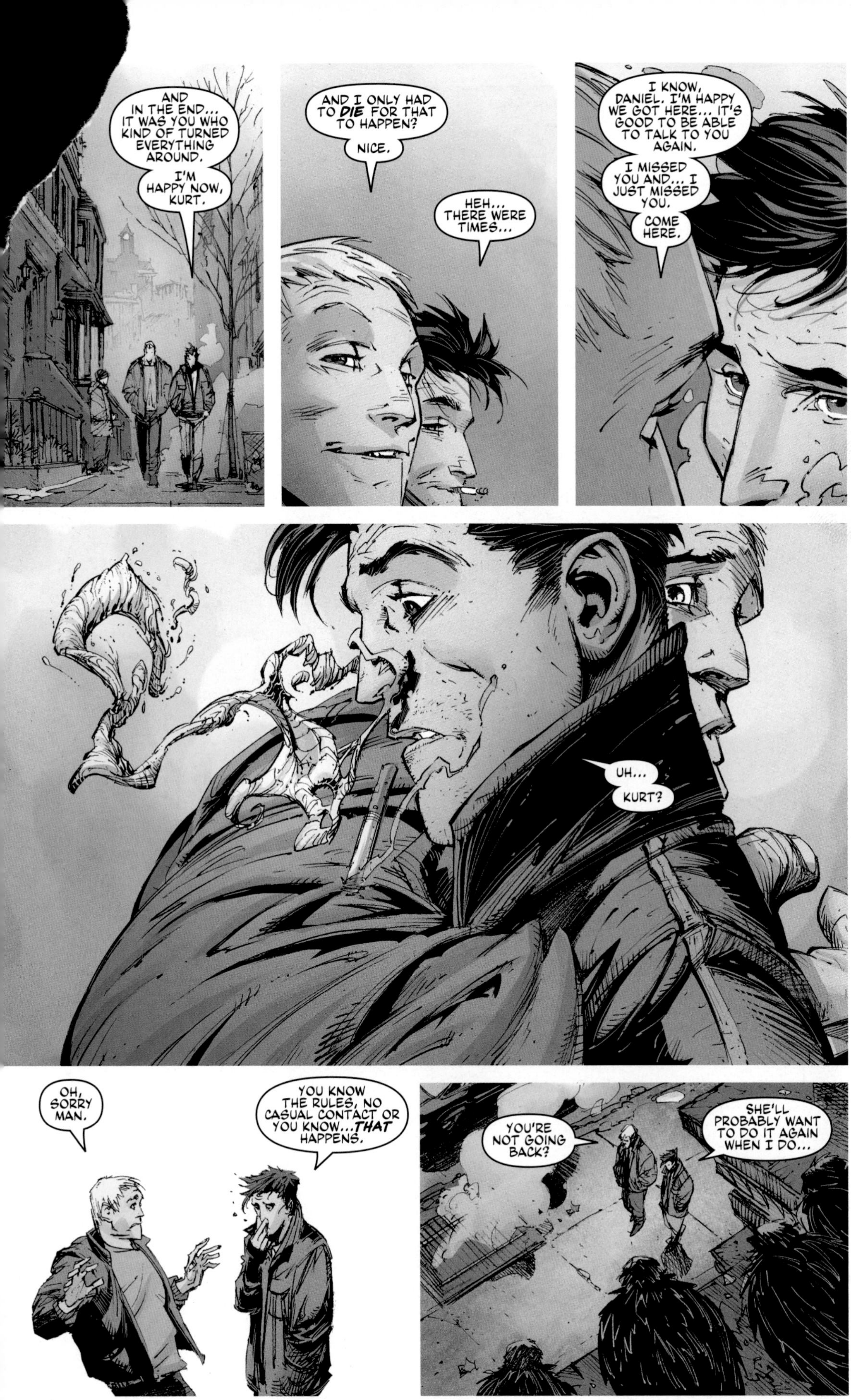

AND IN THE END... IT WAS YOU WHO KIND OF TURNED EVERYTHING AROUND.
I'M HAPPY NOW, KURT.
AND I ONLY HAD TO DIE FOR THAT TO HAPPEN?
NICE.
HEH... THERE WERE TIMES...
I KNOW, DANIEL. I'M HAPPY WE GOT HERE... IT'S GOOD TO BE ABLE TO TALK TO YOU AGAIN.
I MISSED YOU AND... I JUST MISSED YOU.
COME HERE.
UH... KURT?
OH, SORRY MAN.
YOU KNOW THE RULES, NO CASUAL CONTACT OR YOU KNOW...THAT HAPPENS.
YOU'RE NOT GOING BACK?
SHE'LL PROBABLY WANT TO DO IT AGAIN WHEN I DO...

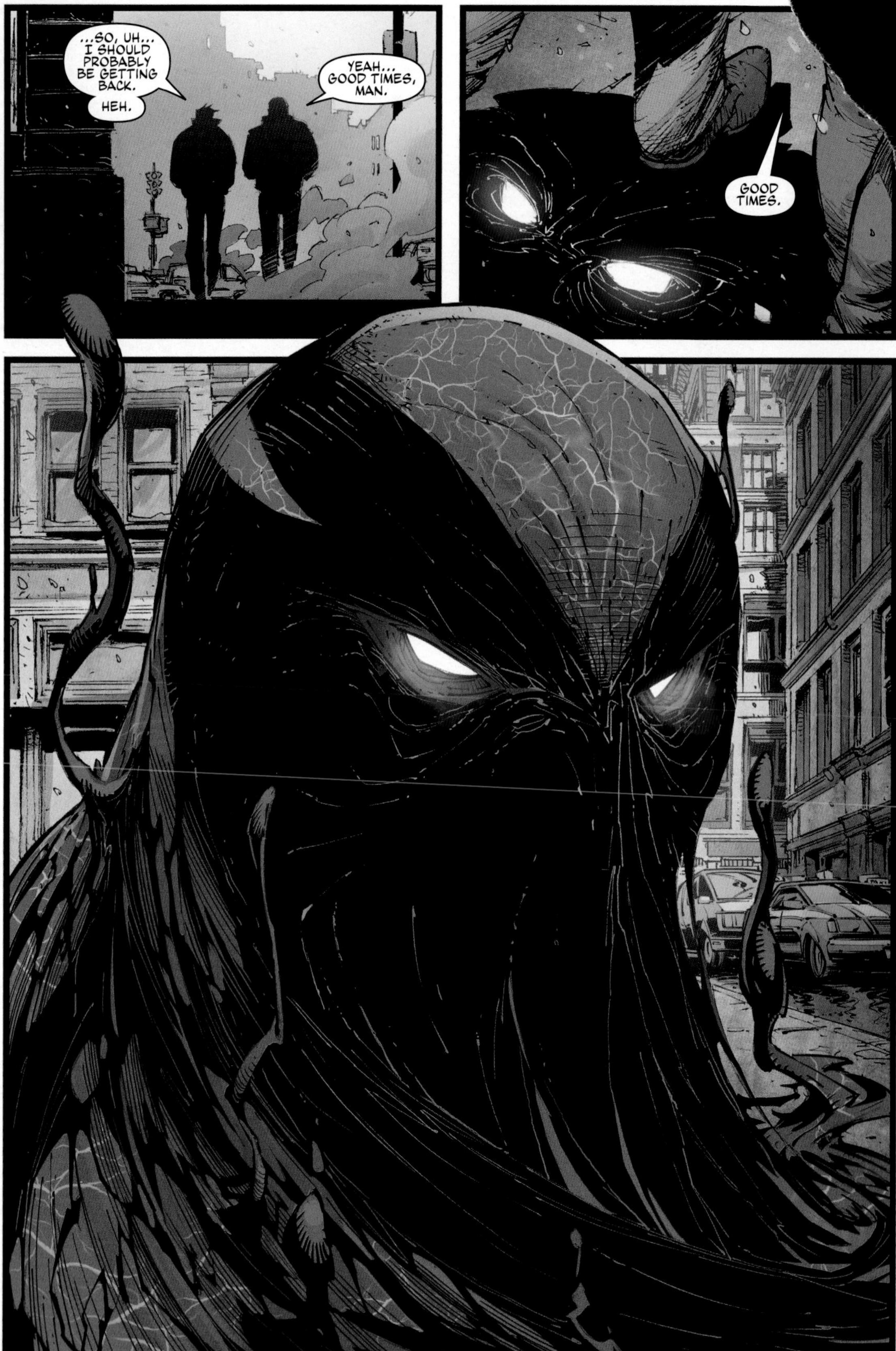
...SO, UH... I SHOULD PROBABLY BE GETTING BACK.
HEH.
YEAH... GOOD TIMES, MAN.
GOOD TIMES.